Praise for
Lauren Dane and *Undercover*

"Lauren Dane deftly weaves action, intrigue and emotion with spicy, delicious eroticism. *Undercover* is a toe-curling erotic romance sure to keep you reading late into the night."

—Anya Bast, national bestselling author of *Witch Fire*

"Sexy, pulse-pounding adventure with a heart twist of emotion that'll leave you weak in the knees. Dane delivers!"

—Jaci Burton, author of *Riding Temptation*

"Exciting, emotional and arousing! *Undercover* by Lauren Dane is a ride well worth taking." —Sasha White, author of *My Prerogative*

"Fast-paced action, steamy romance, two sizzling heroes and a heroine—Dane does it again!" —Megan Hart, author of *Broken*

"Scintillating! Lauren Dane delivers a roller coaster of emotion, intrigue and sensual delights in *Undercover*. I was hooked from the first sentence." —Vivi Anna, author of *Hell Kat* and *Inferno*

Undercover

lauren dane

heat I new york

THE BERKLEY PUBLISHING GROUP
Published by the Penguin Group
Penguin Group (USA) Inc.
375 Hudson Street, New York, New York 10014, USA
Penguin Group (Canada), 90 Eglinton Avenue East, Suite 700, Toronto, Ontario M4P 2Y3, Canada
(a division of Pearson Penguin Canada Inc.)
Penguin Books Ltd., 80 Strand, London WC2R 0RL, England
Penguin Group Ireland, 25 St. Stephen's Green, Dublin 2, Ireland (a division of Penguin Books Ltd.)
Penguin Group (Australia), 250 Camberwell Road, Camberwell, Victoria 3124, Australia
(a division of Pearson Australia Group Pty. Ltd.)
Penguin Books India Pvt. Ltd., 11 Community Centre, Panchsheel Park, New Delhi—110 017, India
Penguin Group (NZ), 67 Apollo Drive, Rosedale, North Shore 0632, New Zealand
(a division of Pearson New Zealand Ltd.)
Penguin Books (South Africa) (Pty.) Ltd., 24 Sturdee Avenue, Rosebank, Johannesburg 2196,
South Africa

Penguin Books Ltd., Registered Offices: 80 Strand, London WC2R 0RL, England

This is an original publication of The Berkley Publishing Group.

Copyright © 2008 by Lauren Dane.
Cover design by Rita Frangie.
Cover photograph by Getty Images.
Text design by Kristin del Rosario.

First edition: December 2008

Library of Congress Cataloging-in-Publication Data

Dane, Lauren.
    Undercover / Lauren Dane.—1st ed.
        p. cm.
    ISBN 978-0-425-22464-9
    1. Undercover operations—Fiction.   2. Sadomasochism—Fiction.   I. Title.
    PS3604.A5U54 2008
    813'.6—dc22   2008027553

PRINTED IN THE UNITED STATES OF AMERICA

10 9 8 7 6 5 4 3 2 1

Acknowledgments

First and most important, none of this would be possible without the unfailing support of my husband and copilot in life, Ray. He's my HEA, my heart and my everything, and I find a new reason every single day to be in love with him.

Thanks to my agent, Laura Bradford, who has been so incredibly supportive since the very first e-mail exchange. You told me this book was "the one," and you were right. Thank you, Laura, for all the pep talks and the book recommendations. You're shiny.

Leis Pederson, my fabulous editor, thank you for never making me feel ridiculous when I asked all those stupid questions. Thank you for your wonderful editing. This book is far better for your touch!

Thanks to my tireless crit partners and BFFs—Anya Bast and Megan Hart—who read this book in no less than three rounds and gave me such wonderful advice and suggestions. Megan: BRRRING ME MY HOOKAH!

To my beta readers and wonderful friends—Tracy Williams and Renee Meyer—you two are part of every book I've written (thank goodness!). Thank you for dropping everything to read my stuff.

Mom and Dad, thanks for always encouraging my dreams.

Last but never least, thank you, Vixenreaders!

Chapter 1

*P*eople scurried out of the way, keeping their eyes down as Sera Ayers stalked into the squat, gray building on the outskirts of the city. Single-mindedly, she made her way through the myriad nondescript hallways at the Federation United Forces. Anger coursed through her as she walked, her boots sounding a muffled *thud, thud, thud* on the laminate floors.

Halting at the subcommander's door, she slammed a fist into it several times. Her hand hurt, but she felt a bit better for the small violence of it.

"Enter!"

She opened the door and went inside. Noting little more than the fact that two men were seated before Subcommander Yager's desk, she opened her mouth to speak.

"Whoa! What's so damned important that you nearly knocked my fucking door down?" Subcommander Yager bellowed before she could say anything.

"I just got your summons. You've reassigned me! *That's* my problem! I'm the best you have out there. My team is good, damn it!" She shoved a hand through her hair, not caring that she probably looked like a curly porcupine.

"Sera," Yager sighed, gesturing to the men in the chairs, "you have a new team. This is Commander Ash Walker and Paracommander Brandt Pela."

At the mention of the names, a roar of white noise filled her ears. In what felt like slow motion, Sera turned and looked into the face of a man she knew all too well many years before. "Ash."

The palest blue eyes she'd ever seen gazed up at her. Eyes she'd given herself to as he was above her and below her. Eyes that had held her down as he'd bound and collared her to his will. Eyes that had haunted her for the last ten years.

It all crashed down on her; the world began to close in, and she fought with an iron will to hold back the impending breakdown. She fisted her hands to stop them from trembling.

"Sera, you're looking well." Ash smiled, his posture relaxed as if she were an old friend he hadn't seen in years. It appeared he wasn't affected at all by her presence. *Prick.*

"Ash?" Sera said sweetly.

He cocked his head. "Yes?"

"Fuck you," she snarled, landing a solid right hook to his jaw.

"Halt. Gods damn it, Sera!" Yager jumped up and, with the other man, held her back as Ash got up from the floor where she'd sent him sprawling. "What the seven hells is wrong with you?" Yager demanded, his face an inch from hers.

"Why, nothing now. I feel *ever* so much better." She hoped her smile was as feral as she felt. At least her hands weren't shaking anymore.

The other higher-up who'd come with Ash barked out a laugh

and stepped back, letting her go. "I'm Brandt. I've heard a lot about you."

Sera looked up at him. Where Ash's beauty was harsh, savage, this man's was elegant. He had almond-shaped eyes of a deep brown so dark they were nearly black. The twist of his braid, dark and rich as his eyes, reached halfway down his back. Lush lips and perfect cheekbones, skin in a beautiful olive tone that made her want to reach out and touch him: *delicious*.

"Look, I have nothing against you, Paracommander. But I am not going to work with Ash Walker. Not now, not ever. I *have* a team. We work very well together."

"Stand down, Ayers!" Yager shoved her into a chair. "You want to do time in the brig for attacking a superior officer? I expect there's an explanation for this—like you've gone insane—but you'll be making amends for your behavior, which you know is horribly out of line."

"This won't work, Subcommander. Just put me back with my team." Sera tried not to sound as desperate as she felt.

"Sera, things with the Imperialists are getting worse. You know that. You see that every day." Ash tried to stay reasonable, despite the pain in his jaw. He'd deserved the punch, he knew that. And at least the pain kept him focused on something other than how much she still affected him, even a decade later.

"Why is he talking?" Sera jerked her head in his direction, speaking through clenched teeth.

"May I speak with you alone?" Ash asked through his own tightened jaw.

"No. You may not speak to me any way at all, at any time or in any place." Still stubborn, that much hadn't changed.

"What the hells is going on here? It's obvious you know each other. Walker, this is something you should have disclosed to me up front." Yager looked back and forth between Ash and Sera, clearly unhappy.

"If you'll excuse me, SC Yager, I don't need to disclose anything to you but what I determine you need to know," Ash growled back.

Sera groaned and got up, heading for the door, but Brandt stopped her. "Sorry about this, Lieutenant Ayers, but you'll need to stay."

Ash watched in slow motion as she centered herself, rocking back enough to give a side kick to Brandt's knees and knocking him down. Using his surprise, she scrambled over him and out of the room.

"Sera! Damn it, woman, hold up!" Ash rushed to pursue her.

Even though he was agitated, he couldn't help but admire her skill. She was quick and limber as she dodged people in the long hallways. Despite his calls for bystanders to stop her, they jumped out of the way and let her pass, indicating a high level of respect for her along with a distrust of outsiders.

Still, he had nearly half a foot on her, and his legs were longer. He caught up to her quickly, grabbing her and shoving her into a room near the front reception area. Slamming the door, he locked it with savage satisfaction. Taking a moment to gather himself, he turned toward her, keeping her only exit through him.

"Don't try and run from me again, Sera. I've had enough of that from you. Just listen to what I have to say." Ash used the toe of one of his boots to shove a chair in her direction.

"You've had enough running from *me*? That's rich." Sera remained standing. Arms crossed, feet apart and eyes narrowed, she looked fearsome and unapproachable.

"Things are bad right now. The Imperialists are gaining the upper hand along the frontier. If we lose any 'Verse in this system, we could lose everything. If they gain a hold here," he paused for a moment, "well, you know what could happen. I need your skills on my team."

"I have a team. Find another person, Commander."

He growled in her direction and ran a hand over his scalp but caught the way she watched his movement. *Ahh*, she remembered. Once, she had loved to stroke her fingertips over the smooth skin of his scalp, tracing along the tribal tattoos marking his family and position that edged the back of his head. All wasn't lost just yet.

"Commander? *Now* you honor my title? Not back before you decided to punch me and be otherwise insubordinate?"

"Commander, I do not wish to be on your team. Period. I do not wish to be in the same room with you. In the same universe with you. I want you to go away. Find. Another. Girl. I'm not interested."

Gods she was magnificent when she was angry. He took in every part of her. The curve of her waist, the swell of her breasts. The way her bottom lip looked so juicy he always wanted to bite it, to savor her bit by bit. He'd forgotten just how long her legs were. Only Sera could make combat gear look sexy. And oh, how she did.

"I don't need to find another girl, Sera. You're what I need. What Brandt and I need. We're heading through the portal, and we need your language skills. More than that, you're an excellent fighter, good on your feet and smart."

"I don't want this! Why are you doing this to me?" She held herself totally erect, still, her arms stiff at her sides.

His heart constricted in his chest at the anguish in her tone. She *was* perfect for their team. He hadn't lied about that. Brandt had run the names through the computer, and hers was at the top of the list. Ash had been surprised to see how far she'd come in the last decade. When he'd been with Sera she'd been a translator in the diplomatic corps. There'd been brief talk of her joining the military corps. She'd certainly had the linguistic and martial arts skills. But after they'd crashed and burned, she'd left the diplomatic job and joined the military. She'd risen quickly and with a great deal of commendation. For a woman of an unranked family to reach lieutenant and to command her own team was nearly unheard of.

All of Ash's feelings for Sera had rushed back as Brandt had briefed him. He hadn't kept tabs on her, because he couldn't bear it. Couldn't bear knowing she'd gotten married and had children with another man or something else like that. It'd been selfish, but he knew his flaws.

As he stood there, watching her anger and frustration, he knew he'd come not just for his team but to make her his again. Period. He may not have kept tabs on her, but he hadn't stopped thinking of her over the last ten years . . . no matter how hard he tried.

There'd never been anyone after her. Not like she was to him. There'd been women in his bed, yes. But no one had held his heart, because it belonged to the very angry woman across the room.

"I'm doing this because it's what needs to be done. You took the oath, Sera. You joined the corps and pledged to do what was best, above your own wishes. You said you'd do what was necessary to fight the Imperialists. We need you on our team. You're wasted here. And I'm not asking. I'm ordering you to get your gear, because we're out of here in two turns."

Sera stared at him, openmouthed, helpless fury riding her hard. She hated him just a bit less than she loved him, and she loathed her weakness for him. Ash Walker made her vulnerable, and she couldn't afford it.

"I'd rather sit in the brig."

He sighed. "You'd be wasted in the brig. I told you, we need you." He pulled a comm unit out of his pocket. "Brandt, send in two guards to escort Lieutenant Ayers to her quarters to pack her gear. They are to stay with her and be sure she gets to our rendezvous point by the proper time."

"Ash . . ." Brandt paused. "Yes, sir. I'll have them wait just outside the front doors. I'm on my way."

"I can't believe you're doing this."

"Get over it, Sera. It was ten years ago."

"I hate you. I hate the sight of you." Sera pushed past him and out into the hall. She didn't resist when Brandt took her arm and handed her over to the guards.

"Ayers, I'm sorry. I didn't know there was a problem," Yager said quietly, pausing to scowl at Brandt and Ash.

"It's not your fault, sir. Please make sure my team gets a good leader." Her people. She'd trained them. They'd been like her family, and all she had left was to hope they'd be all right.

"Count on it." Yager nodded, turned a glare on Ash and they watched as the guards led her out to their vehicle.

Brandt looked over at Ash, his face lit by the yellowish streetlamps they drove past. He could see how troubled his friend was—had been since Brandt had given her name to him.

"You okay?"

"I never should have let her go."

"No. You shouldn't have. But you had no other choice, and you did what you had to do. You can't change the past, Ash. The real question is about right now. What are you going to do?"

"I can't believe I walked away from her to marry Kira. Brandt, you don't understand; Sera was perfect. So strong. She led all day long. But at the end of her shift, once we entered our quarters, she let all that fall away. Gave herself to me. Gods, that pretty skin of hers turns the most alluring shade of pink. I can still see the marks on her ass and thighs after she'd been flogged or paddled." Ash kept his eyes on the passing scenery, so Brandt knew he was thinking back.

"Knock it off, Ash. You're making me hard. And I can't see how this is going to help. Are we bringing her on to help win the war or to get her back in your bed?" Brandt was troubled by the answer he'd give if he had a say. He liked the look of Sera Ayers and couldn't deny her appeal after hearing Ash talk about her through the years.

"Hey!" Ash sat up straight but slumped back into the seat again. "The war. She's a great asset. We need her."

Brandt stayed silent but raised a brow as he drove.

"Okay, okay. Both. I knew I wanted her back, but I thought I'd be able to keep that separate. I didn't realize the depth of what I'd missed until she walked into the room, and I saw her again. Smelled her skin, saw the flush on her face when she got angry."

"Felt her fist connect with your jaw?" Brandt smirked.

"Whose side are you on, anyway?"

Brandt chuckled. "That's a stupid question. Kira may be my sister, but I've always thought you two were wrong for each other. She's much happier now with her spineless, pushover husband in her political marriage. You're a bad memory." He shrugged. "But from what little you've told me and what I saw tonight in how Sera reacted to you, I don't know that getting her back in your bed is a possibility. We need her on this team, Ash. More than you need to fuck her."

"I can have both." Ash was smug as he said it. "I know her buttons, Brandt. Know them better than anyone. I just have to remember how to push them at the right time."

"If you say so."

"He what?" Sera's father exclaimed via the vid screen. Over a secure channel, she'd just told him about Ash showing up, dismantling her team and ordering her onto his.

"Oh, so you weren't good enough to marry ten years ago, but you're good enough when the Federation needs you. Damned Families think they're better than those of us whose sweat and blood have kept the Universes free all these years."

"Dai, I know. You don't have to say it twice. I have no choice. He sent guards with me. They're outside."

Jakob Ayers's face softened when her voice turned strained. "Of course, baby. I'm sorry. You go. You aren't one who shirks her duty. You go and do your job. Keep your eyes on your objective. There's no law that says you have to like your commander. Gods know, I've served under a few dunderheads in my time, too. This'll make you stronger. I know you; you'll make it work for yourself. I'm proud of you."

Sera fought tears. "Thank you, Dai. You'll tell Mai and clear my quarters? I'll check in when I can."

"Of course I'll tell her. She's going to be upset she missed your call. But we love you, and we'll light a candle for you every day at temple. Be safe."

Signing off, Sera shoved her tears down as far as they could go and finished jamming her things into the three allotted bags. Her orders had been for an unspecified period of time, standard language for mobile assignment units. They wouldn't hold her quarters that long. Her mother would come to pack the rest of her belongings so the military could assign the unit to another soldier.

"Lieutenant Ayers, it's time to go," one of the guards at the door said not unkindly. She could see his unwillingness to be part of the situation in his eyes. But he was in the corps like she was. Orders were orders.

"Fine. Be useful and carry this." She tossed him a bag, and he took it, looking grateful to help in some way. She shouldered the two other bags, and the guards led her to the transport vehicle.

As they drove, she tried to process everything. The longer she thought about the situation, the more sense it made that Ash would be so highly connected in the military. He came from a Ranking Family, and the Families controlled the highest levels of the Federation, including the military. Sera recalled enough history to know that the Pelas were another powerful Family, although their territories were far flung from the Walkers'. Something else niggled at the back of her mind, but she was too tired, too wired and angry to grasp it.

She should have been flattered. If it were anyone but Ash Walker, she'd have jumped at the chance to serve on one of the mobile units. She believed in what she was doing. Believed that if they didn't fight against the constantly spreading tyranny of the Imperialists, billions of citizens through all the Known Universes in the Federation would be enslaved.

Still, the idea of submitting to his command again in any way deeply troubled her. At one time in her life she'd loved him so much she'd actually considered his offer to be his mistress. He would have had his Family-approved union, of course. Why should a Family member ever have to suffer? And as an officially recognized mistress, Sera could have even borne his children. But in the end, her pride and self-respect had won, and she walked away.

After twenty minutes the transport slowed at an outlying suburb, pulling into a garage attached to a small series of outbuildings.

She was then loaded into a small helicopter and taken on another lazy, back-and-forth route for a few minutes more until the copter touched down on a pad behind a large estate.

As she pulled her bags from the helicopter, Sera saw Brandt come out of the main house. The precise and predatory walk coupled with the hyperaware gaze told her he wouldn't be caught off guard again any time soon. She was going to have to accept her lot.

She took pity on the guard at her side. "Don't worry, I won't make a break for it."

"I'm sorry, Lieutenant Ayers. I wish . . ." His eyes caught hers for a moment.

"Everyone's sorry. But it's the way things are. You get orders. I get orders. We don't like them, but they're orders just the same. Now go on. Try and have a good night."

She shut the door carefully, hefted her bags and stepped back. The men stayed in the helicopter, and it cheered her that they took her at her word. At least she had that. They took off, and she gathered a steadying breath and moved toward where Brandt stood, waiting.

"Sera, can I get one of your bags?" Brandt asked as she approached.

"Where are my quarters, PC?" Her voice was crisp and efficient.

He sighed. "Are we going to do it this way?"

"What do you want from me? I don't want to be here. You busted up my team, and gods only know who'll lead them now. You put me under the command of a man I loathe. Military code does not require me to like this assignment or to pretend to be excited about it. I don't have to be nice. I just have to obey orders. Which I will do. Now, where are my quarters, or is there a briefing? Perhaps you plan to keep me in the dark?"

Brandt grabbed one of her bags with a snort and jerked his head. "This way. We'll get your bags stowed, and then we'll have a meeting. Ash will want to go over things with you."

She touched her forehead in salute, and he looked stunned for a moment, shrugging before leading her into the large house.

Once inside, he motioned up a stairway, and she followed him, not failing to notice his muscular ass in his uniform pants. There was some solace in the evening, at least.

At the end of the hallway he kicked a door open and flipped on the lights. It was a sizable room with a small kitchen and bathroom unit attached. There was a bedroom with a separate living space. Sera noted the state-of-the-art electronic equipment on the desk. She'd be excited about the new gear after she was alone. There was no way she'd let him see her glee.

"Get unpacked, but keep a kit bag ready at all times. We'll expect you in the main area in twenty. Back downstairs and to the left. You can't miss it. We'll have a meal ready, too." He stood there for a moment. "Welcome, Sera. I mean that. You're a real asset to this team."

He turned and left the room before she could say anything, closing the door behind him.

She leaned against it, trying to catch her breath, trying to still the thoughts racing through her brain as the past pressed against her future. Fear, something she hadn't tasted in many years, began to war with wary excitement. This was a nightmare, yes, but there was no denying the challenge appealed to her. How it would all end up remained to be seen.

Chapter 2

When she came down exactly twenty minutes later, Sera found them both seated in a large common room. The place was homey and lived-in. She didn't doubt they bunked here regularly, although Sera wondered where the *wife* slept. Still, there were hints of the true nature of the inhabitants here and there. The staff were efficient and silent, but every last one she'd seen carried themselves like warriors. On her way down and when she'd entered the house with Brandt, she'd noticed the security. Understated but totally top-notch. Her growling stomach led her gaze to the sideboard against a far wall laden with food. It'd been some hours since she'd eaten last.

"Subcommander Ayers, I'm Ceylon, the house assistant. I'm pleased to meet you and have you here. Should you require anything, simply hail me from any comm station in the house or on the grounds. The others await you in the common room." A tall, rail-thin man who appeared to be constructed from solid muscle bowed slightly.

Subcommander? She bowed in return. "Thank you. And please, call me Sera."

"As you wish, Sera. Again, welcome." He disappeared on nearly soundless feet, and she shrugged, turning back toward the room where Ash waved her inside.

"Sera, come in. Please grab something to eat, and we'll get started." Sera's body responded to the way Ash's eyes roved hungrily over her face and body. Her traitorous nipples hardened at his perusal, and she was glad she wore a thick enough bra to hide it.

Without a word she went to the sideboard and piled a plate with food. She carefully brought it over to the low table and couches where they were already seated, eating.

She didn't ask about anything. She just ate and waited for one of them to speak. Why should she make it easy for them? They'd busted up her life just like Ash had done those years before. Like she was a piece on a game board to play.

Ash sighed. "Are you going to keep this up forever?"

Casually, she wiped her lips with a napkin and looked at him. "Sir? Have I been insubordinate? Perhaps you should find another member of your team you feel more comfortable with."

Brandt chewed his lip to hold back a smile. Sera didn't take any shit, and watching her keep Ash on his toes was amusing.

"Damn it, Sera! Let it go! We have a job to do." Ash clenched his fists on his knees. Brandt knew it was most likely to keep Ash from pulling her body to his.

Her eyes flashed with fury just before she narrowed them at Ash. "Respectfully, sir, I am here to do my job. I am here as ordered. You told me to get something to eat, and I did so. I am a highly decorated military officer. I earned my way to where I am today with blood and broken bones. I have one of the best records in the military in all the

Federation Universes. I don't walk away from my commitments, *Commander*."

Brandt caught the slight tremor in her hand as she held the plate on her knees. Ash was right, the woman was strong-willed. Brandt had been impressed when he read her file. On top of being quite lovely, he could quite easily add intelligent, skilled and deadly to the list. Her ranking in the Federated Universes Martial Arts League was in the top 3 percent.

But right then, she was on the edge, and Ash had to stop pushing, or she'd snap. Smoothly, Brandt stepped in to repair the damage.

"Of course, and I'm sure that Ash didn't mean to intimate otherwise. We've both seen your file and your commendations. You're a fine soldier, Sera. Let's get to the briefing, shall we?" He looked to Ash, who unclenched his teeth.

"Brandt and I run a covert ops team. Our mobile unit has always had three people, but our third retired recently. We're often on the frontier. You'll be receiving a promotion to subcommander, by the way. While we're here in Borran, this is our home base. The doors and other entrances are now keyed to your call. There's transport out in the sheds. You should feel free to come and go as you wish, but only people with level-three clearance and above are allowed at this location."

Sera put her empty plate on the table and crossed her legs. She listened closely as she bit into a piece of purri fruit.

Brandt handed her a file. She ate the last bit of the fruit, wiping her hands before opening the folder to examine the pictures and documents inside.

"The Imperialists have attacked four separate outposts. Clandestine outposts. From these outposts, we believe that they've been able to get more of our classified data.

"We've tracked some of the stolen information back to Nondal."
Ash sat back, and Brandt watched Sera as she read the information.
Watched her eyes as she took in what had been stolen. And, im-
pressed, he watched her piece things together.

"We'll be going in two turns. A bit of scouting of our own to
Nondal. The file has the intel and also what will be your identity.
Memorize the material and leave any and all connection to your
identity here," Brandt explained and then hesitated a moment.
"From this moment on, you're assimilated into our cover as a whole.
Ash and I are seen as Family members with lots of credits and too
much spare time. You'll be playing into that as well. We'll work on
the details when we return from Nondal. It's not easy living a life
where people underestimate you. But in truth, it's quite useful." He
shrugged.

He'd leave off the part about how it hurt to be discounted when
in fact he and Ash were dedicated, intelligent and hardworking. It
wouldn't necessarily always be that way. At some point he hoped
they'd be able to drop the spoiled rich boy routine.

Sera nodded absently as she looked at the evidence in her lap.
Evidence that a member of one of the most important Families in
the Federation had collaborated with the Imperialists.

"That memo pad on your communicator is keyed to your voice,"
Brandt pointed out.

"Don't forget Sera has a photographic memory." Ash nodded
at her.

Brandt raised his brows and nodded. "Ah yes, I remember. Handy
little skill that. I'm guessing it's why you're so good at languages."

"Well, it's not photographic. I'm not perfect. But I do have a very
good memory. Don't ever say something to me and try to insist that
you said something else later on." Sera glared at Ash—who had the
good sense to wince—before going back to read the rest of the file.

Both men waited until she reached the part of the dossier that contained information about her cover identity.

She read it quietly, her body becoming more and more still. Her face flushed, and Brandt could see her jaw clench tighter and tighter until she tossed the file on the table and leveled those midnight-blue eyes at Ash.

"No."

"Look, Sera . . ." Ash began.

She shot up then, hands clenched into fists at her sides as her chest heaved. "I. Said. No. I won't."

Ash stood. "You'll do what you're told, damn it." His hand whipped out and cupped her throat, collaring it with his palm and fingers.

Her eyes widened.

Brandt moved to intervene, but before he reached them, Sera broke Ash's hold, and he was on the ground with her foot on his throat. "You will not *ever* touch me with familiarity. Never collar my throat with your hand. I will kill you if you try it. I'd rather sit in the brig until I die than let you fuck me over again, Ash."

"Sera, stand down," Brandt said, keeping his voice calm and even. Ash had gone too far. Overstepped. That thing with his hand at her throat was uncalled for.

"I am not a whore." Her voice was quiet when she removed her boot and turned, leaving the room quickly.

"What the hell is wrong with you, Ash? You didn't have to push her like that."

"Brandt, I know her better than she knows herself. She needs to be mastered. She *wants* it."

"Ash, this is not about your cock! This is about our mission. She is your team member, and you are her superior officer. You're out of line. You're pushing too far and too hard."

"Don't you tell me what I'm doing, Brandt! You don't know her."

"You don't either, Ash. The person you left ten years ago is gone. In her place is a different woman. Your actions put cracks in her foundation, and you will not exploit that to get into her uniform. I won't allow it."

Before Ash could respond, Brandt left the room and headed up to her quarters.

Sera slammed the door and leaned against it, reaching deep to try to locate some kind of inner strength and stability. Her heart threatened to burst from her chest, and she fought the conflicting shame and desire that rushed through her body.

"You will not cry!" she whispered, taking a deep breath.

That moment when his big hand and powerful fingers closed around her neck—not hurting—it had come back to her with vivid clarity. Each night when she walked into their home, she'd shed her public self. She'd changed into one of the diaphanous gowns with thigh-high slits he'd selected for her. And became his.

The black case lay on her bedside table. Each time, she opened it with care, pulling out the wide leather collar, taking it to him. Kneeling, she'd hold the collar out for him to put on her.

There were days when he would shake his head slowly and put the collar aside. "Tonight, Sera, my words are your collar."

He would often come to her as they prepared the evening meal or some other household activity and put his hand at her neck like that, holding her to him as he devoured her mouth.

It had been a very long time since anyone or anything had made her feel that cherished and safe.

She'd never submitted to another man after the day she moved out. She didn't plan to let Ash lure her into some elaborate mind fuck game now, either. It had been a long, hard road to pull herself out of the pit of self-loathing he'd dug for her with his fancy nuptials splashed over every vid screen and newspaper in the Federation.

There was no way she'd throw all that work away.

She began to pace, working through her options. There was no *technically* about it, she'd been outright insubordinate down there. She'd refused a direct order and assaulted a superior officer and a member of the Families.

"Sera?" Brandt called out softly as he tapped on her door.

She froze a moment and ruthlessly turned off as much of her emotions as she could. She would not give them anything. She would not shed another tear for Ash Walker if she could possibly help it.

Crossing to the door, she took a deep breath and opened it. "Yes, PC Pela?"

"May I come in?"

"If you're planning to help him with this ridiculous ploy, you're wasting your breath."

"I'd just like to try and work through this to find a solution. On my word as an officer, I promise I won't force you to do anything you don't want to do. I just ask that you listen to me and help me to find a resolution here."

Sighing, she stepped back and waved him inside.

"Thank you." Brandt moved past her to the small couch and sat.

Sera went to the fridge and pulled out two bottles of water, handing one to him as she took the chair across from him.

"Sera, you know Nondal is a patriarchal 'Verse. As a woman you'll be forbidden to move freely unless you're a wife or concubine accompanied by your husband or lover. And a concubine won't be expected to observe all the same rules as a wife. You'd have more freedom as a concubine.

"But if you don't go in as a concubine, you won't even be allowed to leave the transport. We need you on the ground. We need your ears and your experience with the Nondalese if we're to get inside. You saw that file; you know who we suspect."

"I won't pose as his concubine, PC Pela. I won't. I'll never allow Ash Walker to make me feel like a whore again."

"Please, can you call me Brandt? A three-person team is very intimate. We'll be out in the field for long periods of time. If we stick to referring to each other by rank, it'll just be tedious, don't you think?"

Sera narrowed her eyes but nodded after a few long moments.

"Okay, good. Now, would it be acceptable to you to be my concubine? Rather, um, to *pose* as my concubine?" He took a quick drink of his water.

Sera thought it over. Brandt was right. Nondal was a 'Verse where she'd be unable to move about at all without a man. A wife would be expected to mix with the other married women and stay separate from her husband except for certain social events and after retiring for the evening. But a concubine could easily move about with her lover. The Nondalese would dismiss her as a pretty piece of fluff. A piece of fluff could hear a lot.

She nodded slowly. "All right."

Brandt smiled at her, and her heart sped up. She realized she'd just agreed to pose as his lover for as long as necessary. It would certainly take some time to get in with the right people on Nondal. They'd be watched closely, and she'd have to be convincing. The Nondalese were notorious for having spy cameras everywhere. But as she looked at him, she realized it wouldn't be very hard to act like a woman smitten with him.

"I'm glad we could work this through. Your clothes for the assignment are in the transport already. You are aware what you'll be expected to dress and act like?" Sera appreciated that he said it so carefully.

"I'm aware. I've never been to Nondal, but I've dealt with enough Nondalese people to know."

"And from your file it appears that you have extensive background in the local accents? We'll be dealing with mainly upper-class Nondalese."

Nondal had a very stratified class system. Each class grouping had linguistic variants and accents. Most citizens in the Federation Universes spoke Standard. In addition to Standard, on Nondal the population spoke Nondalese. But there were small but important differences in the language that varied by group. Those small differences made the language nearly unintelligible to most people. Fortunately for Sera, she'd done extensive study on the different variations, and that would be a big asset to the team.

"Yes. But Ash is very recognizable. How is he planning to get any information at all?" Nondal was a very closed society. The lower and working classes did not have free access to news from the Known Universes. Or contact with outsiders even. Their travel was restricted, and most Nondalese never even left their domed city levels much less folding to visit other universes. But the upper classes did have access to the outside news and information, and they'd hold their knowledge of gossip and celebrity news as a mark of their status.

"How closely have you followed him over the last ten years? Just between us."

She studied her hands. "Not very. Not after his engagement was all over the place. But his wedding was big news for a very long time. It was inescapable. His face was on every vid screen and newspaper and every damned day of their honeymoon, which seemed to last forever."

Sera returned her gaze to him. "After that first year, I made it a point not to see him or hear what he was up to. But given that his Family is so powerful, it's not like you can hide it."

"No. You can't. So we've played on it. I told you a bit downstairs about our general cover. From the outside, Ash Walker is a playboy with too many credits and too much free time. Sure, he has a position in the military, but he doesn't do any more than collect the credits and show up every once in a while. It makes him ripe for approach by certain people, and we've cultivated it for the last seven years now." His smile wasn't a happy one. "Just two irresponsible men out for as much pleasure as possible."

"Playboy? And how does his wife feel about that? Or does she just look the other way?" *Oops, that may have sounded a tad bitter.*

"Kira dissolved their union seven years ago. She's remarried one of Ash's cousins. What Ash does is of very little consequence to her. You didn't know?"

Her breath caught a moment. "I've had better things to do than read the Family pages in the newspapers or watch the vids about you people."

Brandt winced. "That's some chip on your shoulder you've got there, Sera."

"Let's get this straight, Brandt. Ash Walker professed his undying love to me one day, and the next he brought me the paperwork to be his mistress. Because, and imagine my surprise, it turned out he had a fiancée. He'd even shown me the deed to the new apartment he'd purchased for me. Near his house, of course. He could leave her bed and come to mine with impunity. His resistance to marrying according to his family's wishes lasted about as long as his love for me did.

"The Families have walked all over me and mine and acted as if they are better by virtue of blood than people who actually shed it. So it's not a chip, Brandt, it's called experience."

"My father is a decorated military officer who led the troops at Varhana. He lost an arm that day but continued to fight alongside a great many soldiers, including my older brother and my uncles. I've given up a life of leisure to fight against the Imperialists. We're not all the same. I know who you come from. I know you were wronged, but I'm not Ash. My family, although they have their own flaws, aren't the Walkers."

Sera sighed. "You're right. I apologize. I'm being unfair."

Brandt's estimation of her rose. Having the courage to apologize when one was wrong was a quality he wished more people possessed.

"Isn't it difficult? I mean, clearly you're *not* simply rich losers looking for a good time. What do your families think?" She couldn't imagine what it would feel like if her father thought she was a lazy, good-for-nothing fool.

Before Brandt could answer, there was a rap at the door. Sera closed her eyes for a moment before getting up.

"Do you want me to deal with that?" Brandt asked quietly.

She stopped halfway to the door and turned back to him. "Thank you, but no. I have to deal with this if I'm going to be on the team."

When Sera opened the door, Ash was there as she knew he'd be. As she felt he'd be.

"May I?" He jerked his chin, indicating he wanted to enter.

She stepped back, and he walked in, moving to sit next to Brandt.

"Sera, you can't continue to assault me every time I piss you off."

Brandt sighed. "Ash, we've moved past that. Sera is going in as my concubine. She feels comfortable with that, and it's really no difference one way or the other. We were just going over our cover."

"Well, isn't that cozy?" Ash's voice was cutting.

"If this is going to work, you cannot continue to be a 'Verse-class asshole, Ash." Sera wanted to pop him one, but she was too tired to move.

Ash looked at her with surprise and then laughed. "Fine. I see you're still a smart-ass. And you need to teach me that move you pulled down there. You're a lot faster than you were ten years ago."

"We'll see. Now, Brandt, you were about to tell me about your cover." She moved her attention back to Brandt.

"Yes, it's difficult, but we all pay a price in some way. The best rule of this sort of work is to play as close to the truth as humanly possible. My Family is powerful, in ways, even more so than Ash's. But I've not been seen on the front like my father was. All my work has been quiet and behind the scenes. Ash and I have been close since he married my sister. I'm just a guy from a Family full of heroes looking for something to make me stand out."

Sera blinked several times before she could even find the words. That niggling she'd had the night before became totally clear. Kira was a Pela. Just like Brandt. "You're Kira's brother?" She didn't like the sound of her voice. She heard the raw emotion, didn't want them to.

"You didn't know." Brandt said it and felt like a heel. How could he have been so stupid? The whole thing was stupid. He never should have brought her name to Ash. She'd been such a great candidate for the team, and he'd truly thought they could overcome her issues with Ash. But all they'd done since the moment they decided on her was to fuck her life over.

"No. I'm very tired. We have time to go over this. I'll read the file and what you've put in my system." She stood woodenly.

"I'm sorry, I didn't know you weren't aware." Brandt raised his hands but let them fall to his side.

"Please. Just go." The strain was clear on her face.

Sighing, Brandt pushed Ash out the door ahead of him. He knew Ash would want to stay and badger her, and Brandt could see in her face that there was just no more room for that.

Brandt was the one who slammed into his room this time, and Ash followed, tossing himself on the bed with a grumble.

"We've really fucked up, Ash. In less than twenty-four hours we've swooped in, broken up her team, torn her from her life, tossed her ex-lover in her face, and made her feel like a whore. Each surprise we've given her has been worse than the last."

Ash knew it. Her pain tore at him. He wanted more than anything to make it right. He would make it right. "Yes. Okay, I admit it. I shouldn't have collared her neck downstairs. That set her off." Ash watched Brandt as he pulled his shirt off and sat on the edge of the bed to yank his boots off. "But she does something to me. She always has. I just got my roles a little mixed up."

"My, you're the master of understatement tonight. What were you thinking?" Brandt turned, but his hair was tight in Ash's grip, the long rope of it wrapped around his fist.

Ash moved to his knees directly behind Brandt. "I was thinking just how much I wanted to fuck her. How much I wanted to restrain her wrists and ankles and have her spread-eagle on my bed. How much I wanted to use the flogger to tease across her nipples and over her mound until she was glistening and writhing and begging me for more. I want her back, damn it. I want her." Ash's lips brushed against Brandt's ear as he murmured the words, "And you as well."

"I'm not in the mood, Ash." Brandt's teeth were clenched as he said it, but Ash heard the slight tremor in his voice, knew the idea of the three of them together intrigued him, too.

"Oh?" Ash reached around to grab Brandt's cock and squeezed until Brandt moaned, relaxing against him. "You may not be, but your cock sure is. Hmmm, whose turn is it?" Brandt's groan was like a dark caress as he reached back, sliding his hand up Ash's thigh.

"I believe it's mine. But instead of whipping your ass for being such a fool, I'll let you suck my cock instead," Brandt said as he turned and stood, unbuttoning the placket of his pants and looking down at Ash.

For Brandt, switching with a man as powerful as Ash Walker was as much about the exchange of power as the sex itself. Normally, both of them preferred women, but he and Ash had grown so close that after he and Kira had split, they'd ended up together from time to time. Because they were both dominants, they'd had to switch or constantly ended up arguing. So they took turns. Every other time one got to be dominant, and the other submitted.

His head fell back as Ash's hand closed around the root of his cock. He'd deal with the situation they'd created with Sera in the morning. Right then, he just wanted to feel.

Chapter 3

$\mathscr{S}$era woke up at dawn as she always did. Knowing they'd be traveling to another part of the Known Universe, she made a mental note to adjust to Standard Time but knew she'd have to also get used to Nondalese local time as well.

She'd stayed up until nearly two reading the files. Her brother hadn't been annoyed when she'd called in the small hours of the morning to badger him for a favor. Gods knew he'd called her at midnight more than once to get him out of a bind.

Her brother Paul was a clever man, and Sera was glad he was on her side. His results were impressive, and she went over the data again in her head as she showered, continuing to work it over as she got dressed.

It most certainly looked like Giles Stander was a key figure in this whole thing. The Stander Family had a whole lot of influence, especially in the border universes. The bulk of their money and importance came from their trade in goods. They had a lot to gain if the war continued and kept products expensive on the frontier.

Her research on the nifty electronic gear in her quarters showed a distinct lack of ideological stances on the part of the Stander Family. They didn't appear to be true believers in the Federation's precepts of democratic rule nor did they look like they embraced the Imperialists' belief in universe-wide fascism as a tool for greater stability. Still, that it seemed to be a purely economic motivation was worse in Sera's mind. She could understand doing something you believed in, but doing something for profit and all else be damned was lower than low, and she was quite ready to take them down for it.

After reading over everything and piecing together what she had, Sera couldn't help but feel there was more than just the Stander Family involved. The whole thing screamed a wider conspiracy. Each Family controlled different segments of everything the Federation did. So while Stander might be able to get them certain things, and the bombings and other infiltrations could garner more, it seemed logical to bring in more Family members. The big question mark, of course, was, who else? The key would be to note who Stander's closest compatriots were once they got to Nondal.

She made herself kava and noted with some satisfaction her pantry was well-stocked. She made the bread, cheese and fruit into a morning meal as she attempted to compartmentalize her emotions.

It just had to be done. She was right for the job; they weren't lying about that. Her linguistic skills alone would have made her a perfect candidate, but she could handle herself in a bind, too. It wouldn't be easy to deal with them, but she'd do it. She believed in what she was doing, and even though she felt manipulated, she'd stay to do the job.

After her meal she cleaned up after herself, gathered her weapons, and headed out in search of a practice floor and a target range.

Brandt and Ash were already in the common area eating their

meal when she came down. Why did they both have to look so good? It would be so much easier to work with them if they were hard to look at instead of delicious.

"Sera, good morning. Please, have some breakfast." Brandt motioned toward the sideboard, which held as much food as it did the night before.

"No, thank you. I've already eaten. Do you have a practice floor? Target range? I'd like to work out this morning. And then I'd like to speak with you about some of the things I found in my research last night."

"You're welcome to take your meals down here with us. It's what we do as a team. We have a cook who is quite good." Ash's words were harmless enough, but his tone needled her.

Sera took a deep breath to center herself. She would not let Ash rattle her. "I'm sure. Thank you, I'll consider it in the future. Range? Practice floor? If not, I'll head back into town and use the one at my old post."

Brandt stepped between them again. Ash was picking a fight, and he didn't want that. She'd had enough. "Follow this hall and out the back door. The building just behind this one has a target range, a practice floor and various machines for muscle enhancement and strength training. There's a pool as well. As I told you last night, the doors are all keyed to your call."

Sera inclined her head a moment. "Will three hours from now be amenable to discuss the file?"

"Yes, meet us both back here."

She touched her hand to her forehead and walked down the hall.

After Brandt watched her leave the house, he turned. "Ash, knock it off. You promised last night that you'd try and get along with her."

"What? I just told her we have meals here as a team. And anyway, it's my turn now. I'll be giving the orders." He looked smug.

"This isn't about that. And if you want that with her and with me, you're going to have to work for it. She's not just going to fall to her knees for you this time."

With a final look at Ash, Brandt turned on his heel and left the room before he said anything else.

*B*randt watched her from the doorway of the practice room as she moved through her martial arts workout. She was fluid and quick. The muscles in her upper arms and her thighs rippled, her face set in concentration.

It was hard not to appreciate her form: both her physical body and the way she moved. There was no doubt as he watched her, she was a warrior through and through. He liked that.

She worked out hard for at least an hour, and he moved into a corner of the room and did his own workout on the bag. Boxing was an old art brought millennia ago through the first portal from Earth. Brandt loved that it kept both mind and body quick.

After a while he looked up and saw her walking toward the showers. He argued with himself for some time before finally giving in and following.

She was tall, probably around six standard feet. Her legs were long and shapely. Her body, as he'd seen when she'd been working out, was lithe and strong. Small but high and pertly beautiful breasts called out to be touched. A ring through one of her nipples caught the light, and something low in his groin tightened. He bit his bottom lip, wishing it were her nipple instead.

She turned into the water, and her golden blonde hair darkened when wet. Brandt was riveted by her long, graceful fingers massaging shampoo through it.

A tattoo marked her lower back, just above her right hip. The

Walker Family sigil with Ash's symbol in the center. It shocked him to see she hadn't had it covered or removed.

Forcing himself to move, he shed his clothes and headed into a stall to shower as well. Mixed gender showers were quite common in the military, and with them being out in the field for long periods of time, he'd need to at least fake being unaffected by her body.

Sera was aware he'd come into the room and tried not to stare at him as he took his hair out of the braid. When it fell across his back like liquid midnight, she felt its phantom touch. His skin bore the deep olive tone of those who came from the universes nearest the Core and the Federation home 'Verse, Ravena. Muscled thighs and a tight, high ass drew her eyes. Up her gaze went, past the narrow waist and the broad shoulders.

It would be hard to keep her emotions separate on this mission. As his concubine, she'd have to be at his side most of the time once they got to Nondal. She really couldn't feel too badly they'd most likely be engaging in some form of sex play in public and also in their quarters for the cameras. But feelings-wise, he was way off the menu. If he wasn't a Pela and connected to Ash, she'd have pursued him. Sighing, she turned off the water and grabbed for her towel. She'd have to wrestle her emotions back into a deep, deep pit. Feelings for Brandt or Ash would weaken her, and she couldn't afford to be weak in any way.

Quickly, she finished, pretending her eyes weren't drawn back to him every few seconds.

Brandt dried off while she laced up her boots. "You've got excellent technique. I'd really appreciate it if you'd work with me. I'm not awful, but I'm rusty. Martial arts were never my forte."

Sera kept her eyes on her laces after she caught sight of the silky arrow of dark hair leading from his belly button down to what she could only imagine was quite a lovely cock. Oh, okay, she didn't have to imagine; she'd stared at it a few times when she hoped to hell he wasn't watching.

"Well, it takes a bit of time to get to Nondal. How big is the transport?" She stood and tucked her shirt in.

"Ash is a moneyed playboy, remember? The ship is a first-class luxury transport. We have a small crew; most of them are special forces. The others are provided by Ash's Family. It'll be necessary to hold your cover at all times, regardless." He didn't want her to leave just yet. Her scent teased his senses. Tantalizing him.

"If we're going to have company on the transport, I suppose I can't give you much help. We can't risk being seen. It's one thing for her . . . me, to work out to keep my shape, another entirely to be teaching you. When we get back we can work on your skills. I'm a fairly good instructor. What's your specialty? I'm sure you have one, or you wouldn't be on this team."

"Blades. Knives, swords, throwing stars."

She nodded. "Excellent. I'd love to learn from you as well. I expect that it works quite well in combination with Ash's skill with sidearms and blasters."

"I'd forgotten you know him so well."

She jerked back slightly. "I thought I did. But yes, I know he's an expert with anything that shoots."

"You know, there's so much more to what happened than a simple him-leaving-her scenario." Brandt wanted her to understand the immense pressure a man like Ash had felt from his Family over the right marriage with another Family. Ash, as the second oldest son *had* to make a political marriage. He wouldn't have been allowed to find love with a woman of Sera's standing. The Walker Family had a generations-old rule, whereby the first and second sons had to procure the permission of the head of the ruling line to marry at all.

Ash's father would never agree to him marrying anyone other than a ranked woman.

In the end, it was only Kira's fickle nature that had freed Ash. Kira traded Ash in for one of Ash's cousins, and one of Ash's brothers married a Pela as well. The unions were enough, and Ash could walk away.

She held up a hand. "Please, if you're going to talk to me about how I can't possibly understand duty and his choices, save your breath. It's over. I don't want to talk about it."

He grinned. "Okay, so I'm obvious. I just want you two to get past this thing. He's a good man, Sera."

"He's a good soldier and probably a good friend to you. And I said I don't want to talk about it."

He couldn't help but smile at the straight line of her back as she left the room.

Chapter 4

Ash watched her hungrily as she made her way across the court-yard from the outbuildings to the house. He loved the mystery of the way she walked: graceful, filled with an innate sensuality, and yet, as he looked on, he saw the strength beneath the skin. Intriguing.

He let himself think back to the last time he'd seen her. He'd known for months he'd have to marry Kira. There wasn't any way around it. His heart ached every night as Sera had returned home. In the back of his mind he knew there was no way to work things through, but he couldn't admit defeat.

Trying to salvage it the only way he could, he planned to have her as his mistress. He bought her a lavish flat near what would be his home with Kira. He'd have his life with Sera. She *was* his life. They'd have children and a family. She'd be the wife of his heart. It wasn't perfect, but it was the only thing he could do. But he hadn't had the first idea how to break it to her. So he'd said nothing.

Eventually, the news of the upcoming nuptials leaked to the

media, and it had been all over the vids. He'd rushed home and found her there, weeping, her heart broken. He'd tried to explain why he hadn't said anything. Told her he'd been trying to find a way around it, a way out of it, but the bare fact was he'd have to marry or shame his entire family.

He remembered the look of utter betrayal on her face when he'd told her he'd purchased a home for her and had the papers for her to be his mistress. Remembered trying to manipulate her, knowing how weak she was.

He'd have done just about anything to keep her. He adored Sera Ayers with all that he was, and if it had been just him, even just his immediate family, he'd have thrown convention in their faces and taken her as his wife. But there were literally tens of thousands of people depending on him and his decisions: his Family, the people whose livelihoods depended on them. Entire universes' worth of economic systems relied on the Walker Family. The marriage of his Family to the Pelas was something way beyond what mattered to just him.

She'd wavered that night. He'd held her tenderly, and she'd looked up into his face, tears shining in her eyes as he made love to her. From the questions she'd asked, he was sure she'd agree to be his mistress. Not the best situation, but he'd have lived with her, had children with her and kept care of her.

He left for work the next morning and had come back to find her things gone except for her collar and a letter telling him she loved him, but she deserved to be his wife, not his mistress. She'd been right, of course. But he couldn't give her what she wanted—what she deserved—and he'd let her go.

After the wedding, he'd thrown himself into his new marriage. He tried like crazy to make Kira happy. Yes, he loved another woman, but there was no sense in punishing Kira for what she was powerless to change, either. Sadly, they were ill-suited from the start. Kira was a woman who didn't know what it meant not to be the center of all things at all times. She was spoiled and selfish and had no room in her life for anyone but herself.

The sex had been awful, and there'd been no way he could even suggest anything rough. Hells, she'd probably have run screaming from the room if he'd pulled out the cat-o'-nine that had lovingly bitten and kissed Sera's skin.

In the end, it was Kira's own selfishness that had freed him. She'd found someone else, and his little brother married one of Brandt and Kira's cousins. She sought a dissolution, and he'd made no issue of it as long as the contracts still stood uniting their families.

He'd taken on more responsibility in his job and eventually began working covert with Brandt. He'd put his all into the military corps. He believed in what he did and, in a sense, it filled the giant gap in his life. The more it bothered him that the perceptions of him as empty and shallow rose, the harder he worked until he shut out everything but his job and his few friends who knew the real Ash Walker.

For seven years he'd considered finding Sera, but he didn't know how to get her back. Knew he didn't deserve her. He'd figured she'd found someone else. But after they'd pulled her name as a new member of their team, he had her background checked. She'd taken other lovers but hadn't had a long-term relationship since she'd left him.

And now she was there, and he still loved her. He loved her more at that moment than he had when she'd walked out ten years before. He wanted her back, and he planned to move entire universes to make it happen. More than that, he wanted Brandt, too, and the idea of the three of them together teased his fevered brain. Ash Walker had been successful at everything he'd ever tried in his life,

and he didn't plan to let her walk out of his life ever again. Sera Ayers was meant to be his woman. He would make it happen one way
or another.

Sera knew Ash stood watching her through the window at the
back of the house. She'd always known when his eyes were on her.
At one time in her life, that regard had meant everything to her.
There was still a gap in her heart where the pleasure at being first
and foremost in his attentions used to live.

Instead of looking up, she moved into the house. Once inside,
out of his view, she stood a moment, back against the door. Quietly,
she tried to get hold of her rampant emotions. She was better than
this, a professional. There was a lot to do before they left the next
day, and she could not let him get between her and her job. If she
focused on that, she'd make it through.

She was strong, and she believed in their cause. She made a fine
weapon against their enemies. Her mother often spoke about des-
tiny, and part of Sera couldn't help but think she was meant to be
there. Meant to make a difference.

Checking her watch, she noted there was an hour and a half until their meeting. Decisively, she headed out, leaving a note in the
house computer notifying them she'd be back in time for the briefing. They said she could come and go as she needed. They said she
was a full team member. She'd see if they really meant it.

Not twenty minutes later, Ash stormed into Brandt's office.
"She's gone!"

"Not for good. She'll be back for the meeting." Brandt didn't
even look up from his screen.

"How do you know?"

Brandt's eyes found Ash's. "Because she said she would be."

Ash took a deep breath and sat down. "Okay. If she's run off, I'm going to hunt that pretty ass down and bring her back, kicking and screaming. She's run from me for the last time."

"Stop making this about you. You're going to be all right with this, aren't you?" Brandt's voice held warning.

"With what? And in case you've forgotten, I'm the ranking officer here." Ash snorted.

Brandt ignored the dig. "You know she'll have to do more than *pose* as my concubine. I'll be sleeping with her on the transport. I'll be touching her all the time on Nondal. And more."

"And you do know that as your best friend, they'll expect her to be shared with me on occasion."

"Don't push her too far, Ash. We need her in one piece. You can't break her down, not on this mission. It could get us all killed."

Ash's mouth flattened into a harsh line. "I will do my job. But I'll get her back."

"Just be sure you keep the two separate. Know your role here." Brandt shrugged and went back to his screen.

*J*ust shy of the time for the meeting, they heard Sera come in downstairs and got up to greet her, only to stare dumbfounded at her as she walked into the situation room. She stood there, her short curls now so long they hung to her ass. Her eyes bore the makeup common to most concubines, and the beauty mark was there just to the right of her eye.

"What the hell?" Ash breathed out, but there was a weight on his chest at the sight of her. A glimpse of the old Sera. Just a small flicker of his woman, soft, made-up, but still ready for action if need be.

Sera shrugged as she grabbed a glass of juice. "Concubines have long hair. I went and had extensions put in. She'd—a concubine—never be seen without her face made up, so the eyes and lips are long-lasting. I don't know how long we'll be there, so it'll remain on for thirty days or until I remove it."

Both men continued to stare at her, speechless. Her eyes, lined with dark kohl, were exotic and sexy. Her already beautiful lips were even more so with the shiny treatment. Not red, more like the flesh of a pomegranate, that succulent jewel brought from another 'Verse millennia ago. Her hair was thick and lush before, but now it hung in curls covering her back and arms. In short, she was luscious, beautiful and damned sexy. Still in cargo pants and boots and yet utterly delicious.

The smile on her lips told Brandt she knew the effect of her transformation. "What? Don't worry; I went through secure channels to have it done."

Brandt shook off his stunned surprise and moved into the room to the table and sat down, hoping she wouldn't notice the state of his cock. "Of course. It looks great. *You* look great. I like the attention to detail."

"You look more than great, Sera." Brandt glanced up at Ash sharply at his words but was relieved the other man stopped at that and sat.

Sera pulled out two folders and put them on the table before the men. "Okay, I took the liberty of checking into some side channels regarding Giles Stander. He appears to have more credits in the last nine months than he's had before. He's always been on a tight leash and had a regular stipend from his Family. But he used to spend it within days of the first of the month. Apparently he's making it to the last week of the month now. He's even paid down some of his debt."

"Debt? What are you talking about? We've thoroughly checked

his finances, and he seems moderately solvent. And what do you mean, *side channels*?" Brandt narrowed his eyes at the papers in front of him, showing the data to back up what she'd been saying.

"Coming from an unranked family and working with the lower classes has its value. I know people who don't operate on the standard channels, let's put it that way. Anyway, it appears that Stander has a problem with the tables. He's got a wife, three declared mistresses and a concubine as well. Interesting, no? Certainly taxing on his income. Up until not too very long ago, he only had a wife and a mistress, and now suddenly he's got multiple women. It's the kind of thing that might lead a man whose Family has a lot of contact with the Interior to see what he can sell off for more credits to keep his women in expensive jewelry and the hired thugs off his back."

"You can't just use the criminal element for this kind of thing, Sera! You could have very well compromised this mission!" Brandt stood, and she did as well.

"In the first place, PC Pela, I am not stupid. You recruited me to this team because I have certain talents. My contacts are impeccable, and while less than wholesome, they would not betray me. I did not break protocol in my research. If you'd like to see my work and the steps I took, they're all there in front of you in that folder." Her eyes were cold and her voice flat.

He looked down and carefully read over the papers she'd indicated. Slumping back into his chair, he nodded at her to do the same. And she did, only slowly. "Your brother?"

"Yes. My brother runs off-world gaming and money lending. He's not the criminal element. In fact, both your Family and Ash's have used him in the past. Made quite a profit, according to him. I suppose that such dirty money is distasteful, but it doesn't stop you from taking it. And while those of us from unranked families aren't good enough to marry, we can actually conduct ourselves according to the rules." The entire speech was delivered in an impersonal, clipped manner. Every word beat at him.

"I apologize for underestimating you, Sera. This is excellent information and certainly another indicator that Stander is behind the leaks to the Imperialists. For the record, I don't think you're stupid or that simply because you come from an unranked family you're not as good as we are." Brandt felt like shit for yelling at her.

"In any case," she said, not acknowledging his apology, "Stander certainly has a basket of financial problems. That, coupled with his Family connection, seems to indicate that he's a likely suspect. Add it to the other things in the file you'd already put together, and he's head and shoulders above the other suspects in motive and opportunity."

"It would certainly appear that way. I had my suspicions before, but he had no financial motive that we could see." Ash looked through the data.

"That he has a whole series of out-of-system financial dealings isn't so suspicious. I'm willing to bet many people with great deals of money do the same thing. It's the ebb and flow of the credits that's the key here." She held up a sheet of paper, and both men looked down until they found their copy. "This is a rough time line of the attacks and big payouts into Stander's accounts. My brother couldn't be totally precise—the system exists to be imprecise and to hide transactions—but he was able to give a basic estimate."

"This is really impressive work, Sera. Did you even sleep last night to put all this together?" Ash asked, looking up at her, loving that her hair was long again, the way it was when they were together.

"I get by."

Brandt sighed, and Ash felt sorry for him. He'd hurt Sera's feelings, and Ash sure as hells knew what that felt like. "So I think we should focus on him, then. Of course keep an eye on the others, but let's stick close to Stander when we get to Nondal. Our intel says he'll be there in five turns for a general meeting of their trade company. They do big business on the rim. We leave before first light and should arrive the day before he does."

Sera nodded, gathering up her papers. "Is there anything else?"

Brandt reached out and took her hand. "I am sorry. I've offended you. I didn't mean to. I know you've had a lot to deal with in the last day, and my attitude didn't help. I want this to work, and I'm asking for more than is fair, I know, but I'd like to move past this."

She sighed and pulled her hand back. "Fine."

"There's the issue of you being my concubine and also the implantation of the communication chip."

"Communication chip?" Her voice rose a bit.

Brandt explained, "You know what the situation on Nondal will be like. Total surveillance in some instances. We can't speak openly, but it's necessary that we have the ability to communicate. Ash and I have chips implanted, coded to each other. Experimental, but they work. They operate on a special frequency. Ash will need to implant yours."

Her eyes widened with undisguised interest. "Hells. I heard about these things, but I thought it was all silly stories. It's like what, telepathy?"

"Of a sort." Ash held up a small glass tube with a silver cylinder inside. "It's undetectable in almost all cases because it mimics bone. I'll place it against the back of your skull, near your spine. It will establish a neural pathway and connect with ours on the frequency each communicator is set to."

"You can hear my thoughts? I'll have no privacy at all?" How the hells would she survive that?

Ash shook his head. "No, no. I'll give you a bit of instruction, but it's rather simple. You just open a neural doorway to speak and close it when you're done. We can't hear your thoughts unless you want us to."

Sera knew they were right. They'd be watched and listened to almost constantly on Nondal, but the idea of some creepy little brain comm unit was seriously disturbing.

But unavoidable.

"Okay. Put it in."

"Sit there. I'm going to put it in with a needle. I'll have to touch you." Ash phrased it like a request.

She appreciated that he actually asked, and nodded her assent as she sat and pulled her hair away.

Brandt knelt beside her and held her hand. "It's going to be fine. It feels . . . odd until you get used to it, but it doesn't hurt, and it's saved my life more than once. We'll be able to hear you within a twelve-klick radius."

Ash's fingers were warm and sure at the back of her neck. She felt the cool swipe of antiseptic and then the prick of a needle slowly entering her skin. It went deep, and then a strange, metallic taste filled her senses as her spine stiffened and her teeth clenched.

Brandt murmured softly, brushing his hand up and down her arm while holding her hand.

Ash moved away and put her hair back in place.

"It'll take a few hours for the pathway to establish itself and for your frequency to key into ours. Do you feel all right?" Ash helped her to stand.

Sera thought for a bit and nodded. "Now, what was that other bit about me being your concubine?" She looked to Brandt, wanting to focus on anything but the weirdness of what had just happened.

"You need to be used to my touch, Sera. Gentled to my presence. That's not something you can just will yourself to do. You jump when I touch you or when Ash comes into the room. And I know," he spoke a little louder to stop her from interrupting, "this is hard for you, but as a concubine, you'll need to be very sexual with me. I'll need to kiss you and touch you. All over. And more. You know that."

"I do know that, but I can't just be accustomed to a stranger's touch overnight."

"Which is why I think we should start now. We should sleep together on the transport. I'd like to work on small touches and build up from there starting now."

"Build up to fucking." She said it with a subtle raise of her eyebrow.

"Yes, or a very good approximation of it at least. I wish it didn't have to be this way." Brandt shrugged.

Ash snorted, and Brandt turned to him with a glare.

"You mean to tell me you can look at her and not want her?"

Brandt's hands flew up angrily. "I said I wish it didn't have to be this way. I'm not saying it'll be a chore to have her in my bed. But I prefer my bedmates to come to me willingly and not as an assignment. And it would be less of one if you weren't trying to goad her every five minutes!"

"Me? You're the one who insulted her, and now you're trying to maneuver her into your bed!" Ash tossed back.

"Jealous?" Brandt taunted.

"Yes! Gods damned! I am. I want her so much my teeth hurt, and she'll be next to you, naked and willing, and I hate that."

"Not everything is about you, Ash. Have you thought about how hard this is for Sera? For even just a moment?"

"As if either of you actually remember I'm in the damned room." Sera leaned her fists against the tabletop. "If I am to be a member of this team, you'll both address *me*. Stop speaking around me like I'm not here. This is a job. It's better than sitting in a muddy hole in the driving rain, trying not to shiver from the cold. I get why it's important, and okay, fine. But I'm not a thing. I am not even a woman Ash used to fuck. I'm the third member of this team, and you will treat me as such. You need me, damn you both."

"I'm better than sitting in a muddy hole?" Brandt tried not to laugh.

"Marginally so."

Ash snorted laughter but then sobered. "You're right. I apologize. You are the third member of this team, and we do need you. But you're wrong on one thing. You were—are—a lot more to me than the woman I used to fuck. I'm not proud of having to let you go, but it was what I had to do. It wasn't that I didn't love you."

"I don't want to discuss it. I'm well aware as Brandt's best friend, you'll be allowed to show me sexual attention in Nondal. I will tell you right now to keep it to a minimum, or you'll be drawing back a bloody stump. Don't use this to manipulate me."

"Okay, so let's move on as long as we all understand each other." Brandt looked to both, waiting for them to acknowledge what he'd said. Getting it, he nodded and pushed his chair out. "Evening meal back here in two hours. It's time we worked on some team building."

Sera nodded shortly and left the room, needing to get away from them both for a while before she exploded.

Chapter 5

$\mathcal{M}$oving down stairs in a skirt was a lot harder than she remembered. The heels she wore were high and delicate, and if she wasn't careful, she'd step on the hem of the gown. Then she could add to her embarrassment by falling.

Still, Sera hid her secret thrill at wearing something so feminine and sexy. The slits on either side went all the way to her waist. She had to move artfully, carefully, or she'd be showing the world her pink parts. At the waist, the material of the dress was drawn tight with a golden tie that thrust her breasts—such as they were—up over the top of the bodice.

Brandt had been right; she needed to get used to her role as a concubine. Which meant moving at ease in the clothes she'd need to wear as well as being comfortable with his sexual and affectionate touching. At least she had some experience with the clothes. The gown she wore was quite similar to the ones she once wore nightly for Ash.

Showtime, Sera. Sliding her palms down the silk of the dress, she walked into the main room, waiting for them to notice. It didn't take long.

Brandt turned to her, lips slightly parted in surprise. "Where's my drink, darling?" she purred, wearing a sexy smile.

His smile in return was enough to make her stomach flutter. "Don't you look lovely." He approached her with predator-like grace. Stopping just shy of touching her, he reached out, his hand cupping the back of her neck, and pulled her to his body. She let herself fall into him, the cushion of soft to hard. Lush lips passed over her own gently, just a brush, before letting her go.

"Do you still enjoy ale, Sera?" Ash interrupted, voice brusque.

Shaking off the spell of Brandt's touch, she turned and nodded as she took the tall glass Ash handed her. She took a few deep swallows to try to get past that kiss.

"Nicely done, Sera. That's a beautiful color on you," Brandt murmured, his hand sliding around her waist, cupping her hip possessively.

"Thank you. It's nice to know I'm not entirely rusty after years of uniforms and smelling like gun oil."

The sexual tension between them thickened. Her breath caught as his tongue darted out to catch a drop of ale on her lip, sending shivers from her nipples to her pussy. "You're not rusty at all," he murmured, lips just barely touching hers.

"And dinner is here. I'm starved," Ash all but growled as he pushed past them both to the low table where the food had been placed. He plopped down on a pillow and looked up at the two of them, annoyance clear on his face.

Brandt propelled her to the table with a guiding hand at the small of her back. He nodded to the pillows at his feet, and she slowly got to her knees. Warm, lethargic desire rolled through her at the familiarity of the movement. It'd been a very long time since she'd knelt before any man.

One of Brandt's hands caressed the side of her face and neck for a moment before he sank down next to her. Sera realized she might be able to lose herself in the role, to accept her need to be sexually submissive within the context of the person she'd have to be while on assignment.

Whether she could find her way back later was something else entirely.

"Oh, look, your favorite." Sera picked up a small meat roll stuffed with greens and brushed it over Brandt's lips. He opened, nipping her fingers as he took it into his mouth.

Brandt found himself utterly charmed by Sera. He laughed at her playful nature as she fed him and stole bits from his plate and even Ash's a few times. The depth of his attraction for her crashed into his system. Seeing her on her knees there the moment before he sat down next to her, the power of it, of those deep blue eyes blinking up at him, made his cock so hard he'd winced every time he'd moved. It'd nearly brought him to his own knees.

But it was complicated and would only continue to get more so. She used to be Ash's woman. He still loved her. And Brandt loved and respected his friend very much. More than that, Sera carried wounds from her breakup with Ash, and Brandt didn't want to hurt her. And they were all three on a team together.

He had no idea how he'd get through the next weeks with her posing as his concubine. But he looked forward to it anyway.

In truth, he'd dallied here and there, but he'd never actually had a full-time relationship with a woman. The dynamics were far different, more complicated, even as he found himself fascinated and drawn in by the beginnings of just that sort of thing with Sera.

He wanted what he shouldn't want. But that didn't stop him from wanting it.

Sera's heart raced at Brandt's touches. At the warmth of his skin and his elemental scent. His hair caught the light just right, and glints of blue were shot through the ebony strands. His lips had been soft and juicy and hinted at what was to come.

She *should not* want him. It was totally unlike her, which was so very odd. For a very long time she'd simply turned off that part of herself. After Ash, there'd been a dark time when she'd loosed all her anchors and found herself in places she hoped to never return. Part of her had been relieved by the absence of such a powerful bond.

Afterward, though, once she'd decided to live again, she had relationships here and there and enjoyed sex on occasion. But she never craved being topped by any of them. It was as if her time with Ash had been so special, so perfect, that when it ended so horribly, it killed her desire for submission. But there on her knees, the heat of Brandt at one side and Ash's hard, arrogant body just to the other side, she began to lose hold on caution and let herself examine the possibilities.

She should be far more worried about the next weeks in Brandt's bed, but desire began to trump caution. The way he'd touched her as she'd knelt before him . . . she knew their sex play would turn rough and hard-edged, and the knowledge thrilled through her system.

Which made her think about Ash and the way he stared at her with hungry eyes. He'd be touching her, too. She knew he'd push it as far as he could when they got to Nondal, and it panicked her. Not so much because she couldn't take it but that she craved it and had never stopped. Ash had been a part of her for a very long time, and even after she'd left, he'd kept part of her heart. Hells, most of her heart. That's why she'd never been able to get rid of the tattoo on her hip.

Despite loving him still, she couldn't trust him. She couldn't trust herself or the way she felt when he'd dominated her. He'd been her drug, her lover, her friend, her master in the bedroom. No one had ever made her feel that way since.

Until she'd gotten to her knees and looked up at Brandt.

And Ash wanted. He wanted Sera with a depth of longing that twisted his gut. When she'd gotten to her knees before Brandt, he'd bitten his lip so hard he tasted the metallic tang of blood.

His memories of his time with Sera had kept him company for the last ten years. But time had softened the ache. Seeing her there like that sent it racing through him with a depth of clarity and longing he hadn't felt since the first weeks after she'd left. The dull pain of her absence in his life was now sharp-edged. The hunger for her was near desperation, and he knew he'd do whatever it took to get her back.

Watching Brandt slowly begin to seduce her to his power and will had fascinated Ash. He wasn't jealous. He'd expected to be. He just wanted the scenario to include him. Even though Brandt had topped him several times, watching him dominate Sera was a totally different feeling. Bittersweet. It made Ash hot and hard and filled with need. He'd begun to envision a threesome with the two of them topping Sera but sharing their lives as equals in every way. The thought pleased him. And he planned to move heaven and terra to make it happen. It *would* happen.

After the staff had taken the food away, Sera got up and brought a cordial to Brandt and then one to Ash.

"Sit here, Sera." Brandt patted the cushion on the couch next to him.

She kicked off her shoes and pulled her legs up under her body as she reclined into his side. One hand stroked up and down his forearm in dreamy rhythm.

"Would you like to work on using the chip?" Ash's voice was soft, not angry.

Sera took a deep breath. "Okay."

Ash moved a cushion to the floor in front of her and sat on it. "I want you to close your eyes and relax from the tip of your toes up to the top of your head."

She did it.

"Now, think about my finger sliding up your spine." He reached around her body and slid his middle finger up and over each bump of her spine until it stopped at the base of her skull. "Now. The spot where I'm touching is a door. Think of a door, and open it, and when you get inside, flip the lights on."

Sera followed his instructions.

"Now, I'm going to speak to you, and you're going to answer me, but not out loud. Just think your answer, all right?"

"All right."

"Can you hear me, Sera?" Brandt asked.

"Yes, of course."

"Open your eyes." Ash squeezed her hand, and she looked into his pale blue gaze. *"How do you feel?"*

She realized he wasn't speaking out loud and laughed at the novelty of it.

"Amazing!" But she'd thought it, and both men laughed, too. All in her head.

She spoke out loud this time. "That's it? I just have to talk to you in my head?"

"Just open that door. You don't have to do the spine and door thing. You know where it is now, right?" Ash tapped the base of her skull, and she realized his hand had been resting there all along.

She felt it, like a small spot of warmth lying against the bone. "Yes. Weird."

Ash laughed again and moved his hand away. Her skin cooled at the absence of his touch. "You'll get used to it. Just open it and speak. The frequency will alert us, and we can open our chip to speak back. We don't have to be in the same room. Like we said earlier, it's effective up to twelve klicks. To turn it off, just close the door. We can't hear your thoughts if you've shut the path."

She did, and they sent thoughts her way so she'd know what it felt like.

Ash stood and tossed the pillow back on the chair nearby. "Your record is no longer public; we've pulled it. Tomorrow morning we'll start calling you Sela. You'll have to totally take on your cover identity. The name is similar on purpose. Even though you look a little different, if someone thinks they know you and hears a similar name, it should satisfy."

Sera nodded, a bit overwhelmed. It wasn't as if people would recognize her, even if she had been the target of Family gossip when she'd left Ash. She was a thing to them. Amusing to speak of, but none had bothered to look that closely. It satisfied her that such behavior actually served her for a change. "I should be going to sleep now. If we're leaving at first light, I'll need the rest."

"The wake-up call will sound in your rooms. We'll see you in the morning." Brandt kissed the top of her head, totally casually. "You did a great job tonight, Sera. Good night."

She got up and grabbed her shoes, swaying to the doorway before turning back. "Good night, both of you."

Once in her room with the door closed, she looked at herself in the mirror after she'd removed her clothing. There wasn't a huge difference from earlier that day, but the hair and the makeup did mark some sort of step. She pondered just what it could mean if she let herself fall into her role completely.

Chapter 6

$\mathcal{T}$he alarm came even earlier than Sera's normal time. She rolled out of bed and showered quickly. Once they left the house that morning, she'd be Sela Carter, concubine in the service of Brandt Pela.

She tried very hard to keep it in perspective. It was an assignment. It was important to the future of the Federation that they find out who the traitor was and neutralize him.

Looking into the mirror, she laughed a moment. Okay, so there'd be lots of sexual contact with Brandt. It wasn't like she had to lie just then that she'd find it distasteful. And how often did she get to play the part of a glamorous sex kitten, anyway? After the night before, she knew the sex between them would be powerful.

If she hadn't been so attracted to him, if he hadn't possessed such a compelling sexual lure, Sera was pretty sure she'd have felt a bit like a whore. They may have been able to make it look more sexual than it was, faking the actual sex, but if the Nondalese suspected them of hiding anything, no one would trust them enough to reveal anything of use. It was a job, including the sex. But it felt a lot less cold and perfunctory, because she truly wanted Brandt. In a way, just between herself and her reflection, it gave her an excuse to let go and leap, do something she'd never have done without the pretext of the assignment. She didn't know what would happen when the assignment was over, but for the time being, she planned to just go with it and be Sela.

Brandt's Family colors were purple and a deep gold. They'd be seen at the portal that day, and so to cement her role right from the start, she put on a regal, deep purple–colored dress. It crisscrossed just beneath her breasts and hugged her body. Sleek, gold heels completed the outfit. Her hair she wore high on her head, letting it cascade down in a river of curls.

Tucking her current identification into the wall safe in her quarters, she put her new cards and credentials in her bag before heading downstairs.

Brandt had been up an hour already, making sure plans were in place for the mission. Ash had been on the comm, making sure the transport was ready for clearance. He'd been sure to relay their plans to Nondal the day before, arranging for a suite of rooms.

Brandt still bore the marks from the cat-o'-nine-tails Ash had used on him after Sera had gone to bed. They'd both been amped up and needed to work out their excess energy. Ash was good at that.

Both men turned as they heard the sound of Sera's heels sounding down the stairs. Last night she was Sera, trying on a bit of a role for fun. But the woman in the skintight dress and the highest of heels, her hair a mess of curls on the top of her head falling down her back and shoulders—she was Sela Carter. *His* concubine.

"Good morning, darling."

Even her voice had changed. She spoke in a sensual, throaty purr that stirred his blood. And his cock.

He stalked to her and pulled her tight against him. One arm encircled her waist, and his free hand took her chin and angled her head just so before delivering a devastating kiss.

Her eyes widened a moment and then slid slowly shut as she melted into his body with a soft sigh.

At that sigh, his tongue swept into her mouth. Sampled her taste. Slid along her tongue and teasing, seducing. She was warm and minty from her toothpaste.

Shock slammed through Sera, chased away by the heat of desire as Brandt's arm held her tight about the waist. The hand at her chin caressed her jawline and moved to hold the back of her neck.

His tongue in her mouth was sure and skillful, and when she suckled it, his groan vibrated up her spine. Her nipples stabbed into the front of her dress, and she swayed, both under the spell of the kiss but also unable to stop taking more sensation from him.

Her bottom lip caught in his teeth briefly just before he broke the kiss.

"Good morning, Sela. How are you today?" His voice was hoarse, and his pulse pounded against the palm she'd laid against his chest. "Shall we eat a light breakfast here and then make our way to the portal?"

"I find myself suddenly very hungry." Her mouth lifted on one side in a sly smile, and he chuckled.

Letting her go, he held out his arm, and she took it. Only then, as they moved to walk into the dining room, did Sera notice Ash standing there.

"Good morning, Ash." Her voice wasn't quite Sela with him just yet. She'd need to work on that.

"Good morning, Sela. You look beautiful today." He bowed as they walked past and into the room. He didn't seem angry—more thoughtful than anything else. It should have filled her with relief. Instead, it made her wary.

During breakfast they went over their plans. The house was the last place they'd be able to freely communicate verbally. Even on the transport they'd have to be careful what they said and use the chip for anything sensitive. They could be sure no cameras were loaded, but a nearby transport could use modified parabolic equipment to eavesdrop. There was a staff on board as well, and while they were fairly sure most of them were absolutely trustworthy, the Families sent their own people on trips through the portals from one universe to another quite often as observers. Their transport had been chosen, and two representatives of Ash's family would be on board. They weren't people Ash knew personally and so couldn't trust without a doubt.

"Are you ready then?" Brandt stood and addressed them both.

Ash wiped his mouth and stood as well. "As I'll ever be."

Brandt pulled out her chair, and she took his hand. "Wait." He reached into an inner pocket, retrieving a velvet pouch. "You'll look more convincing wearing these."

He pulled out a platinum necklace bearing a stylized *B* in diamonds. Concubines of very important men often wore such identifying jewelry, a status marker for both parties. Reaching around, he fastened it about her neck. Diamond baubles for her ears and a bracelet followed, and he slid a pink diamond ring on her left hand.

He stepped back and looked to Ash, who nodded. "And one more thing." Upending the pouch into his palm, a ring with a dangling row of diamonds slid out.

Heart pounding, she took a deep breath and reached down to slide the bodice of her dress out of the way, exposing her breast. And the ring she still wore in it. A ring Ash gave her when she'd first gotten it pierced.

She heard his sharp intake of breath, and suddenly he was there, next to Brandt. "You're still wearing it." She didn't fail to hear the raw emotion in his voice.

Glib words tried to find their way from her lips, but they faltered when she looked into his eyes. He was satisfied, yes. But there was more. He was moved by the sight of his ring still marking her. She knew that.

All she could do was nod. If she'd tried to speak, her voice may well have cracked.

"I think this one is better, Ash. I understand your feelings on this, but Sela would wear something far more flashy."

Sera nodded, agreeing with Brandt.

"You're right. But I'll take it off. I put it on to start with."

And before Sera could disagree, Ash's hands were on her, fingertips sliding over her nipple to unlatch the ring and pull it loose. She watched his hand on her flesh, and the sense memory of the last time he'd touched her naked breast slammed into her, wrenching out a strangled gasp.

His gaze moved from her breast to lock with hers. The cool metal of Brandt's ring slid into her nipple, and the weight of the diamonds provided a new sensation.

Ash pulled her dress back into place before stepping back, and Sera wanted to run screaming from the house. If he'd done anything but that, she might have resisted the look in his eyes. But he'd touched her with respect, even as she saw the desire in his gaze.

And then it got worse when Ash reached up and unbuttoned his shirt, exposing his chest and his own nipples. In the one on the left, over his heart, he wore the simple ring she'd given him on the same day she'd begun wearing his. He put the one she'd been wearing in the nipple on the other side after he removed a barbell.

All of this without a word. Brandt watched them both. "Okay then, shall we be off?"

Sera took Brandt's arm, Ash fell in on her other side, and they left the house. They loaded into the posh limousine that would take them to the portal, and she left her old life behind.

She still wore his ring. Ash sat, head back against the seat, as he thought about the way her nipple looked in his hand. The ring he'd given her when she'd gotten pierced just for him. It had carried a sapphire, but she'd left that with her letter and her collar.

Hope burned deep within him. He saw love in her eyes. Distrust still, and hesitance, too, but she had feelings for him that didn't all involve wanting to shoot him in the head.

He'd need to be smart about how he went about getting her back. Smarter than he'd been so far, that was for sure. On the ship, he'd have to get her used to his touch again anyway. Originally, he'd planned to work his way into their bed right off. But he rethought that. He'd be more slow and steady, show her she could trust him.

It meant Brandt would forge a physical bond with her first, which was slightly disconcerting. But Ash already had the depth of his memories of her, and they'd share that again. Brandt would help her heal, be the bridge between them.

Once Ash had her back, he didn't plan to let her go again.

She worked through the briefing information in her head as they drove. It kept her from thinking about how her nipple still tingled and burned from Ash's touch. It was difficult. The cool stones rested against the bottom swell of her breast. The new ring was thicker than her old one, so her nipple throbbed, wanting to be touched more.

The drive took about an hour, and she leaned on Brandt, letting herself fall into the way he drew circles on the skin of her neck with a fingertip. They were in full cover mode now, so she said nothing as the two men spoke about business and politics. A pretty accessory.

Finally, they arrived and handed over the various necessary documentation. Sera loved the portal on Borran. Loved the sight of the sleek transports next to the battered freighters, all waiting to slide through the portals interlocking the Known Universes. The Known Universes stacked like a deck of cards with the capital universe at the center and the others shuffled outward from that. A portal was like a door through from one universe to the other. They would travel through several portals from universe to universe until they reached Nondal. The transport was a bit like a train. It would travel over special intra-universe tracks connecting the portals together. The trip to Nondal would take a few standard days of pause and slip, pause and slip.

Sera had never actually even been in a private transport. The Federation kept its own mass-transit ships, and that's how she traveled. The kind of luxury transports like Ash's afforded was reserved only for the very rich and privileged.

The driver opened the door, and Ash exited, followed by Brandt, who held his hand out to help her from the car. She stepped one very long leg out, letting her skirt ride up just a bit before turning to stand. When she straightened, she looked Brandt in the eyes and winked before pulling on sunglasses.

"This way, sweet." Brandt motioned with a hand. She put her head on his shoulder as they walked to the stairs leading to Ash's transport.

The hostess at the top looked over both men with undisguised interest. Sera waited for the woman to look her way, and one eye-brow rose. She didn't need to say more. A concubine of a powerful man like Brandt would be used to seeing other women ogle him but also have some measure of assurance that she was the first in his regard or she'd be replaced. Sooner or later she would be, or her paramour would marry elsewhere and take her as his mistress.

Still, Sela would not have worried in the slightest about that. Sela would have known without a doubt that she had the appeal to hold Brandt's eye. And so Sela looked amused at the hostess and handed her the ticket, making sure she saw the ring and the bracelet before letting Brandt guide her inside.

Transport seemed an inadequate word for the majestic, gorgeous craft they loaded into. Sera wished she could actually squeal with delight. Instead, once they were sealed inside and alone, she turned to Ash and gave him a surreptitious wink and a thumbs-up.

Moments later, the chip pinged, and she opened to it.

"I take it you like her?" Even in her head his voice was teasing and proud.

"I do. It's marvelous."

"I've spent a lot of time on it over the years. Much of the overhaul has been with my own labor. I'm glad you like it."

He withdrew from her head, and it left her a bit bereft. Touched, though, that he'd be sentimental over a transport.

She retired to their quarters while the men went off to the bridge to oversee the process of sliding through the portal. Sera tried not to be jealous as she worked out.

She found the silence and solace helpful for her focus. Because she had to be Sela when she spoke, keeping quiet meant her silence was a refuge for Sera. She poured her confusion and complicated feelings for both men into her workout until she was nothing but a mass of burning, working muscle.

At some point she'd become aware that Brandt and Ash had both joined her in the workout space. When she'd finally done all she could and had broken her concentration, she saw them both watching her.

She bowed to them before taking herself into the showers to clean up. It wasn't so much that she was avoiding Brandt, but she knew they'd most likely be moving to a new level of intimacy after dinner, and she needed to steel herself for it. After the morning's events with the nipple ring, the emotional stakes had risen for her.

She'd meant to take the ring out before they arrived on Nondal so Ash wouldn't see it. But he had, and now things had changed.

The ring had been with her for a long time, and she'd been reluctant to just set it aside for another ring. She supposed in her own way, it was holding on to the good memories of Ash Walker and what they'd been to each other.

Her entire life as she knew it had been upended in such a short time! But the truth was, she'd felt dead inside in so many ways. When she'd walked away, she'd expected Ash to follow. And when he didn't, and she saw he meant to go on, she'd been devastated to see the marriage every time she turned around.

For a time, she sought a replacement for him, fucking rough men who didn't know the difference between mastery and abuse. No one had topped her, and she'd never been able to let go enough to submit. It was self-abuse; she knew that as she looked back. But at the time, she wallowed in it and became another person. It wasn't something she liked to dwell on overmuch because it was weak, and she didn't condone what happened. It filled her with shame, but in the end, she'd risen above it and had found something better than an empty life. She'd found a calling.

Work became her salvation. She didn't become the best at everything she tried. Instead, she worked to be the best she could be at those things she excelled at. Once she focused on languages and culture and martial arts, they took over her existence. She'd been a finely honed tool in the war against the Imperialists. The military became her everything, and over time, she'd stopped dating and even seeing herself as a sexual being except for when the need hit every year or so. She'd engaged in brief relationships for sex only, and when she'd been sated, she'd moved on.

And now she felt it all. So much rage, fear, pain and loss that she would have crumpled to her knees and wept, but the hope burning deep in her stomach saved her. Hope that no matter the outcome with these men, she'd found herself again, the part of her that was more than just a soldier.

Chapter 7

$\mathscr{B}$randt and Ash knew Sera needed some time to herself. They stayed off the chip and let her rest. When she walked into the dining room several hours later, it was apparent to Brandt that Sela was firmly in place.

Which was good, because the Familial representatives had joined them in the dining room. Ash didn't trust the people his Family had sent, and he'd advised Brandt earlier to keep aware. They certainly seemed very interested in Sela.

All four men stood as she entered the room.

"Did you have a good nap?" Brandt reached out and hauled her to his body, and his cock, hard and ready, pressed into her stomach. She smelled sweet and heady, lilacs and warm evenings. Like sex, and he wanted some. He buried his face in the crook of her neck, breathing her in. He didn't have to fake being enamored of the woman he held.

She let her head drop back as he kissed her neck. "Well, I see you missed me. I did have a good nap, darling. Traveling and getting up so early makes a girl tired." She straightened to look him in the eye. "And I know I need my rest to keep up with you." She winked, and he chuckled, leading her to the table.

Both he and Ash watched through half-lidded eyes as she dropped to her knees and put her hands in her lap, waiting for Brandt to sit as well. Every time she did something like that, Brandt understood more why it'd been so hard for Ash to forget her. There was something magical about the way she submitted.

Throughout the meal, Sera served Brandt, doting on him. Each small touch drove him higher. Knowing they'd sleep side by side that night, that most likely he'd be touching her naked body, sent his senses into overdrive.

That and the way she was dressed. A small, gold scrap of diaphanous fabric covered her breasts, but he saw the shadow of her nipples and the dangling diamonds of the ring. Her back was totally bare but for the gold ribbons holding the front of the blouse on her body. The skirt was very short, and his curiosity at what she was wearing— or not wearing—beneath it made his ridiculously hard cock throb in time with his heart.

Brandt felt the chip's call and opened. He heard Ash speak to Sera. *"You play with fire, beautiful. Do you know what you look like there? Makes me crazy."*

"I'm just doing my job." She'd even managed to inject a bit of sarcasm into her thoughts, and it made Brandt laugh. Ash looked up and met his eyes, a smile playing at his lips.

Sela never wavered as she laughed and played charming with the Familial representatives while still remaining wary. They asked a lot of questions he felt were inappropriate and seemed unnecessarily invasive.

"I don't trust these men."

Ash gave an imperceptible nod. *"Me either, beautiful. Be on your guard. I've never seen them before, but they're underlings of my youngest brother, Kendal."*

"Why would your youngest brother be interested in what you do? Can you trust him, Ash?" Brandt asked.

"I have no reason not to. He's got his own piece of the Family business. He's the son of my father's mistress, but he's officially recognized. Still, it's best to keep wary."

The night wore on, and Ash became steadily more drunk. Sera knew what he was like when he got to this point, and she wanted to be out of the room sooner rather than later. It wasn't that she was afraid of what he'd do physically. Ash Walker wasn't a violent man. Not with her. In her years of being with him, all their sex play, even the roughest, was never done in anger or in violence. She'd never submit to anyone who made her feel fear.

No, submission was about trust, and she'd trusted Ash with her body and her heart. He'd been very careful with her body. She wished like hell he'd done the same with her heart.

But when very drunk, Ash was like a dog with a bone. He would pick at something until he'd analyzed it to death, relentless. And she had no reserves for that kind of discussion.

"Brandt, darling." Sera took great care not to look in Ash's direction and get pulled into a conversation with him. "I think I'll wait for you in our rooms, if you don't mind. That way you and Ash can have an after-dinner smoke with your guests."

"No, that's all right." Ash stood up and put his glass down. "I'm off to bed myself. I'll see you both at breakfast. Sela, you look beautiful this evening as always." Taking her hand gently between his, he leaned down and kissed her knuckles. With a final nod at Brandt, he turned and left.

Brandt shrugged. He was apparently familiar with Ash's badger mode and was just as surprised as she was by Ash's graceful good night.

The two guests smiled at them. "I think we should go back to our rooms anyway. If you'll excuse us, it's been a very long day." Brandt bowed slightly, and Sera inclined her head as they walked past and out of the room.

She looked deep into Brandt's eyes and let herself fall into his gaze. He refrained from touching her at that moment, and she knew what he was asking without words. He was giving her a way to back out, but she didn't want it. She could tell herself it was a way to get used to his touch, but she didn't have the strength to lie. She wanted him.

She wanted him to wash away the ache of the Ash-sized hole in her heart. A hole she'd had for ten years and had mostly dulled with work and occasionally play. Being confronted with him and his presence brought it back. It hung like a heavy cloak.

She nodded and put her hand on his forearm.

Just inside the door to their quarters, he backed her against it. Stopping just shy of her lips, he looked into her face, making sure she was still with him. Once he'd ascertained she was, his lips met hers. Softly at first, increasing with pressure and intensity as the moments ticked by.

He took his time as his mouth devoured hers. Lips, hot and soft, brushed over hers. Her bare skin warmed under the hands resting at her hips. She sighed with pleasure, and his tongue slid into her mouth. His taste, intense, spicy and rich, bolted through her system. Sharp teeth caught her bottom lip, and she shivered.

He sucked her tongue into his mouth where the slow, seductive tango of a kiss fried her cells with electric intensity. He dominated her mouth, took, plundered her and fed it back to her until she trembled with need.

Her head fell back against the door behind her as his mouth skimmed over the line of her jaw until he found the hollow just below her ear and feasted on it. Writhing against him, her fingertips dug into the muscles of his shoulders as soft sounds of desire broke from her.

"I love the way you taste," he murmured into her ear as his hands found the ties to her blouse and undid them. The pretty fabric fluttered to her feet. "I want more. Will you give me more?"

Her moan of assent was as articulate as she could manage.

His hips canted forward, holding her there against the door. She watched, immobile with fascination as well as his weight, as his fingertips trailed across her collarbone and down her chest. Skirting her breasts, he touched the sensitive skin between them and circled her belly button. Reversing direction, he reached up and took the weight of her breasts in his palms, eliciting a gasp when his thumbs brushed over her nipples.

"So pretty," he said just before kissing her chin and down her neck.

The heat from his body seared her. She reached out to remove his shirt, but he looked into her eyes and shook his head. "No. Not tonight. It's just you tonight."

He couldn't possibly mean that. She must have shown her distress on her face, because he chuckled softly and smiled.

"There'll be more, sweet. There always is. With you, there always is."

Before she could think up what to say without sounding suspicious, his mouth found her nipple, and all coherent thought was lost. Instead, her hands held his head to her.

Suck. Draw. Lick. Bite. Somehow the man took those four basic things—sucking her nipple, drawing it between his lips and against his tongue, flicking and swirling his tongue around the tip and

biting—to poetic levels. Each time he completed the set of movements and began again, he did something a tiny bit different than
he had before, or he moved to the other nipple. Over and over until
she was little more than a whimpering mass of writhing, begging
woman.

"Please, Brandt, please!"

"Please, what?" He spoke around her nipple, his eyes on her.

"Oh, my! Please make me come. Give me more. Fuck me, spank
me, tie me up, I don't care! Just touch my pussy somehow!"

He froze and gave her nipple a sharp bite that made her shiver
with delight. Looking up slowly, he met her eyes. He was a sight to
behold. His lips were swollen and glistening. His chest heaving to
catch his breath. Thank the gods he was as affected by the situation
as she was!

"Go into the bedroom and take off your skirt and panties. Get
on the bed and spread your legs wide for me."

She opened her mouth once, and nothing came out. She didn't
want to argue. So she nodded and walked past him and into the bedroom.

With trembling fingers, she undid the fastenings on the side of
her skirt, and it dropped to the ground. She looked back over her
shoulder at him with a smile. She hadn't worn panties. The skirt
was so low panties would have shown at the waistline.

"Oh, yes, Sela. That's lovely." He stood immobile, watching as she
got on the bed, first on all fours and then turning over to lie on the
pillows at the head.

It was as if the flash of the pink of her pussy freed his locked muscles. He crawled on the bed after her, still totally dressed. Grabbing her
ankles, he pushed her feet up and then levered her thighs wide open.

She should have been embarrassed. Her pussy was totally bare
and spread open to his gaze, but she was mesmerized by his power

and sexuality. Shivers of desire broke over her body as she watched, breathless with anticipation.

"You're glistening, sweet. I'm going to eat every last bit of you." He said it as he let go of her ankle and idly brushed a fingertip through the furls of her pussy.

With a soft cry, she arched into his touch.

"Impatient little minx, aren't you?"

"Is that a rhetorical question?" Her voice was faint. She couldn't quite draw enough air.

"Hmm." He broke his intent gaze on her pussy and looked up into her face. "Sweet, do you need to be taken in hand?" A smile hinted at the corner of his mouth.

"Oh gods, yes!" Who was he kidding? Of course she wanted that.

He laughed, crawling up her body to kiss her lips. She dragged her nails down his back, reversing them to pull his shirt from his pants. The skin beneath was hot and smooth. Her bare feet slid up and down his calves.

"That will take time," he murmured into her ear before licking the delicate skin there. "We *have* time. I want to do this right. I want you to give yourself to me with all honesty and nothing between us."

And in truth, nothing he could have said would have left her more defenseless. He could have taken her, she was open and offering. The anticipation would be heightened, but also, he wanted to take it slow. Sex was one thing, something they'd do for cover and admittedly, for enjoyment. But her submission was another story, far more complicated.

She nodded, moved beyond words.

He kissed her again with sweet and heady slowness. After a time, when she was boneless with need and he'd pulled her into his spell, he left her lips and kissed down her throat, stopping at the hollow

and then nibbling across her collarbone. Down again to each breast
and the same slow suck, draw, lick and bite rhythm until she'd begun
to whimper.

She was so wet her thighs were slick. Her clit throbbed, but he
held her thighs apart with his body so she couldn't even squeeze
them closed for relief. Her pussy ached to be filled.

A deep moan came from her when he licked across her hipbone
and down the crease of her leg and brought his body to rest between
her legs.

When his hot breath blew over her humid cunt, she gripped the
sheets to keep from screaming out for him to take her. Time slowed
as he moved closer and closer, and she cried out when he took a long
lick through the folds of her pussy and up around her clit. The tip of
his tongue tickled the underside of her clitoral hood, and two fingers slid into her cunt.

"Oh yes. More. Please more."

He pressed his face into her pussy, giving it to her. Giving her
more. Desperate, she rode his hand and mouth.

Pulling his mouth away for a moment, he looked up at her and
licked his lips. A breathy moan was all she could manage as he pressed
the heel of his hand over her clit. Every cell in her body, every drop of
blood, every muscle and bone wanted to come. She felt her orgasm
building deep within her, knew it would be backbendingly intense
when it finally broke over her.

"Touch your nipples. I want to see you show me what you like."

His mouth descended to her pussy again, but his eyes remained on
her fingers as she rolled and pulled her nipples, tugging on the ring.

Fingers, slick with her juices, stroked over her rear passage. It
had been a very long time for her, and when he pressed inside, just a
little bit, that was all she needed to rocket straight into orgasm with
a feral cry.

His mouth continued to devastate her cunt along with his fingers as climax claimed her and pulled her under, battering her on all sides with intense pleasure.

Finally, she went boneless with a heavy sigh and closed her eyes. The muscles in her body twitched and burned as her skin cooled. Dimly, she heard the rustle as he got out of bed. She found the energy to turn her head and open her eyes.

He undressed and came back toward the bed. She smiled and managed to raise her eyebrows a few times. Gods, he was beautiful.

"Not tonight. We have much more time. I'm tired and I've worn you out."

"Are you angry with me?" She rolled to her side to face him as he settled in beside her.

He took her chin in his hand gently. "No, not at all. You've pleased me very much." He tapped her temple, and she opened the link. *"Step by step, Sera. This is Sela and Brandt on one level, but I want Sera. Do you understand?"*

Her breath stuttered a moment, and she managed a nod. *"I don't know if I can,"* she thought back.

"You can, and you will. I'll earn it, and we'll work it through. You're beautiful, Sera. Beautiful and special and I want you. All of you."

Sighing, she let herself believe just a bit before she allowed him to pull her in to his body and wrap his arms around her.

He lay there, wrapped around her, listening as she fell into sleep. He finally understood the depth of Ash's desperation. Yes, she was smart and sexy. But there was something else, something he didn't even have words to do justice with. It made him crave her deeply. Made him want to sleep like this with her every night.

And not as Sela and Brandt. As *Sera* and Brandt. He wanted to see if he could have something real with Sera Ayers. He'd caught a glimpse of what kind of sub she'd be: saucy, irreverent. He smiled against her hair.

He didn't want some fun D/s play, he wanted Sera's submission. All of it and without hesitation and with total abandon. That first time between them wasn't the right time. He didn't just want her to submit because it made her wet to get dominated. He wanted her to submit to him because she desired to with all her being.

For now, they'd continue to get to know one another and move forward sexually and emotionally. He wanted more than to fuck her. Wanted more than her submission. He wanted it all. He knew it was beyond the cover for her as much as it was for him, so he'd enjoy each step they took, knowing she wanted it as much as he did.

Good thing, too, because his cock throbbed angrily. It didn't care that he had a plan to slowly woo Sera into a real relationship with him. It just wanted to be in her pussy or her mouth.

He thought of Ash, pinged him through the link.

"You fucked her," Ash said before anything else.

"No. I wanted to. What is it you envision this being?" It was important for Brandt to know. He didn't want to lure Sera into a place where she got hurt, and he wanted Ash to understand what was happening between them.

"I see the way you look at her. It's more than cover, and you want her as more than a plaything. I want that, too. We can be together, all of us. I know I love her. You're my best friend, and I love you. We can make this work. You need to build something with her. When the time is right, I'll move forward, too."

"You're going to be all right with me topping her?" Brandt couldn't not be that with her. He couldn't have the same switch relationship with her he had with Ash. He felt much more deeply and intimately for Sera. What he felt was more than an urge to play and blow off steam.

"As long as you understand I will be, too. I'm not jealous. I thought I would be, but I love her, and I love you. I can share that with you both. I think we could be a powerful unit, not just intimately but as a military unit. I'm tired. My cock is hard, and I need to come. Unless you want to be in my head when I stroke off, I'll see you in the morning."

Brandt laughed through the link and sent a little help for Ash's problem.

Chapter 8

When Sera woke up, she was alone in bed but not alone in the room. Brandt sat shirtless at the desk nearby, working on his computer, his forehead creased in thought. She took that moment to watch him for a bit.

He finally heard her rustling to sit up and turned around with a smile. "Good morning. Sleep well?"

One of the corners of her mouth quirked up at the sight of his sexy smile. "I did. I was extremely relaxed when I fell asleep last night. And how are you?"

"I'm good. We've got some other traffic out there now. All on their way to Nondal or Ceres." With that veiled warning to watch what she said and did, he stood. "I'm off for a meeting with Ash. Family business issues. Will I see you at breakfast in an hour or so? Or shall I have someone bring you a tray?"

Air strangled in her throat when he reached up to stretch, pulling his arms over his head. Her bottom lip caught between her teeth as she watched the play of muscles in his abdomen and upper arms.

"I'll be in for breakfast I think. Thank you, darling."

He raised one eyebrow, catching her staring at him hungrily. "I am a lucky man indeed to have such a treasure in my bed who looks at me that way."

"Oh? Do you need to hunt for buried treasure then? If so, I think I know where you need to look." She spread her thighs.

Throwing back his head, he laughed, a deep, rich baritone. "You do tempt me. But I just hit Send on a message that I'd be in the meeting in ten minutes. And I never do anything quickly when the job needs a lot of attention to detail."

Sera pouted and got out of bed, letting the sheets fall away. When she attempted to pass him to enter the bathroom, he grabbed her, lightning quick.

"You do know how much I wish I could stay in here all day and make love to you, don't you?" His words were quiet and for Sera. "I really do have to duck out and meet with the representatives and Ash. And then there'll be breakfast."

"I had a slight inkling." She squirmed against his erection. "But I do thank you for saying it anyway."

Leaning down, he captured her lips in a brief but thorough kiss. Breaking away, he set her from him with a sigh.

Her tongue slid over her bottom lip, still tasting him there. Still feeling the delicious pressure of his mouth. "I'll see you in a bit then. Don't work too hard."

"Always. That's my motto."

Laughing, she left him there in the room while he finished dressing. She closed the door to the bathroom behind her and thought of the pleasure of waking up with a man's presence in the bedroom.

There was something inherently safe about it, warm. Yet another thing she'd missed but hadn't recognized until she had it again.

*H*er next two days were roughly the same. The Familial representatives took up Ash and Brandt's time, and she was left to her own devices for most of the daytime hours.

She'd found the small screening room on the lodging deck, and the staff brought her snacks while she watched vids and movies. Leisure had been a scarcity in her life until that point, and it was truly a luxury to laze around watching movies, tucked up under a soft blanket with no one to answer to.

There still hadn't been any fucking, which frustrated Sera to no end. Brandt did, however, order her in a very dark and velvet voice to suck his cock. Which she eagerly complied with.

He still hadn't overtly topped her. It was there between them, the unspoken air of command, her desire to be controlled and dominated, his to exert that control. But neither had stepped into it fully. She knew he waited for the right moment, and that made sense, but it still made her achy all over even as it scared her.

On the afternoon of their last day, Ash came to the door of the screening room.

"Sela, may I join you?"

His presence had been respectful and considerate since they'd left Borran, but it still filled her with apprehension. But she knew she hadn't spent much time with him in establishing a cover. Mainly because her feelings about him were so damned complicated.

"Of course." She waved to the spot beside her on the large couch.

His scent invaded the space along with the heat of his body.

"Are you enjoying my screening room? I thought perhaps you'd enjoy watching films while Brandt and I were occupied all day." He knew she did, of course, they'd spent many an evening going to the cinema or watching at their home.

"I am, thank you."

The movie queued up and began, and they settled back to watch. The cook had prepared little crackers with cheese and fruit and sandwiches of all kinds. The two of them ate while they watched, slowly growing comfortable again.

He took her hand in his and massaged it between his own in exactly the way he remembered she'd loved before. Heat spread up her arm and into her chest. Big, gentle hands kneaded the space between her fingers and over her knuckles, up her wrist and forearm. If he'd been so inclined, he could have easily snapped any of her fingers right in half, or broken her wrist. But he only gave gently to her.

She looked up into his face, and the shock of his eyes shining with love made her take in her breath sharply. *No!* Damn it, not him. She could not feel for him.

"Don't fight it, or it might pull the tendons I've just loosened." His eyes gave her the multiple layers of that sentence. Hellsfire.

She shook her head sharply and mouthed, *Stop.* And to her utter surprise, he did, but not before bringing her hand to his lips and kissing the space on the inside of her wrist.

"I'm sorry if I hurt you."

Oh gods. His cover words referred to the hand and wrist, but he meant ten years ago. And his eyes meant it. He wasn't the belligerent man he'd been before, blustering to save face. There was so much laid bare for her to see. He'd done it on purpose. And it worked. She felt for him. She believed what he said was true.

She pulled her hand back gently. "Thank you for your apology.

I'm fine now." She motioned to the screen with her chin. "Next movie's starting. You going to stick around to watch with me?"

She saw his surprise at her invitation and then the pleasure. He settled back against the couch cushions. "Sure. This is one of my favorites."

They both sat there, cuddled up but not quite on each other, for another few hours. As each minute passed, Sera relaxed with him again. He didn't press, didn't use the chip to speak to her; he just let things *be* between them.

After the movie was over, Ash stood up and stretched. Sera closed her eyes to keep from watching him. "Come on, I'll walk you back to your quarters, shall I?"

Opening her eyes, she saw he'd extended his hand and watched her with exposed hope.

With a sigh she reached out, taking it and allowing him to help her stand. He kept her hand wrapped in his as they walked to her door.

"Thank you for spending your afternoon with me. I quite enjoyed myself." Ash leaned in, and before she knew what to do, he'd brushed his lips across her brow.

"I'll see you shortly at dinner." Proud her voice hadn't gotten breathy at his close proximity, she managed to take a step back.

With a nod of his head and a smile, he turned and walked toward his rooms, whistling.

Frozen, she watched his retreating form. The phantom of his touch still radiated on her skin. The gentle brush of his lips across her brow was worse than if he'd laid a lascivious tongue kiss on her. The startling sweetness of his behavior was incredibly alluring, and it put her off balance. Just when she'd begun to expect one thing, he did another. Damn the man!

Sera walked back into the living room feeling slightly dazed. Brandt was there, dressed for dinner and looking like a wickedly handsome reprobate. It suited him. Probably because he was the opposite of that. She wondered if it bothered him when people thought of him as a lazy, shallow, spoiled rich boy.

"Hello, there. Why didn't you come and get me? I didn't know you were free." She kicked off her shoes and padded over to him. She slid her hands up his chest, over the fine material of the shirt, and into his hair.

Clearly pleased, he dipped his mouth down to claim hers, his hands moving down to cup her ass.

"I just got free not too very long ago and came back here to get ready for dinner. The representatives will be going on to Ceres, so this is their last night with us."

"Well then, I'll go and get ready." She stretched up and kissed him quickly before ducking out of his grasp with a laugh.

In the mirror of her dressing area, she realized there'd been no acting just then. She'd been pleased to see him and kissed him. He'd been pleased and returned her affection. Her hands gripped the side of the sink.

In six days she'd fallen for Brandt Pela. Six frigging days. She stomped her prettily heeled foot in frustration. She'd held off feeling anything for anyone for years, and now she was falling in major like for the man out in the living room and considering forgiving a man she'd pretended to hate for ten years.

She shook her head at herself. Weak. Damn. It was what happened when you denied yourself sex for so long. Your brain ceased to work in a coherent fashion.

Her hands shook as she put on a midnight-blue gown. It was sheer; gods, all of her clothing was sheer these days. She'd begun to miss wearing comfortable clothing that didn't make her feel so exposed. She wasn't sure how concubines did it. Being on display all the time was tiresome.

$\mathcal{B}$randt knew that Ash had spent the afternoon with Sera. It hadn't bothered him at all, which was puzzling. Brandt understood he and Sera were building something far deeper than their mission, and that excited him.

At the same time, he knew she and Ash had a complicated history, but there'd been a lot of love there at one time. And he sure as hells knew Ash still loved her. Each time Brandt saw Ash's eyes and body language when Sera was in the room, it was totally obvious. Not to mention, Ash had come out and said it. If Ash had been an asshole like he'd been back at the house, it might have been a different story. But he'd shown a side of himself Brandt hadn't seen before: soft, humble. His love for Sera had made him into a better man.

As each day passed, Brandt began to feel more and more strongly that the only way he could be with Sera was if Ash was with her, too. They'd be working together all the time in close quarters. A couple would not work between two of the three. If it were he and Sera, they'd drive Ash away, and Brandt couldn't imagine watching her with anyone else and not having her, too.

All of that fell right out of his head as she walked back into the room. "Good gods, Sela, just when I think you can't possibly look any more beautiful or sexy, you outdo yourself."

"It's the clothes, darling. Spend a great deal of money on something, and it generally makes you look or feel better."

She was an excellent actress. In his time with her, he found her to be one of the most genuine and nonmaterialistic people he'd known. But mind to mind through the chip, it was different, a sort of knowing on two levels. She'd let him into her real self.

"Hmm. I think I need to spend a great deal of money on you once we get to Nondal tomorrow then." Winking, he caught her hand and kissed it.

She laughed, low and throaty. "You've already done that. I'm quite eager to make you feel better at any time, in any place. You just say the word."

"All right then. I'll be saying that word after dinner. If you're ready."

The weight of what he was saying hung in the air between them. "Well then, I'll try not to drink too much and keep my strength up, shall I?"

He took her hand and put it on his forearm, covering it with his palm. "That's a very good idea."

Chapter 9

Sera found it nearly impossible to concentrate at dinner. The heated looks Brandt sent her seared her, shooting straight to her pussy. Each movement she made brought home just how he affected her as the slick lips of her sex slid against each other.

The Familial representatives made her nervous and suspicious. She didn't like the way they watched her with Brandt or the way they scuttled around the ship. Yes, she knew she had issues with the Walker Family, but this was more than that. She'd been wary at first, but now she was convinced they were up to something.

One positive was that they seemed to completely write her off as a nonthreat, because while they had watched her and Brandt, they spoke as if she weren't even in the room.

"Ash, your uncle is concerned about your lack of interest in re-marrying. There are suitable matches for you, and yet when they've been proposed, you refuse them all." One of the representatives sneered down his nose at Ash.

"You can tell my uncle the exact same thing I do: I'm not interested in another match made by anyone but myself. I did my duty at great personal cost. Kira has married back into the family. Our future with the Pelas is secure."

Sera admired her own very fine acting, because she wanted to hurl her drink across the room, and no one even detected her rage. Instead she sat serenely, looking at the vid screen against a far wall playing various nature scenes. All the while she imagined kicking the representative who'd spoken in his testicles.

"Yes, but there are other Families who have eligible daughters to marry. It's not seemly to have a Walker of your age running about, frittering away his future. You need to get married and produce heirs."

Sera heard the click of Ash's jaw locking from across the table. If there was ever an intractable man, it was Ash Walker when he clenched that jaw of his. She knew if she turned to Brandt she may well start to laugh so she took a drink and continued to act as if she were bored.

"It is not up to *you* what I do or don't do, Representative. I will produce heirs when I'm ready. In my own time. You and my uncle have no say about it."

"Be that as it may, Ash, we, that is, your Family, want you to make better choices about the woman you choose this time."

Brandt leaned forward. "Are you maligning my sister, gentlemen?"

Oh big whoop, his sister was a coldhearted, shallow bitch. Every time Sera had seen an interview with Kira, she'd felt even more horrified Ash had chosen *her* instead. And then the infernal cow had dumped Ash for someone else! It might have been a sort of poetic justice, but really, the woman was too much. Not that Sera was biased or anything.

"Oh no! Of course not, Brandt. Your sister was eminently suitable for Ash. No, we refer to the woman he'd been cohabbing with before his marriage to Kira. A lowborn woman of a wholly unsuitable nature. No better than a whore. Ash's family wants to be sure there will be no repeat of his request to marry any such unsuitable candidates."

Sera had to hold on to her glass tightly but not break it. She ignored the ping over the link. She couldn't hear them right then, or she'd lose it. Concentrating on not shattering the glass was the only thing that kept her from jumping on the representative and snapping his neck.

"You'll *never*, ever say such a thing about her again. Do you understand? She was not a whore. She was a good, kind woman who worked hard and earned everything she ever received. You have exhausted my hospitality, and I will ask you to keep to your quarters until you disembark tomorrow morning on Nondal. You will tell my uncle to keep his nose out of my business and my bed. I will not have this discussion with *you* or him again. Now, get out of my sight before I toss you out the door in between portals." Ash's voice was low and deadly, sending shivers down Sera's spine.

"Now see here!" The representative stood up, sputtering with indignation. Slowly, Ash unwound his body, standing and leaning toward the representative. The other one grabbed his compatriot's arm and pulled him from the room.

Ash sat back down with a long exhale.

He'd asked his family for permission to marry her. He'd been telling the truth about that part. Her hands trembled, but the pings stopped for the moment as each of them realized she couldn't deal with it right then.

Ash turned to her, and that pale blue gaze met hers. "I apologize that you were exposed to such vulgarity."

Brandt sat quietly next to her, his body sending out warmth.

Sera nodded. "I understand, Ash. They want the best for you."

He shook his head vehemently. "I had the best, and I had to give it up. My life has been empty ever since. I made the choice I had to make to save hundreds of thousands, if not millions of people in our universes who needed that union between Families. But I don't have to do that anymore, and I won't."

Speechless, Sera's mouth was dry as he pushed his chair back and stood. "Good night, both of you. I'll see you in the morning."

Brandt stood as well. "Shall we retire for the evening? I'm sure you're quite tired and would like to sleep."

She saw in his face that he was giving her an out. Right then, though, she needed his strength as an anchor, to hold her steady in the tide of emotions running through her. She needed to feel a hand around her throat and the command in his voice.

"Well, I think we should retire, but I'm not ready to sleep just yet. Perhaps you can help me get sleepy." A slow smile curved her lips.

She'd been staring into his eyes, so she saw his pupils grow so wide it was hard to tell where the pupils stopped. Deep, dark eyes looked back at her, eyes filled with intent.

"If you say so, I should endeavor to serve just such a purpose." He bowed slightly, and they walked rather quickly back to their rooms.

When the door closed behind them, it clicked into place. Reaching back, she untied the ribbons holding the top of her gown together, and it fell away from her upper body, leaving her breasts and torso bare. A tremor of need passed through her, rendering her light-headed at the intensity of it.

She wasn't sure when it happened to her. When her attraction and like of him had turned into a craving. She'd readily admitted to herself she wanted to fuck him, but this depth of desire to have him inside her was shocking. His mouth opened and closed a few times. She could tell he struggled with his feelings, too.

"Take me." Her voice was a whisper as she leaned back against the door for support. "Please." She'd been hiding in Sela, letting Sela be the one who needed him so much, but she couldn't hold the illusion any longer. The eyes that pleaded for his touch were Sera's.

He raised a brow, asking her with a look if that's really what she wanted. In answer she undid the side of the skirt and let the gown fall to the ground in a pool of blue silk at her feet. Reaching up, she pulled the pins holding her hair loose, letting the curls tumble free. Taking a deep breath to steady herself, she walked toward the bedroom.

She fell to her knees at the foot of the bed and waited, hands clasped in her lap. She'd not done that, naked anyway, since Ash. Brandt would have his own rules, she was sure, but it seemed a safe enough place to start.

It felt right there, kneeling for him. Her submission, which had seemed so foreign in the last years after Ash, fit her again. Molded to her form like a glove. There was no discomfort, no unease or fear in it. Sera wanted to gift him with her submission, wanted to abandon herself in the sweetness she hadn't felt in a decade. Wanted to feel sub-space again.

This man who stalked toward her, intent plain on his face, had been very careful with her since she'd joined their team. He'd protected her from Ash's temper and behavior and had gone out of his way to make all of this all right for her. He'd incrementally seduced her into submission, waited for her to be ready to give it instead of him having to take it. His kindness, his patience, his respect for her attracted and touched her deeply.

So she'd kneel and see what he did with the power. The rest could be negotiated as they went. She wanted to please him, and she'd handle her feelings when the mission ended. She wasn't going to think about it right then when her pussy was slick and swollen and ready to be fucked. She needed the strength of his dominance to help her through the revelations of the evening.

He halted in front of her. His hands sifted through her hair and down her neck. "Are you sure you're feeling well, Sela?" he murmured.

"Yes." She met his eyes, letting him know she understood what she consented to.

"Let's begin then. Before you suck my cock, I'd like you to help me get undressed."

"May I stand to do that?"

A visible shiver ran through him, and the remembrance of the intensity of power a submissive had over her Dom crashed into her, made her glow with adoration and desire to please. Craving more.

"It pleases me that you're asking. Yes, you may."

Standing, she moved to him. She slowly unbuttoned his shirt, leaning in to kiss his chest as she exposed a bit more skin. Her hands skimmed over his chest and down his arms as she pushed the shirt from his body. Quickly, she folded it and laid it across a nearby chair before coming back to him.

He was beautiful. She'd certainly noticed that in their time together up until then, but she hadn't really examined him as closely as she'd wanted to. Moving behind him, she pressed herself against his back, the heat of his skin burning into her. Her cheek rested on the muscle there as she breathed him in.

Her heart leapt, and she took a deep breath before reaching around to undo his belt, zipper and button. Moving to face him, she got back to her knees to help him out of his pants and underwear after he'd toed off his shoes and socks.

When she looked up again, his cock was at eye level, and she had to swallow her amazement. *My*, she did love his cock. Fat and wide.

His chuckle was dark and seductive, and it made her giddy with excitement.

"May I?" She looked up the line of his body.

"Oh yes, please do."

She slid her palms up the hardness of his calves and over his knees. Her thumbs slid in the line of his leg where it met his body. First, her hair slid over his cock and then her cheek.

His scent was hot and spicy, elemental, like him. Wrapping her hand around him, she angled his cock to take the head into her mouth, swirling her tongue around the ridge of the crown. She hummed her satisfaction at the salty taste of precum that'd beaded on the tip.

The weight of his hands resting on her shoulders was just right, reassuring and strong.

Her mouth engulfed him as her palm cradled his balls. The surface of his cock changed, the closer he got to climax. Ever harder, the skin tightening and vibrating with energy under her tongue.

She loved to hear the intake of his breath when she flicked the tip of her tongue against the sweet spot just under the head.

His hands moved from her shoulders and up into her hair. After she'd gotten a rhythm down, he began to guide her movements. Slow at first, gauging just how much she could take, and then pushing her limits more and more as time went by.

Sera knew if she thought about him pushing her down onto his cock, she'd gag or lose her rhythm. Instead, she let go of her worries and began to float, letting herself flow through the experience. She let him control her movement and the depth of his thrusts.

"That's the way. You're making me feel so good. You're so beautiful there, like a dream." His voice was soft but laced with command, and her body responded, nipples hardening, pussy softening.

What did she look like to him? On her knees, cock in her mouth, serving him, pleasing him. She hadn't wondered that, hadn't wanted to, in so long. The feeling of rightness settled into her.

Tears washed through her, and he stopped, pulling back and kneeling before her. She answered the call to her link.

"Se . . . Sera, are you all right? Honey, did I hurt you?" Silent with his voice, his hands still on her head, smoothing over her hair.

She wiped her eyes, laughing. She sent back to him, *"I'm sorry. I'm fine. Really."*

Standing, he pointed imperiously at the bed, back in charge. "Up and on the bed right now."

Quickly, she obeyed, and he followed, lying next to her.

"You're crying. Are these breakthrough tears?" Hearing his voice in her head was so intimate, a brush against her soul.

Sera was no stranger to tears during or just after sex. The kind of deeply emotional tears that happened after something Ash had done touched her or moved her in some way. Sometimes the emotion of feeling that deep connection when he topped her would make her cry.

She nodded and thought back. *"It just felt right. No pain. I'm not sad. Well, I learned some things tonight that have made me reevaluate what I've believed for the last ten years. But I'm really okay. And you haven't fucked me yet. I'm going to die if you don't."*

He looked surprised for a moment, and then laughed. Leaning in, he kissed her shoulder before flipping her onto her stomach.

She yelped when the first crack of his palm landed on her ass. One side, then the other.

"On all fours. Head down, ass up. Now." His voice sounded through the room, the command in it like a whip. She shivered as she obeyed.

His fingertips traced up her thighs and over her ass, bringing gooseflesh in their wake. "You're so beautiful." This delivered just before another crack with his palm. But the man knew his spanking, and his placement was percussive and aimed just so, carrying the vibrations from his hand up to her clit.

The fire on her thighs and ass emanated outward. She squirmed back against him with small sounds of entreaty.

Suddenly one of his hands moved up, wrapping her hair about his fist, while the other sent fingertips sliding between slick labia, testing her readiness. She nearly laughed at the very idea. She'd been ready for days. She thrust herself back against his hand and earned a yank on her hair.

"Tsk, tsk, sweet. This is my time."

Still, she didn't complain when his fingers pulled out and she felt the fat, blunt head of his cock nudge against her gate. As he slowly pressed into her body, her spine curved to take him in deeper. The wiry hairs on his thighs tickled the backs of her legs, still on fire from the spanking.

A low moan came from her as he fully hilted within her body. The fingers of his hand at her hip dug into the flesh so hard she knew she'd be bruised the next morning. He dragged out of her cunt and pushed in again. Over and over. The way her body was positioned, she could watch where they were joined, see his cock pull out, slick with her honey, and then disappear inside again.

Brandt looked down at the long curve of her back, the perfectly toned ass, still pink. He loved the way her superheated skin felt against his cooler flesh. Loved the sounds she made while he'd spanked her, loved her lascivious little squirms and squeals.

He'd never had a serious relationship with a woman he'd topped before. It wasn't so much that he'd been afraid to commit to anyone, but his life was complicated. He had a double life, and that wasn't something you could share with just anyone. And sure, he had a connection—physical and emotional—with Ash, but it wasn't the same. He thought of Ash as a friend he blew off steam with sexually from time to time. Sera was, or had the potential to be, much more.

The sight of her sucking his cock on her knees nearly did him in and then the tears. He knew that sometimes after a particularly emotional scene a sub might cry, but after the upheaval of the evening with the representatives, he'd worried he'd pushed her too far.

Her confession that things had felt so right when he'd been thinking the very same thing had done something to him, changed him deeply. Now as her pussy clutched his cock, not wanting to let him go each time he pulled out of her body, the feel of the silky hair wrapped around his fist—she moved him.

His orgasm was close, but he wasn't going alone. "Make yourself come around my cock."

He felt the movement of her arm and then the brush of her fingertips to gather her honey. The pull of her pussy as she began to stroke over her clit, tug, tug, tugged against his cock. Deep within her cunt, her muscles began to flutter and clench as her climax got closer. Soft sounds came from her, drawing him in deeper.

Her movements back against him grew more frantic and needy, and he knew her time approached. He deepened his thrusts and quickened his pace. The sounds of her moans wrapped around the wet sounds of fucking and his own grunts.

"Oh!" she cried out softly, and her cunt spasmed around his cock like a greedy fist as orgasm slammed into her body.

Not too many thrusts into her later, his own climax followed, his head tipped back, a long, guttural groan coming from low in his gut.

He let it wash over him for long moments, his cock still spasming within her and her pussy still fluttering. Finally, with a long sigh he fell to the bed, still inside her.

A few minutes later Sera placed a soft hand on his chest as she got out of bed. He grabbed her wrist, but she leaned down and kissed his fingers. "I'll be right back."

Sera went into the bathroom and ran water, getting a washcloth to cleanse him. She liked taking care of him. And it kept her from thinking too deeply on how good it had felt, his heart pounding against her back as he held her just moments before.

She gathered herself and tried to put Sela back in place before going back into the bedroom. It was shaky at best as she caught the look on his face when she bent over to use the warm cloth on him.

"Come, let's go to bed. We slide through the portal tomorrow on Nondal, and then things will get busy." Brandt's voice was sleepy and lazy as he pulled her back into the covers, and she settled in beside him. His arms around her, she felt safe.

The brush of his thoughts brought her awake, and she opened the link to the chip.

"You were beautiful tonight. More than I could have ever imagined. Thank you."

Unable to respond, even mentally, she shook her head and snuggled against him, letting hope grow.

Chapter 10

When Sera awoke, her muscles were pleasantly sore in the right places. All the physical exertion in the world could keep her body in shape, but nothing took the place of a hard sexual workout. Stretching those deliciously tender muscles, she opened her eyes to find Brandt watching her, a smile on his lips.

"Good morning, darling," she purred, moving to rub her body against his, sleep-warm and very hard.

Slowly, lazily, his palm stroked up the curve of her thigh and came to rest on her waist. "Good morning to you, sweet. I've become quite spoiled waking up next to such a beautiful woman every day." Part of their cover was that she'd just begun to see him a few weeks before, so things were new between them.

"Mmmm." She sighed softly as she reached down and found his cock beginning to show signs of life. "I think I see the truth of that statement. I rather like spoiling you."

Forty-five minutes later, Sera rolled off Brandt's body and lay on the mattress, breathing hard.

"Well, that was a lovely wake-up call, I must say."

He laughed, planting a kiss on her forehead before getting out of bed. She levered to rest on her arm and watch him walk naked to the comm unit on the other side of the room.

"We're due to arrive at the portal a bit after breakfast. Let's get ready, shall we?"

Ash was already waiting in the dining room, reading through some files, when they walked in. Seeing her, he whistled low and raised an eyebrow.

They'd decided a barely there gown of gold would be a great entrée into Nondal. There was no back at all, the waist low-slung, and the skirt a series of light panels that moved around her like the tide as she walked. The color highlighted the honeyed tone of her skin and hair. She was every inch the kind of woman who could hold the attention of a rich and powerful man like Brandt Pela.

"My! Well, Sela, the Nondalese aren't going to know what hit them when you walk down the gangplank at the portal. You look beautiful."

She inclined her head a bit, hoping she wasn't blushing. "Thank you, Ash."

Brandt stepped in neatly. "Have the representatives made any noise this morning?" Brandt sat, thanking Sera for the cup of kava she'd poured for him.

A sour look marred Ash's face. "I awoke to a message from my father and another from my uncle demanding I remove the travel restrictions at once."

Sera bet that only served to make him more intractable. "And did you?"

Ash winked. "Hells no. We'll see them when we all disembark. Before it's time to dock, they're confined to quarters."

She felt the ping and opened her link. They conversed about what the plan would be when they arrived on Nondal. Although Nondal, like every other Federation universe, held to standard time, their daylight hours were longer because the universe was farther from the Core and closer to their system's sun. Plenty of time for mixing with the other concubines. Stander would undoubtedly bring at least one with him, and if anyone knew any dirt, she would.

Nondal was on the border between Federation and Imperialist territory. It wasn't a capital universe but fell under the jurisdiction of the Licht Family, who held this part of the Known Universes. As a frontier 'Verse, it was much more heavily inclined toward trade and more apolitical than those 'Verses closer to the Central Core of the Federation.

Sera agreed with those who said the reason was because Nondal was structured far more closely like an Imperial Aligned Universe. There was no democracy at all: strict class structure with all the power at the top and none at the bottom, little freedom of the press, and a lack of basic information for most of the population.

Nondal was ideal for anyone hatching up ways to trade information or sell it to the highest bidder. It was one of the last stops before the Edge and then Imperial territory. It also served as a departure point to catch a portal to Ceres, a resort-themed universe ringing the next Familial quadrant. Nondal was a tourism destination in and of itself for wealthy Federation citizens who came to catch the space light phenomenon: beautiful, colored explosions of gaseous compounds that turned the evening sky brilliant shades of every color imaginable.

Anyone could be there for any reason. And because of that, it was the perfect cover.

They also had an invitation to a dinner party at the home of a prominent Nondalese businessman, a ranking Family member, the following evening. They'd loosely decided that while Sera attempted to flatter her way into the confidence of various powerful men present, Brandt would poke around a bit to see if anyone made him any offers. Meanwhile, Ash would try to hack his way into the Familial computer servers. There was a hub in the home they'd be visiting. Fortunately, they were all three quite handy at a great many things, so the plans could be loose enough to change if need be.

After breakfast, they slid through the portal and docked. Their baggage was sent ahead to the shuttle that would take them to the city, and they moved to disembark.

The representatives stayed well away from Ash as they boarded the shuttle. They'd make their visit to the Nondalese governor and leave for Ceres later that day. Sera couldn't wait for them to be gone. They both stank of trouble.

The trip to the city was relatively quick, but as they walked onto the concourse and were greeted by several Nondalese, the representatives moved ahead of the three of them and turned. Everyone stopped, waiting for a good-bye.

"I understand your agitation when we questioned your plans for marriage now, Ash." The troublemaker from the night before had the audacity to leer at Sera who, with iron will, cast her eyes down according to her social place as a concubine.

"Is that so?" Ash's eyes narrowed as he moved closer to Sera.

"I see she bears your mark. You only had to say you were involved in a triad. But you certainly know you can keep a concubine after marriage."

Sera's stomach sank. *How could I have been so stupid?* The tattoo must be showing because the dress was so low in the back. She was an utter fuckup!

Ash put his arm around Sera's shoulders. "My relationship status is none of your business, Representative. Yes, I'm in a triad with Sela and Brandt. This was information we wished to share on our own terms."

Great. Now she'd have to be Ash's concubine, too. Just when she had absolutely no reserves against him. She kept her eyes lowered.

The Nondalese governor chuckled and reached out to clap Brandt's shoulder. "She's a lovely one. Sometimes a little sharing is in order. Nothing to hide. We're on the frontier, but we're modern enough the closer you get to the sky, you know."

"The closer you get to the sky" was a way of denoting class rank on Nondal. The upper classes lived in the topmost levels of the domed cities with more sunlight and where the air circulators were. They literally got first dibs on fresh air and light.

Ash turned his body away from the representatives, and Sera heard a few people gasp softly at the slight. His arm remained around her shoulders and Brandt's around her waist.

"Shall we go then? I take it we'll be in the guesthouses on the top deck? Sela has never seen the space lights. I told her about the rooms with glass ceilings so that one might lie in bed and watch the sky that way." Brandt took the change in plans smoothly. The man was a professional, after all. Sera was grateful they were both so fast on their feet. She wouldn't have been so quick to gloss over her mistake. She'd make her apologies via the link when they got to their quarters. She couldn't bear to deal with it just then.

"Yes, of course." One of the Nondalese spoke to two men waiting off to the side, ordering them to take the bags to their accommodations. "Right this way, Mr. Walker, Mr. Pela." Like she wasn't even there. She'd have been offended if their stupidity hadn't suited her needs.

Sera was finally able to look around and, hopefully, hide her revulsion. The lower concourses were dark and the air close and stale. They loaded into an open elevator to take them to the upper levels of the city. Their liaison entered a code into the panel, and they began the ride up toward their rooms. The higher they went, the nicer the walkways were—wider, cleaner. The storefronts cheerier and better stocked.

"Here we are." They got out at the very top level.

Sera looked out over the city, Nondal Major. It was an architectural marvel, really, the way it was spread out. The dome was created with a semiporous substance much like glass that let in light and also served as a filter. The radiation levels were deadly to citizens who lived without protection of the domes.

Despite the danger, Sera knew there were some who'd left the cities behind and lived out in the open. They'd taken the risk to be rid of the stench of the lower levels and the lack of freedom. The luckiest ones had special filters in their homes that didn't cut the risks completely but lowered them.

Knowing what she did about Nondalese culture, Sera didn't blame those who'd chosen a shorter life span in the open air over the stifling conditions in the lower levels.

By contrast to those lower levels, their accommodations were quite luxurious. Nicer than any hotel she'd ever stayed in before. And true to Ash's word, the ceilings in the bedroom were glass.

Lush green plants filled the rooms, making the air fresh and cool. The furnishings were plush, the kind of chairs and sofas that called for you to lie on them and dream the afternoon away.

Their guesthouse was built in a circular pattern, and in the center there was a small courtyard with a fountain and a lovely table and chairs.

"Please feel free to move about this level and the two below it at will. Should you desire a tour of the middle strata, please contact the concierge, and he'll arrange for a Nondalese representative to accompany you." He bowed, reminding them of the fact that Nondal was a very closed culture and to keep on those levels that were preapproved. "There are several requests for your company at social engagements. Just check the console in the living area. Welcome to Nondal and Nondal Major."

With a nod from Ash, the man turned and left them alone.

Sera sighed and fell into a chair, trying desperately not to show how upset she was with her major mistake.

Ash came to kneel before her, taking her face in his hands. "I know we'd decided to keep our status quiet at first, but it's all right. No one is angry with you." He leaned in and brushed his lips over hers with such tenderness it tightened her stomach. Saying things he couldn't say specifically, trying to make her feel better.

Before she thought about it, her hands slid up the wall of his chest and over the soft skin of his skull. How long had it been? But her hands remembered; her skin remembered and rejoiced at the feeling.

He growled low in his throat and deepened the kiss, his tongue sliding across the seam of her lips until she opened to him. His taste burst over her, the sweetness of the memories rushing through her until they overflowed, and she thought she'd drown in them.

With a soft sigh, Ash pulled back, slightly trembling. She realized he trembled with need and was holding himself back. She didn't want to feel this for him again. Didn't want to care about him again. It was easier to hate and resent him.

But it was there, back like it had never gone, although fear existed there, too. Fear in her heart that she'd lose him again, and so she couldn't let herself love him or anyone else. She'd care about him, and they'd all make this work, but she mustn't allow herself to fall for Ash Walker again.

"Are you all right?" Brandt asked through the link. He sat on the arm of the chair and tucked her hair behind her shoulder.

"I'm sorry. I can't believe how stupid that was."

Ash took her chin and turned her gaze back to him as he replied via the link, *"You're not stupid, Sera. It was a mistake, but it didn't cost anything. It gives you more protection while we're here. And I'd be lying if I said I didn't rejoice to see you still wear my mark."*

"We'd both be very annoyed if you decided to punish yourself over this."

Sera smiled up at Brandt, who managed to sound arrogant through the mental link. Having to pose as a concubine to *two* incredibly handsome, virile men wasn't such a bad situation after all. They'd have to deal with the aftermath once they left Nondal.

"Would you like to sightsee a bit?" Brandt asked aloud.

She stood. "Of course. Let me change into some shoes more appropriate for walking. Shall I change gowns?" She pointed to the mark on her back.

Ash stood, and with his body he pushed her into the bedroom until she fell on her back onto the very large bed. Above her the sky, a deep blue, shimmered through the glass.

"I don't want you to cover my mark any more than I want you to take off the ring in your nipple or the necklace that marks you as Brandt's. You're ours. I like that a lot."

Brandt stood at his side, wearing a wicked smile. "I do think I need to see that ring in your nipple." He reached out and yanked. The top of the dress ripped as he tossed it over his head, leaving her upper body bare.

"Oh . . ." The power of coherent speech left her.

Nimble fingers flicked across the hardened nipple, and she caught her breath. She looked down the line of her body and watched his hand, the skin tawny gold, against hers, just a shade or so lighter.

"It's been very hard not sleeping in the same bed at night. I'm glad the representative saw my mark on that sweet skin of yours." Ash moved to the bed, tossing his shirt aside before he lay beside her.

She turned her head, feeling snared in the slow honey of time, and caught sight of him. Allowed herself to see him in a way she'd denied herself since she walked into her commander's office the week before.

Still so ruggedly beautiful. All very hard muscle, his stomach was lightly furred and his chest hairier. Both nipples bore rings, one hers, the other one she'd given him. His narrow waist led up to a broad, wide chest. He was so masculine it took her breath away. It always had. From the first moment he'd unveiled his body to her fifteen years before.

Her hand sought his cock through the material of his pants. "How hard has it been, Ash?" Her voice was Sela, a sex-kitten purr.

"Pull it out so we can see," Brandt said . . . no, ordered. And the remnants of the skirt followed the top of the dress.

Sera paused a moment, surprised by Brandt's seemingly easygoing attitude about suddenly sharing with Ash. She couldn't deny the allure of being topped by two men at once. By *these* men. She wished they could talk about it, but at the same time, she worried they'd lose the intensity of the moment. She wasn't a stranger to either man at that point, and there'd be time for talking later.

"That was a very expensive gown, darling." Managing to not sound too breathy, she smiled at him as she rolled onto all fours. Why not make the best out of it?

"Worth every credit, I assure you." Brandt lay down on the bed to better watch her.

Her hands went to the waist of Ash's pants and unfastened them, finding him bare underneath. She pulled the pants off and moved from the bed to put them across the arm of a nearby chair before hopping back up between the two men.

"Well." She looked back over her shoulder at Brandt. "It certainly looks hard."

"I think we need a test. Just to be sure," Brandt murmured, his body close to hers. Reaching around her waist, he took Ash's cock in his hand. Coherent thought became nearly impossible as she watched.

Ash looked up into her face, reaching out to caress the line of her jaw. "Like silk. Always so soft."

So much was happening all at once. Despite being slightly overwhelmed, her attention was seized by Brandt's fist, lazily pumping around Ash's cock.

"Oh, that's not the test. You know I just like to touch Ash's cock." He did? Well, things were just getting better and better! "You need to suck it. I'll think up the rest of the test as we go along." Brandt moved his thumb up and over the head, spreading the moisture gathered there, and brought it to her lips. She sucked it inside and tasted the spice of Ash and the tang of Brandt's skin.

She moaned breathily around Brandt's thumb and bit it gently before sucking on it.

"Sweet holy gods," Ash breathed out, and her attention turned back to him.

Brandt pulled his hand back, and Sera leaned over Ash's body to kiss his lips. Their tastes mingled. She heard the rustle of the rest of Brandt's clothing being removed, and he was back behind her body within moments.

"You know the way I like it, Freka." Ash moved the caress from her jawline to her neck.

She froze at his use of the name he'd long called her, the name of a goddess he'd said she reminded him of. The pain of what they'd had and lost knifed through her, and she sat up, moving out of his reach, her hand pressed over her mouth as if to hold in the scream of agony that threatened to flow from her.

Ash's eyes closed for a moment and he moved slowly toward her. Brandt put his arms around her and murmured in her ear, "Be calm now."

Ash stopped just in front of her body. He wasn't touching her, but a deep breath by any of them would have achieved that.

In her mind he spoke as Brandt listened, too. *"There has only been you. Forever and a day, and it's been you. There are so many things I want to say but cannot just now. I don't have the right words. But I know you know me."* His eyes pleaded with her to understand him. To hear around what he could not say.

How long had she wanted to hear these things from him? Wanted to *believe* them? Looking into Ash's eyes, she did believe it, without a doubt. There were a lot of things to work out. She wasn't sure what would happen when she wasn't Sela Carter, concubine. But for that moment, she was Sera, and he was the man she'd loved all those years before—before the pain.

A long, shuddering breath came from her lungs, and she cocked her head slightly, inviting a kiss. With a groan, he moved toward her that last bit, and their bodies touched just before his lips came down upon hers with crushing force.

It was a kiss of claiming as well as healing. Ash marked her with those scalding kisses as much as the tattoo on her back did. It was a melding of teeth and tongue and lips with a depth of intensity that felt as if he wanted to crawl inside her body.

All the while, Brandt stayed behind her, pressed against her, whispering in her ear that she was beautiful and sexy and how much he wanted her.

Ash broke contact and stared into her eyes for long moments, letting the unsaid be spoken through his gaze. "Now, I believe you were given an order."

She gulped and barely suppressed a shiver of need at his tone. Her hands caressed the hard planes of his chest and stomach. She leaned in to skate her lips down the warm line of his jaw and to the hollow just below his ear, swirling her tongue there, feeling the frantic beat of his pulse.

Hands braced on his thighs for balance, her mouth skimmed downward until she found his flat, hard nipple. He moaned as she brought the edge of her teeth over first one and then the other. Her mouth remembered what he liked and where he liked it as she moved it over his body, reading his desire by touch.

It was a good thing she'd been braced. Brandt bent her body forward a bit more and slammed his cock deep into her. Her ass rested on him, her thighs spread and leaning against his. His thrusts weren't slow and easy. He pounded deep and hard, making her breasts sway, the diamonds clicking quietly with the movement.

"Suck his cock, sweet. Suck his cock while I fuck you." Brandt's voice was a feral growl, and instead of speaking, she whimpered and found the head of Ash's cock with her mouth, slowly sucking it inside.

Ash was not a quiet man in bed. He owned his sexuality in a raw, dark way. There was something so sexy in the running commentary he made, even the naughtiest, dirtiest things he said were so hot they never failed to make her wet.

"That's right, Freka, suck me the way I like. Your mouth is so hot and wet, Gods, you make me hard. I can't wait to come, to fill you up. And later, I can't wait to put my cock deep into your cunt and feel how soft and hot you are when Brandt is done. Would you like that?"

Brandt groaned behind her, and his cock jerked within her in agreement. She took Ash deeper, breathing through her nose to keep her rhythm steady. As she dug just under the head of the crown with the tip of her tongue, his guttural groan let her know he still liked that very much.

Moving one of her hands, she cupped his balls in her palm and pressed his perineum with the pads of her fingers.

"Yesss," he hissed, rolling his hips and thrusting into her mouth. His hand moved to her hair and gripped it so tight tears sprang to her eyes. But the pain rode that line, just on the right side of the pleasure/pain divide. He knew her body, knew how to make it sing just for him.

Sliding her hand forward, her fingertips stroked over his anus, and his cock stiffened even more.

"Oh yeah, that's the way." Ash's body arched back as he rolled his hips, thrusting into her mouth. One of his hands held her hair, controlling her movements. She began to slip away into the sweet haven of sub-space. Brandt's fingers digging into her hips anchored her there between them. Kept her from drifting off completely. Instead, she felt warm and desired, cosseted and revered.

"Aw, fuck," Ash groaned as he began to come. His taste flooded Sera again for the first time in so very long. It was as if her entire system celebrated his return. Her body tingled, her skin was ultra-sensitive.

Sera continued to suck and lick his cock until he'd softened, and she pulled back with a kiss to the head.

Ash leaned forward and dragged his nails up her back, and she shivered and stuttered a moan. Gods how she loved to be scratched like that!

"Oh, I see." Brandt chuckled as he and Ash must have shared a look over her body.

She felt Ash bend over her body and cried out as he sank his teeth into the back of her neck. Only he knew that line she loved to walk, only he'd known just how far to push her and keep her safe.

"Oh, sweet, you're so fucking beautiful," Brandt groaned out as his cock jerked inside her body, filling her as he came.

Panting for breath, she found herself quickly flipped over, with Brandt still between her thighs. "Now it's your turn."

"Indeed." Ash moved down and settled in next to Brandt.

There was no way she had the power to reply to them, so she arched her hips and made a sound of entreaty.

Both heads bowed. Brandt moved upward and licked up her stomach and over her nipples, biting and laving until she squirmed. Which was nothing compared to the way it felt when Ash gave her pussy a long lick, pressing the flat of his tongue over her clit and sliding it from side to side.

"Brandt, come and help me."

Sera grabbed a pillow and put it behind her so she'd be able to look down her body and watch as their heads met at her pussy: Ash's soft, gleaming bare skin with those red tribal marks on the back of his skull and Brandt's midnight, soft-as-silk hair. When Brandt's tongue joined Ash's, she cried out, fingers digging into the soft blankets beneath her body.

Her breath came ragged around soft sounds of desperate need. Head moving from side to side restlessly, she knew the time had come to beg. She needed to come.

"Please, oh please!" she managed to gasp out.

Both men stopped and looked up at her and then turned to each other and kissed, sharing her honey and Brandt's taste as well. Her eyes widened, and her gasp turned into a squeak of surprise.

"Shall we stop?" Ash asked, eyes half-lidded, lips glistening.

Her mouth moved a few times. "*No!* No, more. More!" As much as she wanted to come, watching these two men kissing had been even more compelling. She'd come in a few minutes.

Brandt laughed. "It's your turn. Then more. Always more." He bent his head down and sucked her clit into his mouth.

"Beg, Freka. You know what I like to hear." Ash's voice whipped up her spine, and orgasm hovered just out of reach. How that conditioning had lasted all these years, she didn't know. She did know her body wouldn't find release until he gave her leave.

"Please, oh Ash, please make me come. Brandt, please make me come." Her words were breathless, but they squeezed from her lungs anyway.

Ash's fingers found their way into her pussy and hooked, finding her sweet spot, stroking over it with clever precision. "Show me how beautiful you are when you come, Freka."

Orgasm, intensely blinding, rocketed through her. Her back arched, and a cry erupted from her lips as wave after wave of pleasure rolled through her. On and on it went until she was sure she'd die from it.

Finally, she fell back to the bed, boneless and sated.

Both men crawled up her body and settled on either side of her, each tossing a thigh over her.

"That was really lovely," she mumbled from under her hair.

"It was, indeed." Brandt gently pushed the hair from her eyes, and she opened them to see him smiling. She returned his smile, and he moved to kiss her. He tasted of her and of him and of Ash, and it was deliciously intoxicating.

Ash nudged Brandt out of the way and took over. His kiss was coming home. Touching her, touching her without her anger or fear had been intensely satisfying. He'd thought he'd never have that with her again. Thought he'd never have that sort of intimacy and connection with anyone.

He'd given up in many ways after she'd gone from his life. After his relationship with Kira had failed, he realized just how truly unique and miraculous what he'd had with Sera had been. He'd known they had something good, but over time, he'd figured out it had been singular. The loss of it had laid him low, had closed him off and numbed him.

Numb no more, emotion swelled through him with Sera there in his arms again, her scent on his skin. She'd filled in those gaping wounds, soothed, nurtured, made him whole again in a way only she could.

He wasn't even sure he could grasp just what it meant to have her back, so he decided to leave it for the time being. To celebrate instead of question.

They lay there, entangled in each other for some time, drifting in and out of sleep until Sera tried to sit up. "I'm hungry," she said, her voice muffled.

Ash chuckled. "Sex does do that to you."

"Hey! I haven't eaten since this morning before we arrived."

Brandt sat up and kissed her forehead and swung his legs out of bed. "Come on then. You get cleaned up, and I'll check our dinner invitations." He nodded at Ash as well as Sera, and she understood he was giving them some time alone. She wasn't sure she was ready for it, but before they'd even reached the door of the bathroom, someone knocked at the outer doors.

Ash groaned. "Go on and get cleaned up. I'll see who that is." He caressed her shoulder before turning to grab a robe and then left the room.

She watched him leave with mixed feelings of relief that she'd have time to get herself together after that intense interlude and missing him already.

Chapter 11

*O*nce the concierge had gone, Ash looked through the sheaf of papers in the file he'd delivered.

"The representatives didn't waste any time talking to your father, did they?" Brandt looked at Ash over the rim of his glass.

"He knew I would ignore any messages he sent via server, so he does this. A folder full of eligible women, like they were pretty cattle and I a bull for stud! He says he's happy to see I've found a concubine for my *physical needs*; a Walker should have a concubine and a wife as well. He's alarmed, though, that I'm sharing a woman with you when I should have my own."

Brandt chuckled. "Well, it's not as if I'd imagined myself in this place either."

"*Does it bother you?*" Ash sent over the link.

Both men were painfully aware of just how much they couldn't say out loud.

"*Surprisingly, no. I've thought a lot about it. Three is the only way to proceed here. Or nothing at all, and I don't think any of us wants that. Now that I've had her, known her, I can't pretend not to want more. I do."*

Ash paused. *"You formed the bridge back to her, and I love you for that. Gods know I love being with her again. I've missed her so much, more than I could admit to myself and still get through every day. Missed her cries and moans, missed the way she felt with her mouth on my cock, her taste."* Even just the way she filled the room with light whenever she entered it. Sera Ayers made living that much better just by existing.

Ash knew it'd be a slow road to something with her. Not back to what it was before; too much damage had come between them for that. But they could build something together. With Brandt.

Ash could see enough to understand that his friend felt deeply for Sera and she for him. The extra person took the pressure off them in a sense. There was a kind of refuge in Brandt that Sera could take from him. Ash appreciated that. That extra angle in the relationship enhanced it rather than harmed it. Helped them forge a new future. And he'd still have his best friend and his woman back again.

Brandt nodded, speaking out loud again. "My family will hear the news soon enough, I'd wager. Now that your father has sent this missive, mine will hear. He's already on me to marry and have children. I'm not the oldest or even the second oldest, so it's not as bad for me, but still . . ."

Brandt didn't care, because he meant to share his future with Sera Ayers. In whatever way he could. One of them would have to marry her to give her status. He certainly wouldn't leave her as a woman he only had sex with. He wanted to protect her, and yes, it would bind her to him as well. He didn't have any problem admitting that to himself.

"Well, it's a good thing I'm just an unranked concubine then, isn't it?" Sera walked into the room, pain clear on her face. Her link hadn't been open to them. He and Ash had been a team long enough to have it open most of the time in situations like this, but it was new for her. Damn.

The bitterness in her voice cut through the casual air she tried to give off. She waved them away. "Oh, tell your father not to worry! You'll find yourself a wife. Gods know that you're both handsome, intelligent and rich—qualities women do so adore. It's not as if we're setting up house, for goodness' sake! Now, we had some dinner to attend to?"

Brandt got up and stalked to her. "Sela." His voice held a warning. He would not brook her holding herself away from him for whatever happened between her and Ash. "Don't be jealous, sweet." He teased, but he looked deep into her eyes and shook his head. Hard. Her gaze slid away, and she kept her link closed. He could push though it, but he knew she'd hate that invasion.

When she wouldn't meet his eyes, he took her chin in his hand and moved her head. Ash came up behind him and put his arms around them both. "Freka, don't pout; you're too lovely to mar that face. I'm a bad boy to make you look so forlorn. I must make it up to you."

"Don't be silly. Darlings, a woman of my status knows several things. First among them is that she must accentuate her talents to hold on to that status as long as she can. I did not imagine you would marry me. That would be silly. Now, come on, get rid of those long faces! Truly, I know what my role is; neither of you has anything to worry over. When my time is up, it's up." She said it in her best Sela purr, and it made him angry. She'd used it to hit at them because they'd hurt her.

Brandt narrowed his eyes at her, hampered by his inability to speak freely.

"I think it's rather late for a walking tour, though. Tomorrow perhaps I'll find some of the other concubines and go exploring a bit. But I will expire of starvation if you two do not feed me soon. I cannot live on your bodies alone."

She tried to move away, but Ash pulled her tight against him and spoke against her ear. Her hair blocked his face from view. "Open up, Sela."

She sighed, slumping a bit, and opened to them.

"You didn't hear the whole conversation, Freka. Don't think the worst of me. I'm not walking away; I don't want to. Brandt isn't walking away. You're not just anything to either of us." His voice was so low, even through the link, laced with so much emotion Brandt felt it as much as he heard it.

Ash kissed down her neck and released her, letting her get away with not replying for the time being. "Before you lure me back into bed, Freka, we have dinner plans. Brandt accepted an invitation, and you look perfect. Shall we go then?" He held out his arm, and she put her hand on it.

Brandt saw her hesitation and kicked himself. She'd obviously misread what was being said, and it only played against her experience. They'd have to walk carefully and prove to her that she was first with them, regardless of Family issues.

Her link was still open, at least. *"You need to keep the link open tonight. If something happens, you'll need instant contact."*

She nodded at him and looked back to Ash. "Where are you two dragging me off to then? Somewhere nearby, I hope?"

"Tobin Fisk's home. He's one of Nondal's leaders. A close friend of my Family's." Ash raised a brow for a moment, and Sera understood.

"Oh, let me go and get my bag, I've forgotten it in the bedroom." She needed to be sure she had some of her tools in her bag, tools that looked quite innocuous. A small signal jammer made to look like a brooch and a pretty hair comb that had a data miner in it.

The men might be searched for such items but they'd leave her alone because she was a woman. That gave her satisfaction. Using their own stupid attitudes about women against them held a lovely irony.

Putting her hair back with the comb holding it in place, she tried not to think about the conversation she'd overheard between Brandt and Ash. She'd been stupid to let herself even imagine a future with them. They were important men, and of course they'd need to marry according to status. No matter what Ash said, she, more than most, understood the realities of the situation.

So she had to hold herself back, take refuge in Sela, because she could not afford to let herself care for these men knowing that they'd still be on a team when they both had wives. There was no way she'd be a mistress or concubine while anyone else held the honored title of wife.

She brushed down the front of the burgundy gown, smiled at her reflection and hoped like hell she didn't look as bitter and fake as she felt.

Chapter 12

"*I see the room with the network. I'll need you to just keep people's attention for a bit. I'm going to let this gentleman show me his technology and get that miner into play,*" Sera sent over the link.

"I just love your home." She put her hand on the arm of the man who'd ogled her breasts all evening long. She wanted in that room, and he was her ticket.

"Would you like a tour?" He placed a hand over hers on his arm.

It was an obvious enough game. He'd flirt, she'd flirt. He'd try it on, not seriously enough he couldn't talk his way out of it should he be discovered by her men. But some concubines would take him up on the offer for the thrill and possible presents. His money was the only thing he had going for him. He lacked the manners to stare at her discreetly, so she didn't feel too very bad about turning that around on him and using it to her advantage.

"Oh absolutely." She fluttered her lashes and tried to appear helpless. Certainly not the kind of woman who'd maneuver him into that data room and mine his network for any information she could use to toss him to the Federation authorities if he was helping the Imperialists.

She pretended to be fascinated as he walked her through the house, pointing out the art on the walls. She also pretended not to be annoyed at the women who kept throwing themselves at Ash and Brandt the moment she got three steps away.

They weren't hers, anyway. She had to keep remembering that.

"Oh, what's that?" She turned to the room with the electronics. "It seems so dark and isolated." Blech. The last thing she wanted was to be in the dark with this man, but it would serve her purposes, and she'd take an extra hot bath when she got back to their cottage.

"Ah, come in and see, Sela. I'm sure you've seen more modern gadgetry back near the Center and all, but I'm quite proud of this."

He led her into the room, and she reached into her hair to let it fall, as he backed her against what was conveniently the data hub.

One-handed, she managed to place the data miner and set it to copy as many files as it could grab. He ground his erection into her thigh as he babbled on about the specs. Specs he had at best a weak grasp on.

"Can you get away from your escorts for a while?" he asked her, his mouth very close to her neck.

She swallowed her revulsion as she grabbed the miner and palmed it.

"I don't think so. I do appreciate the invitation to what I'm sure would be a satisfying interlude. But my men are quite perceptive, and I'm quite happy where I am." She brushed past him on the way out.

Ash watched Sera out of the corner of his eye as she glided back into the room. He was relieved she'd been able to get out of that network room without any problems. He and Brandt had hoped to get near that room themselves, but she was far better suited for it. Clever. Still, an unsettled feeling had remained around her.

Outwardly, there was no real change in her behavior. But since they'd left the cottage earlier, he'd sensed a careful drawing away just beneath the surface. It made his skin itch. He needed her to know he was true. Needed her to believe he'd risk anything to be with her. Especially now that she'd allowed him back into her life.

She charmed the men at the dinner party carefully and stayed well within her role. The party was absent wives. They'd be off somewhere safe from the likes of mistresses and concubines. The women in attendance bore the same coquettish manner. Sera stood out like a golden light. The others' eyes held a calculating gleam. He understood it. He knew it was a matter of survival for them to keep from those lower levels. At the same time, he was glad Sera had other choices.

Sera had a wit about her and a mischief that drew people. None of the other women appeared to be threatened as soon as they knew she was with him and Brandt. After all, she had no need to trade down to one of their protectors. Still, Ash had had to tactfully turn aside several pointed invitations from women looking to escape Nondal.

One such woman rubbed herself over him shamelessly as she repeatedly tried to grab his crotch. Brandt hid a smirk of amusement as he glanced back now and again, never taking his eyes from Sera for more than a few moments.

Sera looked up from the knot of men who'd surrounded her and saw him, raising a brow at the woman's behavior. He sent her a pitiful look, and she patted several arms and made her way over to him.

"Excuse me," Sera purred, waiting for the other woman to notice she was standing there. She did, with a slight jump away from Ash, guilt on her face.

"Oh, hello, Sela." The other woman kept her eyes down, and Sera sighed.

"Branwen, is it? Yes, that's it. I'm going to pretend this behavior isn't beneath us both. If you want out of here, you must use subtlety. Especially if you wish to bump another concubine or mistress out of the way. That's not going to happen with me." Sera fluttered her lashes at the other woman. "Now, I believe your escort is in need of a drink, and the yellow-haired girl is trying to take care of that."

Branwen's anger at Sera's speech died when she heard the last bit, and she jumped up and ran off.

"Thank you, Freka. Come and sit with me to protect my honor, please." Ash patted the couch next to him, and she rolled her eyes before sitting, curling into his side.

"You're going to have to be a big boy and protect yourself. Whatever will you do when I'm gone?" Her tone was teasing, but Ash's brow furrowed.

"It's a good thing we have no plans whatsoever to get rid of you, then, Freka."

She waved his comment away, and Brandt sat on her other side, taking her hand and kissing each finger.

Ash felt her brush up against the link and opened to her. She leaned into him, her lips against his ear, making it look as if she were propositioning him. Instead, she spoke through the link to fill them in.

"I was able to attach the miner, but I'm not sure what I was able to procure. I did hear Stander will be here first thing in the morning, and he's bringing a male guest. Someone no one here seems to know. Stander has referred to him as a business partner, and there will be meetings of some sort with the guest and Nondalese officials."

It was hard to think with her so close, but the details sent his brain into analytical mode. *"We'll need to keep an eye on who this partner is. I think you're right when you say he can't be doing all this alone. The data they were able to procure to set up this last attack was so sensitive it had well-connected Family all over it."*

She sucked on his earlobe a moment, making it difficult for him to hold that train of thought. *"I agree. The dinner tomorrow night will have this guest attending."*

He grabbed her hand and nibbled on her fingers before moving to kiss her neck and then up to her ear. *"All this you got tonight?"*

Her laugh was velvet seduction, rendering him harder than stone. *"Never underestimate the power of breasts, even small ones."*

Brandt looked lovingly at the body parts in question and stifled a groan. *"When you're attached to them, I have no doubt."*

"Flatterer." She spoke aloud, fluttering her lashes at him, and suddenly his need for her worked through his body, leaving him flushed.

"I think we should be making our good-nights, don't you?" Brandt stood, holding out his hand for her to take.

"I don't want you two to end your time before you're ready. I was just fine over there with my admirers."

He pulled her up and against his body. "We're the only admirers who matter, sweet."

"Indeed." One of her eyebrows rose as she shot him a flirtatious smile.

Ash stood behind her, pressing her tight between them both. Well, no time like the present to be out as a threesome. "I know what you're doing, and it's not going to work." His murmur was delivered against the flesh just below her ear and sent shivers down her spine.

She planted a palm in the middle of Brandt's chest, vainly attempting to push away from him and distance herself from Ash, trying not to drown in them.

"I'm not letting you go this time, Freka. You're mine."

She pushed back a bit and laughed, a bit shaky. "Shall we go, or are you two planning on staying here?"

"When this is over, we're having a long talk." Brandt kissed her softly, reaching around her shoulders to put her wrap on. They made their good-byes, and Sera ignored the smarmy smiles the men wore. It was more than just two men sharing one woman. Two men sharing with each other was acceptable and even seen as a novelty in some quarters. Ash and Brandt had become even more desirable with the discovery of their relationship.

"I think we should enjoy the evening. Let's take a walk." Brandt bowed and she laughed.

Strolling down the wide plaza lined with trees and flowers, they headed back to their quarters. Each man had one of her hands, and it made her feel cherished and imprisoned all at once. She wanted to believe her feelings, wanted it to be an expression of how they truly felt, but she knew the danger in that and tried to remember reality. She'd locked up the link, needing the mental space from them, but she knew they'd only be patient so long.

"It's lovely here. There seem to be quite a lot of outlanders here right now, though, I noticed." Ash spoke casually as his eyes flicked around the area, taking it all in.

"Apparently now is the height of the year for the lights. It's sort of a mini-tourism season for them, and the visitors then move on to Ceres."

Brandt looked at her, surprised. "That's interesting. I didn't know that."

She laughed. "People tell beautiful women things all the time. One of my admirers tonight was a sort of tourism minister. He'd love to create a resort, apparently, just for outlanders to come and watch the lights. He wanted to sell packages for connections to Ceres as well. Isn't that clever?" The minister seemed very unconcerned about their proximity to the frontier. She'd faked a bit of nervousness about the Imperialists, but he'd waved it off far too comfortably.

"Yes. But I'm surprised they'd think so, this close to the frontier and all." Ash's eyes flicked over her quickly and then away once she'd nodded nonchalantly, answering his inferred question.

"Yes, darling. It's so awfully close to the Imperialists. I'd be frightened if you two weren't with me. But he assured me it wasn't a problem. He said he's got the support of powerful friends near the Center. I suppose that's very clever." She looked up at Brandt, wide-eyed.

"Brandt? Is that you? Ash?"

Both men froze at the sound of the female voice and slowly turned, bringing Sera around with them.

"Kira, what are you doing here?" Brandt let go of Sera's hand and went to embrace the beautiful, ebony-haired woman. The woman who was once Ash's wife. The woman he'd left Sera for.

Nausea swamped Sera, but she had to keep her damned cover in place. She tried to let go of Ash's hand, but he wouldn't release her. Both men repeatedly pinged her through the link, but she left it slammed closed. As if she wanted to have an argument in her head with them right then. Men!

"Sera, talk to me, damn it!"

"You said you couldn't hear me unless I let you in!" At least her anger at Ash helped her to get past the nausea.

"Not usually. But I can break through the link if I need to. In an emergency."

"I can't do this right now, Ash. Don't push me. I've had quite enough for one day, and we need to hold my cover."

But before he could say anything else, Kira cleared her throat as she spoke to Brandt, looking Ash up and down as she did. Her lip curled as she took Sera in.

"I'm here with Perry." She jerked her head toward the watery version of Ash who stood next to her, eyeing Sera like he was a hungry animal. "We've been at Ceres and are on our way back home. What are you two doing here?"

"We're here to see the lights. We knew it would be something Sela would enjoy."

"Sela? I suppose that's the name of your little plaything? Or is she Brandt's? Ash, really, you need to get over it already and remarry."

Sera felt better when she dug her nails into Ash's hand, and he winced. Brandt took a step back to Sera's side, brushing her hair over her shoulder.

"Her name is Sela Carter. Sela, this is my sister, Kira Pela-Walker."

Kira stepped back, her hand over her chest. "Brandt! How dare you? It's bad enough you've had her in my presence and she's looking at me. I'd certainly never lower myself to speak to her."

Sera took a deep breath and yanked her hand free of Ash before turning and heading away. They both called to her through the link, but she ignored it.

Less than two minutes later, with the guesthouse in sight, Ash caught up with her, grabbing her around the waist and turning her in one easy movement. She had to fight her natural urge to defend and repel. She'd pushed it far enough by walking away, but there was no way she could have continued to stand there facing that horrid woman.

"Don't fight me, Freka." He didn't bother with the link; he spoke aloud, his voice frustrated and rough against her ear as she pushed against his chest.

"Let me go. I want to rest. I've had quite enough this evening."

"I know you have. Let's go inside. You can't roam freely here. I don't want you to get hurt."

His arm around her waist, he allowed her to turn and then propelled them to the guesthouse and through the door.

"Where's Brandt?" She tossed her bag and wrap on a nearby chair and kicked her shoes off. She wanted to throw them at his head but refrained.

"*I know that look on your face, Sera. You're furious. I didn't plan to have her come here. Why are you angry with me?*"

"*You, you . . . There aren't even words!*"

Sera stomped out of the room, wanting to throw something but knowing they were at least monitored on some level.

"Brandt is having a late drink with his sister." Ash followed her into the bedroom before she could close the door on him.

"*How nice for him. I assume her venom only kills those foreign to her instead of family.*"

Ash's lips trembled a bit, and he shook his head. "I'd love for you to rub my neck. It's very sore." He unbuttoned his shirt, and her traitorous hormones shot to attention at the sight of his naked upper body when he took it off. He did have the good sense not to hand it to her, though.

"Hmpf." Ignoring him, she glided into the bathroom and removed her gown before turning on the water for a nice, long soak. She may not be able to yell at him, but all women, even concubines, were allowed fits of temper, and she was going to have one.

Chapter 13

She'd just stepped into the large soaking tub when Ash strode in, naked, erect and bearing glasses of wine. She slid under the water so her nipples wouldn't show.

"I take it you're upset with the presence of my ex-wife. You have nothing to be jealous over." He placed a goblet of wine at her hand and stepped into the water, hissing a moment. "You like the water too damned hot."

"You're a baby. Feel free to get out, and you won't have to deal with the water temperature."

"You know you're going to pay for this, don't you? I'm going to enjoy it, too."

He sat, back to her, and leaned into her body. Without thinking, her hands went to his neck and shoulders. She kneaded the knotted muscles there until he groaned softly.

"Your ex-wife is a beast, Ash."

"A spoiled, horrible woman. Yes." He sighed. *"And nothing like you. I'm sorry. I'm sorry she acted that way, but that's who she is."*

"I can't believe you married her. You walked away from me for that?"

"You walked away. We've been through this. Sera, I had no choice. I did what I had to do, and I hated it, but I had people depending on me. I don't now, not in the same way. I did my duty, and I won't put anyone before you, not ever again."

Despite knowing he spoke the truth, her feelings were still bruised. Her rational self understood his actions before, but the hurt made it hard to let go of the fear. She decided to be irrational for the time being until she could process everything better.

She leaned in and bit his earlobe hard enough to make him sit up with a yelp. Water splashed everywhere. He turned, eyes flashing, and she knew she was in for it. He stood, water sluicing down ridge after ridge of well-defined muscle, and hauled her up.

One-handed, he pulled her hair from the neat nest on top of her head and stepped out of the water, carrying her like a sack of goods.

"I'm very tired, Ash." She kept her voice bored even as she was slightly upside down as he carried her.

"I don't care, Sela."

The nerve of that man! And Brandt? Where the hell was he? There, apologizing to her for his sister's horrid behavior? No, having a drink with the poisonous creature. Probably apologizing to *her* for Sera!

Ash tossed her on the bed, but she scrambled up. He anticipated her direction and met her.

"I'm wet. The bed will be ruined. Let me get dry."

"No."

"No? I'm a concubine, Ash Walker, not a slave."

"You're mine, Freka. That's what you are. You're angry with me, and we're going to work this out with some flesh and some sweat.

When you've come a few times, your opinion will soften." His grin was arrogant, self-assured.

"You're a pig. An ass. A man. That's what you are. A man."

"I am. I'm your man. Now get on that bed before I make you."

Her head swiveled a bit at his audacity. *"You think you're going to master me after your bitch of an ex-wife treats me like scum on a public street, and your friend goes off to drink with her? Oh, how they must laugh. Poor Brandt and Ash, stuck with the low-class whore."*

His eyes narrowed, and in two steps he'd closed the distance. She found herself on her back as he loomed over her on all fours.

"I'm going to be there in a very short time, Sera. And then we'll talk about your low opinion of me." Brandt's voice whispered over the link.

"He's with her so you and I could talk alone."

"There is no alone! I'm being watched every minute of the day by the Nondalese. You and your friend bust into my head at will. I have no defenses against you, and you're using that against me! I can't take it. I gave you everything, and then you left me with nothing. I can't do that again. I don't have anything left." She put an arm over her face.

"Freka, I love you." He kissed her wrist where it covered her eyes. He said it out loud, and the words, familiar and beautiful, cracked her facade until she had nothing to fend him off with. The tears flowed, and he gently moved her arm, kissing her cheeks and eyelids.

"You can't love me, Ash. You aren't meant for me," she mumbled through her tears. The inability to react completely honestly only frustrated her more.

"Don't tell me what I can't do. No one but me is meant for you. And Brandt, I suppose."

Sera opened her eyes, met his, and fell in. Deep. Still, that woman galled her. "She's very skinny. And her nose is reconstructed. She looks like a bird. How could you fuck a woman who looks like she'd break, Ash?"

He grinned. "Not everyone is high capacity, Freka. Although I have to admit I like when you're jealous and petty. It's attractive, I don't know why."

She laughed. "Such a way with words when you think you might be climbing between my thighs."

He pressed up, his cock sliding between her now slick and ready labia. "Looks like I'm already there."

She watched his face change, watched as he went from her lover concerned for her emotions to the man who needed to top her. A shiver rolled through her at the transformation.

"Sera, I never dominated her. No one has worn a collar for me since you. No one has been worth it to me."

His lips met hers, and there was no gentleness, only possession and heat. She managed to gasp, "Please, Ash, please fuck me," between kisses.

"Roll over," he ordered and sat up so she could obey him. He moved off the bed, and she heard him rifle through a bag and come back.

Cool, soft fabric covered her eyes. One of her scarves that masqueraded as a blouse. Darkness settled in as the bed moved and he straddled her back, tying her wrists together and then securing them over her head, most likely to the posts on the bed.

Electric jolts of red lit the back of her eyelids when his fingernails scored down her back from shoulders to the curves of her ass.

She gasped and arched into his touch. He scooted down her body, and his nails followed down the back of her thighs to her ankles.

He picked one foot up, and his teeth found her instep, so sensitive the sensation shot straight up her legs to her pussy.

In the dark behind the blindfold, her hands held captive, she waited to feel what he'd do next. A warm, wet swirl of his tongue at the back of each knee. The edge of his teeth nipped the backs of her thighs, the meat of her ass cheeks. The tip of his tongue trailed up her spine.

Each touch sent her deeper into herself, each sound of his appreciation made her pride swell. She was his, on display for his eyes, for his pleasure. A beautiful vision made for him.

"Lift your ass for me. I want you on your knees so I can touch every bit of your pussy while my cock is buried deep inside you."

Levering one and then the other knee up to keep her balance, she kept her ass up and her head down, her hands still stretched before her.

"Your pussy is so wet, your honey is on your thighs. You don't know what it does to me to see the effect I have on you." As he spoke, he drew his fingertips through the furls of her sex, drawing the slickness up and over her clit, making her gasp.

"Tell me, do you want me to eat your pussy? Or fuck it?"

She moaned at the words as heat flushed through her system, setting her skin aflame with desire for him.

He moved back, the warmth of his body fading as he did. She whimpered in response. She didn't know which she wanted. She wanted to come, yes. But his body was a feast for the senses; no matter what he did to her, he'd please her. It was hard to think with her clit throbbing in time with her nipples and pounding heart.

"Whatever you want. Ash, take from me in whatever way you want."

Ash groaned. She got to him. Always had. She'd just given herself to him with a few words, and it wrecked him. His control weakened as he watched her ass sway. The lines from his nails rode down her perfect back, already beginning to fade.

He moved back to her, widening her thighs and the sound of her sigh slithered through him. He didn't deserve her, but it wouldn't stop him from taking her anyway. He needed Sera. The emptiness he'd felt had settled into him and had felt normal. It wasn't until he'd seen her again that the desolation of his life had become so achingly apparent.

He'd had her. A beautiful, lush life with a woman who completed him. And then she'd gone, and he'd lived half a life with Kira. She'd left, and he'd had nothing but the military and a series of impersonal brief sexual interludes. Sex without connection. He hadn't been celibate, but it wasn't the same. It hadn't filled the empty spaces.

His heart swelled with what she was to him.

Guiding his cock, he teased her entrance with it, rolling the head through the inferno-hot wetness of her cunt. She strained against the scarves holding her wrists, and he cursed himself for not bringing any gear with him. When they got back he'd spend weeks playing with different things, remembering her body and learning her anew. For now, he'd make do with scarves, his hands, and his cock.

"Please."

Her voice had gone into a slur as sub-space settled in. His beautiful Sera, so quickly into sub-space when they played.

In one thrust he filled her until his balls slapped against the wet flesh of her pussy. Her inner walls fluttered around him, clutching and rippling as she made room for him.

He dragged out and pressed in deep. Over and over. Her hands were restrained, so he brought his own to her clit, playing with it and bringing her off quickly to take the edge off her desperation.

She writhed against him, pressing herself back into his thrusts to take more of his cock into her body. Her pussy slid around his cock, gripping him, luring him closer and closer to climax even as he worked to stave it off, not wanting the time spent inside her to end.

"You feel so good, Freka. Your pussy is hot and juicy for me. Tonight at the dinner I wanted to grab you and slide you down over my cock and have you ride me. Brandt watched you. I knew his cock was hard. He'd have come to stand next to me so you could lean over and suck his cock."

A guttural moan broke from her as a pulse of her wetness nearly scalded him. The room was heavy with the scent of sex.

"Would you like that? To have everyone know what you do to Brandt and me?" he teased as she squirmed.

"Not a single woman in this 'Verse equals your beauty. Not in this system. Not any woman I've ever known. Give me another orgasm."

At one time, all those years ago, he'd been able to command her orgasms, control when she came with a word. He'd been so in tune with her and her with him. He wanted that again.

"I don't know," she began, but he felt the telltale tightening of her pussy around him, and her sentence ended on a soft cry as she came when he flicked his thumb over her clit.

"You're mine." It was true. She was written into him.

She was silent for long moments until she burst out with a cry, "Yes. Damn you, Ash, I am."

The admission broke his control, and he came hard, his teeth clenched around a hiss as he unloaded deep inside her.

That moment was total perfection.

"Well now. Someone is going to have to bring me to speed. I think I've missed a few things in my absence."

Ash looked over his shoulder at Brandt, leaning in the doorway and smiling at the scene before him.

Chapter 14

*B*randt turned back to his sister and brother-in-law after Ash left to deal with Sera. He'd wanted to go as well. It'd been difficult to watch her run, knowing she was hurt. But he'd understood it was time for Ash and Sera to work out their issues over Kira once and for all.

"Really, Brandt, one would think you would have better taste." Kira wrinkled her nose. "Is this the reason I've received several messages from our mother in the last day?"

Brandt loved Kira, but he really wondered how they could come from the same family. "My taste is excellent, Kira, and I'll warn you now to keep your opinion to yourself on this matter. Instead of discussing this and knowing we won't agree, do you have time for a drink? We've not seen each other in some time."

Kira looked as if she wanted to argue but held her tongue. She wasn't totally stupid. Perry continued to look down the avenue where Sera had departed, and Brandt barely repressed the urge to pop the other man in the nose for disrespecting Sera and Kira that way.

"Of course. A visit would be pleasant," she said somewhat sincerely.

They walked to a nearby cantina and sat, ordering drinks. He listened absently as Kira babbled on about their trip and all the new baubles she'd acquired. He'd winced when he heard Sera's comments through the link and sent back his own.

Sometime during his sister's interminable blathering, Brandt had heard Sera's comments about him joking to Kira about her. He'd blanched at her estimation of him, but it was her pain that made him so antsy. He knew she'd been made that way by what she'd suffered, but he needed to comment back her way.

He itched to go back to the guesthouse and touch her, to show her with hands and mouth, with heart and head, just what she meant to him.

"You aren't paying any attention to me, Brandt."

He forced himself to focus on Kira and sent her a smile. "Of course I am. But there are only so many stories about new gowns any man can take. How long are you here in Nondal?"

His brother-in-law finally spoke. "Another few days. We have a friend coming in. We haven't seen Giles for some time." While his slight resemblance to Ash was discomfiting, the other man was nothing like Ash in personality. He was perfect for Kira really, weak, shifty, greedy.

And then he realized what his brother-in-law had said and stilled mentally. A connection to their chief suspect made Perry a suspect as well. Certainly, a connection to a Family like the Walkers and to the Pelas, too, would serve the Imperialists quite well.

"Oh really? I suppose we'll most likely bump into each other at the parties, then." He'd make a point of it.

"I suppose you'll be bringing *her* with you? I do know how you men love to parade around your pets at these parties. Nondal gets worse and worse every time we come, I must say. Not that I'll be at that party tomorrow. I'll be safely off with the respectable women while the whores fetch things for you all. Giles has so many women now I don't know how he can afford it. His poor wife doesn't even bother with him. Why must you share a concubine, Brandt? There are plenty of women out there for you and Ash. You can each afford more than one of your own if you wanted. I suppose Ash has never really gotten over my leaving." She sipped whatever frothy concoction women like her drank and happily lived in her own world.

He clenched his jaw for a moment, wanting to defend Sera, but it wasn't part of the cover, so he let it pass. "I can't see why anyone would have so many women. Perhaps they just haven't found the right one yet. Are you speaking of Giles Stander, by any chance? I've heard he's got so many concubines and mistresses he can't keep up with the bills." He tipped his chin at Perry.

"He does like the tables. But he'll work it out; Giles always does. He's very resourceful." Perry's smarmy smile made Brandt's skin crawl.

Brandt stood and indicated to the cashier to charge his credit for their drinks. "I must get back. Kira, you look lovely as always. I will be seeing you and Perry soon, I'm sure."

"Well, be sure not to expose me to your pet next time, Brandt. That was wholly unseemly." Kira allowed a brief kiss of her cheek.

"I'm sure it wasn't any great pleasure for her to have you react that way, either." He waved, turned on his heel and headed back to the guesthouse.

The moment he entered, he heard them. His adrenaline kicked in as his cock hardened. Ash's grunts played over Sera's whimpers and moans as Brandt tossed aside his jacket and, on his way to the bedroom, unbuttoned his shirt.

Standing in the doorway, he watched Ash fuck into Sera. He found himself entranced by the glow of her skin as she strained against the scarves binding her wrists to the post at the head of the bed. The fire inside him rose along with his need for her. His urge to reassure her overcame his anger at her mistrust of his dealings with Kira.

"Well now. Someone is going to have to bring me to speed. I think I've missed a few things in my absence."

"Well, Sela and I had a spat and were just making up." Ash pulled out, cock glistening with Sera's honey.

"I can see that." Her back bore faint tracks where Ash's nails scored into her skin. She still wore the blindfold, still remained bound.

"Should I untie her?" Ash asked, one hand idly playing over Sera's clit.

"No." Brandt pulled off the rest of his clothes and Ash moved to the side, lying next to Sera.

"Open up, Sera." Brandt got onto the bed, kneeling next to her head.

"My mouth?"

He sent a look at Ash over her body, and his friend shook his head and grinned.

"On your back."

She slid back down to her belly and turned carefully, her arms crisscrossed at the wrists. "Like this?"

"You know I'm not going to let you avoid the issue, don't you?"

"What issue would that be?" Even through the mental link he heard her emotion.

He straddled her body and tapped her lips with the head of his cock, already slick. "Suck my cock."

Her mouth opened, and he rolled his hips, pressing himself

between her lips. She lost herself in him, he knew, took refuge in the act. But right then he didn't want her lost. He wanted her attention.

"Did you really think I'd make fun of you to Kira? Do you think so little of me and my care for you?"

The link remained silent, and he fed more of his cock to her until she breathed deeply through her nose, and he bumped the back of her throat. Her body stiffened a moment, but she adjusted.

Reaching down, he removed the blindfold, but she kept her eyes closed.

"Open your eyes. Your eyes are mine when my cock is in your body, Sela."

She shivered and slowly, reluctantly, opened her eyes. He saw the anger, the hurt there.

"All of you. I want every bit." And he didn't plan to negotiate on that point.

She blinked quickly but not fast enough that he missed the flash of fear. He slowly fucked into her mouth, keeping his gaze locked with hers. Keeping the link of intimacy between them.

"Well?"

"It seems to me this link should be about necessary communication only."

He nearly laughed at how she'd sounded in his head.

"If you don't think my feelings for you and yours for me are necessary communication, I've misjudged you terribly."

She blinked quickly; he saw the tears welling in her eyes, and he pulled out, scooting down her body. His face close to hers, he stared into her eyes until the tears broke free and trailed down where he dipped his head, catching them with his lips.

"Sweet, why would you let the appearance of my sister upset you so?" He kissed down her jaw. *"I wanted to give you time with Ash, and I wanted to see what they were doing here. We'll talk about that later. For now, Sera, you're pulling away, and you must know Ash and I aren't going to let that happen.*"

"She's poisonous. And vile." Some of her vitality came back as she squirmed against the scarf. Her nipples hardened as he traced over first one and then the other with a fingertip. "*And she took what was mine.*"

He nodded. "*But I'm yours, and I'm right here. Ash is yours, and he's right here. Neither of us is leaving you. Not ever.*"

She hmpfed, and he rolled her over quickly and landed three sharp blows on her ass.

The squeal of outrage she made into the pillow was partially muffled, but he grinned at Ash as he scrambled over her body and went into the vanity area adjoining the bath. A quick scan of the surface of her table, and he found what he needed and grabbed it.

Ash saw what he held and laughed. "How could I have forgotten? When you leave your toys at home, you can always improvise."

Sera had gone still, but when she heard that comment, she turned her face from the pillow to look up at him. Her eyes went straight to the wooden hairbrush he held, and they widened.

"Ahh, I see. Now, I've left my paddle at home so . . ." He knelt over her and gave the fleshiest part of her ass a smack. The resulting red mark was very attractive, and she wasn't complaining, either.

"Ass up in the air."

The quickness of her compliance told him she was still very interested. He landed the blows carefully, not wanting to hurt her, only wanting to push her into sub-space, to bring her the increased serotonin of pleasure/pain. They'd both pushed her and would continue to do so until she admitted the truth of their relationship, but he wanted to be smart and not scare her away.

She moaned softly, and Ash moved in, his hands sliding beneath her body to play with her nipples. When her ass was a lovely shade of pink and the heat rose from her along with the scent of her honey, Brandt tossed the brush to the side and pressed his cock into her cunt quickly and without preamble.

A shuddering groan rocked through her as she rippled around him. Three short, hard digs, and he pulled out, much to her distress.

"Is there a problem?"

"Make me come, please," she begged, trying to turn to see him fully, but the way she was bound, arms crossed at the wrist, made it difficult.

"I will. But I don't want your cunt just now."

His cock was wet with her juices, with Ash's come, and he brought that slickness from her pussy up around her anus. Gooseflesh rose on her skin, and his cock throbbed in time with his pulse.

"I'm going to fuck your ass. Because I want to. Because I can. Because I want to be in every part of you."

A flush moved up her skin, and Ash surged to his knees to band an arm around Brandt's waist and kiss him. The kiss tasted of Sera, of Ash, of Ash's boldness, of his passion for their woman. Sharing Sera, having that unified depth of feeling for this woman, had deepened their connection as well.

"I want to see! I know you're doing stuff and it's not fair I can't see." Sera struggled to turn more fully, but Brandt pressed the fingers he'd been teasing around her rear passage into her to the first knuckle.

She hissed, and Ash craned his head to watch while stroking his cock.

"Tight. Hot and tight and silky smooth." He scissored his fingers to stretch her a bit, and she thrust back at him. *How long has it been, Sera, since you've been fucked in this tight little hole?*"

"*Since Ash. Ten years.*"

He shuddered, and Ash exhaled softly.

"Ash, don't let her clit get lonely." Brandt spread her and began the slow push into her. She loosened when Ash's fingers found her clit and began to work it. Her body contracted around his, rippled as he got deeper and deeper with each slow thrust.

"Please, all the way."

"I don't want to hurt you. You're very tight." The strain in his voice matched the strain in his muscles as he worked to keep control over his need to fuck her hard and deep.

"I want it to. It'll be fine after I get used to it." Her voice was thick with emotion.

That was all he could take, and he began to fuck her in earnest as she writhed back against him. Ash moved his head so he could kiss her, and her desperate, needy sounds echoed into his mouth.

Pleasure was a vise around Brandt's cock as he drew closer and closer to climax.

"Come for me, sweet." His fingers slid into her pussy, fucking her as he plunged into her ass and Ash worked her clit. Her hands fisted as she pulled frantically against her bonds.

"Give it to him. Come on his hand. I want your climax, he wants your climax. Give it up now." Ash's voice held a note of command Brandt had never heard before, and it turned him on even more.

It must have worked for Sera, too, because her scalding-hot honey rained on his fingers and hand, her anus contracting around his invading cock as she cried out, Ash swallowing the sound.

With a low groan, Brandt gave up and let loose, gave in to the waves of sensation that buffeted him until he had to collapse next to her on the bed.

Sera barely felt it when Brandt untied her hands and massaged her wrists. Ash came into the room with a wet cloth and cleaned her up, turning her over and helping her get beneath the blankets.

Ash snuggled up against her left side, slinging an arm over her belly, and Brandt against her right, his thigh over hers. He played idly with her nipple ring as her muscles jumped and trembled.

She'd lost herself in the oblivion they gave her. Let herself fall deep into the way Brandt touched her, the feel of his cock deep inside her as Ash kissed her.

"Sera, don't think to try and hide yourself from me or Ash. You gave yourself to me on the transport."

"And you gave yourself to me earlier," Ash added over the link.

"I'm very tired. You two fucked every part of me today. I need to rest." She didn't want to answer over the link. She just wanted to hold Sela around her like a shield until they left her alone.

Brandt snorted in a very undignified manner, and Ash laughed. *"Interrogation is going to be so much more fun with you than with the enemy."*

Oh gods above and below, was she in trouble.

"What hour must I wake up tomorrow morning? Will you two be off for the day so I must find my own entertainment with the others?"

Brandt pulled her a bit closer, and Ash pushed in. They surrounded her, cocooned her.

"We have a dinner party tomorrow. My sister won't be in attendance. Wives will be off elsewhere. Let's wake up when we wish and then make our decisions from there."

"Stander will be at the party tomorrow night. Perry seemed quite happy to see him, by the way, said they were friends. I hate to say it, but that makes him a suspect, too, Ash. Kira expressed disgust at his many women, said his wife doesn't even bother with him anymore. Perry made a comment you might find interesting. When I mentioned Stander's money problems, Perry said Stander would work it out; he always did."

"Well, of course his wife doesn't bother! What woman would accept

such a thing quietly?" Sera wanted to punch Giles Stander's testicles so hard he choked on them. Men!

Ash nibbled on her shoulder, and she sighed quietly.

"A man wouldn't have need of that many women if he had you. It takes two men just to keep you satisfied." Brandt had the gall to wink at her, and she raised a brow at him.

"He wouldn't need to have that many women if he cared about satisfying any one of them. A real man doesn't need all that."

Ash kissed her forehead. *"Back to business for a moment, if I may. If Giles is indeed feeding information to the Imperialists as our evidence suggests, and if he's getting help, also as our evidence suggests, Perry has a lot of opportunity. I don't like thinking about anyone in my Family being involved, and I can't imagine why Perry would do something so heinous, but it's something we must think on."*

"I'm sorry, Ash."

"We'll deal with this tomorrow. After we take care of our woman again." Brandt touched Ash's arm briefly.

Ash chuckled softly and hummed his agreement as he nuzzled her neck.

"I'm boneless. Exhausted. I need sleep."

Which didn't stop his nuzzling of course, it only brought Brandt up to do the same on the other side, and she closed her eyes, letting herself fall into sleep.

Chapter 15

*A*sh awoke early and stretched. He couldn't recall the last time he'd been so damned relaxed, especially on an op. On quiet feet, he padded out of the bedroom. Her scent still lingered on his hands, on his lips. *Where it belongs*, he thought as he took a shower.

He shaved, not wanting to scratch her with his beard growth, pulled on a pair of pants and headed into the common area to order in some breakfast.

It wasn't until he'd opened up his communications folders that he wanted to hit something. His cousin Perry had run straight to the Family with news of Sera. His father and uncle had both written him angry missives defending poor Kira's feelings in the matter at being exposed to a fallen woman in such a way.

He wondered if it was the normal interference or if Perry had something to hide and was trying to divert attention away from himself.

Whatever the case, he dashed off a quick text to his father, ignoring his uncle for the time being, reasserting his right to make his own choices. The Family made its profits, political alliances had been made and he'd done his duty. He didn't plan to be answerable for his private life at this point in his life.

There were several invitations for Sera to accompany different groups of concubines on sightseeing trips that day. Taking a quick glance through, he saw the two most likely to have Giles Stander's concubine attending and made a quick mental note to talk with her about it when she woke up.

"Morning," she said in a warm, sexy voice as she entered the room. She wore a robe tied loosely around her waist, and her hair was bound in an intricate braid. The scent of her soap and shampoo tickled his nose.

He rose and took her into his arms, swaying with her for long moments until she smiled against the bare skin of his chest. He'd missed that lighthearted love they'd shared.

"Good morning to you. I've ordered some breakfast for us. You have several invitations for social engagements today. You're a very popular woman, it seems." He sat, pulling her down with him, and she peered at the screen to view her mail.

"Some of these girls grate on my nerves, Ash. But I suppose if I can't be with you and Brandt all day, I'll find the company of Tifrit Alder's concubine, Rina, and her group amenable. It is a shopping trip, after all."

She quickly sent a note back indicating she'd attend and her regrets to the others before he spun her around and nuzzled the hollow of her throat. "Well now, hello."

Her hands moved up his back and over his skull, caressing, kneading, tracing the tattoos. *"I've missed this part of you."*

"I've missed having you love me this way."

"So smooth." She pressed kisses at each temple and then traced her tongue over the top of his head. So ridiculously simple but totally erotic that she'd find him that attractive.

A knock sounded on the door, and he groaned.

"Sit, I'll get it." She stood, but he moved past her quickly.

"I don't want to share your beauty with anyone else right now. I'll get the door." Her laughter accompanied him as he opened up to the delivery staff, who set up a very large, very fine breakfast in their interior courtyard.

When he went back to get her, Brandt had come in, and she stood behind him brushing and braiding his hair. It wasn't an act, the way she touched Brandt, ministered to him with such a small thing. She clearly wanted to take care of him, loved it even. Brandt's eyes were closed, his face totally relaxed. Ash had seen a snarl of bloodlust on that face, had seen him in a killing rage, and no shadow of that man existed in the presence of their woman.

Her hands moved slowly, rhythmically, as she brushed, long strokes through Brandt's dark-as-deep-night hair. Her lips were slightly parted, her eyes halfway closed as she held the brush.

The moment was so intimate in its normalcy Ash felt a tightening in his gut, touched beyond measure by both of them. What he had with her wasn't conventional, but it was right. And it just made sense to have Brandt there as well. Not between them but with them.

When she finished, she leaned down and kissed the top of Brandt's head.

"Thank you, sweet."

"Breakfast is ready," Ash announced, and they both looked to him with a smile. Inside him there was no pang, no fear there'd be nothing left for him once Sera gave Brandt her attention.

* * *

$\mathcal{T}$he filtered light from the glass of the dome above them shone over her as she tipped her head toward it, eyes closed. Funny, this toughened soldier would look so at home in the guise of a creature of indulgence. Ash made a promise to himself to show her more luxury after this was over.

"Did Sela tell you she'd be heading out on a shopping expedition later today?" Ash said it casually, but Brandt's eyes lit a moment.

"You'll need to replace a few things we so oafishly destroyed in our eagerness to get you naked," Brandt teased.

Like a cat, she stirred, stretching in the sunshine before reaching over to pat Brandt's hand. "Don't worry, I will."

"Be sure you do. I wouldn't want anyone to think we didn't spoil you enough and try to steal you away."

When her spine stiffened, Ash sighed. *"He didn't mean it that way, Sera. It was a Sela comment, also urging you to not hesitate to spend credits to fit in. Gods know both Brandt and I have them, but this is also our cover. Neither of us thinks you'd leave us for another male with more money."*

Brandt took her hand and kissed it, and she nodded slightly, her spine loosening a bit.

She nibbled on a piece of fruit. "There's no one in this 'Verse who can compare to you two. Thank the gods, because I don't think I could handle any more of you." She winked and laughed.

Calls started coming in shortly after they'd finished eating as other men of powerful Families began to awaken. Brandt and Ash might be posing as indulged sons of powerful Families, but the need to constantly network was a reality. And in Nondal, it would be done without females unless the males needed to show off their prowess in some way other than financially.

Because of how society worked in Nondal, a certified chaperone showed up some hours later to collect Sela for her outing. Someone had come over to do her hair and makeup, and she wore some complicated getup that barely covered her but concealed enough to make a man curious as to what was beneath the fabric.

She took Ash's credit chip with a wink, and he pulled her against him, letting her feel just what she did to him. Needing her to know.

"Mine. Now, buy some pretty wrapping for your pussy. I don't have to tell you to stay alert, but I expect you to be safe today."

"Me as well." Brandt strolled to them and embraced her from behind, kissing her neck.

"You two will rumple me," she said without even a small amount of annoyance in her tone.

"I like you rumpled," Brandt said as he nipped her earlobe.

Ash sent a look to the chaperone, who lowered his eyes, and she was gone, swallowed up by a bevy of chattering women.

*S*era wanted to die. These women would be the death of her. How they could stand themselves, she didn't know. But one thing she did know was that among Rina's little group was Giles Stander's alpha concubine, Delia. Sera figured it would be so and had taken a calculated risk in accepting this particular invitation. Rina's keeper was a powerful man, not the most obviously so, but the one with the most financial power based on gaming and other gray market areas not so closely regulated by the Federation. They'd move in the same circles, and Stander would want his females moving with ones like Rina.

"You are quite fortunate to have two such gloriously masculine protectors," Delia said as she tossed an obscenely expensive gown at the clerk.

Sera smiled serenely as she fingered the undergarments, selecting several things to entice her men with.

"News travels so fast in Nondal," Rina said in a voice so low and sensual, Sera figured it had to be enhanced. "They are very fine-looking men. I hear you had a run-in with Walker's former wife last evening."

"News does travel fast." Sera offered nothing else. She wanted to know what else they'd heard and how.

"Giles is close with Perry and the she-demon. When they're together, it's the only time Giles's wife ever has the nerve to say anything about all his women on the side." Delia sniffed as if offended by that. Sera thought Giles's wife would make a better point with a large, blunt object while her wayward husband slept. Still, Sera did quite enjoy the characterization of Kira as a she-demon.

"Have you met her?" Sera asked nonchalantly.

"Of course not. Do you think she'd lower herself to speak to one of us? Is it true they introduced you to her? I would have loved to have seen it with my own eyes." Delia laughed.

"She gasped as if she'd been injured and stepped back, hand over her heart, when Brandt introduced me. As if being a concubine would be something she could catch." *Venomous, evil, horrid woman.*

"Not so perfect herself. Her or her precious Family."

Really now? What did that mean? "This is lovely but this," Sera held up another gown in a deeper color, "would suit your coloring so much better."

Flattered, Delia took it, and in the middle of the boutique, stripped out of the gown she wore and tried on the delicate one Sera had handed her. "You're right. I'll wear it tonight, I think."

Sera waited until they'd entered yet another shop to hedge around the topic again. "I'm just relieved *she* won't be at the party this evening."

"Perry will be. She doesn't know what a beast he is when she's not around. Wouldn't be so superior-like if she knew. All she cares about is credits, anyway."

"I've seen Perry. A girl has to get something out of a relationship, and since Ash is in my bed, I think credits must mean more to her than sex." *Whoo, way to channel Sela.*

Delia and Rina laughed. "I've seen Perry's cock; it's nothing to put on a vid and report over. But as long as he's willing to keep certain people happy and doesn't have the morals of a speck, she'll stay with him, and the Walkers will be happy." Delia put yet another pair of shoes on the teetering stack she'd already created. Stander must be operating in the gray in a major way to finance this woman's shoes alone.

"Certain people? Should I be worried about Ash ending up in some off-'Verse brig for dealing with the criminal element?" she asked as she handed a pair of shoes to the clerk with a smile.

"Doesn't seem the type to play on the wrong side of the fence," Rina said. "Oh, I love that bag!"

Sera let it go for the time being, she couldn't push too hard about it. Sela wouldn't care overly much, anyway. She'd find ways to bring it up at the party later that evening and whenever she could without looking suspicious. Certainly the comments Delia made didn't cast Stander in a very good light, and the stuff about Perry was worrisome.

One thing that did bother her was the possible involvement of Kira in the dealings with the Imperialists. Not that she gave a purri seed one way or another about the stupid woman. But she worried for Brandt and Ash, for their feelings and their Families. Sera hoped the things they'd said about credits and that sort of thing just indicated Kira's nature and not any sort of knowledge of what was going on between Stander and the Imperialists.

By the time the afternoon was over, she entered the quiet guesthouse. The shops had sent over her packages, and she was halfway to drunk from all the liquor they'd imbibed at each boutique.

As Ash and Brandt were both gone, she stripped down, got in the large bath, and soaked while she tried to figure out just what the hell Kira and Perry had to do with Giles Stander and what she could do to protect her men from whatever trouble might arise.

"*L*ook what I found in our bed, Ash," Brandt called back over his shoulder.

Sera opened her eyes, and when she saw him standing there, the smile she gave him pushed all his exhaustion away.

"I see by the mountain of packages in the common area you had a good time today." He pulled his shirt off, kicked out of his shoes and pants, and got into bed with her. She immediately snuggled into him, warm and sweet-smelling.

"I missed you today."

That meant something to him. More than a million credits. "After hours with a bunch of men trying to brag and drink each other to death, I missed you, too. Your company is far preferable. Ash had to make a communication to his family. They've pinged him several times today."

"I learned something today he may want to deal with."

"What is it, Sera?" Ash asked through the link.

She related what she'd heard during her outing with Delia and Rina. *"I'm sorry."*

"Why are you sorry?" Brandt caressed her jawline.

"I wish it didn't possibly implicate your sister and Ash's cousin."

"None of that is yours to be sorry for. We'll see what we can see. I'll be in momentarily." Ash broke off, and Brandt held her close.

Brandt didn't like thinking Kira could be so selfish she'd betray their own people for credits. She wasn't the most forthright person he knew by any means, but he'd never thought her so very heartless and without even basic values.

"Did you fetch yourself any finery today?"

"More than enough." She licked over his nipple, and he shivered at the sensation. "I've missed your taste, too."

He moved, rolling her so that he lay atop her, her softness cradling him. "Well, I'm here to be tasted now."

"But you're on top."

In one easy thrust, he filled her totally. "You're right. You can suck my cock later."

He kissed her over and over as he slowly fucked into her body. And she opened for him, opened her cunt, opened her mouth, made a home for him within her body in a way no one else ever had.

In Sera Ayers, he'd found something he realized he'd never known he was missing: sanctuary. He loved her, he realized. It'd gone far beyond a depth of affection. Beyond wanting something lasting. The exact moment it happened, he didn't know, but he'd do anything to keep her, even deal with her wounds and prove to her he was real, and his feelings were true.

Their fingers intertwined, gazes locked, he made love to her like nothing and no one else mattered.

Sera was unsettled by the way Brandt touched her, by the tenderness he showed her. Much like the hand massage Ash had given her back on the transport, that gentle touch was her undoing. To be in the hands of men who could easily break her in half but who instead touched her with reverence was her downfall.

She'd given herself to him. Body and soul. And heart. Too late to panic, although beyond a doubt she was scared. She believed they cared about her. They'd shown her quite clearly. She believed what she felt when they touched her. Yes, they were undercover, but there were things she knew they weren't faking.

But that was also part of the problem. She couldn't really process all of what was happening, because she needed to wear Sela all the time. She couldn't think with them in her head. She needed the emotional space to work through it without them instead of having them inside her brain when they discussed things.

And ultimately, despite *knowing* they cared about her, she was scared. Scared of ever feeling what she had ten years before when she'd had to leave Ash. The desolation had made her into a different person, had darkened and broken a part of her she couldn't quite ever put back together. It had taken everything she had to recover, she didn't have it in her to do it again. So even though she could admit she loved both men, she wasn't sure if she could trust herself to believe it all the way just yet.

"Please don't look at me with fear in your eyes. Do you think I could ever bear to hurt you?" Brandt's voice whispered through the link as his cock continued to invade and retreat.

"Not with your hands."

He leaned down and kissed her face. Gently, softly. *"I love you, Sera. You're meant for me."*

She closed her eyes, but he leaned down and whispered in her ear, "You're beautiful, and it's inevitable. Give in and love me."

"I do," she said back, the tears bleeding into her voice.

The bed dipped as Ash got in with them. But he did nothing more than lie there, one hand stroking over Brandt's back and down his thigh before moving to Sera.

"Does his cock feel good inside you?" Ash asked, a fingertip circling her nipple.

"Yes," she sighed.

"Good. I'm next." The hand he'd been using on her nipple slipped down her belly until his fingertips dipped into her pussy, bringing her honey up to slick over her clit.

"Gods, when you touch her clit, her cunt ripples around me like liquid heat." Brandt's voice was pleasure-taut. "Make her come, Ash. All over my cock."

Ash's chuckle tightened things low in her gut as he danced the pad of his middle finger over her clit, drawing the pleasure from her, pulling her climax closer and closer.

She wanted to lose herself in the oblivion of climax, but more than that, these men looked at her and knew her. It made her want to weep and also laugh. Instead, she shrugged it aside and grabbed her orgasm, forcing it through her system as it took over in a rush.

A surprised groan came from Brandt as she felt his cock jerk inside her, unleashing his climax, filling her with his come. He leaned down and licked across her collarbone and then moved to her lips.

"Believe it. Believe *in* it."

"I don't know if I can." She wasn't able to mask the fear in her voice.

"On your belly. I'll make a believer out of you yet," Ash said teasingly as Brandt rolled off and pressed a kiss on her hip.

*A*sh sipped his drink and waited with Brandt as Sera finished her preparations for that evening's dinner party. His muscles were pleasantly loose after the extremely satisfying sex the three of them had shared.

"So, what'd your father have to say?" Brandt asked casually.

"The usual. Kira must have run back from drinks last night to call your mother. Who in turn called Perry's mother, and you know how that all works. Somehow it's turned into a scenario wherein Kira has been humiliated, when she's been remarried for seven years, and she's the one who left me."

They both watched the door, not wanting a repeat of the day before when Sera had caught only part of the conversation.

"Sera, we're having a talk out here regarding what Ash spoke to his father about. I don't want you to hear only part of a conversation and get hurt," Brandt said through the link. Her distinctive snort of derision came back through.

They looked at one another and laughed.

"I simply reiterated, again and again, that my life was my own. What about you?" He'd been beyond irritated at having his ex-wife interfere in such a ridiculous way. Ash didn't know what she thought she'd gain other than to be troublesome.

Brandt sighed. "I only texted my father back to say hello and ask him to trust my judgment. My sister manipulates men quite well, but my father isn't as easy as most men."

Sera swept into the room, and their conversation halted. Her gown was high-necked, and the sleeves touched the tips of her fingers. Her hair twisted in a long braid down her back where one swath of bare skin showed at her tailbone and nowhere else. The deep purple shot with threads of gold brought out her coloring, enhanced by a dusting of gold powder on her cheekbones.

As she moved, the dress swirled around her ankles. The soft fabric clung to every curve so that even though she wasn't as exposed as she'd been so far, every outline of her body showed. Her nipples pressed through, swaying sensually, even the dip of her belly button appeared when she moved a certain way.

By covering up what others had so blatantly shown off, she'd made it taboo and thus created a heady sexuality in doing so. Ash had no idea if she'd done it on purpose or not, but it was brilliant. He admired her tactical skill as well as her skill as a woman.

"My, don't you look incredible." Brandt bowed low from the waist as he took her hand.

When he kissed it, he slipped on a bracelet they'd seen earlier that day. Pale purple stones from Ravena, the home 'Verse.

"Ash and I thought this would look lovely on you, and look, it does. Later, I think it might be lovely to drape these over your nipples. They stand up so nicely when anything touches them."

"Stop that, darling. You'll make me all moist before we even leave." She examined the bracelet, her eyes bright with pleasure. "This is quite beautiful. Thank you both."

Ash held his arms open, and she slid into them a moment, kissing him.

"We need to get started, or I'm heading back to the bed." Ash groaned at the feel of her against him.

"You say that as if it's preferable to be out and about all night than alone here with me. Naked and thanking you for this bracelet." She arched one eyebrow.

Ash laughed. "Quit it." He swatted her ass, loving how toned and muscular she was.

As they walked through the evening, people stopped and admired them and the picture they made. Brandt with his long, dark hair and nearly pretty face; Ash with his tall, broad and fierce handsomeness; and in between them, Sela, a beautiful, sexy woman who held them in the palm of her hand.

"I doubt you'll be able to get near their network hub tonight, Sera. Although, looking the way you do, no one can refuse you anything you ask," Brandt said.

"I think so, too. Last night I was lucky, but this house, this group is *different. But Stander will be there. I'm curious to see what he'll be like in person. I do have the feeling he'll be drunk with his own perception of power. He's seen it all. So I'll dazzle him a bit. It's going to take a different approach to see what we can see."*

"No, Sera. You won't seduce him into telling you anything."

She sent him a withering look before rolling her eyes. *"Ash Walker, I need not shove my cunt in his face to get information from him. That's clumsy and beneath me. And such an accusation is beneath you. Not too long ago you were happy to have me shove my cunt in Brandt's or your face to help get this information from Stander. Remember?"*

"Brandt and me . . . that's different. I'm happy to have your cunt in my face anytime. But you don't need to whore yourself. You're worth more than anyone ever asking."

"Ash! That's absurd. I appreciate your saying so, but in truth, of course I'm not. I'm one person exchanging part of my physical self to get information that could save tens of thousands of lives, if not more. But I have no intention of fucking Giles Stander."

"Ah, I believe this is the home," Brandt broke in.

Ash kissed her, and she allowed it; she even tugged his earlobe playfully. She did pinch the lobe tight though, to make her point.

Chapter 16

*E*very eye was on her as they entered. The women ranged from admiration to outrage, the men, just admiring.

"Oh look, darling, it's your brother-in-law."

Brandt would paddle her ass later on for that amusement in her voice.

Perry stood in a knot of men—Giles Stander among them—at the far end of the room. Stander had turned to lock his gaze on Sera, who'd begun to laugh and chat with Rina, one of the concubines she'd been out with earlier that day.

"Quite the coup! I'd wager eight of the women in this room will have a dress just like yours within several days." Rina smiled at Brandt and Ash. "Welcome to my home. Tifrit is over there somewhere." She waved in the other direction. "Please, do be at ease. I'm going to spirit away your woman, if you don't mind."

"I'd like to hold on to her for a while." Brandt put an arm around

Sera's waist. "She's too beautiful to just let her wander off." He knew he should let her go, but he felt oddly possessive of her, protective. In any case, he'd be getting close to Stander, and she should be with them.

"Ah, of course. I can't blame you. I wish Tifrit looked at me the way you two look at Sela." Rina winked at Sera. "You come find me when these boys tire of you, and we'll gossip some, all right?"

Rina wandered off, waving and greeting some others who'd just entered, and Brandt steered them in the direction of that group in the corner.

"Brandt, Ash, greetings!" Perry said in a too-loud, too-drunk voice. He bowed, his hungry eyes roving all over Sera's body. Brandt paused a moment. Not Sera's body. Ash's body. But then Perry's gaze returned to Sera, quite happy to look at her breasts. "And Sela, am I correct? When you get tired of these two, you know where to find me."

"I'll keep that in mind." She'd rolled into full Sela mode. Her eyes half-lidded, her voice down an octave. A throaty purr that hardened his cock. Even her movement had changed. She turned to Ash. "Darling, would you like a drink?"

Ash collared her throat, and Brandt, standing to the side, saw her nipples stab through the front of her dress. Leaning in, Ash captured her lips slowly, surely, and aggressively. Sera allowed it, reveled in it. Sela *used* it to spill her sensuality outward, catching Giles Stander in her web.

"I'd love one. You know what I need." Ash's voice was thick with emotion, and Brandt had to stifle his desire to push her flat and shove his cock down her throat.

She turned, a smile at the corner of her lips. "Brandt? You? Can I do anything for you?"

He grabbed the rope of her hair and pulled her close, taking advantage of her gasp to sweep his tongue inside to taste her. "You have," he said as he broke the kiss. "You did just half an hour ago. But I'm always happy to have you do anything for me again."

She laughed. A real laugh, straight to her eyes. "Oh darling, you make me gooey in all the right places. I'll be back with drinks."

He turned as one with Ash, and they didn't have to fake being entranced by the movement of her ass as she walked away on those very high heels.

"Well now! I'd been wondering why any man would share a woman when he had enough money to have his own, but now I see the way of it."

Brandt turned, proud of himself for not leveling the man with a fist to the temple.

"Giles Stander. It's a pleasure to meet you. This is Owen Alder; he's a friend visiting from the Edge."

Brandt and Ash shook hands and nodded. The Edge was undefined universe, where neither Imperialist nor Federation held sway, when in reality it was far more likely the Imperialists were running illegal activity through to destabilize Federation rule. And Owen Alder was a shadowy figure, with ties to criminals and the weapons runners who made the Edge their private playground—especially those who trafficked in explosives. The situation got more interesting by the moment.

"Lots of credits to be made out my way, gentlemen. Just ask your cousin." Owen's beady eyes gleamed as he spoke. "Speaking of money, your woman, she's quite interesting. I'd be willing to pay quite a nice sum for her."

"*Easy,*" Sera whispered through the link as she approached.

"Sela isn't for sale. There are whores, should you desire one." Ash crossed his arms over his chest, and Sera approached.

"He's lucky I don't knock his teeth out for that," Ash said through the link.

"Hello, darlings, did you miss me?" Sera handed them their drinks.

Brandt took the drink she'd procured and kissed her fingertips. Ash did the same.

"Of course we missed you." Ash moved closer on one side, and Brandt did on the other.

"By the way, Ash, I think I'm wasted on Perry. It's you he seems to be salivating over. Not that I blame him." Sera's mouth curved up.

"Ah, but he's taken, isn't he, sweet?" Brandt teased back, winking at Ash.

"I see Delia and Rina just over there. I'm going to go say hello so you can keep up the man talk, shall I?" Sera cocked her head and leaned into Ash a moment.

"Oh no, please stay. You liven our lowly circle." Owen beamed at her in what was supposed to be a paternal manner, but it made Brandt's skin crawl.

"Oh now, you!" Sela waved at him and laughed. "What were you all discussing then? Did you see this lovely bracelet my boys gave to me earlier today? It's the little, very shiny things that make a girl happy." She slid back her sleeve, slowly. The movement was seemingly innocent but filled with an inherent sensuality.

"The Walkers have been doing very well lately." Perry puffed out his chest, and Sera touched his arm with a smile.

"How you all manage to be such smart men with all these 'Verses to deal with and the Imperialists just a few slips away is so very impressive! I can't believe you aren't worried!" She'd widened her eyes at that point, and Brandt noticed the way the others scrambled around to appear more impressive to her. Her artful question, designed to pull information from Perry, impressed Brandt.

"Nothing to be afraid of. The Imperialists want to make credits just like we do. Politics is a silly waste of time, you know." Stander insinuated himself closer to her, his eyes directly on her breasts.

"Do you really think it's that simple?" she asked, voice breathy, eyes wide with sincerity. Brandt wanted to laugh, but the act clearly worked on the men in their group.

"If the Federation simply let us make our profits without interfering, the Known Universes would be far safer. Especially for our credits." Stander laughed suggestively and moved a bit closer to Sera.

"Ugh. How can she stand to let this pig touch her? Delia must use some kind of mind-altering substance."

Brandt smiled and reached out to touch her hair. Stander caught the movement and stood back a bit.

"I can't complain about the lovely baubles coming my way." She laughed, deep and throaty, and Brandt shivered. Ash caught his eye, and Brandt knew his friend was as affected by her as he was.

But they had a job to do.

"Sela, sweet, I'd love a bite of something." Brandt ran his fingers down her jaw.

"Of course, darling. I'll get you a plate right now." She turned to Ash, who played with the end of her braid. "Are you hungry?"

"Yes." He paused, and Brandt's cock hardened at the sexual tension between Ash and Sera. "And I'd be grateful if you'd prepare me something to eat as well."

She kissed him quickly. "You're a very naughty boy. One of my very favorite qualities. You two behave yourselves." She winked at the other men. "And you, too. Stay out of trouble."

It got quiet as she sauntered away toward where the banquet tables lay at the other end of the room.

"She's quite something. I suppose the rest of us will simply wait impatiently until you tire of her." Stander sent them an oily smile, and Ash wanted to shoot him.

"She is. And we won't. Tire of her, that is. And in truth? I think she might be a bit more than most men could handle. It's why she needs two of us."

Brandt laughed and changed the subject. "But as far as sharing business with you? Well that's another matter entirely."

Stander's eyes lit. "Ah yes. Perry can talk with you on that as well. We have friends in all sorts of places who like to hear things, things you might come across here and there."

Ash's stomach clenched a moment, but he kept his expression bland.

"Although perhaps we should move into this back hallway." Tifrit, the Nondalese who owned the house and the party's host, indicated with his chin.

"Probably a space with less surveillance. Sera, hold off for a while. Speak with the women and see what you can find out that way." Once Ash had sent that to Sera, they took their drinks and followed the others.

"So, do share this new Walker economic plan, Perry." Ash leaned against a wall and watched his cousin.

"Your woman is wearing the benefits, Ash, so don't take that tone with me." Perry was a sloppy drunk. Weak. Perfect for Kira, he supposed.

"No tone, Perry. But as my credits are involved here, I admit to having concerns and being curious." Ash shrugged.

"Calm down, Perry. No one is picking a fight but you." Stander turned to Ash. "There's more to the Known Universes than our part of it. Credits to be made, information exchanges to be had. Profit changes hands much more easily when politics isn't in the way," Stander interjected.

"Information? Like what?" Ash sipped his drink.

"There's information and then *information*. Our friends need a helping hand to get a toehold on this side of the Edge." Stander smirked, and Ash wanted to know what Owen Alder had to say about the whole thing. Stander was a pompous braggart, but it was fairly clear Alder had more power in this little group.

"Forgive my saying so, Giles, but what is your expertise here?" Brandt asked.

"I know how to spend credits. I know many other people who do as well. And I know the people who help me spend them." Giles looked smug, but Ash had no idea what the blasted man meant.

"Yes, Giles, your expertise is racking up great deals of debt and having people hold it over you so you get leveraged into a corner. Don't forget to mention the people you owe the credits to." Perry sneered, and Ash thought there was more to the spat than simple intoxication. Perry sounded jealous.

"Gentlemen, gentlemen!" Owen stepped in between the men, and Ash realized his good-natured facade had fallen away. Owen wasn't the fool he tried to portray himself as.

"You're just jealous, Perry. I've got the *women*, and I've got the deals. Without my connections, you'd have nothing." Giles pushed Perry's shoulder. Brandt and Ash took a step back. Ash wouldn't lift a finger to protect either drunken fool.

"If you call those men who hound your every step and threaten to kill you if you don't pay your chits from the tables *connections*, I suppose you're right. Face it, Giles, you're only part of this because they can use you." Perry shoved him back.

Owen's mouth flattened into a tight line. "That's enough."

"I agree. This is my home, and there's no call for this sort of behavior among civilized people." Tifrit sniffed indignantly as if working with the enemy was civilized.

"No one uses me! I have useful information. And some people want more than they'll ever have." Stander glared at Perry, and Ash knew where the jealousy lay. He'd seen desire on the face of many people, but Perry didn't just want power, he wanted *Giles*.

But Stander said nothing else as Owen and Tifrit grabbed him and harshly told him to be quiet.

People had turned to look, and Owen shook his head at the others. "You've attracted attention, Giles. That's not healthy."

"If you'll excuse us, we're off in search of Sela and a bite to eat. If and when a serious discussion about business happens, please contact me." Ash drained his glass and placed it on a nearby table before walking away with Brandt. He knew they'd come to the end of any useful discussion at that point. But in the short time they'd been at the party, they'd discovered quite a bit of information, and it most certainly looked like Stander and Owen Alder were very strong suspects. Unfortunately, Perry looked guilty as well.

Sera was relieved not to have to deal with Giles Stander or his friends. Even the company of Delia and Rina was preferable.

"Hello there!" Rina waved at her as she approached. "Boy talk get boring?"

"Did Giles get tired of looking at your breasts?" Delia asked with a smile. "He's rather tedious that way. One-track mind. Three-pump fucking. It's a good thing he's got money."

"I'm sure he must have some redeeming qualities," Sera said, but doubted it. She nibbled on a tasty bit of cheese.

"He's unhealthy, so he'll probably die young. He can only get hard with enhancers, so the other concubines are bored. He'll most likely wean down to me and one mistress. That's redeeming." Delia rolled her eyes. "For a while it looked like none of us would be around for very long. He not only has a problem resisting the tables, he loses at them and attracts the attention of the wrong sort."

"Wrong sort? That sounds frightening. Oh what's that little dainty there?" Sera pretended to be interested in a tiny cake and not in working Delia for intel on her lover.

"I've eaten twelve of them already, and my legs will show it if I'm not careful. Yes, it was just me, the mistress, and his idiot of a wife, and suddenly he's rolling in money. Perry and the she-demon are part of his circle, and now he's got more women than he can satisfy. But I don't care, because my wardrobe is far nicer than before he started going on his little trips out here and to the Edge." Delia's smooth exterior had rubbed off a bit. A calculating woman lived inside, and Sera needed to tread carefully.

"Trips are nice. Shops in other 'Verses. New things. Shiny things." Sera laughed and showed off her new bracelet.

"Most of the time he doesn't take any of us, but he does toss credits my way when he returns."

"I've never been to the Edge. It seems awfully lawless and scary out there. Whatever could any man be up to?" Sera really did enjoy the savory bit she snacked on, even if her stomach had dropped at the news that Giles traveled to the Edge.

"It is lawless, Sela. Silly, why else would he go out there? No prying Federation eyes." Delia shrugged. "It's him and . . ." her sentence trailed off as the shouting from the hallway echoed out to where they stood. "Perry has been drinking again. Fool. And Giles is bragging, no doubt. Since the two of them are joined at the hip, I imagine I'll end up sucking Perry's cock while he pretends I'm Giles. And Giles will pretend he doesn't know what Perry is thinking." Muttering, Delia headed toward the noise, and Rina snickered.

"Well now, that was unexpected," Sera said dryly as she watched Delia leave.

"Perry's interest in men is pretty well-known with our set." Rina shrugged and leaned in close. "He's in over his head. They all are. No one can deal past the Edge and stay alive. If you were a smart woman, and I think you are, you'd get your men away from this crowd."

"What do you mean?" Alarm raced through her at the thought of losing either one of them. And at the risk Rina had just taken by admitting they'd been dealing with the enemy.

"I can't say more." Rina closed off and began to chatter about her new furniture, and Sera wanted to sing for joy when she caught sight of Ash and Brandt moving toward her.

"If you'll excuse me, Rina, thank you for your words of caution and for your lovely hospitality. I'll be off with my boys. Hopefully to be ravaged well and truly."

Rina kissed both her cheeks, blew kisses at Brandt and Ash, and Sera's men each held out an arm for her to take.

"I do believe I told you two to behave yourselves," Sera said in a purr as they moved toward the door.

"This time it wasn't my fault, Freka. Some men need to watch their liquor." Ash said it without humor, but he did lace the words with condescension.

Owen caught up with them before they reached the doorway. "Ash, Brandt, I do apologize for that regrettable exchange back there. I wanted to invite you to brunch tomorrow. The Nondalese have a lovely gaming hub just south of here. It's an annex to Nondal Major. Perhaps you'd join us for the afternoon? We could speak of business without shouting, and your lovely lady here could do some shopping with the others?"

"In other words, 'Keep her back here, because the wives are on this trip.'" Sera thought if she could grind her teeth mentally, she would.

"Of course. That would be amenable," Ash said smoothly, like he shunted her off to the side to hang out with more suitable companions on a regular basis. It was one thing to know they needed to get next to these traitors to discover what was going on, but it was another to experience it. Kira would be there basking in the attention, while Sera stayed back with the other women—women they fucked but never took to places official women were invited. It was a stupid system.

"We'll send someone for you both tomorrow then. It was a delight to meet you, Sela." He took her hand and bowed over it, kissing it with his papery lips.

"And you as well, Owen. I hope we'll have a chance to visit again before we leave Nondal." She smiled, even though she wanted to wipe her hand on Ash's shirt.

One of the younger men who'd flirted with her and tested her availability saw she was leaving and rushed over. "Are you leaving then, Sela? The evening would be so much sweeter for your presence." He looked to Brandt and Ash briefly. "Why do you take this beauty from our presence?" She wanted to laugh at how silly he was in comparison to her men.

"Ash Walker, Brandt Pela, this is Decker Wilhelm."

"We're taking this beauty home to bed. You wouldn't know what to do with her, pup," Brandt nearly growled. He was jealous. Interesting.

Ash just sized the other man up without a word, and they moved her outside. "Good evening, Decker!" she called over her shoulder as they continued to walk her away from the house and into the cool evening air.

Brandt wanted to hit something. He'd had quite enough for one day. Traitors, assholes, double dealing, and men slavering over his woman right and left. Jealousy coursed through him, and it wasn't a pleasant sensation nor one he was accustomed to.

"Slow down, please. These are very high heels, and the gown is long. I'm going to fall." The amusement and agitation in her voice were evident.

He bent, shoved his shoulder into her waist and stood. She squealed as he held on to her with one hand on her ass, totally bare under the dress.

"You two seem very fond of carrying me upside down this way. But it messes up my hair, and all the blood rushes to my head. It's not very pleasant."

Ash laughed and patted her ass. "You're bare under there!"

"Of course I am. The dress is very form-fitting. If I had panties on, they'd show through. Put me down."

"If I put you down, you'll complain about how fast we're walking," Brandt said, not stopping.

"You could put me down and stop running. That would be a start."

"I like you up here. At least while I'm carrying you, no one is offering to buy you or asking me to send you their way when I'm done with you. As if I ever plan to be. Which I don't. Let's get that clear, woman. I'm not ever going to be done with you. And then some boy who's barely left his mother's breast tries it on with you in my presence like I'm not even there." Brandt was working on being quite angry.

"He was a *boy*, Brandt. In case your years are now so advanced you don't remember what it was like to be his age, it's what they do. They swagger and throw their attitude around and try it on with women who are much older and completely out of their league."

Her voice, muffled, was patiently amused.

He put her down gently and hauled her to him not so gently. He took her mouth without pause and devoured her.

"You don't have to be so amused by my jealousy," he said, struggling for breath after he broke the kiss.

"Darling, a girl has to enjoy these moments. We never know how long they'll last."

"No, don't you throw Sela in my face right now. I'm damned serious."

"In case you've forgotten, we're in public with three spy cameras pointed at us right this very moment. Sela's all I have to throw around myself in this situation."

"What does that mean?"

"Brandt, you're going to make our lovely Sela very grumpy. So stop." Ash sent him a look, and Brandt swallowed his anger for the moment.

He took her hand and walked back, more slowly this time.

"It's a lovely night. Too lovely to be so cross." Sera's voice soothed his edgy mood a bit. He tired of the ruse. Hated putting her on display and having her in the position of an inferior. It bothered him because he knew it bothered her, and yet she did it without complaint and quite well. In point of fact, she'd proven quite indispensable. Her ability to get that data the night before had been ingenious.

"Mmm, that looks very tasty," Sera said as she paused before the window of a small bakery and sweet shop.

"Your wish is my command, Freka. What would you like?" Ash kissed her lips softly.

"One of those, with lots of frosting." She indicated a frothy-looking concoction, and Brandt winced.

Ash laughed. "I'll be right back. Brandt, would you like anything?"

"A mulled purri juice would be nice."

Ash disappeared into the store, and Brandt pulled her close to look into her eyes.

She smiled and reached up to brush the backs of her fingers over his chin. "So handsome. I like looking at you."

He tasted her lips because he needed to, needed to connect and know she felt the same. "I want all of you."

Her eyes closed for a moment before opening again, that deep blue looking into his.

Ash came out then, holding a bag in one hand and Brandt's drink in the other. "Let's go. I find myself very hungry."

Chapter 17

"I'd like to say for the record, I'd much rather be back in the cottage with my cock deep inside a warm, willing pussy." Ash had been annoyed since Sera had grumpily slapped his hand away and buried her face in the pillow that morning when the men had awoken to leave.

Brandt snorted. "Don't take it out on me. You're the one who kept her up until nearly dawn licking frosting off all her best parts."

"Yes, well, that was quite pleasant. But I wanted to fuck her before we came out here, too. She slapped my hand away."

Actually, she'd slapped his hand away and told him she'd shoot him in the head if he didn't let her go back to sleep. Good thing she'd added that bit about the shooting through the link. He'd forgotten how she could be without enough sleep. Ash smiled at how bloodthirsty she was.

"This would be a lot better if she was here," Brandt said.

The conversation certainly would have been. Ash hated this sort of gaming outing. Casinos and gaming halls were not entertaining to him in the least. Men with more money than sense losing more of both than they could afford.

And he'd have appreciated her take on the whole situation. When they'd returned to the cottage the night before, sex had pushed most discussion from the schedule, but they had gone over, just briefly, the increasing evidence pointing to Giles Stander and Perry as well as the very real belief that Owen Alder and his connections with weapons runners might be the key. Whether Kira was involved was still a big question. Rina and Delia's comments the evening and day before about Kira weighed against her. But Ash, while convinced of Kira's general worthlessness, didn't know if she was a traitor.

Brandt sipped his drink. "She's not, so deal with it. She slept in and then got a massage before heading out for a late lunch with her new friends."

"Lucky her. And that masseuse better have been female."

"Ash, you actually sound jealous over a hired woman. Have you fallen so very low since we parted ways?" Kira insinuated herself at Brandt's elbow.

"Kira, behave yourself," Brandt warned her.

The wives were on this outing, which meant Kira was there and had been skirting around them all day. Giles Stander had been glaringly absent from the gathering, and all Ash wanted was for Owen to stop parading around and get to the damned point. He had a woman waiting back in the cottage, and he wanted this op to be over so he could get back home and start a real life.

"It's so like you to play with your food," Ash said without heat. He was bored with her blasé nastiness. It was her second nature to be a bitch, and all he could do was be fucking glad she'd set him free. "What's it to you, anyway?"

"You're lowering yourself, and because we used to be married, it reflects on me. It's pathetic that both of you are involved with her. I expect that sort of thing from a woman of her status. But you two are born better. Ash has always shown poor judgment. He has a taste for lowborn women. But you, Brandt, how do you think a woman of marriageable status will look upon this," she sneered as she waved a hand between Ash and Brandt, "thing you're doing?"

Brandt actually growled low in his throat, and Ash touched his friend's shoulder. "I see Owen, let's go and speak to him, shall we?" With that, he got up, turned his back on Kira and walked away.

*B*randt leaned over to his sister and narrowed his eyes. "Be careful where you tread, Kira. Cease with this troublemaking and communicating back home. It's none of your concern. It seems to me, you have a bit of your own trouble to deal with."

"What do you mean?" Her gaze, which had glittered with malice, slid from his.

He'd known her and covert work long enough to see the slight alarm in her eyes. He had to know if she was involved.

"I mean, the company you keep isn't as upstanding as you portray. If you invite closer scrutiny, you should be sure you can withstand it."

"Are you threatening me? My own brother?" She tried to recover by using her aloofness against him, but he waved it away.

"No, Kira. I'm warning you. If you have anything you're worried about, you know you can come to me or to Father, right? We'll protect you, help you. But there are some things the farther you get into them, the less we can do. These people Perry is involved with, do you know what they are?"

He stood, hoping she'd take him seriously and confide in him.

"I don't know what you're talking about, Brandt. I'm going to find my husband now." Her body stiffened.

"You do that, Kira."

He shouldn't have said as much as he had, but she was his sister. He had to think if she was involved, she couldn't know or have really thought out the consequences.

He saw Ash with Owen and headed in that direction.

Sera awoke alone and smelling of frosting. She smiled as she stretched, still a bit sticky from the late hours when Ash had teased her with his tongue until she'd begged. He'd tried to wake her up for yet more sex before he and Brandt had left, but she'd not gotten nearly enough sleep and smacked his exploring hands away. She remembered vaguely sending a threat through their mental link, and he'd smacked the bare cheek of her ass in warning. And promise.

Not like she'd complain. Sometimes a girl simply needed to misbehave, because the punishment was so delicious.

Loving being alone, despite all the cameras and spy equipment—damned nosy little deviants, the Nondalese—she ate a leisurely breakfast before taking a long bath and heading out.

Her chaperone stood back and let her shop without interference. She'd purchased plenty of things for herself but wanted to pick up gifts for Brandt and Ash. She also grabbed a pair of earrings for her mother. She'd send them home once she returned to Borran.

The clerks in the shop gossiped about her, not knowing she understood Nondalese. It wasn't anything too awful, some commentary about what Ash would be like in bed, a bit of sniffing about fucking your way into comfort when some women worked and didn't demean themselves. It was something Sera felt an affinity with, but after taking on this assignment and having met some of the other concubines, she understood them more. Understood the lack of choices that had brought some of them to the lives they led.

In truth, she felt much less sorry for those who thought it a business arrangement than those who truly loved the men they served. Those men weren't Ash and Brandt, and while she was sure many of them showed their women on the side some measure of warmth and affection, it wasn't official. And in their world, it wasn't enough protection.

The vagaries of fate meant women without official status would be bound to lose any position they had when their protectors got bored or died. Sera shivered, glad this was all a ruse. She wasn't a concubine, and she had a career to sustain her no matter what happened.

The wide avenues on their level of the city were lined with foliage: large trees, planters overflowing with beautiful flowers. Up there, life was good. A slow-moving trolley ran up and down the middle of the avenue, ferrying people where they needed to be. No other vehicles but the trolley and bicycles for deliveries ran, so the streets were open and safe. In the quiet, birds chirped, and the sounds of people laughing and mixing at the various outdoor cafés and small greenbelts rang through the air.

It was as if those dark, dank and suffocating levels of the city didn't exist. The workers for the upper level were housed in a level a few down, not nearly as bad as the others but not this good, either. So, if trading your body to a rich man got you into the sunshine and fresh air, was it really so awful? Could she really make such a harsh judgment?

She'd had rock-solid moral opinions, and the last ten days had challenged her severely. She'd been forced to look at herself and examine her own reactions to Ash and his marriage, and it wasn't comfortable.

"Sela, darling, whatever are you up to?"

Sera turned from the window of the shop to face Rina.

"Hello. I've been shopping before I went to your luncheon. You look lovely as always."

Sera kissed her cheek.

"Well, do come along with me then. I've received a communication from Tifrit. They're all still playing, so it should be some hours yet before they return. He believes I have nothing better to do than sit around and wait for him to appear." Rina rolled her eyes.

"Don't you have a chaperone?" Sera looked around.

"No. I'm supposed to, but they'd have to deal with Tifrit's wrath if anyone harassed me. Tifrit's wife doesn't need an escort; why should I?" Rina sniffed, and they began to stroll toward her home.

"I imagine it becomes tedious to have to be escorted everywhere."

"Among other things, yes. It's bothersome to always be on display." Rina laughed when she caught Sera's look. "What? Did you assume we didn't know? Or wouldn't mind?"

"I suppose I figured you'd made peace with it."

"Have you?" Rina unlocked her door, and they swept inside. The chaperone took his leave, and for the moment it was just Rina and Sera there.

"Have I made peace with being supervised at all times here in Nondal Major?"

"Here, let's drink while we get philosophical, shall we?"

Well, women often knew things because men either told them or spoke as if they weren't there. Rina was far more clever than Sera had given her credit for.

"I like that you're not an idiot." Rina handed her a glass of smoky amber liquor, and Sera took it, breathing in the scent.

"Well, thank you. So tell me? Or is this not the place?" Sera wanted to hear whatever Rina wanted to share.

"It's as good a place as any up here." Rina shrugged and sat. "Have I made peace with my place? With being in the shadow of another woman for as long as Tifrit suffers my presence in his life? What do you think? How does it make you feel, Sela? I see the way you look at them, this is more for you."

Sera sighed. "How can you ever be at peace with a tiny portion of what you should possess fully, but don't, due to birth? Am I less worthy because my mother is unranked? Less worthy than a woman like Kira Pela-Walker?"

"At least Tifrit's wife is a fool. Women like Kira aren't. But she treads dangerously, and your men do as well. My Tifrit plays in waters too deep for a councilor from Nondal, but his pride pushes him far from shore. And men like Owen and Perry thrive on people like Tifrit."

Sera wanted to tell her to get to the point she danced around, but that wasn't Rina's style, so she waited, trying hard to be patient.

"But there are others who are in even more precarious positions, like Delia, for instance. Giles isn't a fool; he's worse. He's in debt and hungry for money and attention but too weak to get it in the way a normal man should. The thing about being born where you and I were, we know what it means to dig our way out, to climb and work. These ranked people don't. And so they end up drunken, indebted messes like Giles, sad shadows like Tifrit, or soulless traitors like Owen. The Brandts and Ashes of the world are rare, but even Ash dumped aside his prior love for Kira Pela." Rina's eyes narrowed a moment, and Sera's heart beat a bit faster, wondering if Rina knew.

"What is happening, Rina? If my boys are in danger, I would

know. You said yourself you saw how I looked at them. I love them both deeply." Sera didn't have to act at that point.

Rina squeezed her knee. "I know you do. Even if they'll leave? Choose a wife from women who are not of our class strata?" She paused and looked at Sera again. "I suppose I have the answer with you sitting here, don't I? Times are dangerous, Sela. Some associations are best severed. If I knew someone who considered getting involved with the likes of Stander or Owen, I'd tell them to get on a transport and head back toward the Center. The Edge is less and less secure. The people Owen is involved with, the things they do . . . I'm afraid, and it's probably too late for me. But not you. Get out while you can."

Before Rina could say anything else, the chimes at the door rang.

"Ah, guests. Let's go then and have a nice luncheon." Rina stood, and Sera touched her arm.

"Thank you. Can I help you at all? Perhaps you would like to come and visit with me on Ravena?" If things were that dangerous, Rina had just risked her life to speak up to warn them. Sera couldn't just walk away without trying to give in return.

"I may contact you later," Rina said quietly as they went to the door. By the time she opened it, her seriousness had gone, replaced by the sultry, playful Rina; the one Sera was used to.

"Perry tells me you've been very disinterested in Family economics. Why now?" Owen Alder looked Ash over with a careful eye.

Ash leaned back and lit the tip of a smoking stick. "My disinterest, as he terms it, has been keeping my Family as powerful as its been for generations. It's my work, together with my father's, that has kept us strong. But the thing I find most interesting is how my cousin has a lot to say about my motivations when he barely knows me. Why is that, do you think?"

"I believe it's because he doesn't trust you."

"Ah, honesty. Refreshing in a compatriot of my cousin's. Unusual, and a quality he doesn't have in great portions."

"I've dealt with him; he's made me money and helped me with problems. You're an unknown. Why should I trust you enough to let you in on our dealings?" Owen asked.

Ash blew out the sharp smoke and raised one brow. "I wear the marks; he does not." The marks on the back of Ash's head were an indicator of honor and rank. His older brother didn't even bear them. He'd proven himself an honored member of the Walker Family, and his place and rank were unquestioned. Ash had earned those marks by his twentieth year fighting in interverse wars and proving himself loyal.

Owen nodded. "And therein lies the problem, does it not? Those marks are of an honorable man. Honor that is unquestioned. I'm not looking for honor, I'm looking for loyalty. Perry is loyal. You are honorable."

How could Ash argue with that? It was the truth, and Owen understood the difference in a way Perry never could. Perry just didn't like having to share the power.

Ash shrugged. "It's up to you. I'm sure you're aware it's my father's line who controls Walker finances and not my uncle's. One way or another, you will have to go through me, because we both know Perry is weak and will create problems down the line."

Owen looked at him again, a vague smile on his lips. "Our business isn't so typical that would be necessary, Ash."

"And what business is that, then? I don't like this vague pointing and inference. Show me something tangible."

"You seem very interested in details."

"Of course I am. You brought me here to offer me a business partnership, and now you play coy. I can buy and sell grain or women's clothing with anyone. Why should there be so much secrecy here?"

Owen's eyes flitted around the room, taking stock. "There are some *issues* we're clearing up right now."

Ash didn't like the sound of that. He pinched out the end of the stick and disposed of it. "You know where to find me when and if you really want to do business."

It was best for Ash to act that way. Desperation would bring suspicion. Standoffishness would serve him better.

Owen nodded. "Things are a bit unstable just now. But shortly they should even out, and I'll be in contact."

Something had changed. Ash was nearly certain it wasn't his cover slipping. He'd be dead or at the very least, someone would have tried if that were the case. No, it was something else, and he had a very powerful urge to connect with Sera.

He nodded and turned, meeting Brandt's eyes. *"Something is up. Sera, are you all right?"*

Brandt made his farewells, and they headed for the private transport that would take them back to the guest cottage.

"Yes, I'm here. So much to tell you when I see you. There are too many people here right now, I can't concentrate on two involved conversations at once."

Ash relaxed a bit when he heard her voice and knew she was safe.

"What the hells is going on?" Brandt demanded.

"Something has changed. I don't know what, but I want you to be on your guard. We're coming for you. Don't leave with anyone or go anywhere until we get to you," Ash told Sera.

"*I'm quite capable of protecting myself.*" The annoyance in her voice was so clear, Brandt looked at him and laughed out loud.

"*Indulge me.*"

The ride was over relatively quickly, and Brandt went with him to gather Sera from Rina's home.

Chapter 18

Brandt didn't like the look on Ash's face. Not one bit. It was one thing before Sera was on their team, but now the two people who meant the most to him in the world were there. He'd protect Sera with his life, whether she liked it or not.

Rina opened the door herself and sent them a sexy smile. "I don't suppose we could work out a trade? I could come with you two, and Sela could stay here?" She winked.

Ash leaned over in a bow and kissed her hand. "As lovely as you are, I'm afraid Sela has spoiled us for all other women."

"And she'd find you and cut out your hearts," Sela said as she sauntered to the door.

"That, too, sweet. We've come to collect you and take you to dinner. Are you amenable?" Brandt relaxed a bit when she took his hand, and he spun her neatly against him, loving her laugh.

"How can I refuse two such pretty men? Rina, thank you for a lovely afternoon."

"Any time, Sela. I know you'll be leaving soon, but I do hope we see each other before you go."

Brandt thought that odd but stayed quiet.

"Of course." Sera kissed Rina, hugging her before turning back to them. "All right then. I'll need rest first, I've only eaten not too long ago."

"*Now, tell us what is going on.*" Brandt walked quickly, keeping Sera in between himself and Ash.

Ash told them about the conversation he'd had with Owen and of his suspicions that Owen was up to something. "*Something is up. Or it's about to be. He's skittish, and his comments were ominous.*"

"*I think we can go forward with a pretty safe assumption that this is the group dealing with the Imperialists. The coincidences and inferences keep piling up.*" Brandt worried his bottom lip between his teeth a moment. "*What did Rina tell you?*"

Then Sera told them of her conversation with Rina. "*Her warnings were pretty dire. I believe, given what she said, she's discussing the mess with the Imperialists.*"

"*You're not going back there! She may know who you are. I can't believe you stayed.*" Brandt wanted to haul her over his knees and spank her.

"*I don't know how, there weren't pictures of me at the time, and I do look different now. She didn't come straight out and say it, but I certainly got that feeling from what she said. But not that I'm covert. She just thinks I'm back with Ash after all these years. She risked a lot to tell me what she did, to warn me. If she wanted to hurt me, there'd have been police at the door. We have to get her a way out. She doesn't have to take it, but I want to give her the option. If she stays and this breaks open, who cares about a mistress or a concubine? Especially here. She has no real protection.*"

"*We'll get some credits to her. Enough to get herself some new identity papers and a ticket toward the Center. She can't come to you, it's too*" *dangerous for you both. But we have people who will help.*" Ash kissed her hand as they strolled.

"*One last thing: Delia was very nervous today. She showed up late and not in the fashionable sense. She was jittery and not her usual put-together self.*"

"*Giles wasn't at the outing today.*" Brandt sighed, opening up the door to their cottage.

"*Stop. Someone's been here.*" Sera walked in. "Darling? Did you come back here before you two came to collect me?"

Brandt pulled her back, trying not to be obvious about it. "No. Why?"

"I left the room in a bit of a state when I left earlier. But not like this. My things have been moved."

"*Experts or novices?*"

"*There's enough of a difference that I'd notice even if I weren't specially trained. They're clumsy. I think we should notice, and I think you need to notify the authorities. They won't find anything to implicate us unless it's been planted.*"

"Do not enter the room. I'm going to call and get someone up here right away." Ash had her sit on the bench just outside the front door.

"Why would someone do this? Did you leave anything of value in front of a window?" Brandt ran a hand up and down her arm. Fear coursed through him at the thought of her being threatened.

"Darling, I'm a big girl. All my expensive jewelry is in the safe. I'm wearing everything else."

"*The data miner?*" If whoever had broken in had found that, they'd be exposed.

"*The chip is in my hair. I've had it with me all the time.*"

Moments later, Ash returned with two Nondalese officials in tow along with the hospitality manager.

"Stay here. We're going to do a walk-through of the cottage," Ash said before disappearing through the front door.

He returned sometime later. "It appears nothing has been taken." Ash looked to the authorities for a moment before speaking through the link. *"But the communications console has been tampered with. I didn't mention it to the authorities, but we'll look when we're alone."*

"We'll move you immediately. We're terribly sorry and very relieved none of your belongings were taken." One of the hospitality liaisons looked slightly panicky under Ash's scrutiny.

"I'm very uncomfortable just now. While our things are being moved, I'd like to go to our transport for a while." Sera stood up, her hand at her throat.

Normally, it wouldn't be allowed. The transports were outside the realm of Nondalese surveillance. Speaking of surveillance . . .

"We'd like to see the surveillance footage. Have it sent to our communications unit in our transport, please." Brandt looked at Sera a long moment before turning to the officials who looked doubly uncomfortable.

"Sir, we do not have private areas under surveillance," the police officer in charge stated.

Ash crossed his arms over his chest. "Of course you do. It wasn't a request. Send it. Sela, come in and let's get all packed up. We'll have our bags sent to the new quarters before we go back to the docking rings."

Brandt followed them, closing the door. Sera quickly packed her things, and Brandt grabbed their comm unit before letting the liaison know they'd return sometime later.

"Mr. Pela?"

Brandt turned to the liaison.

"We'll have whatever footage we can obtain sent to your comm unit. We're very sorry about this. This is an unacceptable and unusual occurrence here in Nondal Major." The liaison looked distinctly uncomfortable.

"I'm sure it is."

Chapter 19

*A*sh did a thorough sweep when they walked inside the transport. Their own security had reported that no one had attempted to board and break the seal, but Ash wanted to be doubly sure.

Still, Sera knew they'd still be monitored with high-powered microphones and other listening devices, especially in light of what had happened back at the cottage. The ruse weighed heavily on her shoulders, and she didn't know how the Nondalese handled it every day.

"Viewing room. Let's see what they've sent. We'll watch the surveillance footage while Ash checks out the comm unit to see what he can find." Brandt pulled her to him. "Are you all right?"

"Just a bit rattled. I'll survive."

In truth, she *was* rattled. It was one thing to be shot at and deal with warfare in the trenches. That was straightforward. You got shot at, and you returned fire. It was clear. But what she did, what they did now, wasn't clear at all. It was all bound up in complicated deceptions, and it ate at her.

Beyond discomfort at having to take abuse from people like Kira because of their perceived—and actual—differences in status, having to pretend to be someone she wasn't grated on her. All of it did, because everyone else around her played a role as well.

She didn't know what to believe. Was Rina trying to help her? If so, was it about herself and her lover? Would Rina turn on her if she thought it benefited her? Sera hated to believe the worst of people, other than Ash, but that'd been self-preservation. And yet, what they did brought her distrust into sharp focus.

"You okay in there? You look lost in thought." Brandt sat her down and loaded up the surveillance footage while Ash sat with a grunt and began clicking on the keyboard as he hacked into the comm unit to see what had been tampered with.

"I'm all right. Really. They suspect us. Someone does, and I worry about you and Ash."

He grinned, and his pretty face transformed into something innocent and beatific. Sera's heart seized as her breath caught. She touched his face. "You're so beautiful."

His expression softened, and he kissed her, brushing his lips across hers. "You're good for me."

"I hope to be. I hope I am. You both mean everything to me. I want to be worthy of that." She said it knowing it was a risk but not wanting to hide from it for even just a brief moment.

The clicking of the keys halted as Ash moved to join them, kneeling in front of her. He put his head in her lap, and Brandt, sitting so close his thigh touched hers, simply smiled.

Unbidden, her hands went to the smooth skin of Ash's skull.

"These times when you don't hide yourself mean so much."

Brandt's eyes saw right to her very heart, a heart thundering in her chest because she'd exposed herself so much.

"It's us who need to work to be worthy." Ash's breath warmed her thighs.

Brandt's hands undid the fastenings holding the top of her gown, his fingers brushing over her neck and chest. Cool air met her breasts as the material slid away.

"I've been dying for you all day," Brandt breathed out. "I've never needed anyone the way I do you."

Ash's hands moved up her calves, spreading her thighs as he pushed her dress up and out of the way, exposing her barely covered pussy.

"These are sexy," Ash said in that deep-as-night voice. Unerringly, his middle finger stroked her lightly, finding her clit swollen and begging for attention, even through the whisper-thin material of the panties she wore.

Brandt pinched her nipples between his thumb and forefinger just shy of painfully, and she arched with a cry as the sensation burst through her.

The sound of fabric tearing broke through her sensual fog as Ash tossed her panties—another ruined pair—over his shoulder and spread her wide open to his gaze. "So beautiful, wet, pink. Your scent goes straight to my cock." Dipping his head, he delivered a devastating kiss to her cunt, one that left her gasping for breath.

"Hands on the back of the couch. On your haunches, thighs open wide." Ash looked up at her, lips glistening with her honey.

She nearly fell over in her rush to comply, and he chuckled darkly. A moan of pleasure slipped from her lips when he got back to work, licking and eating at the flesh of her pussy, paying special attention to her clit. Her fingers dug into the sumptuous material of the couch, gripping tight to keep her balance.

"You're so beautiful there, Ash's mouth worshipping you like the goddess you are." Brandt stood. She watched, rapt, as he unbuckled and unfastened his trousers. He pulled out his cock, stroking it a few times, although it didn't look like he needed any help.

Sharp hits of electric energy zapped through her as Ash devoured her. It took all her concentration not to let go, not to let her head loll back. But the sight of Brandt moving toward her kept her focus.

"Do you want my cock?" Brandt's voice was low, velvet, compelling. Her cunt loosed more honey, and Ash's groan of pleasure echoed through her body.

She nodded her head, licking her lips. Her nipples stabbed forward, her hips rocked against Ash's mouth. She couldn't take her eyes from Brandt or from the head of his cock, glistening with a pearl of semen. Ash pressed two fingers into her gate, high, hooking them and stroking over her sweet spot until she burst out a surprised cry.

And still Brandt advanced, getting up onto the edge of the back of the couch and sitting, one leg on either side. He scooted toward her as she began to pant from the relentless driving pleasure of Ash's mouth.

"Suck my cock. Take it all, keep me wet." Brandt's fingers undid the pins holding her hair and grabbed it in his fist, guiding her head down as he held his cock in the other hand.

His taste, salty and spicy, filled her as she swirled her tongue across the head and around the ridge. He grunted as she used the tip of her tongue to dig into the sensitive spot just below the slit.

In the background, the comm unit pinged as if it had found something. But Ash didn't stop, and Brandt's fingers tightened in her hair, urging her on, increasing her speed as he arched, bringing his hips up to meet her mouth.

She found that place within her, the quiet, calm space where she wrapped herself in her submission, and her throat eased. She breathed through her nose, kept Brandt's cock nice and slick, and swallowed him over and over. His groans and other sounds of pleasure were like a physical caress.

"That's it," Brandt crooned.

Ash moved his mouth away, and she cried out at the loss of sensation, but his hands adjusted her so she faced the back of the couch and held on again. Brandt moved to stand behind the couch, and his cock ended up at eye level.

When Ash's cock slammed into her pussy, she squealed around a mouthful of Brandt's cock, and he chuckled. "I'm going to fuck your pretty mouth while Ash fucks that delicious cunt."

She whimpered at the sheer eroticism of the words, at their taboo as Brandt pressed into her mouth. She held on, finding her quiet place again as he thrust into her. The sounds of the room, the wet slap of cock in cunt, the soft sighs and grunts met the scents of sex, the musk of maleness, the sweet, heady scent of her juices and combined into a potent brew.

Brandt's hands tightened in her hair as he got closer to climax. Ash's thrusts into her pussy drew into short, hard digs. Her nipples abraded the couch, and one of Ash's fingertips found her clit and pressed hard, sending her headlong into an orgasm she hadn't expected.

Brandt groaned and began to come, filling her with his taste to nearly overwhelming as she struggled to take him while her climax buffeted her senses. He finally took a step back, kissing the top of her head.

On and on, Ash fucked her. The couch bumped back a bit each time he thrust home. He whispered against the skin of her back, told her he loved her, he adored her. All she could do was hold on physically. Barely so, emotionally. Finally, with a harsh roar, Ash came as he pressed in deep one last time.

"You're mine, Freka. Always." He pulled out, kissing her shoulder.

She collapsed to the cushions, and Brandt laughed. "And mine. Rest, why don't you, while we look at what we can see?"

$\mathcal{A}$sh stared at the comm unit screen and growled with inarticulate rage. *"They tried to hack into my financial records. Not successfully, but they did try. Yours as well, Brandt."*

"That could be good and bad. They may just be trying to see if they can use anything against us like Stander." Brandt watched the vid screen as the surveillance video uploaded.

"It's almost as if they knew exactly where the cameras were," Sera said as she sat up, putting her gown back to rights.

"Indeed." The intruders kept their faces down and away from the cameras in the room. They headed straight for the comm unit and began to poke around while another man idly went through their things.

Ash watched while one of them answered a personal comm unit, and they scrambled to get out.

"Looks like they were warned."

"Darling, it looks as if someone called them home for dinner." Sera shifted, moving to look closer, and Ash walked to the screen.

"Interesting." Ash looked back to Brandt. There was no real audio except for the chirp of the personal comm unit and the person's brief sound when he answered.

"The time stamp is right around when you called me through the link and asked if I was all right."

"I do think it's too big a coincidence to overlook. It was someone at the gaming hall or someone acting for them." Ash ran a hand over his head,

a physical gesture he fell to when he was thinking, but the sparkle in Sera's eye caught his attention.

"Stop that, Freka. I've just had you, the scent of your cunt is all over me, and I still want more." Ash grinned, and she laughed.

"Do we have to go back there? Can we not stay here until we're ready to leave?" Sera asked, tucking her feet beneath her on a nearby couch.

Ash was ready to get out of there. He wanted to get back to Borran; he wanted to throw off this op and be able to enjoy Sera openly. But they had to deal with this and not just as operatives; Ash had to deal with the very real possibility his cousin was aiding their enemies.

"The Nondalese aren't much for that sort of thing. We can stay here a while longer. I've just received notice our things have been moved to a new cottage. They've even provided a catered dinner for us at our leisure." Brandt brushed her hair back from her face.

"We also need to deal with the authorities about this." Ash waved to the screen. Anyone would be upset by the infringement of their privacy and safety. It was suspicious not to follow up. He also wondered just how involved the Nondalese officials were. At the very least the hospitality liaison, because the intruders knew the exact placement of the surveillance cameras.

"*I suppose they've all just let us know there's something big to hide. That's one positive way to look at it. I'm going to take a few minutes to set up an account for Rina.*" Sera went to the wall of computers near the door and began to work while Brandt made a copy of the film and Ash went to deal with the Nondalese officials.

"I'm going to head to the security offices here in Nondal Major. I want to know what they plan to do about this. What if Sela had been there?" Despite knowing Sera was quite capable of protecting herself, she'd have been limited by her cover, and Ash didn't like the idea of anyone trying to harm her. Rage simmered in his gut, and he wanted to hit something.

"We'll meet you at the new cottage." Brandt's face told Ash he held the same anger at the situation. He knew Brandt wouldn't leave Sera alone for a moment now that someone was so boldly trying to find information about them.

Sera knew she didn't have to help Rina. Knew she couldn't trust Rina totally, either. Yet she could have been Rina but for the accident of birth. In a place like Nondal, what options would she have had being born unranked? Sera supposed she felt a sort of kinship with the other woman, and she wanted to give her an option if things got worse and she wanted out. And whatever her motives, Rina had risked herself to warn them; that counted for something.

After she'd taken care of that, she headed to their rooms, cleaned up, changed clothes, and slid Sela firmly back in place. Brandt had watched it all with a smile, taking in every moment. It wasn't the same weighty surveillance she'd have to deal with once they stepped outside the transport. No, he watched her because it pleased him.

Being with Brandt was entirely different than being with Ash. There was no heaviness of the past between them, no pain. And while there was fear, the absence of the hurt she'd had with Ash created an ease between them. An ease that felt totally natural and right, which scared Sera down to her toes. Losing it terrified her. This situation was a fairy tale. She wasn't Sela, she was Sera. She didn't walk around in slinky gowns and cast her eyes down unless sex was involved. When they got back to Borran and the ruse was gone, when the real Sera surfaced, would they both still want her? Moreover, if they decided they did, would they regret it later?

Still, it was inevitable the ruse would end and reality reassert itself. She may as well ride it out to what she hoped would be a positive outcome.

"Are you ready to go back and meet up with Ash?" she asked Brandt.

"As much as I love having you all to myself, I think we should. Do you feel all right? You do know we'll keep you safe?"

She laughed and snuggled into his arms. She could strike several killing blows with her bare hands, but they worried for her. Annoying but sweet.

"I trust you both, yes."

He kissed her temple. "Good."

He held his hand out, and she took it, giving herself to him in more ways than one.

Chapter 20

*A*fter the small privacy the transport afforded, being back in the city was oppressive. Sera sat, her body curled into Brandt's, as they were ferried to their new cottage. This one was even grander than the last, but she felt a thousand eyes on her when they went inside. Where she found Ash having a very gruff conversation with none other than Kira.

Sera froze, feeling invaded. Brandt squeezed her hand. "Why don't you go into the bedroom and rest a while?"

It was *her* cottage, and *she* had to leave because poor Kira shouldn't even be exposed to her presence. Sera pulled her hand from his, ignoring his pings through the link, and stormed into the bedroom. It was only mildly satisfying to slam the door in her wake when she really wanted to knock Kira's smirk from her face.

What Sera hated so much was that she wasn't a whiny woman. She wasn't the type to stomp her foot and have tantrums, but this entire situation turned her into one, because she had no recourse.

She had no ability to say to Kira exactly what she'd say if she were living her normal life.

She growled at the impotence she felt. She couldn't confront Kira, she couldn't speak openly to Brandt and Ash about their relationship, and she had to act like a silly piece of fluff. It galled her because it was the opposite of her normal way of being.

Ah well, at least Sela would stomp out of the room, so she had that one small solace. Of course, Sera would walk up and kiss her on the lips as if being unranked was a disease she could transmit to Kira.

She laughed at the image as she tossed herself on the bed.

"$\mathcal{I}$ see you've finally learned some manners," Kira said archly as Brandt approached.

"Too bad you haven't. Why are you here?" Brandt demanded. He'd had enough of the whole fucking situation, and his sister's presence just capped it.

"Giles Stander has been murdered." Ash looked at Brandt, one eyebrow slightly raised.

"What? Here in Nondal Major? Well, have they made arrests?" Brandt's thoughts went to Sera, not in his sight. He wanted to know she was all right.

"*Damn it, Sera, answer me.*"

"*What?*"

Ash actually laughed a moment but covered it with a cough.

"*That answers my question. I just wanted to know if you were all right. Stander has been murdered.*"

He turned his focus back to Ash. He knew Sera would wait for them to tell her more once they'd dealt with Kira.

"No. They have no suspects at this time." The sarcasm in Ash's voice was clear.

Kira interrupted Ash, placing her hand on his forearm, and Brandt shot his friend a confused look. "It's just awful! What kind of place is this? I've always felt safe when Perry and I visited, but Ash tells me you've had a break-in, and now this murder. What is the 'Verse coming to?"

"What are *you* up to, Kira? Why are you here to tell Ash instead of sending a comm or letting us learn from the authorities? And just how often are you out here, anyway?" Brandt crossed his arms over his chest, seeing right through her histrionics.

"Is it wrong to seek out some comfort from my former husband and my brother? Why are you so suspicious? Is that pet of yours trying to turn you against me?" Her artful pout only made Brandt more suspicious.

Ash took her upper arm gently but firmly and led her toward the door. "Kira was just leaving. She's delivered her news, and now she needs to get back to her *husband* where she's safe."

Kira tried to shake him off but was unsuccessful. "I don't have a chaperone or an escort back to our rooms. Ash, would you take me?" She fluttered her lashes at Ash, who let go and took three steps back rather quickly.

"I'll take you, Kira. Although you seem to have made it here just fine." Brandt hid his smile at Ash's response.

"I was so shocked, I didn't stop to think." She held her hand out, and Brandt took it, placing it on his arm.

"I'll be back shortly," he called over his shoulder as he steered Kira out of the cottage and away from Sera.

Once they'd gotten a bit away from the cottage, he turned to his sister. "Now, as we're out and about and things are noisy and a bit chaotic, why don't you tell me what the hells you've gotten yourself into? This isn't playtime; just ask Giles. Oh, but you can't."

"I don't know what you're talking about or why you keep accusing me. Giles was a friend of my husband's." She sniffed, offended, and Brandt wanted to grind his teeth.

"You're out here frequently; you're involved with these people. I'm warning you, Kira, for your own safety, stop to think about whatever it is you and Perry are involved in. People are dying."

"Here we are. Thank you for escorting me. Perry and I are leaving in several hours, so I suppose this is farewell." She kissed the air above his cheek, and he sighed as she rushed inside without a backward glance.

When he returned to the cottage, Sera and Ash stood stiffly side by side watching a vid screen. He moved to catch the footage of another destroyed outpost, one he knew was an important relay station.

"Fifty-three people were killed." Sera answered the question he hadn't asked yet.

"They're saying it was an accident. The electrical station had a malfunction and set off a series of explosions. The enviro-tent over the settlement was destroyed, and the pressure killed those the explosions hadn't." Ash's eyes lit with anger. They had friends at that station. More than that, they'd just met a man who had connections to weapons traffickers who dealt in the kinds of explosives that Brandt suspected had been used.

"We need to make our way back toward the Center." Brandt couldn't tear his eyes from the scenes of devastation on the screen.

"I'd like to say good-bye to Rina."

"That's not going to be possible, Sela. We should get moving now. I don't like you here with all this anarchy." Brandt moved to brush a hand down her arm, but she stepped back and narrowed her eyes at him.

"Don't you even try to tell me what to do. I'm going to see her. I have something for her. And you can fuck right off, along with Ash and your stupid sister, too," Sera said through the link.

But Sela simply smiled. "While your worry for me is touching, Rina is a friend. I will say good-bye."

"Every time with this, Sera. It's really rather tedious. You get angry for something I can't control." Brandt didn't bother to hide his annoyance.

"Well, don't let my tedium at repeatedly being treated as a whore get in your way then, Brandt. And don't tell me she was just here to deliver the news about Stander. She was here for Ash. I'm not stupid."

Brandt turned to Ash with a smile, hoping to look casual, but Ash's face told him Sera's accusation was on the mark.

She moved to the comm center to arrange for a chaperone, but Ash negated the order.

"I will escort you. You have no need of a chaperone when you have Brandt and me here."

"Fine," she said through clenched teeth and went out the door without waiting for either man.

Sera moved rather quickly toward Rina's home. Instead of her usual towering heels, she wore flat sandals, and she didn't care a bit that Brandt and Ash had to rush around people to keep up with her.

Men were so blind sometimes! She wasn't mad at them for having to leave the room when Kira was there. That was work; she knew her cover, and even though it galled her, she did what the job called for.

She wasn't jealous of Kira, either. She saw the way Ash reacted to his ex-wife, and he didn't look at the two of them the same at all.

She was sick of the ruse and sick of the situation, and then they had the nerve to try to forbid her from helping the one woman they'd dealt with who did deserve the help. Of course, that went right over Brandt's head, and she would have just told him that via the link, but then he'd gotten all snotty and high-handed, so he could just wait now.

As for Kira? Sera snorted. Kira was a sly bitch, but it didn't escape her notice how often she'd been around, and it sure as hells wasn't to visit with her brother. Sera did see some measure of affection between brother and sister, but what she saw on Kira's face was the same thing she saw on the faces of children. Kira didn't necessarily *want* Ash, but she didn't like it one bit when he didn't want her. What made it all the more irksome was that Sera couldn't simply tell the woman off and stake her territory.

The atmosphere had changed, even up there on the higher levels. More police milled around, and the normally carefree-looking Nondalese upper classes didn't look so comfortable. They'd been faced with something pretty unheard-of for them. The constant supervision by cameras had rendered their society one with very little violent or property crime. She supposed it was an exchange many people were willing to make.

Rina came to the door, her normally beautiful face drawn. "You heard?" she asked as she drew them all inside.

"I did; Kira came over to relay the news."

Rina's eyebrows shot up as she laughed. "Thank you for that, I needed to laugh." Ignoring the men, Rina led Sera into the living room and sat down.

Sera sat next to her, close, and put a small chip in Rina's hand. Without pausing, Rina took it and continued to speak about her shock.

"How is Delia?" Sera wondered what would happen to her after Giles's death.

"She's been turned out by Stander's wife. All the others have been as well, or so I hear. Delia is resourceful, she's already found protection from another as I'm sure her compatriots will. Giles may have been irresponsible on many levels, but one couldn't fault his taste in women."

Sera nodded. "We're going to be leaving. There's not much enjoyment in the lights when someone you know has been murdered. I suppose you heard about the break-in at our guesthouse?"

Rina nodded. "I did. Nothing was taken?"

"News travels fast here." Sera winked.

"Yes. We're all in each others' pockets. A result of being on camera every moment of the day. I trust you'll travel safely?" Rina stood and hugged her again. "I have a little something for you. Hold on a moment."

Rina left the room, and Sera didn't bother looking at Brandt and Ash. She felt their presence, knew they stood in the entry, waiting for her.

"Here, it's nothing fancy, but I think it would look lovely in your hair." Rina handed her a pretty box with a black lacquer hair comb inside. "I hope to see you again sometime."

"Me, as well. My ear is open should you need it." Sera worried for Rina, but there wasn't much she could do. Rina's care in how she spoke compared to the day before told her the authorities had ramped up their surveillance in the wake of Stander's murder.

"Thank you." Rina kissed her lips gently. "Have a care, all right?"

"You, too. Please be safe." Sera headed for the door and bypassed the men.

Out on the avenue, heading toward their cottage, Ash caught

her about the waist, and she slowed her pace, not wanting to make a scene.

He grunted his satisfaction. "That's better. Do you plan to be angry with me for the rest of the day?"

She sighed. He thought it was about Kira, too. "Since we haven't unpacked, we can get things sent back to the transport right away. We could even take them ourselves, but I suppose that's out of the question." She ignored him. She'd started to say something to him back at the guesthouse when Brandt had taken Kira back, but the story about the relay station being attacked came on, and they'd simply watched in shock.

This had to end, and if it involved Kira, so be it. Anyone who could so blithely cooperate in an attack like the one on the relay station didn't deserve to be protected.

"I've already had it sent back. We've received clearance and are ready to make the first slip." Brandt took her other side, slipping his arm around her that way. Did they think she'd just melt? Stunned into quiescence by their utter manliness? She snorted, not bothering to hide her annoyance.

"No monitors this time. Just the crew, so should you decide to be naked the whole trip back, all the better." Ash spoke with his lips against her ear.

"You wish." She hadn't snarled, but it was a close thing.

Ash took a deep breath and led her onto the lift with Brandt right behind them. She was extraordinarily angry, and he understood part of it. He didn't chalk it up to simple jealousy. She'd known exactly what Kira's intentions were even before he'd figured them out.

And she couldn't say a damned thing about it. She had to go into the other room to keep up the ruse of being a concubine. Just like she'd had to be set aside those years before. He realized that when she came from her room when Kira had left with Brandt. It hurt him deeply, knowing she felt that way again and that he was the cause, even in a corollary way.

It was different this time. He didn't sense her planning to run off, and he hoped it was due to her understanding he had no feelings for Kira at all.

And Kira, he wanted to kick Perry's ass for not getting a handle on his wife, but hells, Ash hadn't, and he was twice the man Perry was. Kira needed to be dealt with. As to whether or not she knew or was involved in Perry's business with Alder remained to be seen.

Clearly Perry was involved with this plot. Just how deeply, Ash didn't know. If he was working on some secret plan with the enemy, he wouldn't trust Perry to keep it quiet, but he was there, he was part of the conversations, and clearly Owen considered him part of their group. If his cousin had anything to do with that bombing at the relay station and the other attacks, he'd pay. Ash would make sure of it himself.

There were a lot of things he and Brandt had to make right.

Sera remained totally silent on the trip to the port. But her relief at leaving Nondal hung in the air. He couldn't blame her. He felt the same way.

They loaded into the transport after Nondalese authorities had shown up to apologize profusely about the break-in. This after they'd played dumb about the way the intruders had known where the cameras were.

Theirs wasn't the only transport readying to leave. Others had lined up to get out, and Ash knew the Nondalese would lose a lot of credits as fallout. He could only hope it hit the people behind the murder.

"I'm going to speak with the crew to get them started, and then we'll all talk." Ash sent a pointed look at Sera, who waved it away over her shoulder as she stalked down the corridor.

Brandt chuckled as he took a deep breath. "We're in trouble."

"Been there since I saw those eyes the first time." Ash headed out to deal with his crew.

Chapter 21

$\mathcal{B}$randt headed toward their quarters and found her hauling her things across the corridor to an empty room.

"What is it you think you're doing?" He blocked her way.

"Moving my things to an empty room."

He walked her back into their room, using his body and the look on his face. The transport made the first slide through the portal, and he felt the tug in his gut as it happened.

"I don't think so. I like waking up with you in my bed."

"And it's all about what *you* like, is it?"

Her face was flushed, her eyes narrowed and she looked ready to spring at him. Gods, she made him hard.

"Well, certainly I prefer it when it's about what I like." He kept his voice calm as he cornered her near the bed.

"I'm not having sex with you right now." She tipped her chin up.

"Not now maybe, but in about three minutes? Well, I'd not be laying any odds on that."

Her dress, like all the others she'd been wearing, simply fell to the floor when he yanked on it.

Her eyes widened, and she blew out a frustrated breath. "You can't just give me those eyes and lick your lips and expect me to jump on your cock."

Ah, Sela was fading, and Sera was surfacing. Fine, he preferred the real woman anyway. Unfortunately, that one was extremely vexed at that moment.

"It doesn't matter if Kira wants Ash, sweet. He wants you." Giving up on seduction for the moment, he moved around her body and lay across the bed. He patted the mattress, but she perched on the far edge instead.

"That's not the point. She doesn't even want Ash. Not really. She just doesn't want anyone else to have him, either. It's a female thing, Brandt, just take my word for it." She rolled her eyes at him, and he laughed.

"*I'm sorry I said you were being tedious. At the time I hadn't thought about the Kira and Ash thing. And I didn't take into account how much you must have hated it to have to go and hide from my sister.*"

"*Your sister is a vile, vile creature, Brandt. Once this is over, I won't be running to the other room when and if I see her. But it was my job to do just that.*"

He grinned. "Sweet, you've made my cock very hard with your attitude."

"*And for your information, I'm not mad because of Kira. I mean yes, she's an idiot, and it escapes me why anyone would be able to resist smacking her face a time or two just for fun. But now I can be angry that you've missed the entire point of why I'm mad and think I'm as shallow and insipid as your sister.*"

"*So tell me then. Why are you upset if it's not Kira? And I don't think, by the way, that you're shallow or insipid.*"

"You didn't think twice before scampering out to escort Kira back, but you actually tried to forbid me from helping the one person on Nondal who needed it most. And then, on top of that, you got all high-handed with me. For a moment there, Brandt Pela, you were the Ranked man, and I was the unranked concubine. That's what it felt like, and I don't like it one bit."

She watched his face as he got it. He sighed, very tired sounding.

She stood, and quickly, he lunged, bringing them both to the very thick rug, rolling so his body took the impact. "Oh, no you don't. I want you here. You gave yourself to me, remember? I do. I'm not giving you back." He kissed down her bare chest to her breasts, where her nipples stood hard and proud.

"I'm not a thing."

"No, you aren't. Nor did he say you were. We want you. You're beautiful and sexy and neither of us likes it when you're angry with us." Ash knelt beside them.

"Then neither of you should act like idiots."

"You're right. But, Freka, as you pointed out just the other day, we're just men." Ash whipped his shirt off and tossed it behind him. "Is this bed big enough for three?" He nodded to the bed next to where they lay.

"You want me, but you don't need me. I'm a complication neither of you needs."

Brandt looked her straight in her beautiful eyes and shook his head. They'd slipped and moved through the portal. They didn't have monitors on board, and damn it, he wanted to say what he meant. Out loud. "Fuck this whole thing. I do need you. More than I expected to, more than I planned to, more than I knew I could need anyone. You're not going to push me away because of how complicated things are. I may be heavy-handed, but damn it, I love you. I'm not going to allow it."

"You may change your mind if we find something out you didn't want to know." She held up the comb Rina had given her. With a flick of her wrist, it split open, and a data chip fell into her palm. He didn't miss the emotion in her voice.

Ash sighed and stood, helping her up.

"No matter what we find, it's not your fault." Ash grabbed her waist and pulled her against his body, and she moaned softly.

Brandt knelt behind her and nipped, hard, on one delicious cheek of her perfect ass. He ran his palms over the smooth skin of her legs, over the taut flesh of her belly, and she writhed between them.

"Don't get too involved back there," Ash said, looking around her body and down at him.

"I'm changing into clothes. Real clothes. And then I'll do a bit of reading."

"No more of this nonsense about changing rooms." Brandt frowned.

"My room is bigger; it might be a more comfortable fit for the three of us." Ash shrugged, and Sera threw her hands up.

"Fine. It's not like I have any say."

Brandt grinned and watched as she dug through the drawers until she located a pair of soft pants and a long-sleeved shirt. And for some reason, she looked even sexier in them than she had in the scant little things she'd been wearing on Nondal.

She turned and saw his perusal and snorted. The sweet smoothness of Sela had been replaced by the sharper bite of Sera. He preferred it. *"I like you much better this way. Sela was sexy and all, but Sera is vibrant, sharp, vivid, and far more sensual than I'd started to learn back in Borran. And Sera?"*

She cocked her head.

"I love you. A thousand times over until I cease to live, I love you."

He didn't fail to notice the quirk of her lips as she fought a smile or the way the stiffness of her spine softened.

"I'm sorry." He said it genuinely and out loud.

"I know." She rolled her eyes and sashayed from the room. "Oh, and I love you, too."

Smiling like the fool he was, he trailed after her into Ash's room just down the corridor.

*A*sh hadn't lied; it *was* a much larger room. Sera's eyes widened a bit as she took it in while heading straight for the computer and other electronic gadgetry in the far corner. First she loaded the data she'd mined that first night and hit a wall straight off. Encryption. She'd need to set a program up to try to get through whatever locks so they could access the information.

Once that was set up, she loaded the chip Rina had given her and ran it through a virus program before uploading the information it contained.

*S*era looked at the screen and frowned. It wasn't concrete proof, but it was a host of things Rina suspected Owen Alder had been up to on the Edge. She believed Perry was part of it and that Tifrit was also becoming involved. She felt quite strongly that Giles's murder was arranged by Owen because Giles had been talking too much and had outlived his usefulness. Rina wasn't sure just how involved Kira was but felt she had some level of knowledge of the situation.

Ash sat heavily behind her, and Brandt sighed and began to pace. She may not like Kira and Perry, but their possible involvement hurt the men she loved, and that hurt her. *She loved them.* She wanted to run and hide from it, but she couldn't. Instead, she tried to focus.

"This isn't good."

Brandt undid his hair and shook it out, sending sensual shivers through her despite the seriousness of the situation. It was so long and so dark; she knew the feel of the cool, dark silk as it glided over her skin. She swallowed hard and dug her nails into her palms to focus on the issue.

"*I may need to make a trip home to follow up,*" Brandt said.

"*Me, as well,*" Ash agreed.

"*Why don't you both head on, and I'll change transport in Pilus? That way you can keep going, and I can go back to Borran. The data I got the first night is encrypted. It's a very sophisticated program, actually. It may be a few days before I can get it translated. No use wasting time when you two can get on your way.*"

Ash looked at her, spun her chair to face him, pulled her up, and grabbed her hair. "We'll be together, Freka." He tipped her head, angling her mouth just where he wanted it, and stole a kiss. She'd expected a ferocious one, but instead, he delivered a touch so gentle and reverent, tears stung her eyes.

"*We'll all go back to Borran and then head out once we're there.*" Brandt moved behind them, pressing his cock into the flesh of her ass.

"Now that we've taken care of work, some play is in order, wouldn't you say?" Ash asked her with a wicked smile.

"Are you suggesting a vid?" She smiled. They were both ridiculously incorrigible.

She found herself slung over Ash's shoulder, and she growled, "I believe we've discussed how unamused I am by this position."

Ash laughed and tossed her to the bed, and she bounced.

"You're very saucy today."

Sera couldn't pry her gaze away from Ash's hands working the fastenings on his pants.

"Something here you find of interest?" He looked particularly feral in that moment; shirtless, bare skin on his skull gleaming, deep concentration on his face. All for her. It made her heart beat faster just to watch him look at her.

"I'm saucy every day, Ash. It's just that your diet has apparently been quite bland."

Brandt burst out laughing and quickly undressed, standing at the foot of the bed, naked, hair loose around his shoulders.

"So, um, you two," Sera licked her lips, "are you *together*? I mean, I know you're together." She couldn't believe she was blushing. "But I meant, like as a couple?"

Ash's smile turned wicked as he reached out, sliding his hands through Brandt's hair. "Does the idea please you?"

"Look, I'm all about the boy-touching, let's make that clear. As long as I'm involved, I can watch, and you come back to me, I'm on board."

"Like this?" Brandt turned and kissed Ash's jaw and down his neck. Ash hissed, arching into Brandt's touch as Brandt tugged on one of Ash's nipple rings.

Sera got rid of her shirt and pants before piling some pillows to lean against so she'd be better able to watch. "How long? How long have you been lovers?"

Ash encircled Brandt's cock in his fist and pumped slowly. "I wouldn't say we're lovers. Not the way we are with you. We've given each other pleasure; he's let me use the cat on his ass and back. I like to make him come. He likes to make me come. It works out."

Sera idly tweaked one of her nipples and spread her thighs wide. Both men homed in on her pussy, and she smiled. Yes, she was the submissive, but in submission there was power.

"Who tops?" The idea of the two of them together, all that male strength, all that dominance writhing and moaning together made her wet and achy. She'd never actually been in a threesome before, so the whole thing was new. But watching her two men together, the small glimpses they'd given her was beyond titillating. It was comforting, too, in some sense. At first she'd had a twinge of unease, of jealousy. But they clearly needed her, wanted her, desired her, and the jealousy had eased until all that remained was how sexy it was.

"We switch." Brandt lifted his lips from where they'd been on Ash's collarbone. "Finger your cunt for me."

A flush of heat rose from her toes as she slid her hand down her belly. She wasn't surprised to find herself already wet as she played her fingers over her clit. Still, she wasn't going to let go of the subject at hand. "Can I watch? You know, you two going at it. Or, well . . ." She paused as a wave of sensation echoed through her, her clit hardening against her fingertips. "Be in charge, too?"

Ash laughed and raised a brow in her direction. "I didn't say you could come. Hold off." He waited for her to slow her fingers down before going on. "We don't need to with you around, Freka. We can both top you. And I don't need Brandt that way, not with you in my bed."

She frowned dramatically, pulling her glistening fingers free and painting her nipples with them. "Well, I can't deny the appeal of that and all, but you know, it would make me so happy to see it. Like, say, one of you could top the other two." She sat up, looking hopeful.

"You're very mischievous." Brandt's eyes didn't leave her nipples.

"Yes, and saucy and disobedient and a whole list of things. We've established that. But surely you can't be all hot for each other and just, you know, turn it off."

Ash turned to Brandt. "Whose turn is it?"

"Mine, and it's not that we just turned it off. Ash is still sexually attractive to me. How can he not be? But you're the center of everything. I want you the moment my eyes open each day until they close at night. What turned me on the most with Ash was topping him. Dominating a man as dominant as me. He's got an able hand with the cat, yes, but you make me witless with desire in a way no one ever has." He turned to Ash. "On the bed with her."

Ash kicked his pants the rest of the way off and crawled to her. The look on his face made her wet. Wetter.

"It's you, Freka. You're it. We can be three. It works because I love Brandt, too, and it's no punishment to have him in our bed. But you make me whole. You make us whole. Do you know that?"

She pressed the back of her hand against her mouth. Why did he get to her the way he did? No one else, not even Brandt, could touch her that way, so intimately.

"My cock is awfully lonely over here. You two had better remedy that," Brandt ordered from his place at the foot of the bed.

Sera looked to Ash, who tackled her on the way, rolling her over and kissing her. She arched into his body, loving the way he felt: hard, male, in charge. His mouth sought her nipples, moaned as he tasted her.

She opened her eyes to see Brandt still there, just inches away, a smirk on his face and his cock in his hand. "You're taking your time about it. Both of you."

"He feels so good." She sighed as Ash bit her nipple and pinched the other one until she writhed.

"She tastes spicy and sticky. Like her pretty little cunt." Ash licked downward, but when the tip of his tongue touched her clit, Brandt put a stop to it.

"I gave you both an order."

Ash chuckled and got off the bed, holding his hand out to Sera. With a frown at him and then Brandt, she reached out but soon found herself being picked up, spun, and splayed facedown over Brandt's lap.

Three quick, sharp slaps to her ass, and she squirmed against the very hard cock poking her belly.

"Silly me, I've forgotten all my toys at home. However," he leaned down, still holding her in his lap, "as we know, everyday objects can be put to our use. And if anyone's ass needs a little correction, it's yours."

She smiled into the taut flesh of his calf, head upside down, hair hiding her satisfaction.

The cool edge of something, something flat and hard even as it was smooth, touched the heated skin of her ass. *What is that?* She tried to place it until he used it like a slapper and she sucked in a breath and then found the sense to breathe through it as he continued to use it on her thighs as well as that lovely place where ass met thigh and cunt.

The scent of her pussy painted the air as the flush in her skin built. With that, the presence of that hard cock on her belly grew, pressed, became insistent.

She slipped away, letting the sensations take her, envelop her in a fluffy bed of serotonin, into that dreamy place.

*B*randt tossed away the flip-top notebook he carried his data cards in. It'd served as a very fine slapper substitute, although he preferred something with a handle to save his wrist. He liked a better gauge on the strength of the slaps. He held back this time, not wanting to overdo it.

From the heavy weight of the woman spread over his lap, he need not have worried. She'd slipped into sub-space, her muscles pliant and loose, her fingers open against the rug at his feet.

"You're so amazing. So beautiful." He said it as he softly caressed her skin, feeling the warmth of it radiate from her.

Ash stood there, still bound by his orders, and Brandt sent him a wicked, unrepentant smile as he dipped his fingers into her from behind and she moaned, stirring a bit and pushing against his hand.

His gaze still locked with Ash's, Brandt took those fingers to his lips and tasted her, laughing at Ash's reaction.

"Ah, ah, ah. I'm topping, and you didn't submit very well, now, did you? As I can't tie you up and . . . oh but I can." He stood, Sera still warm and soft in his arms, and laid her on the bed. "Just a bit, sweet. I'll be right back."

He grinned as he rifled through the drawers and found what he needed.

Ash still stood, waiting for instructions.

"On the bed, and don't touch her. Really, why you don't have toys in your damned transport is beyond me. I'll have to make do." Brandt straddled Ash's body, and Sera's eyes cleared a bit to watch Brandt take each one of Ash's wrists and fasten it to a bedpost with one of Ash's own belts.

Fire raged in Ash's eyes as he realized what Brandt was going to do, yet he kept quiet but for a growl as Brandt dragged his cock over Ash's on his way down to secure each ankle.

"Very nice." She lazily fanned her face.

He grabbed a chair and set it at the foot of the bed and settled into it. "Can you see me, Ash?"

Ash lifted his head. "Yes, you bastard."

Brandt laughed. "Sweet, put a pillow under Ash's head so he can see us better."

Sera moved, languid and slow, obeying. She planted a kiss on Ash's forehead, and Brandt let the infraction slide.

"Come here."

She slid off the bed and walked to him, waiting for him to tell her what to do next.

"Face Ash, hands on the footboard."

She turned, showing off the long, feminine line of her back and the still-pinked cheeks of her luscious ass.

"Spread your thighs and fuck me. Make sure Ash can see my cock sliding deep into your pussy and coming back out all shiny with your juices."

"Fuck," Ash snarled, pulling against his bonds.

"Her cunt is on fire, Ash. Hot, wet, and so tight." Brandt watched, entranced as hunger took over Ash's face, before transferring his gaze to the sight of the deep red stalk of his cock, shiny with her lube, disappearing into her.

"At least let me make her come, Brandt. Let me suck on that sweet little clit until she comes all over me and your cock."

Brandt smiled at Ash's begging. This was better than cuffing Ash and making him suck his cock. Topping them both at once was a heady thing, but he got the feeling it would be very short-lived, given the gleam of fury in Ash's eyes. Sera, on the other hand, was juicy and soft, made for him. For this.

"How about this instead? You watch while she makes herself come? And maybe, if you're obedient, I'll let you lick me clean when she's done." Brandt couldn't resist teasing.

With an inarticulate growl, Ash flexed his biceps and yanked, pulling one wrist free while Brandt laughed and shook his head.

Ash undid the other wrist and moved to his ankles while Sera continued to slide up and down Brandt's cock.

"I knew you wouldn't last." Brandt laughed.

"You're a fucker."

"Yes. On your knees, mouth on her pussy. You can touch my balls; you know how I like it."

Sera whimpered and showered Brandt's cock with honey, the heat of it making him moan.

$\mathscr{A}$sh squeezed himself between the bed and where Brandt sat with Sera and inhaled the scent of sex. Of Sera mixed with Brandt. And he quickly moved up, sliding his tongue through the wet, swollen folds of Sera's pussy until he got to her clit.

Her squeal shot straight to his cock. When Brandt finished, Ash had every intention of sliding that sweet pussy down his own cock until he exploded within her.

"That's it, Freka, let me taste your pleasure." He didn't waste any time working on her clit to make her come. He wanted her climax, knew it would take Brandt with her, and then it would be his turn. No more of this switching stuff now that Sera was with them. He couldn't turn it off, his need of her, couldn't watch without wanting to touch her, too.

Her thighs trembled, and she ground herself down over Brandt's cock, pressing into Ash's face on each downthrust. Her breath had sped to pants, quick puffs of air filled with desperate moans and whimpers.

He pressed two fingers hard against the ridge of flesh just behind Brandt's balls and wanted to laugh at the resulting groan and tightening of his friend's sac.

"Ash, oh gods . . ." she murmured. "Brandt, harder, please."

Each man worked her, licking, sucking, fucking, until she cried out, body taut, and came so hard it was almost as if Ash felt it like it happened to him. It echoed through their mental link.

Brandt gave a strangled moan and held her tight down over his cock.

After several long moments, Ash surged up, pulling Sera with him, spinning her and depositing her on the bed facedown, spreading her thighs and entering her from behind.

"So fucking wet," he said through clenched teeth.

Her moan echoed through the walls of her cunt, and his eyes nearly rolled to the back of his head. Her butt and thighs still burned pink from Brandt's work, and it only made her more beautiful. His mark on her hip, he loved to see it, made him believe they were meant to be together, had always been meant to be.

Brandt got on the bed and turned her face to take her mouth. She clung to the kiss like a drowning woman as she arched her back, thrusting onto his cock.

"That's it, fuck me. Give yourself to me." Ash delivered a sharp slap to her ass, and she whimpered and writhed back against him.

The need to slam into her cunt brought Ash to the brink. The mindless seduction of her body, the way she made him feel—strong, hard, masculine—swirled around within him until he fucked into her body, teeth bared. He watched as Brandt devoured her mouth, alternating that with the sight of his cock disappearing into her.

A cocktail of pleasure so intense he was nearly blinded with it.

His fingers dug into the muscles of those high, firm ass cheeks, leaving white impressions there against the fading pink. He leaned down over her body, still pistoning his cock, and kissed up the line of her spine. Kissed until he met the tangle of her mouth and Brandt's. Their kiss became something more, of connection and desperation, of pleasure and contentment, heat and comfort, movement and sighs.

And just like that, he lost it and began to come, unexpected but in a rush that left him blind and numb on the soles of his feet. It seemed to go on and on as she took him in, the only person who ever made him feel safe and welcomed within the shelter of their body, and he knew he was home forever.

*S*era was wrung out. Tingly, sweaty, wet, sore, tired, invigorated, and completely overwhelmed.

Even so, after Ash came, he turned her gently, and his mouth found her again as Brandt's skimmed to her nipples. Both men gently drew her pleasure out, so sweet and sharp she came in a series of tremors that left her unable to do more than sigh.

She kept her eyes closed. Something had happened. The price of her love was too high; she couldn't pay it. But it was too late. Too late because she did love them both so much it changed her irreparably. If they had to marry wives of their class, she'd face the pain then.

She wouldn't think on it for the time being. She loved them both, achingly, deeply, and totally. The wondrous part was that she loved them both in completely different ways, and yet between them, they occupied the space inside her mind, inside her heart and soul.

"You're not a very good sub," she mumbled as she turned in Ash's arms. Brandt had come back to bed with a wet cloth and cleaned her up gently.

Brandt laughed and slid in behind her, fitting against her like he was meant to. "He isn't. Neither one of us really is. I'd love to punish him for breaking loose, but I guess we won't be topping anyone but you in the future."

Ash snorted. "I think not. It was fine as a mind fuck and some rough play before. But with this precious thing we have nestled here between us, there's no need to. Although I will get even with you for making me watch you fuck her so beautifully. Bastard."

"I'll have you know my parents were married when I was con-ceived."

They bickered effortlessly around her, and she smiled as she slipped into sleep.

Sera needed the workout, so she woke up and headed to the gym nestled in the aft section of the transport. It'd been some time since she'd been able to work openly, so she relished the long, slow warm-up.

Her hair was bound up in a tight braid, but she missed the free-dom of her shorter curls that never got in her face. Missed wearing pants with many pockets. Missed carrying a weapon. Hells, she missed being Sera Ayers. Who'd have thought? She'd trade in the life of a pampered plaything for her battle-hardened existence any day.

She fell into a rhythm as she moved through her martial arts workout, losing her mind and letting her body take over, letting her muscles do what they needed to. She lost herself in her work, as she had time and again, which had been the reason she'd come to love martial arts in the very beginning.

There was nothing but the reign of her muscles and the flow of her energy. It wasn't until much later she came back to herself and felt the burn of use, the soreness that came with hard work. It felt good.

When she came out of the shower, she saw Brandt working at the bag, boxing. His body gleamed with a fine sheen of sweat. Her gut clenched at his raw beauty.

She left him to his workout and headed to the electronics center on the transport, a place she hadn't been able to use on the trip to Nondal because of the representatives.

She sent a coded message to her brother. She had a feeling his connections could prove helpful as she tried to find answers. The encryption on that data was beyond her skills, so she knew he'd be a big help with that, too.

She needed to get back to Borran, to her own sources and her own life, so she could dig in the best way possible. At that point, there were no cameras on them, but the threat of being listened to still existed.

Ash wandered in and put a cup of kava at her elbow. "Have you eaten anything?"

She stood, stretching, before turning and straddling his lap, wrapping her arms around his neck. His surprised smile of pleasure warmed her, and she kissed his forehead.

"Hi, there. Thank you for the kava. I slept longer than normal, but that'll warm me and wake me up."

His skull felt solid against her palms as he skimmed his lips down her neck, and she held on, arching back to give him access.

"There are better ways to wake up." His clever hands had worked their way beneath her shirt, and his thumbs slid back and forth over her nipples.

"Mmmm. That may be, but my ass still hurts, and I'm barely able to walk this morning from the workout you two gave me last night."

He laughed softly. "You haven't eaten, or you would have said so." He stood, holding her around him with a hand cradling her butt. "Come on. You need to eat."

She rained kisses over his face as they walked down the corridor, and he grinned. *"I've missed you. Not a moment has passed in the last ten years when I haven't ached for you. To have you here wrapped around me, loving me freely, is such a gift, Sera. Thank you."*

"I love you," she said softly, knowing she shouldn't but wanting to free the words she'd held in her head.

He hugged her tight to himself as they entered the dining room. "I love you as well, Freka," he said against her hair.

"Here I thought I'd just get breakfast, and you walk in with something sweet to snack on."

Ash dropped her carefully, and she turned to kiss Brandt. "Good morning. You looked very fierce and handsome earlier when you were in the gym."

His hands on her were gentle but possessive, protective. She curled into him, and he kissed the top of her head.

"Enough of that. Apparently she's a bit sore from last night. Eat, Freka." Ash sounded gruff, but he wore a smile, and she got up to fill a plate.

*E*ach day for the rest of the trip they worked and played. Their bond grew stronger, and despite her streak of hard common sense, a tiny spark of hope grew that they might be able to salvage something to stay together, even as she knew in her brain their world was set up in such a way that Brandt would *have* to marry at some point. He couldn't stay single with a whatever she was in reality, not forever.

The ruse of their original cover began to wear off, but still they didn't speak quite openly of their mission. Over the link they discussed some of the issues they needed to look into.

Ash had received a coded file detailing the attack on the relay station. It had clearly been an inside job, as the bombs had been placed in the deepest, most secure part of the settlement. The explosives used were of the type traded along the outer Edge, precisely what a man like Alder helped put in place. It appeared some electronics were missing, but they couldn't say for certain just what, because the damage was so extensive.

Some chatter had been intercepted after the fact, and it had come from the quadrant of the 'Verse where Nondal was located.

Sera's sinking feeling got worse as they investigated. It was clear from the evidence Owen Alder was involved and a given Giles Stander was, too. They'd uncovered evidence of his visits to the Edge, visits with Alder, credits flowing into his accounts, and then attacks on their stations. Perry's involvement also became more and more clear, but the information path she'd been researching was still partially encrypted. It boiled down to the trips and the flow of credits.

She needed to push some sources about breaking into the Stander Family's personal communication system. She hadn't had the chance to pursue it before they'd left Borran, not through gray channels. She added it to her list of things to do when they returned.

$\mathscr{B}$randt stepped off the transport, Sera, regal and beautiful, on his arm, wearing a smirk. She should, he'd just fucked her like there was no tomorrow against the bulkhead no more than moments before they'd been given permission to leave.

Ash had come upon them just as they finished and snorted. "I can't leave you two alone."

"I can't leave her alone." Brandt grinned, and Sera had simply rolled her eyes.

They walked through the spaceport until they'd reached their private vehicle and took off. Once they'd cleared the gates, their cover slipped away, and all three of them stepped back into their roles nearly immediately. Their driver took them to a hangar where they'd changed clothes and taken a small helicopter back to their compound.

The freedom to let go of his cover and speak without concern for being overheard again warred against his worry. Brandt dreaded his sister was involved in something horrible and unforgivable, and he'd have to be the one to take her down. How could she not know her husband was doing all he was? She was with him on many of those trips he took to meet Stander and Alder. If she was guilty, she'd be executed. Traitors weren't tolerated, especially not in this time of heightened tension between the Federation and the Imperialists.

Could he do the work that led to the death of his sister? Even if she was a traitor? The thought had nagged him since Sera had told him of Kira's possible involvement.

But whenever he weakened, he remembered the footage of those destroyed stations. Of the people who'd lost lives, and all for nothing but profit. Then he knew he could do whatever he had to, to make things right. At that point, what was done, was done, so all Brandt could do was hope he was wrong, and Kira wasn't involved.

Once back inside their house, the three of them headed in different directions. He knew they needed to sit down and have a very long discussion about what would happen next with their relationship at some point. But first he had to attend to his trip home. He had to find Kira himself, if he could, to deal with her. Tossing himself in his office chair, he booted up his comm unit and sent a message to his Family's social secretary to set up travel arrangements. He'd be getting a personal call later from his parents, but it was best to get things started right then.

A smaller transport could get him home in less than one turn. Borran wasn't too far from Majar, his home 'Verse, just a few slips between Borran and Ravena. Kira had a home there with Perry. She'd mentioned heading back, so he'd try there first. If not, he'd have to meet up with Ash and try Sanctu, the Walker Family–controlled 'Verse.

After some speaking back and forth, he found himself scheduled to leave before nightfall. He'd wanted some more time with Sera, but it looked like it wouldn't be possible.

As he made to get up and look for her, his comm pinged, and a vid call from his father came in.

"Hello, Father." Brandt smiled. His father was the only person in his family who knew of his military status. It took the pressure off Brandt to know the man he respected most in the Known Universes didn't think him a layabout with more credits than sense and duty.

"Brandt, I hear from my assistant you'll be coming for a visit. Your mother is pleased; she's inviting half the city to a meal in your honor."

Brandt knew that meant eligible women as well. They were angry at him about the concubine thing. His father had known enough to realize what he shared with Sera was genuine. Not that he'd be pleased in either case. Sharing a woman, a woman from an unranked family most especially, was not something a Pela did. Not in the long term, anyway.

He needed to talk to them about Sera, to make it clear he was going to be with her and no one else. But he needed to deal with this business with Kira as well.

"Father, please tell her not to worry about female companionship. I can't stay long, I've got work to do. Will Kira be in attendance?"

His father paused and then spoke to someone else before turning back to the screen. "Her house manager says she and Perry should arrive within the next turn or so. Is there a problem?"

"I ran into them both in Nondal Major, and I need to follow up. I'll be seeing you soon then. Send my love to Mother."

His father's worried frown was the last thing he saw before he terminated the call. Brandt didn't want to involve his father in this mess. *He* didn't even want to be involved in it. Eventually, when it all came to light, everyone would be involved. There was no help for it.

He looked up at a tap on the door and saw Sera standing there, looking hesitant. Her hair was back to normal, and the elaborate makeup had been removed. And yet she was so beautiful his heart ached.

"Hey, come in." He motioned to her appearance. "I see you took care of that."

She perched on a chair across from him, and the closeness he'd felt on the trip back to Borran evaporated. A small smile touched her lips as she drew her fingers through her hair with uncharacteristic self-consciousness. "I know. You were used to high-glamour Sela. This has to be a bit of a shock."

Cocking his head, he sighed. "I love the way you look, long hair or short. The first time I clapped eyes on you, you had on combat gear and, if I recall, a dirt smudge across one cheek. You took my breath away then, you take it away now."

She smiled, her back straightening a bit. "Mmm-hmm. Listen, I've put out some feelers, and the data should start coming in shortly. Would you like to meet tomorrow so we can go over it?"

"I have to leave in just a bit to go home."

Her face fell, but just as quickly, she reassembled herself and nodded. "Oh, of course."

"I had to catch a quick transport, and it leaves tonight. I won't be gone too long, hopefully. I need to catch Kira before she has a chance to assemble a story. Or while her conscience might sting. Something. She has to know." He blew out a frustrated breath.

Placing her papers on the edge of his desk, she moved toward him, kneeling at his feet and laying her head in his lap. A deep tenderness, so sharp it caught his breath, rolled through him at her gesture. His fingers sought the softness of her hair, took comfort there.

Brandt wasn't sure what he had done, but he thanked the gods for her. He bent and kissed her head. "You mean so much to me," he said, lips still pressed to the cool, sweet-smelling softness.

"I know this is hard for you. I'm sorry. I wish I could help."

So kind, his love. "You *are* helping, and it's not your fault. Our job is to find who's been giving information to the Imperialists, and we may very well have done that. I'm the one who's sorry for having to leave so soon after we arrived. I'd been hoping we could have some time together, to talk and get things settled."

"You've drafted me into this team and taken away my old one," she said with humor. "Where else am I going to go? Go and do your job. I don't expect any less of you."

*A*sh came around the corner and saw the rich gold of Sera's hair, short once again, in Brandt's lap. The look on Brandt's face brought a smile to Ash's lips.

How many times had that simple act—Sera putting her head in Ash's lap or on his shoulder when he'd had a hard day—made the exhaustion or agitation fall away? The *what was* haunted him at times. Kira never offered such kindnesses, just a touch or a moment of quiet. Certainly never to him and most likely not to Perry, either.

Brandt looked up, noticing him in the doorway. "Hey, come in. I was just telling Sera I had to leave at nightfall. I'm hoping Kira will return to her home in Majar, so I'm going to try to get her while she may be feeling bad about what happened. She might be a way in, a weak link."

"Ah, yes. I was on my way in to relate similar news. I'm actually on my way out now. I've been called in to HQ to report, and then I thought I'd head home to speak with my uncle and father, see what they know."

Sera stood and dusted her knees off. "I'll be here working. Keep me updated."

Ash didn't like the way she'd physically pulled away from Brandt and saw her hesitance.

"I wanted to be here with you. We have a lot to talk about."

She nodded slowly. "That seems to be the general consensus. But there's work to be done, and people's lives are in the balance. Go. Both of you. We'll talk when you return."

Three steps, and she was close enough for him to draw her to his body. "We will, Sera, so get that look off your face. It's different now. You know that. Don't tell me you didn't feel it between us not only in Nondal but on the way back. I love you. I need you, and we *will* be together."

"We *are* together." Brandt spoke from behind her.

She didn't speak but looked up into Ash's face. Every part of her—he remembered thinking he'd memorized every part of her. He used to lie in bed at night after she'd gone and think about the curve of her cheek or the line of her jaw, but as he looked just then, he noticed parts of her he hadn't before. Like a new puzzle, a gift.

He laid kisses across the bridge of her nose and over her cheeks. She held on to his shoulders without speaking, only holding her face up to receive his affections.

"I wish I had the time to take you slow and deep."

Her cheeks plumped as she smiled against his kisses. "You were just inside me this morning. It isn't as if you'll die from an over-abundance of seed."

"No. I just want you. I need you. Now that you're with me again, I don't want to walk out that door. Even for just a few days." He dreaded it. The idea of not seeing her, even for such a short time, brought back a ghost of the misery he'd felt those days just before she'd found out about his engagement. He simply didn't want to be away from her now that she was at his side again.

"You put a chip in my skull; you can find me within twelve klicks. It's not like I can run." She gave him a lopsided grin.

He held her face gently between his palms, tipping it so he could see directly into her eyes. "Don't. Don't make light of it. Not for me, or you. Ten years without you. I never want that again."

Her bottom lip quivered just a moment before she firmed up and nodded. "Are you trying to make me weepy?" Her hands fisted and relaxed in the front of his shirt.

"I'm trying to make you understand. Things are different this time." A universe different, thank the gods.

Ceylon, their house manager, buzzed through the house comm system. "Your vehicle is here, Commander."

He kissed her lips softly, taking in her sweetness and that sharp edge of her, too.

"Be safe. Please." She tugged his earlobe. "And Ash? I know. I know it's different."

He relaxed, happy she'd admitted it. "You're everything." He kissed her again quickly. "I'll be in touch." He looked around her to Brandt. "Travel safe. Report anything you find."

When he left, she watched him from the front door, and he touched his fingers to his lips, still feeling hers there.

$\mathcal{S}$era had watched each of them leave. She stood in the doorway and tried not to hurt that they'd had to leave her behind. She understood it. It was part of the assignment, and they all had their own specialties and jobs.

But watching Brandt's face as he contemplated his sister's involvement in an executable offense tore her apart. Sera had been the one to uncover the first evidence of her involvement. How could he not blame her at least a little bit?

And Ash, when he got to HQ in Ravena, he'd be surrounded by ranked people. His own class. Would he remember the importance of his station then? She couldn't lie to herself anymore; he'd married

Kira because he'd had to. What did the future of his position hold
for them now?

If his cousin was involved, it would cause terrible upheaval in the
Walker Family. One thing she was pretty sure of, Perry Walker had
involvement with Owen Alder and whatever in hells Giles Stander
had been doing.

She needed someone who could get her in some back channels to
do some snooping in the Family networks. And she needed to think.
Or maybe not to think.

Shaking her head, she returned to her rooms and tossed herself
on the bed. Just as quickly she got up and moved to the comm unit
and pinged her brother. Not surprisingly, he was out, so she grabbed
her firearms and headed to the range. A little target practice was just
the thing to clear her mind while she worked through the puzzle of
the whole situation.

Some time later, after she'd showered the acrid scent of cordite
from her body, she'd headed back inside to see that Paul had mes-
saged her back.

"Ceylon!" she yelled as she headed downstairs in search of the
house manager.

"Subcommander Ayers, I apologize. You shouldn't have to come
and find me." He bowed.

"Don't be silly. I came to find you rather than summon you like
royalty. I need for you to make travel arrangements for me. To
Sanctu."

Chapter 23

"I've got the pretty blonde, thanks Georges."

Sera rolled her eyes as the assistant at the front gates backed away, and her brother came forward to grab her bag.

The trip to Sanctu had been relatively short. The Walker Family–controlled territory neighbored Borran. A little under a standard day, and her military transport had dropped her away from the main dock, and she'd been met by her contact, who'd driven her to Paul's place and left without a single question. She could really get used to that sort of power.

She'd grown up in Sanctu. It was where she'd met Ash. As a young woman she'd been enrolled in the language academy in the capital city of Mirum. He'd been—oh, gods—handsome and refined. Older, wiser, powerful. He'd worked in the same building as she had her first internship. She'd pretended to bump into him as often as she could, and he'd finally asked her name.

Within months they'd begun sharing a house. Their connection had been so fast, so deep, and she'd thought so enduring. Three years later, she'd walked away from Mirum and Ash Walker.

She shook it off, focusing on her brother instead. His spacious and yet totally off-the-grid compound was in the mountainous region to the south of Mirum. He paid his bribes to the Walker Family, and they pretty much left him alone.

"Welcome. It's been far too long since you've been here." He hugged her, kissing each cheek. "You look good, a bit sad. I expect you'll share what you want to and know I want to hear it. Come on up. Lina is here, and she's made a large meal for us. You know Mai and Dai will be crushed if they hear you're here and you don't go to see them."

Their parents lived in a small working-class suburb outside Mirum. She couldn't involve them in this mess nor could she even begin to explain Ash's presence in her life again. Not yet. She'd have to face them sometime, but she couldn't deal until she had the rest all tied up.

"I'm here on business. I can't involve them right now. I'll be back later, when it's just a social call. Right now, Paul, I need every connection I can make." She paused a moment. "Let's go inside and see Lina first."

Lina, her childhood friend and Paul's on-again-off-again lady love, met her at the door with a hug and a smile. "It's so good to see you. Come in! Paul, put her bag in the guest room and meet us in the kitchen. Be quick, or we'll eat all the good stuff."

All through the meal Sera itched to check her comm to see if Ash or Brandt had been in contact. They hadn't in the day before she'd been able to get out of Borran, and then she'd traveled for some time, too. She knew they'd be busy with family and in meetings. It was unreasonable for her to expect them to message her so quickly. Didn't mean she wasn't disappointed. Funny how she missed them so sharply. They'd only been a part of her life a short time and yet had become totally integral to it.

Despite her impatience, the meal had been truly fabulous, and the company relaxed her. Paul was an easygoing person. They'd always been close, even when he'd chosen a life she never would have. And Lina, well, her brother was a fool for not marrying her. They were together in some way, that much was clear, and Sera certainly had no place to question it, given her own circumstances. So she just rolled her eyes at him when Lina took her leave at the end of the night.

"Did you have something to say?" He grinned.

"Yes, show me your electronics. The good stuff, and don't waste my time with any denials. I need to break into a Family network, and I need to do it quietly and quickly."

He locked the house and took her down a stairway and into a room totally packed with machinery. "What do you need? I'm not leaving you alone in here. This stuff is my life, and you need me. You know you can trust me."

She snorted. "Of course I can trust you. I had no plans to ask you to leave. You can do this way faster than I can." She held out the chip with the encrypted data. "Oh, and this, too. Do you think you can unlock it?"

He just looked at her as he snatched the chip from her fingers. "Don't insult me. Anything else?"

She explained what she needed, and he moved via a chair with wheels from station to station, mumbling to himself. While he worked, Sera updated the information she had with supplemental material Ash had uploaded. He must have received it when he went to HQ.

The picture it painted, as she added her own intel, was one of a cold-blooded greed that made her skin crawl. Each new thing she pieced into the overall puzzle pointed more and more in Owen Alder's and then Perry Walker's direction.

Among the information Ash had sent there'd been a note, a quick one. But he'd said he missed her. It made her smile.

"Gods, what the hells is that?" Paul had moved behind her, and he saw the pictures on her monitor.

"That's what's left of a relay station. A relay station the Imperialists attacked. Everyone there was murdered, and vital information was stolen."

Her brother stilled. "A Family member did this?"

"I don't know for sure. I think so, yes. That's why I want you to get into Kira Pela-Walker's personal network and into Perry Walker's as well. Someone fed the Imperialists information about the location of this station."

"What have you gotten into?"

"Don't ask. It's better you don't know, and of course, you know to never breathe a word about it."

"We're going to crack into that network. This sort of thing can't be allowed to continue." He rolled back to his station and began to type quickly.

Brandt eased himself down from the high window. On soundless feet, he crouched and waited for any other sounds but his breathing.

Satisfied he was indeed alone in Kira and Perry's home, he stood and adjusted his night-vision glasses.

The security had been easy enough to outwit. Two guards on a timed sweep of the property. The internal security had been coded to the main Pela estate, so one quick adjustment back at his own home, and he'd been able to create a window in the system for himself to get in.

If his sister and brother-in-law weren't traitors, he'd have to speak to them about how woefully inadequate their home security was.

He'd been in the house a few times, enough to know where the home network was located, and he quickly made his way there. Where he found some real security. Interesting.

The panel on the door took some time for him to get past, and he was glad he'd brought his tools with him. One ear listened for external noise while he focused on the intricate task of hacking their electronic locks to get into the network room.

When he finally did get in, he discovered the room was empty of the central processing unit for the network as well as Kira's and Perry's personal comm units.

He blew out a frustrated sigh. It was one thing to take a personal unit—he did that while traveling all the time—but another entirely to remove the central unit. Totally unnecessary unless one had something of great value to protect. Or something to hide.

Leaving the room, he reset the door and did a sweep of the rest of the house, just in case they'd left any other comm units. But he quickly discovered all other comms had been removed as well.

He made a mental note to see if there was a way to look into the Family network to get into Kira and Perry's personal system. He'd tried but had run into walls. The Families had built major protections for themselves into the legal framework of the Federation. Their networks were protected by the law in all but the most extreme cases. It did seem as though this sort of situation would qualify, though. He'd need to run it by Ash when he spoke with him again.

He thought of Sera as he let himself out of the house, this time through the back door. He missed her and needed to get the hells back to her side as soon as he spoke with his father.

"*B*randt, you can't be serious."

Brandt looked at his father and scrubbed his palms down his thighs. "I am. I'm in love with her."

"She's a concubine! You can't be thinking straight." His father pushed up from his chair and began to pace.

Kira had been nowhere to be found, and Brandt needed to tell his family about his intentions with Sera before he left to get back to Borran.

"She's not. She's on my team. She was only posing as a concubine."

"Well, that's a small mercy, I suppose. Who is she then?"

"Her name is Sera Ayers. She's from Sanctu. And I'm old enough to know what love is. I'm thinking just fine."

"Bah, love." His father waved a hand and then paused, picking up on Brandt's not giving Familial affiliation for Sera. "Did you say she's *unranked*? She may as well be a concubine, Brandt, for all the good it does you."

"I'm not with her for status, Father."

"That's clear. She has none, and she'll give you none. She'll drag you down. She's nothing."

Brandt stood, a flush heating his face. He physically jerked back, fists clenched at his sides. For a few long moments he had to concentrate on his breathing to keep from saying something they'd both regret.

Brandt respected his father more than any other person he knew, and he couldn't recall ever actually standing up and feeling as if he wanted to strike out in anger at him.

It wasn't absolutely necessary that he have the permission of the head of the Family to marry, but he wanted it anyway. Not that it would stop him from saying what needed to be said. "Don't you dare ever speak that way about her. She is *everything*. I love her. She's strong, smart, self-made. You think Kira is self-made? You think these women Mother parades past me every three minutes are self-made? Have any of them ever earned anything on their own? I thought that was important to you."

Viktor Pela sighed and touched his son's shoulder. "This is a mistake. You have a duty to your Family."

"I'm doing my duty to my race right now. Every day. As does Sera. I'm not a first or second son. Marius will marry politically, you know that. Ivan has already. It isn't necessary for me to do it, too. Stop making excuses."

"Your mother will tear the walls down around us all." His father threw his hands up in the air.

"I imagine so. Which is why I'm telling you and not her. I would like your seal on the papers. And then I need your quiet on the situation until my mission has been completed."

"You want me to give you permission to marry an unranked woman, and then you want me to keep it a secret? You don't wish to have a joining here in Majar? On the grounds?"

"It's going to take all my charm to convince her to marry me to start with. I don't know that I can also work in a ceremony with eight hundred attendees. Right now, it needs to be quick and quiet, and then later, we may do a joining here."

His father took the papers and looked them over. Brandt breathed a sigh of relief when his father finally signed and stamped his seal on them.

"Why the hurry? Is she with child?"

"No. I want to extend my protection and status to her." He took the papers from his father's hands and tucked them in an inside pocket. "It's complicated, but, oh gods, do you remember the woman Ash was with when he married Kira? The one he loved and wanted to be with?"

His father shot to standing again. "You told me *after* I signed the papers? This Sera is *that* woman? I thought she left?"

"She did. Ash offered to make her his mistress, but she didn't want less than marriage, less than the total love and attention of her man. She left and rose in the ranks of the corps. To lieutenant."

His father's eyes softened as approval replaced his outrage. "An unranked female? And she's young. She must be an exceptional soldier."

Brandt hid his smile. "She is. And she's on my team. You may as well know she's with Ash, too. But only one of us can marry her, and I want it to be me. I want to protect her from any retribution that may come of what we reveal in this investigation. And I want to protect her from any censure for being involved with us both." He paused. "She's a good person. Honorable. Strong. Courageous. Everything a man would want in his mate."

"You have to tell your mother. Not right now, I understand your situation. But I'm not risking life and limb, hells, I don't even have all my limbs to risk! You have to do it when the time comes. Go, go with my blessing."

Brandt grinned, relieved. "Thank you."

"She sounds like the kind of person I'd enjoy. I'll look forward to meeting her."

"Thank you for that, too. You'll like her. But in the meantime, I'd like you to lock Perry and Kira out of the Family Network. Just say it's technical problems or something like that. I can't say more, so please don't ask. It's imperative for everyone."

"I have to know. Is Kira in trouble?"

"She could be. And if she is, she's done something horrible.

Something she can't take back. I hope my suspicions are wrong, but I can't know for sure yet, so in the meantime, lock it all down."

*A*sh stalked from his office at HQ and headed to his CO's. As he went, he dodged yet another woman who fluttered her lashes at him. The news that he'd been involved in a threesome had made him some sort of irresistible quantity to women. Not that he'd had a problem before. He smiled inwardly. But it was worse now, as if he emitted some special pheromone or something. Women were all over him.

He needed to get back to Borran, and he needed to straighten everything out. He'd made his intentions clear, but until they got it all out in the open and settled upon, he'd be uneasy. They hadn't been able to simply come out and be specific about the future when they'd had to rush off. They needed that.

Sera's communications with him had been short, but she'd told him she loved him and missed him. She was opening up, taking a huge risk, and he wanted to be sure she never regretted it. He needed her. Needed to be tied to her in some sense.

He had a few more things to do, and then he needed to get back. To see her again, to hold her in his arms and tell her he loved her, preferably with his cock buried inside her.

The female assistant who'd been giving him the eye finally spoke. "He'll see you now."

"Thank you." Ash didn't say anything else as he headed through the large doors to Comandante Ellis's office.

"Ash, good to see you." Wilhelm Ellis sat, all nearly seven feet of him, behind an enormous desk. The thick file of intel they'd gathered was before him on the blotter. "Sit, please."

Ash sat. And waited. Ellis was a man of few words, but they'd come when he was ready and not before.

"Her work so far had been exemplary. Subcommander Ayers is a credit to your team and the corps. Getting the info chip from the woman on Nondal was a fine stroke of luck."

Ash nodded. "Not luck, sir. The woman trusted Sera before she knew Sera had taken care to set up a way to get free from Nondal if she chose."

"Beautiful, too, eh?" Ellis's perceptive gaze landed on him, daring him to argue.

"Why do you say so, sir?"

Ellis laughed, startling Ash a moment. "Why do I get the feeling your cover has bled into your reality? This Sera is the woman you had to leave aside when you married, isn't she?"

"Yes." How Ellis had known wasn't something Ash questioned. A man didn't sit in Ellis's chair without a great deal of insight and knowledge.

"Don't play coy with me, Walker. If this situation is going to be complicated by anything, I should know. I should have known from the start. Her previous commander, Yager, sent me a very terse note about you. This woman is an asset we should use here if you're going to muck it up there."

Ash leaned forward and barely leashed his snarl. "I think not, Comandante. She is mine. In all ways."

Ellis's eyes met his for long moments. "Ah, it's that way. All right. Keep it all in line then. How is your Family going to handle this? I assume Ayers isn't any more inclined to stand aside for a political marriage now than she was then."

"She'll never have to step aside for another woman again. We're together, end of story. As for the nature of our covert operations, they'll have to change after we break this open; you know that. But with the advances in implants and the ability to change appearances, we can simply take on new identities instead of using the ones we have now." Ash realized at least he'd be free of their cover now. Thank gods.

"You've been thinking about it. Good. Yes, I was just speaking to Councilor Holmes about this whole mess, and he suggested the same thing. You'll be held up for what you've done. Honored. There's no way to hide your involvement, not really, and it's good publicity for the citizens to see Family members out there doing their part. It'll help counteract the fact that Family members have collaborated with the enemy to murder their own."

Ellis sat back and blew an exhausted-sounding breath.

"I'll get back to Borran then, sir. Paracommander Pela has gone to Majar to attempt to gather information, but his sister hasn't returned. He did some reconnaissance in their home, but the electronics had been removed for travel, so he found nothing."

"All of them?"

Ash nodded.

"Well now. That's unusual. I mean to say, *I* remove my central unit when I vacate my home, but these two aren't dealing in the kind of information I am. Or, I suppose, perhaps they are." Ellis's brow wrinkled with thought.

"Yes, sir. Brandt and I both find it highly irregular, and I must say it's another indicator they're hiding something. We'll be looking into other ways to access the information. I'll get you the results when we garner them."

Ellis nodded. "Fine. I won't ask where this information comes from. Or where this was gathered." Ellis indicated some data Sera had sent along.

"That's how I operate as well." Ash didn't ask. It was better that way.

"You have full clearance for this case, Walker. Use whatever channels you need to. It's all been approved. Keep me apprised, and

use my direct comm when you contact me. I don't know how far up
this goes or who else may be involved. Makes me sick." He leveled
sharp green eyes on Ash. "Catch these people, Walker. I'm sorry if
they're your Family. But they must be eradicated."

Ash stood and bowed slightly. "I have every intention of doing
just that, sir."

On his way out, he tried to remember why he'd once thought
he'd have liked to relocate to Ravena permanently. The spires of the
government buildings rose up into the clouds. Majestic. Ravena was
old-world glory. The capital city went on for as far as the eye could
see in all directions. It was the heart of the Known Universes, the
seat of Federation governance.

His palatial apartments lay within walking distance of his office.
The place, which he'd often craved staying in when he was away, felt
empty without her. Sera had filled him up again and in doing so had
only highlighted how lost he'd been before.

He'd bring Sera here. This place would be theirs. He'd have to open
himself up to Brandt's presence not just as a friend and teammate but
as a member of his relationship with Sera. A balance had been achieved
between the three of them. His need for Sera rode his senses, filled his
head with thoughts of her. Brandt had his own feelings for Sera. Something different than what Ash had and felt. That's why it worked.
That's why it would work. There was no threat. Neither man wanted
her more or less, loved her more; they simply loved her differently. And
he knew without a doubt she felt the same for him, for Brandt.

Certainly there was the added spice of the sexual attraction he
and Brandt held for one another as well as what they felt for Sera.
There were no sharp edges in their threesome that way.

He grabbed his bag and headed for the door and the dock without even a backward glance.

Chapter 24

*B*randt stalked into the house and knew immediately she wasn't there.

Growling with annoyance, he headed to her quarters and found she'd taken some clothes and her personal comm unit but most everything else remained. His agitation eased a bit. At least it appeared she hadn't made a run for it. He opened their link but got nothing. She wasn't in the immediate area. He'd been traveling and hadn't rested so he could get back to her quickly. He dragged his ass into a shower and felt a lot better once he'd finished.

She'd been working on the case. He saw the information she'd gathered and had forwarded to him and Ash. Where in hells was she?

He headed down to find Ceylon to see if the other man knew anything.

*A*sh regretted his choice to take the first transport he could. Unfortunately, he'd been forced to mingle with people he did his best to avoid in his everyday life. He didn't have an individual berth. The ship was a quick-slip and more like ultrafast mass transit.

"Fancy seeing you here, Ash." Byn fluttered her lashes.

He wanted to groan when he realized Byn and Allen Thorndyke had just taken a seat across from him. "Not really so unusual. We travel back and forth between 'Verses all the time."

"I hear you've taken up with a concubine."

He sighed, ignoring them. The Thorndyke Family was part of Walker Family provenance. He'd pretty much always hated Allen Thorndyke, and his wife was as big a fool as he was in addition to being one of Ash's far-flung cousins.

"Come on, Ash, don't pout. I'm certain we could find you another wife. There are many women who are appropriate for a Walker of such high rank. Your mother has been the talk of society ever since your ex-wife began to tell everyone about this new pet of yours. Really, don't you think it's time to start being more responsible?" Byn smirked.

Rage flushed his skin. "*You're* telling me to be responsible? Two more useless people other than Kira I can't fathom. Don't worry about who I'm with; it's none of your concern. The funds flow, contracts are fulfilled. Family business gets done, and it enables you two to be completely useless while the rest of us work. My ex-wife has been remarried for seven years, so forgive me if I find her timing and ire on the issue of who I'm putting my cock into and how to be none of her fucking business. It's none of yours, either."

"You're a public face of the Family, Ash. You don't do us any favors with this attitude," Allen said.

"Did you just sniff at me like what you said carries any weight? Take yourselves away from me immediately. Let's pretend we don't know each other." Ash looked back to the book he held, but the words on the page swam.

This is what she had to look forward to. This sort of treatment would drive her away if he didn't make his intentions official. Thing was, as the second oldest son, his right to marry was governed by his Family, namely his father. There was no way Ash could get permission to marry an unranked woman. Not ever.

Brandt looked up when he heard the front doors open. The heaviness of the tread indicated it was Ash.

"She's not here," Brandt said as he came out to the landing at the top of the stairs.

"Do not tell me she ran. I will hunt her ass down."

Brandt laughed, startled at the vehemence in Ash's tone. "No. She's in Sanctu. With a man."

"What! There's got to be an explanation. She wouldn't do that. She's been updating us with information regularly. She's working, not playing."

"I believe it's her brother. At first I wasn't sure, I admit. She'd gone, and it worried me. But her clothes are still here for the most part, and yes, she's been sending information. Ceylon gave me an update on her travel plans, and after I thought it through, I figured her brother might be a good source for gray market information." Brandt wasn't proud of jumping to conclusions, but he was glad it hadn't lasted long.

"She told me she'd found a source for some off-books information. I should have assumed it was her brother. We need to go to Sanctu anyway. I have to deal with my family. But before we go, you and I have to talk. We've got to figure out what to do with Sera." Ash tossed his bag to the side and headed into the common room where Brandt followed.

"We have to give her status. You can't imagine how many times Ranked people brought it up to me." Ash threw himself into a chair.

"Actually, I can. It's not just your Family, but mine. Everywhere I went back home people commented. I don't want her exposed to that. It'll make her feel bad, compound those insecurities she's already got about rank and position. We have to protect her and, yes, give her status." Brandt paused. "My father signed marital papers."

Ash shot up and got in his face. "Convenient isn't it? So you marry her, and then what? What about me, Brandt?"

Brandt ran a palm over Ash's skull gently. He softened his voice and looked Ash straight in the eye. "It's not convenient, Ash. In a perfect world I would have Sera all to myself. She'd be mine, and I'd shower her with everything she's never had. I'd make sure everyone in the Known Universes understood how much I adore her. But it's not a perfect world. I can't have her all to myself, and you can't marry her. But I can. It won't mean you aren't part of what we're building. What it means is she'll have the protection of my status and my name. The three of us can be together." Brandt brushed his lips across Ash's.

Ash's chest heaved as his face hovered just inches from Brandt's. "We can't force her to choose, and I'm not giving her up. I've been so damned empty without her."

"Did you not hear a word I just said? I know. I accept that. Do you think I'm complaining that I have both of you in my bed? This way, I don't have to close off how I feel about you, either. As long as she *and you* understand she's my primary concern and my wife in every way, I don't see that we can't all be together and make this work."

Ash sighed and moved back to his chair. "I can't believe this rank business is going to keep me from her again."

"You're being stupid. It's not keeping you from her. So you can't marry her. Make her your mistress. You don't need permission for that. It has the added bonus of letting everyone know she's yours, too. If and when children come, they'll be yours as well as mine."

"You've given this a lot of thought," Ash said, his voice losing some of its anger.

"And you haven't? What were you planning? To sever yourself from House Walker to marry her? And for what? You'd lose your rank as well as your family, and she'd hate that you gave it all up. She'd feel responsible, and in the end, it would eat her alive. She understands your marrying Kira a lot more than she did ten years ago. She's intelligent, and she gets the big picture. She wouldn't want you to make that choice. She loves you, Ash."

Ash paused while he thought. "All right. I'll have Ceylon get the papers filed and ready when we arrive in Sanctu. I take it you have the marriage agreement with you? We can have the marriage performed there. I want it done before we see my family." Ash pursed his lips. "Should we tell her we're coming?"

Brandt grinned. "No. Let's surprise her. I think we're going to have to keep her off balance until she agrees to the marriage. You propose the mistress designation at the same time, so she knows we both want her to be given our status. I don't want her to panic at having to choose."

"Let's go."

Sera's eyes hurt from staring at data streams for so long. Her back ached, and her stomach growled. They'd uncovered so much information she hadn't wanted to look away for very long lest she miss anything.

She was close to finding all the pieces, and she wanted the whole situation over and done. Wanted the culprits caught and taken into custody. Wanted to live her life without this business hanging over her any longer.

"I told you to eat. Stubborn." Paul pulled her from the chair and up the stairs.

He pushed her toward the table and began to place food on it between them.

"Now you can tell me what the hells is going on in your private life. I can see you're dealing with Ash Walker. He's alive, I presume, and you're not hiding from a murder charge?"

"Oh Paul, it's so complicated I don't know where to begin." She was horrified at the tears in her voice.

"Stop being ashamed of having emotions, Sera. Has he harmed you again? Because if he has, *I'll* be dealing with a murder charge." He shoved a plate at her and began to eat as well.

"He hasn't. I-I understand why he did what he did ten years ago. I'm not making excuses, so don't give me that look. But it wasn't as simple as I've made it out to be in my head, you know? They're not married anymore, by the way. And so he comes back into my life, and I'm doing all I can to resist him, and then I fall right smack in love with Brandt Pela, Kira Pela-Walker's brother. Yes, I know. So he and I are in this situation I can't go into just now, and then suddenly Ash is involved, and it's the three of us." She put her head down on the table, blushing. "I'm in love with both of them."

Paul laughed. "Who'd have thought you were so wild."

If he only knew! "Anyway, gods know the situation is nearly impossible. I'm unranked, and they're both sons of very important Houses. I can't have either one of them, much less both. Not permanently. Can I?" She groaned again. "I have to work with them. What am I going to do if they have to marry? How can I live with that?"

"What makes you think you can't have either one of them? Or

both? Sera, it's not as if triads don't occur; they do. Do you think they love you?"

She nodded. "Yes. I truly do. They're good to me, they've both said they love me, and I believe it."

"Then why would you assume they'll have to marry else-where?"

She sighed. "The Walkers have the marital rule. Ash can't marry without permission, and there's no way they'll let him marry me. You know that."

Paul sighed and shrugged. "Yeah. But that doesn't mean he'll marry anyone else. You're a wonderful person. How can you not see it?"

"I don't know, Paul. Why can't *you* see how wonderful you are, and just be with Lina already?"

"This isn't about me." His mouth flattened, and she laughed.

"You've made that face since you were two. Did you know that?"

"Shut up. But come on, since we've known each other since I was born and all, let's be totally honest. You know they love you. You love them. What's the real issue here? Why are you really so afraid?"

She caught her breath. "Curse you for being so astute." She tossed a piece of fruit at his head. "Partly it's that I've just uncovered evidence that will tear the Walker Family apart, and I'm still unsure as to how involved Kira is."

"Dangerous to know, I'd wager. And you know I do love to wager. How will Ash react to the information? And if Kira is involved, what will her brother do?" Paul asked.

"I don't know. I want to hope they won't blame me. But I'm the one who discovered the information to begin with. I just don't know. And as much as I don't want to admit it, I'm leaning more toward Kira Pela-Walker not being an active participant. Oh, she knows something illegal is going on, and I do think she's involved. She had to have known. But at the level Perry is? I don't think so. I have some more data to look over, but I've been looking at monitors for the better part of the last two days, and I think after I eat, I'm going to bed."

Paul went to her and hugged her, kissing her cheek. "You're ducking the rest of it."

"I know. I'm working it through. There's all sorts of stuff. I'm a mess, you know. But I will work it through, and I know I can talk to you."

He chuckled. "It's going to be fine, no matter what. You're strong. You will get through, and the people who truly love you will be here when the dust settles."

She agreed, but she was tired of recovering and being strong. She wanted things to be fine. Normal. Happy. She wanted a life with her men. Both of them. Without fear and without regret.

Chapter 25

"Sera, I think you should come up here," Paul yelled from upstairs.

She stood, stretching. She had what she needed, anyway. Now it was just a matter of arranging to get the information to Ash and Brandt.

"You bellowed?" she said, yawning as she reached the top of the stairs.

But instead of Paul, it was Ash and Brandt who stood there.

A horrible bout of shyness hit her. Uncertainty.

"You know, a note informing us of your whereabouts wouldn't be such a problem to write, would it?" Ash took a few steps and suddenly pulled her to him.

His scent, familiar, comforting, sensual, wrapped around her senses as she held on tight.

"I didn't run off. Ceylon knew where I was. I've been sending you updates." She spoke against the wall of his chest, not wanting him to let go.

"Um, I need to go and see Lina about something. I'll be away for a while." Paul looked between them. "A long while."

"Paul, this is Ash Walker and Brandt Pela. This is my younger brother, Paul." She took a step back as Paul looked Ash up and down with narrowed eyes as they shook hands.

"Paul, we realize how much you've assisted Sera in this investigation, and truly, we're indebted to you." Brandt held his hand out to shake Paul's.

"I'd do anything to help Sera. She's very special."

He was so very protective she wanted to burst out laughing and hug him at the same time.

"I understand, and I agree." Ash said it first, and Brandt nodded.

"All right then. Don't touch the settings on my electronics." He turned and squeezed Sera's hand. "I'll be back, well . . ." He looked at the three of them again and sighed. "Tomorrow."

Once they were alone, Brandt went to her and embraced her, holding her to his body, feeling the steady beat of her heart against his own when they stood chest to chest.

"I've missed you. More than I'd thought, and I thought it was pretty bad." He captured her lips quickly, relieved when she immediately opened to him, receiving his tongue eagerly.

Her hand slid into the waist of his pants and found his cock. He moaned into her mouth, and she swallowed the sound, pressing against him.

"Gods, before I fuck you right here . . ." He lost his train of thought as she brought her thumb over the slick eye of his cock, smearing, delivering nearly painful sensation to him.

"I haven't come in four days, no wait, five. I need it. I need you two." She spoke as she delivered kisses to his neck while pumping her fist around his cock slowly.

"Oh, you'll get it. Lots of it." Ash picked her up and pulled her back. Brandt's knees nearly buckled when Ash licked her thumb, biting it gently. "But we need to talk first."

"I don't want to talk. There's time for talking, and that's after we have lots of sex."

Brandt laughed at the sight of her pretty pout. "Are you trying Sela on now? Like a costume? I like that, I think. But let's all get settled and have a drink while we *talk*."

"Talk? Is this the *it was nice while it lasted, but we should just be friends* talk?" She stopped, her arms crossed, looking partly defiant and partly scared.

Brandt went to her, caressing her cheek. "You're not very smart sometimes. Try listening to your heart. Does it tell you I'm going to break things off? If I didn't know how frightened you were, I'd be offended you had such little faith in me."

"In us. Now, get that sweet ass in the other room. We need to talk, and *then* we will fuck." Ash hefted a bag. "This is full of toys, Freka."

Brandt barely withheld a moan of pleasure at the fine tremor vibrating from her.

She nodded and led them up a stairwell and into a large set of rooms. "I'm staying here. Paul keeps a place for me, when I need to get away and unwind."

Brandt watched her wince as she reached to grab a tray with their drinks on it. "Are you all right?"

"I've been hunched over reading data, breaking all sorts of laws looking for information."

"Well, let me take the tray; you sit."

Ash widened his legs, tossing a pillow on the floor at his feet. "Sit there, and I'll massage your back and neck."

"You're both being very nice to me." She sat, and Brandt snorted, handing her a drink.

"Then I won't feel so bad when I flog you for distrusting the fact that Ash and I want to take care of you." He sat across from her on the floor. The lines on her forehead smoothed when Ash began to knead her neck muscles.

"Mmm. I'm supposed to complain about that? And that wasn't distrust, it was a compliment."

Brandt scooted forward to touch her. "Oh. Well, thank you. First, let's just get this all laid out, shall we? I love you. Ash loves you. We both want to be with you. In a relationship. Permanent and exclusive. How do you feel about that?"

She twisted her fingers together in her lap for long moments before speaking. "I'm all right." She shook her head and chewed her lip. "No. I'm afraid. Because I love you both, and I don't know if I can choose. The last time I loved a man, my heart broke, and my life was nothing but work for so long. I'm afraid you'll go against your family for me and not marry and lose everything. I'm afraid you'll force me to choose, and one of the three will resent the other two. I worry if I had to choose, I'd yearn for the one I didn't pick. I'm afraid you'll choose each other and not me. I'm afraid you'll both ask me to be a mistress while you marry a woman of your rank, and I won't have the strength to say no this time. I'm afraid I'm not good enough for you. I'm afraid you're both going to be exposed to censure for being with me. I'm afraid you don't really love me, but this is exciting and fascinating, and once it wears off, you'll be bored. I worry I'll have to keep up the Sela ruse because how can we be together and say who I am without exposing what we've been up to?" She took a deep breath. "Yeah, I think that covers it."

"Thank you for being so honest. I'm—I'm touched you trust us enough to share yourself so intimately." Brandt took her hands, kissing the fingers she'd been wringing as she'd spoken.

"We worry about some of those things, too, you know." Ash moved down to the floor with them, still rubbing her shoulders. "*Some* of those things. Not that you're not good enough, because that's so far from the truth it's laughable. But we worry about people using this to hurt you or one of us, too. I worry you'll feel more deeply for Brandt than for me. I love you so much. I'd forgotten what it felt like to be with you like this, and now that I have it again, I don't think I can survive losing it."

"We can do this," Brandt said. "We can make a triad work. It will take energy to be totally open and make sure everyone feels like they're getting enough attention and love. But I'm not going to force you to choose, and while I love Ash, I'm not choosing him over you. I choose you, Sera. Always. But I'm not sorry I can choose you both, because you choose him as well as me."

"Agreed," Ash said. "You're it for me, Sera. Forever. The three of us can do this."

She swallowed hard and blinked quickly.

"So." Brandt reached into his pocket and pulled out the sheaf of marital papers. "Will you marry me?"

"Only one of us can marry you, Sera, or I'd ask, too," Ash said quickly. "And there's the matter of my being a second son and needing Familial permission. But I want to give you the protection of my status, also, to make a statement, a public statement, about who you are to me. What this relationship is. So I've filed papers to declare you my mistress." Ash pressed his finger to her lips. "No, it's not like last time. I swear to you on my life. There will *never* be a wife for me again. You will marry Brandt and be my mistress and the three of us will be together. You'll be my wife in every way that matters. I wish it could be different." He shrugged, looking pained. "But it can't. The important thing is we're together, and we can make this work."

Brandt nodded. "Please say yes. I want you to be at my side forever. I want to walk out with you on any avenue in any 'Verse and have people know not only that we're together but that I honor you, and Ash does as well."

"People will talk. They'll say, gods, they'll say all the stuff they said about me when Ash married Kira."

Brandt heaved a sigh. "They will. I'm sorry about that. But they'll say worse if we don't do this. And I don't want anyone thinking you aren't worth marriage. That you aren't worth status. Because you are. People will understand why Ash can't marry you."

"And I'll tell them. Please say yes," Ash added.

"I don't want to be the biggest mistake you ever made."

Her voice was so small, so threaded with emotion, that Brandt's own tears threatened. There it really was; he could tell from the way her body bent, the sound of her voice, this was what had bothered her most and kept her so wary.

"My beautiful Sera. You're the best thing that ever happened to me. You make me whole. Look into my eyes and see the truth of what I feel for you. That's not going to change. You said you gave yourself to me. To Ash. Well, it's time to take that final step."

Ash knew what had to happen. She was scared, frozen, and worried any choice she made would be the wrong one. He finally truly understood why. She hadn't the luxury they had to make mistakes. He'd always thought of himself as a victim of circumstances, too, when it came to marrying Kira and in a sense, he was.

But it was Sera who'd paid the price. Yes, he'd lost the love of his life, but he'd gone on, gotten married, and there had been some good times with Kira during the time they were together.

Moreover, he'd enjoyed the luxury of what came with his rank. He had homes in several cities all through the Known Universes. He traveled, he continued to rise within the ranks of the military corps. His place in the world had been secure. While the choices he made did affect people, mistakes she made would be far more harmful to her own situation than he'd given thought to before.

And here she was, worried for *them*. Worried they'd regret choosing her. Gods, he loved her so much for being so giving, so loving.

Which was, of course, why he and Brandt needed to protect her and make her officially theirs.

Chapter 26

"Sera, stand and remove your clothes."

Her eyes widened a moment, but she took the change in activity well and unfolded herself gracefully. Her beautiful hands moved to the hem of her shirt.

Brandt understood what Ash was up to and moved back, standing and watching her as she pulled her shirt up and over her head.

"I love your body. I love the curve of your breasts, the line of your belly." Ash knelt before her and pressed kisses to each hip, taking a sharp nip at her belly button.

Her fingers traced his tattoos, sending currents of sensation through him.

"I love that," she murmured, arching into his lips.

"What? You can take your pants off while you answer." Ash leaned back, watching as she shimmied out of her pants. He nodded when she raised a brow and indicated her panties.

"Your head. I love how smooth it is. How soft, with the smallest bit of a rasp when I touch my fingertips to it." She shivered, and he did, too.

"Undress me." He stood as she slowly unbuttoned the front of his shirt.

"May I touch you?"

"Gods yes."

Brandt exhaled sharply, and Ash laughed.

"Come here, Brandt. Sera, undress him as well."

Her eyes went to Brandt. "And may I touch you? Take your hair down?"

"Does that please you?" Brandt asked.

She dragged the edge of her teeth over Ash's nipples, tugging on the rings before moving her attention back to Brandt.

"What? Touching you? Seeing your hair down?"

"Both. Either."

She walked around him as Ash watched, watched her own her submission and then wield it. She knew they saw her, knew they adored her, and she gloried in it.

*P*ressing herself against Brandt's back a moment, she hummed low. "Yes to both." She breathed him in, his unique scent that tightened things low, made her wet.

She took her time undoing the bottom of his braid, running her fingers through it over and over to free it bit by bit. It fell over her hands in all its dark glory.

What a contrast they made standing side by side. So breathtakingly hard and male. One all angles and muscle, the other taller, more beautiful, and from what she'd seen, he wore his savage nature on the inside more than Ash did.

Reaching around his body, she buried her face in his hair as she skimmed her hands up his belly, taking his shirt with them until she had to step back to bare his upper body.

The muscles on his back rippled as his arms raised and then fell again, and a soft, "Oh," whooshed from her.

A step to the side, and she reached around Ash to grab the open halves of his shirt and pull it down and off. Her nails made a lovely trail of light pink when she scratched down his shoulders and spine.

He arched with a groan, and she couldn't resist smiling at Brandt, who watched her with a greedy gleam in his eye.

"You're playing with fire, you know that, right?" Brandt's lips pursed in a smile.

She laughed and kissed his biceps before sidestepping in between the two men to face them again. "I certainly hope so. If I recall, someone mentioned a flogger." How long had it been? Since Ash. So very long. Her body fought the memory, wanted to fall into that place of heat and sharp pleasure/pain.

Now the fun part: pants. She knew both men wanted her, really wanted her, given the way their cocks pressed against the plackets of their pants.

Catching her bottom lip between her teeth, she considered her options while displaying herself in a way she knew appealed to them both.

In truth, she was caught off guard in a big way by their proposal. It filled her with hope, elation, and a fear so deep she choked on it. Everything she wanted was right there at her fingertips. She could take it and know they offered it truly. But the worry that they were throwing away their futures for her remained.

Bending her head, she licked across Ash's flat, hard belly as she undid his pants. She dropped to her knees, and he put a hand on her shoulder as she removed his shoes, socks and pants.

Breathing in the heady musk of his sex, she drew her cheek over his cock, luxuriating in how soft the skin was. Bending, she started at his ankles, kissing her way up his calves, over his knees and thighs. She nuzzled his sac, and he widened his stance to allow her more access.

Slowly, patiently, she licked long lines from his sac to the crown of his cock and back again until he caught her hair, stopping her.

"Enough. For now."

Keeping her head down, she smiled and inched over to Brandt. She put her arms around his waist and hugged, loving the way he felt against her. His hair was so long it tickled her hands and wrists at his back.

His cock practically leapt into her hands when she pulled the rest of his clothing off, and she couldn't resist giving it a few dozen kisses and licks.

"Take it all, Sera. I want you to take every bit of my cock." Brandt's voice was low, nearly hoarse.

She closed her eyes and centered herself, letting go of everything but pleasing him, of everything but his cock and her mouth. Bracing one hand on his thigh, she angled him with the other hand and began a slow in and out, taking a little more each time. She set a hypnotic rhythm, keeping him wet, keeping her throat relaxed.

His hands pet her shoulders, caressing. "Yes, yes, that's it. You're perfect."

The embers inside her banked and rose into flame. Needing to please, wanting to serve, she managed to take him all the way until the head of him tapped the back of her throat. He groaned when her throat closed around him a bit, and she breathed again as she pulled back.

"Stand up, Sera." Brandt helped her up, and she swayed slightly.

He pushed her toward the bed, Ash on her other side, hands all over her body.

They pushed her hands aside when she attempted to touch them, and she found herself looking up into Brandt's face, his hair all around his shoulders, sliding forward to caress her nipples.

Ash pushed her thighs wide and settled between them, kissing up her belly, licking and nipping the underside of each breast and then tugging on her nipple ring.

She touched him, the rough suede feel of the skin on his head. He didn't have to shave his head, he was naturally bald, but there was just a slight roughness as she eased her palms against him, her fingers seeking the slightly raised ridges of the markings at the back.

There were times he'd rub his head against her, often after sex. The abrasion against her nipples, against the skin of her belly would send delicious aftershocks through her body.

"Your nipples just got harder," he said, lips against her sensitive flesh.

"I was just remembering."

Brandt took her lips briefly and ran a hand, next to hers, over Ash's head. "Remembering what?"

She shivered again as the scent of her cunt, aroused, needy, filled the air. "Ash used to rub his head against me, against my skin, and it felt so good."

"Did you ever rub it against her cunt?"

Sera's entire body went rigid, her clit bloomed, her pussy fluttered. She'd imagined it in her dirtiest fantasies, but she'd never said it out loud. Never asked. Which, given the manner of naughty things they got up to, seemed rather silly in retrospect, but still . . . It just seemed so . . . *naughty*.

"Well, now." Ash spoke, but his gaze locked onto hers, knowing. "I haven't, but it seems to me our woman would like that very much. Is that so?"

Her heart raced as she licked suddenly dry lips and finally nodded.

"Say it. Tell me what you want."

Her mouth opened, but no words came. The idea of it stunned her.

He gave her nipple one last lick and headed down her body where he spread her pussy and dove into her like a starving man.

All the air rushed from her lungs as she watched his hands, large and powerful on her thighs, pushing them wide apart.

"He's beautiful while he's licking your cunt," Brandt whispered in her ear. "Say it, Sera. Tell him you want it."

She squeaked instead when Ash speared his tongue deep into her pussy. He ate her ravenously, mercilessly; he wanted her to say it, and she knew she would.

The width of his shoulders now held her open as his hands teased and played. "Brandt, lube."

Brandt moved from the bed, and she craned her neck to watch him rustle through the big bag Ash had brought with him.

Brandt handed him a blue bottle, and Ash looked her straight in the eyes as he played with her rear passage, his fingers sliding through the lube he'd just poured there.

Bright colors streamed when she closed her eyes a moment. His fingers began to work their way into her, and she tried to keep relaxed.

"Your eyes belong to me. Open them and see who owns your pleasure."

Oh gods, she was afraid to. The man who spoke truly owned her heart and soul, shared it with the other man in the room, but she'd never stopped belonging to Ash, she knew that now.

And when she opened her eyes and met those pale blue ones, he knew it, too. Just as he belonged to her, heart and soul.

She swallowed the lump in her throat and watched the muscles in his forearm cord as he played with her. The set of his mouth, still glistening with her honey, was one she'd seen many times before. Implacable. He wanted what he wanted and nothing else. And he'd get it.

"Clamps, I think," Brandt said as he plucked her already hard nipples to elongate them.

She tried to keep her presence of mind enough to breathe out, to breathe through the pain as he put the clamp on first one nipple and then around the ring in the other. The bite of the clamp was sharp, but as she rode it, forcing herself to give in to the sensation rather than fight it, the pain bled into a dull pleasure.

But it wasn't until Brandt moved down to Ash and their lips met in a kiss, sharing her honey, that her desperation grew to unmanageable proportions.

And they knew it. When they broke the kiss, both men looked straight at her with matching wicked grins. Brandt walked his fingers over her bare mound and flicked the pad of his middle finger over her clit relentlessly until she began to pant, and the first tendrils of orgasm began to wrap around her, and then he backed off, giving his fingers to Ash, who licked them clean.

"Oh gods!" She wanted to close her eyes, but she didn't dare.

"Say it, Freka. Are you ashamed of it? Of wanting me that way? I love you, you love me, what is there to be ashamed of? I know you want it, your cunt weeps every time I bring it up. You're *panting*! You want me to do it; just ask me to."

"Oh gods, just do it! Please, please rub that soft-rough head over my pussy."

"Brandt, hold her arms." Ash looked back to Sera. "Arms above your head, legs wide. I want every bit of your pleasure. Every moan and gasp. Do. Not. Hold. Back."

Brandt crawled up her body, stopping briefly to kiss her, and she moaned at finding her taste on his lips. He settled in behind her. She put her arms above her head, her wrists crossed as if she'd been bound by more than Ash's command. Brandt leaned in and put his weight on her, holding her at her elbows, pressing her arms to the bed.

It didn't hurt. But the effect was immediate, right straight to her bones. Being restrained in word and deed thrilled her and then smoothed out all her inner turmoil as the heaven of it, as the *rightness* of submission settled in and took her away to that quiet, white space.

"I love it when your eyes blur like that. I've never seen anything more breathtaking in my life." Brandt whipped his hair over her nipples, against the flesh bound by the metal clamps, and she groaned deep.

In the position she was lying, she couldn't see Ash clearly, but she felt him rustle and then the first ridiculously good brush of the round, smooth-rough skin of his skull against the swollen, needy flesh of her cunt. She nearly shot off the bed.

He stopped and touched each ankle briefly, a reminder to keep her legs wide for him.

And again. Press, press, rub. The curve of his head, the way his skin felt, the absolutely dirty, naughty nature of what he was doing brought a chatter to her teeth and a tremble to her thighs.

He moaned. It got to him, too, she'd bet by the raw sound he'd just made.

"*Fuck*," Brandt said.

Even as Ash pressed against her pussy, his hands reached up, and a rush of sensation flooded her when he pulled the clamps free. Bright, white, vivid pleasure shot from her nipples straight to her clit, and like a cup that'd been filled and filled, she began to overflow.

She cried out as orgasm hit her with an intensity she rarely experienced. So good, so all-encompassing it rendered everything else irrelevant as it coursed through her.

A tingle moved through her hands and fingers as Brandt let go. He paused to kiss her and then, just when she thought she'd never seen a sexier thing, Brandt leaned in and slowly drew the flat of his tongue over the curve of Ash's head.

She pounded her fists on the mattress and laughed. It was so fucking beautiful, so hot, so sensual and naughty, she nearly came again just watching them.

"You taste even better on his skin." Brandt held a hand out, and she came to her knees, meeting his lips in a kiss, tasting herself, tasting Ash, tasting the three of them. Ash joined them, his tongue sliding into her mouth, teasing Brandt's.

"So, was that as good for you as it was for me? There's never been anything taboo between us before. It seems a simple thing, but oh gods, as I did it, my cock throbbed in time with my heart." Ash took her fingers and kissed them.

"It was amazing. A fantasy come true."

"You never have to be afraid to tell me what you want. What we do among the three of us is beautiful. As long as everyone wants it, we'll be all right." Ash smiled. "Your desires are so sexy to me."

"And me." Brandt raised a brow. "Now, go in the bag and bring me the longer-handled flogger. Ash has taunted me all these years with how beautiful you are when you've been flogged. It's time I saw for myself."

She nearly lost her footing as she stepped off the bed and made her way to the bag. Her heart sped at what lay inside it. A coil of rope, wrist and ankle cuffs, a slapper and two floggers, a short- and long-handled one. Together with the clamps on the bed, the lube and several phalluses, she'd be a busy woman if they decided to use their whole arsenal.

"You're taking a long time over there," Brandt said lazily, knowing full well what she was looking at.

"You two have been very busy, I see." She turned, holding the flogger in her hands. The scent of leather wrapped around her senses, and the slither of the tails over her wrists as she handed it to Brandt forced a muted gasp from her lips.

"We're about to be." Ash bent and fished the wrist cuffs from the bag.

"Your brother has great taste in furniture." Brandt indicated the posts on the footboard. "Bend forward, hands on each post."

The diamonds on her nipple ring swung merrily as she obeyed, the weight tugging to send a warm rush of sensation through her.

Ash fastened first one wrist to the post and then the other. He then knelt on the bed, his cock right in licking distance.

She looked up at him, seeing his smile when she gave him her eyes. Behind her, Brandt readied the flogger.

The soft, cool leather of the flogger tails slithered over her back, down her ass. The creak of the handle slowed down time, and her eyelids grew heavy with expectation.

And then . . . the rush of air breaking over her ass cheeks just before the first strike landed.

She arched with a soft gasp as the tendrils of heat rose, infused her cells. Her hands convulsed around the warm wood of the bedposts. She didn't yearn to be free; she yearned to be kept by them, an object to be adored and cherished.

Hearing was submerged, murky through the gentle static of sub-space as it crept through her. Ash said something, she saw his lips move as she struggled to keep her eyes open.

Another strike, the multiple tails licking her flesh like ribbons of flame. Her breath fell deep, slow, intoxicated with serotonin as her limbs grew heavy.

Again and again, licks of fire over her flesh, converted from pain to a pleasure so intense it nearly drowned her. Her bound wrists and Ash's gaze held her, kept her from floating away on the tide.

*A*sh looked down at her, his beauty. Her eyes were glazed, lips parted, fingers gripping the bed. "Gods, you're magnificent. I've missed this so much."

And he had, so much a dull ache spread through him at the sight of the marvelous pink hue of her ass and back. Brandt had a fine hand with the flogger, wielded it like an expert. Her body came alive under his strokes, just hard enough but never to cause pain.

Ash caressed her face, and she turned to press a kiss into his palm, her breath warm there against his skin.

Originally he'd intended on having her suck his cock while Brandt worked her with the flogger, but he simply wanted her to enjoy it, *he* wanted to enjoy her response.

Brandt looked up, asking silently how Sera was doing. Ash nodded once. It was time to stop and bring her down a bit.

Brandt laid aside the flogger and grabbed a small container, opening it and rubbing the sweet-smelling ointment on her skin.

Her eyelids fluttered, and Ash undid her restraints, easing her to standing and then helping her onto the bed on her belly.

"Shhh, close your eyes, Freka, and let us take care of you." Ash kissed her forehead and ran his fingers through her hair, murmuring to her softly.

"How are you?" Brandt lay beside her, drawing his fingers up and down her spine. She stretched under his touch and moaned with satisfaction.

"I'm wonderful. And wet." Her voice was muffled by the pillow, but they heard her and laughed.

"We've got the cure for that when you're ready. Just relax a bit and enjoy the comedown," Brandt said.

She rustled around and turned, wriggling into the covers. "Oh, my! It's been a very long time since I've felt this." Her words were becoming more distinct, losing the slur of sub-space.

Ash couldn't help it. "How long?" The curve of her shoulder called to be kissed, so he answered, tasting her.

"Ten years," she said simply. "After you, there was no one else I trusted enough to let in."

"I'm so honored you trusted me enough," Brandt said, moving over her to kiss her lips.

"Then one of you needs to fuck me. Please. I'm wet and achy, and I'm the kind of girl who likes sex with her domination."

Brandt needed her, needed to be inside her to share the intimacy he'd missed while they were apart and to seal what they'd just become to each other. A new level of trust and love existed between them.

But he knew Ash needed it, too, for the same and yet totally different reasons.

"Shall we stuff you with cock then, Sera? Me in your cunt and Ash in your ass?"

Her skin rose in gooseflesh, and her nipples hardened, darkening to a deep pink.

"I think that's your answer, Brandt." Ash chuckled and leaned off the bed to grab the lube.

"Ride me, then."

She moved to straddle him, reaching up to arrange his hair around his head with a sly smile. "One bald, the other with hair to his butt. Like a continuum of incredible masculine beauty. I don't know how I ended up here, but I'm glad I am."

Brandt touched her face. "Are you then? Glad?"

She nodded slowly.

"Then say yes."

Ash arranged himself behind her body, and Brandt reached down to stroke a fingertip over her clit to keep her ready. She arched her hips forward, grinding herself into his touch, taking his cock into her cunt.

"Mmmmm."

What should she say? What a stupid question. She knew what she was going to say. Had known it seconds after they proposed the idea. Scared, yes, stupid, no.

Ash spread her, and the cool lube eased the passage of his fingers, first one, then two.

She'd never actually been double penetrated. Well, Ash had used toys while he fucked her for ass play, but she'd never had two real live cocks fucking her this way before.

The idea had been exciting enough, and she'd entertained it plenty since they'd started a physical relationship, but the reality was better if not more complicated. Overwhelming.

Brandt barely moved within her as Ash loosened her up, preparing her for his cock. The sensation of his fingers stretching her while a cock nudged into her pussy was incredible.

But it was nothing compared to the feeling when Ash gently pushed her forward with a hand at her back, and she felt the blunt head of his cock begin to press into her rear passage.

Some low, guttural sound came from her as he pushed into her body in small, short digs, filling her to the point where she was quite sure she couldn't take another bit of him. And yet, he continued.

"Say yes," Brandt whispered.

"Yes. Yes to both of you. But if it's a mistake, you can never say so or I'll have my revenge on your dangly bits. Ahhh!"

Ash pressed all the way in, and the three of them remained still for long moments as her body adjusted. The threefold beating of hearts echoed through her.

"It's not a mistake. I'll spend the rest of my life proving it." Brandt wriggled his fingers against her clit, and her cunt spasmed around his cock and must have affected her ass because Ash groaned low.

"I love you. I adore you, and if I don't move this instant, I'm going to die," Ash ground out behind her.

"Fuck me. Both of you. Own me, mark me, make me yours and mean it."

In a slow, alternating motion, Brandt slid in as Ash pulled out, reversing as Ash pushed back in.

She couldn't move, so she held on, buffeted by her two men, by chests and hard, muscled thighs as they took her and made good on her request. In that moment she was well and truly marked forever as theirs. And they as hers.

"Come for me, Sera," Brandt urged, his fingers speeding against her clit.

Ash filled her, sparking those nerve endings so seldom used, it felt unspeakably good, just a hairsbreadth away from being too much, from pain. She writhed between them, trusting them to keep her just on the right side of that line, and they did.

She sobbed as climax hit. Her body didn't know what to do. Her inner muscles clamped down on Brandt, and Ash sped up, fucking into her deeper as her body loosed with orgasm.

Brandt reared up and bit her shoulder as he groaned, coming deep inside her, and with a muffled curse, Ash shoved forward, and his cock jerked as he came.

"I love you both so much it's like you're written into my very soul," she said softly as Ash picked her up and they carried her into the bathroom adjoining her rooms.

"*I*s she all right?" Ash asked over his shoulder as he tested the bathwater.

Brandt cradled her in his arms and nodded. "Yes. Just overwhelmed, I think."

"Let's get her cleaned up, and then we'll feed her before we get the marriage taken care of and file the paperwork for her to be my mistress."

She grumbled, and Ash laughed. "Don't be so argumentative. You already agreed to do it, so why waste any more time?"

Brandt stepped to the bath, carrying her with him and gently put her into the water. He and Ash knelt next to it.

"We'll need a bigger tub in the future, I think." Brandt chuckled.

"Ash, sweetness, why don't you get in and clean up?" Sera's eyes were half-closed and dreamy, her voice languid.

"I'll shower when you finish. Let us take care of you for a change." Ash picked up a fragrant bar of soap and lathered a washing cloth, leaning in to grab a feminine foot and start to scrub.

"For a soldier, you have lovely feet. Mine are all beaten up."

Brandt began to wash her back. Ash loved the satisfied smile on her lips.

"Thank you. And darling, I promise when I look at you, your feet are the very last thing I notice." Sera still hadn't fully opened her eyes.

"Oh yeah, what do you notice then?" Brandt kissed the top of her head as Ash began to move the cloth up her calves.

"Needy," she teased, a sparkle in her eye. Ash couldn't remember the last time he'd seen her mischievous like this. "Well, the first thing I noticed were your eyes. I thought how while Ash's beauty was harsh and savage, yours was elegant." She peered at Ash and took his hand a moment. "And I mean that as a compliment to you both."

Ash felt better at that and realized she was making an effort to love them both as much as she could. He liked that.

"And then the hair, your lips, oh my, I wanted to kiss them right there."

"Before or after you knocked me down?" Brandt teased.

Ash stifled a snort.

"Before. And after, too. I've thought of one word consistently when I see you." She smirked.

"I'm afraid to ask." Brandt's mouth quirked into a smile.

"Delicious."

"You're very good with that." Ash saw the blush even through Brandt's skin tone.

"Oh, all right. Me?" Ash wanted her to stroke his, um, ego, too. He'd reached her pussy and gently used the cloth, knowing she'd be sore.

"Well, as you know, I bumped into you on purpose for a month before you finally asked my name. I saw you in your uniform, and you were so handsome and refined and there was this edge to you.

Of course, I had *no* idea how much of an edge until you brought out a coil of rope the first time I slept at your place."

"The first time, Ash?" Brandt snorted. "You don't waste time on preliminaries, do you?"

She sat up and cupped Ash's chin. "Overwhelming. You've simply owned my heart since the first time you looked at me with that smile and said, 'And since you've made the effort to press yourself against me so many times, why don't you tell me your name.'"

His breath caught. Disarming. "I love you, Sera. I hope to show you that every waking moment until I pass from the universe." He kissed her softly.

"Come on, then. Stand up so we can rinse you off, and then I want you to march back to bed and get in. Wait for us, and we'll eat." Brandt helped her up as Ash began to rinse her.

"Are you two going to do stuff with each other while I'm in the other room?"

Ash was taken aback. "Do you think that's why we want you to rest? Haven't we made it clear it's *you* we want? I'd never go behind your back like that. If I found I wanted Brandt and couldn't wait for the three of us to be together, I'd say so."

She grinned, toweling off. "No, silly. I just wanted to watch. I trust you both. We should probably talk about that sort of thing. What's okay and not okay. I'm not bothered if you two are together when I'm not around. Or even when I am. Especially when I am." She laughed. "You're beautiful when you touch each other. I'd feel bad if I felt you were ignoring me. I'm sure we can deal with that, though."

Ash got into the shower under the spray but kept speaking to her. "Well, I appreciate you saying that. And I don't care if you're with Brandt when I'm not around, either. And I expect there will be times when we'll want it to be just the two of us as well."

He stepped aside as he soaped up while Brandt got in. She leaned against the counter and watched them both.

"Brandt?" Sera asked.

"What both of you have said. I know I'm going to want you all to myself sometimes. But I agree we can work it out. We all love each other; it'll take work, but we can do it."

Chapter 27

Sera padded into Paul's large kitchen and began to assemble a meal while Brandt poked around in the cabinets to find the items they'd need.

"I've found a lot of things. You want to know now, or do you two want to tell me what you've learned first?" She sliced bread and motioned toward the jar of fruit preserves on the counter.

Ash poured them some juice, and they began to ferry the food to the table and finally sat down.

"Why don't we eat first, and then we can compare data. We've been traveling, and you've been working nonstop by the looks of it." Ash began eating, and she agreed, turning to her own plate.

"Sera, how long has it been since you've eaten?" A smile hinted at the corners of Brandt's mouth as she realized she'd practically inhaled her food.

"Long enough. I ate this morning before I went downstairs."

"Now that we're here, you'll take care of yourself." Brandt said it in the way of a man totally sure he'd be obeyed.

She laughed and patted his hand. "Two things. It's very sweet you two want me to take care of myself. I like that. But I don't bottom outside the bedroom. Got it? I'm not saying you were ordering me to take care of myself as my top, but I just wanted to be clear on it."

Ash laughed, a deep, masculine sound that made her smile in response.

Brandt shook his head as he drank the last of his juice. "I'd figured that. It's enough work—and pleasure—to top you sexually; I need to get my strength back when we're not fucking. Truly, I respect your independence. As long as you're on your knees in the bedroom, you can stand tall everywhere else. You were made to."

She cocked her head at Brandt. "You're very smooth. Sexy. Thank you for that. What you just said."

Ash snorted. "Show-off. All right, let's clean this up and head down to the data room. We can go over everything there."

"Afterward, we're heading into Mirum to get the marriage taken care of. Right?" Brandt stood, and they all cleared up and headed downstairs.

"Yes, all right. If you two are absolutely sure, I'm still willing."

*B*randt stood in the doorway of the room filled with fancy electronics and nearly sighed with happiness. What a space!

"It's pretty impressive, isn't it?" Sera caught the gleam in his eye and grinned.

"Gods, you're the perfect woman." He pulled her to him, kissing her soundly.

"Come and sit here, let me open up the files, and I'll show you what I've found." Sera motioned them over to a table with several stacks of hard copies neatly lying on top.

She opened one up. "Shall we just get to the worst stuff first? Things I can prove clearly?"

"You may as well. The comandante is quite clear on wanting to eradicate this threat now. Any way we have to." Ash leaned in.

"All right." She pointed to the screen. "Paul was able to get past the encryption and unlock the data, I um, liberated. Together with what we found elsewhere and with what Rina gave me, this is what I've got." She took a sip of kava and looked back at the data. "This is the basic sketch of the ring of communication. Owen Alder is involved with Imperial credit schemes up to his neck. You can see here, he's been communicating with Supreme Leader Fardelle him-self. Here's also a transfer of credits from Edge banks to Alder's ac-counts. Each time has been between three standard weeks before to right until the attacks on the different outposts and then immedi-ately afterward. But technically, he's an Edge citizen, so this isn't entirely illegal for him."

"Just the part where he was instrumental in the deaths of Fed-eration citizens and aiding our enemies. Where did you get this information?" Brandt asked.

"I gave you an overview. Do you really want to know the specif-ics? I can't say anything that would potentially harm anyone who aided me at extreme risk." Sera waited for his reply.

"We've got an emergency powers waiver. I assume you used channels however you did to gain information on this investigation. Anyone aiding you is protected, as you are. Where you got it isn't an issue. Not officially, anyway." Brandt tapped the papers. "This stuff is beyond what we could get hold of before."

She sighed. "We cracked into Family networks. Several of them. This is partly from Owen Alder's own comm unit and his banking records. He didn't make much of an effort to conceal any of it. But for corroboration, I also managed to get into the banking networks. I've tracked and logged it all."

"Who else, Sera?" Ash asked.

Sera chewed her lip a moment, and Brandt was suddenly afraid of the answer but waited anyway.

"I'm sorry, but Perry is involved and has been for the last standard year. He's made a considerable sum of credits and at key points after outpost attacks, he's been paid. He was also in receipt of an influx of credits immediately after Giles Stander's murder." She paused and touched his arm briefly. "I'm sorry. There's no doubt he's part of it. And there's more. Your uncle . . . Ash, your uncle has had communication with Giles Stander and then Owen Alder quite a bit. I don't know if he's been trading information, but it stands to reason your cousin doesn't have enough power to get this high-level information on his own."

"Have you found any communication between Perry and anyone else in the military or governmental corps? Any place he could have gotten the information he sold to Alder?" Ash's voice was flat, but Brandt knew he was upset.

"I checked. We did an exhaustive search, looked through a lot of inane banter between Perry and his man on the side. Don't think Kira knows about that, though." She shrugged. "I need to get a list to the comandante, because there are military people who appear to be helping, but they are not ranked high enough to do much. They shouldn't be allowed in the system regardless."

"Get me the list now, I'll send it to him. We can't have these people roaming free," Brandt said.

Sera nodded to Brandt, and he saw just how seriously she took the job, not for the first time. "Go to that terminal; the list is on the screen. Everything in here is secured."

"Ash, fill her in on what you learned, since I've already heard it. I'll be back in a moment." Brandt moved to the terminal and looked at the list with shock. "This list is two screens long."

Sera moved to sit next to him, and Ash joined them. "Next to each name are links to the evidence I gathered. Communications, meetings, in some cases credit transfers. As far as I can tell, the credit transfers were in exchange for access to low-security sites where the suspects are stationed."

"How did you know about the meetings?" Brandt asked while he typed out the message to the comandante.

"Communication trails, entry and exit logs, in a few cases, vid footage. Not a whole lot isn't in a network or on a screen these days." Sera shrugged.

"Why would they take such risks?" Ash asked.

"Please don't be offended, but Family members are pretty untouchable. You control everything. You run the government and the military. That can lead to a very heady state of invincibility. Family network communication is protected, so why even worry about it? In this case, that behavior was the key, because it provided us with screen after screen of incriminating evidence." Sera's voice was calm, but Brandt knew she was right.

"Okay, sent. Kira?" Brandt turned back to face Sera.

She chewed her lip a moment. "I just don't know. There was some activity in her personal comm channel, but as much as I hate to say this, I don't think she's smart enough to have orchestrated this. What I could find looked a great deal like Perry's signature. It *is* damning. But I don't know for sure. The majority of her communications are ridiculously inane. Beyond stupid and irrelevant. Filled with commentary on clothes and the cost of homes and other status markers. I find it suspicious that she'd be so stupid one moment and suddenly vicious and bloodthirsty the next. Not that I'm rescinding my opinion that she's an evil, venomous creature or anything. But I'm not convinced she's as culpable as Perry is. She *is* involved, and it's fairly certain she understands what she's doing is illegal. That makes her a criminal. But I don't know if that makes her a traitor."

Relief poured through him. Brandt couldn't imagine what it would do to his father to have his child be a traitor. But more than relief for his family, he was relieved his woman was so professional, so righteous that she'd protect his sister when Kira would not do the same for her.

"So, we've got Perry Walker involved, Owen Alder involved, this list of military corps and some government corps people involved. My uncle looks like he's involved, and Kira may or may not be involved. Anyone else?" Ash rubbed his palm over his head.

"Several members of the Stander Family have some fairly obvious ties to Owen Alder. I've got that, too. Military corps had some of this already, but without all the key pieces I was able to get through back channels, it wasn't complete enough to see the big picture." Sera closed the folder.

"In sum, there's a conspiracy aided by several of the most powerful Families to aid and abet the Imperialists to destabilize our governance and take over. Is my father involved? My uncle, yes, I see all the evidence, and I think he should be tried. Anyone else in my family?" Ash asked.

"Kendal, your youngest brother, the one closest to Perry's age. He's accompanied Perry and Kira to Nondal and Edge 'Verse several times. He's been in the Family network trying to break into your father's accounts."

*A*sh deflated a moment, hanging his head. Pain, sadness, and then rage rolled through him at this entire situation. "I can't believe this. My own family? Why? We have plenty of credits. We control huge chunks of 'Verse space. Kendal is a recognized son of my father's mistress. He has an empire of his own. I don't understand."

Sera went to him, putting her arms around him, and he instantly felt better. Comforted. "You can't understand because you have a sense of right and wrong. I didn't find anything on your father at all. Or anyone else in the Walker Family. Kendal might believe in universal fascism. He might believe in the power of credits no matter the cost to humanity. He might hate your father or you or your older brother. He could resent being born to a mistress and not a wife. People's motivations are often a mystery. But yours aren't, Ash. You're a good man. You're doing the right thing, even though it will cost you and your Family. I wish I found other things, I really do. I'm sorry."

"It's not yours to apologize for. Brandt, send this list to the comandante, and let's get some arrest and extradition papers drawn up to have people brought to Ravena." Ash stood, keeping an arm around Sera. "We'll go to Mirum and handle the marital papers and the mistress situation first. You will have the protection of both our status as well as your status as military corps. Then we go to my Family's compound. I need to tell them about you, about us, and then confront them about this mess."

He had a lot to deal with. Resentment that he'd done the right thing and nearly lost Sera and would never be able to marry her made him edgy. He'd done the best thing for the Family, while Perry had turned his back on a millennia of rank by the Walkers.

By the time Ash finished with them, everything he'd needed to say for years would be said. He could only pray his father backed him against his uncle.

"And then what? Our cover will be blown for all future operations. What do you suggest we do about that?" Sera asked.

"I brought this up to the comandante. He feels it's time for Brandt and me to be open about our military service and loyalty to the Federation. At a time when people's faith in the Families will be shaken, we can be a symbol that not all of us are traitors. It keeps the people having faith in rule by the ranked, keeps the peace. And it helps us openly be with you as well." Ash leered at her, and she rolled her eyes.

"And the perfect cover of two obscenely handsome playboys?"

"With all the prosthetics and other image-enhancing capability, it won't be difficult to go undercover in different ways now. Other teams do it all the time. It's just another cover. I'm sick of people thinking I'm some moneyed spoiled brat." Until he said it just then, Ash hadn't really articulated it out loud. The saying of it liberated him.

She shrugged. His lovely woman just raised her shoulders and sniffed. "Okay. Well, let me change. Because I can't get married and be a mistress in work pants and my hair a mess. And I need to tell my family. I can't get married and have them find out via vid screen."

"I understand. I'd like to meet them after this is all settled." Brandt kissed her forehead. "Can they keep it quiet until we've announced it? I think the surprise will keep everyone off balance, and that will work in our favor."

"Absolutely. My Dai is career corps." Sera winced. "He's, well, he doesn't like you much, Ash. So let me talk to them alone first, to clear things up a bit. They're not likely to take the triad thing well at first. Mai is very religious."

Ash sighed. "I understand. You've not gotten much of a great reception from my world, either. We'll work this through. Go on. Brandt and I will deal with all this stuff down here, and you conference your parents and get changed."

$\mathcal{S}$era trudged up to her rooms, lightened a bit from telling them about the involvement of their families but also burdened by Ash's personal pain. She couldn't imagine learning Paul had betrayed their people, or anyone in her family.

She wished Paul was with her right then to call her parents, but she had to deal with that on her own. She changed into a pretty skirt and boots along with a dark sweater and fixed her hair. They may as well see her dressed up a bit, hopefully take the edge off at least a small amount.

Settling in, she took a deep breath and connected to her parents' home.

Her father's face popped up, and when he saw it was her, he smiled broadly. "Hello there!" He turned away from the screen. "Malta, it's Sera."

Sera heard her mother in the background, and soon her face joined her father's. She loved them both so much. They were both the kind of people she strived to be; courageous, honest, hardworking, kind, loving to one another.

"You look beautiful, Sera. Are you back now?"

"I am. Listen, Mai, Dai, I've got this on secured, so I need to tell you something you can't repeat until I give you the all go."

They both nodded, giving her their assurance. "First of all, I'm here in Sanctu, but I'm finishing up a mission. When I complete it, I'll come straight to you. Second of all, you're going to start hearing news, so I need to tell you first. I'm marrying Brandt Pela within the hour."

Her mother began to cry, and her father demanded answers. Sera held her hand up.

"Wait. There's more."

"Sera, that's never a good sentence," her father said.

She laughed. "It is good. I'm also going to file as Ash Walker's mistress."

Instead of screams, both her parents got utterly silent for a long time.

"Did you just tell us you're marrying one man and becoming another man's mistress? A man who you left for asking that very thing ten standard ago?"

She knew that tone. Her father often got grumpy about things but rarely truly angry. He was truly angry just then.

"It's so much more complicated than I can go into right now, but please trust me. Ash is a good man. Better than you and I knew. And Brandt is a good man as well. I'll come to you after this is over. We'll talk. Please."

"You can't just throw something like this at us and expect us to take it without an explanation."

"Mai, I love you both so much. I will explain, I promise, but I can't now. I need to go. I just wanted you to hear it from me first." Sera pressed her hand to the screen and ended the communication.

$\mathcal{S}$era came downstairs to find them changed into military uniforms and looking unbelievably handsome.

"Wow. Look at you two." She fanned herself and walked around them to catch the look from behind. "Impressive. I feel underdressed. Shall I change into my uniform as well?"

Ash took one hand and Brandt the other. "You look beautiful. You can change after we deal with the ceremony and paperwork. For now, let yourself enjoy it a little bit." Brandt kissed the hand he held and slipped a ring on. Sneaky man.

Sera looked at it. The flat band was embedded with stones. Nothing flashy but beautiful, classic. Totally her. "Oh. It's perfect. I love it. I'm, well, I don't have anything for you." She blushed.

He laughed and kissed her quickly. "I'm glad you like it. I thought it was perfect for you. We can deal with rings for us later. This was a surprise for you, I know."

She turned to Ash, who slid a ring on her other hand. "What?"

He grinned. "You didn't think only Brandt would give you a ring did you? You're mine, too. I wish with all I was we could marry, but we will declare our forever anyway."

Ash's ring was the mirror of Brandt's, only with a warmer-colored metal.

Emotion choked her. "I'm so . . . I just never expected to feel this way for anyone again. To have this with you, Ash, when I thought it lost forever . . ." She shivered, without words, turning to Brandt. "To find it with you when I least expected it. To feel it for two men and have it be all right, it just seems like a dream."

Both her men looked at her, stepping forward to embrace her.

"We love you. We have the forever you've deserved for so long," Ash whispered in her ear.

"I know. I believe it. I'm so happy. I love you both so much."

"Then let's go and do this," Brandt exclaimed.

"We can borrow one of Paul's vehicles. I've left him a note about it." Sera led them outside.

"Were you able to get in contact with your parents?" Brandt asked as they got in.

She winced as she navigated out of the drive and headed toward Mirum. "Yes. I told them we'd come to see them after everything was taken care of. They'll keep the news quiet until then."

Ash laughed from his place just behind her. "That was a fine bit of avoidance, Sera. I take it they didn't react well?"

"They're shocked about the triad thing. They're not that opposed to me marrying Brandt, but they're upset about my being anyone's mistress, much less yours. They'll get over it once I can explain. Once they see things are different now. But after . . . after things ended, I was a mess for a while."

"How much of a while? Tell me," Ash asked quietly, his normal demand absent from his tone.

She sighed. "It's not important. It was a long time ago. I'm not there now. We're together again. Let it go." She didn't want to be in that place again, and she didn't want to take him there, either.

"I'm sorry. I just want to know."

"Why? And don't be sorry; it's over and done. What good would it do to know now, Ash?" She focused on the track in front of her. "It can't help you."

"How do you know? I thought of you every day, you know. But I forced myself to let you go, to never look to see where you'd gone or what had happened to you. I couldn't know. Selfish. But when we called your name up for the team, I looked and learned a bit. But so much is missing."

"Tell him," Brandt urged.

"Why? It will only hurt. I don't want to hurt you, Ash."

"Please."

She sighed, frustrated. "What do you think I was like, Ash? I believed in you. In us. I believed in love and forever and all that good stuff. In the span of a day, it was all a lie. It sent me reeling. I fucked my way through many men in the following months. All of them incredibly unsuitable. It was dark, self-destructive and bad. My parents were distressed. And then I found my way into the military corps, and I had a regimen to guide me. Structure. I was so busy and inundated with rules and tasks every moment of my day, it stopped hurting so much, and I stopped hurting myself instead of you." She swallowed. "My family had one Sera one day and a stranger the next. It took a while before I got back in my own head. But I was never the same as I'd been with you."

"So of course they resent me. I resent it, too, Sera. I wish I could take it back." Ash's voice was quiet as he touched her shoulder.

"Don't. Don't, Ash. Yes, they resent you, but as I told them, you're a better man than I gave you credit for then. It hurts, I can't say it doesn't. But I *understand* what you did. I don't think you could be the man you are if you'd walked away from your duty then. Doesn't mean I like the ranking system and what it does to everyone who doesn't agree with choices made for them. But I understand your choice." Sera blinked back her tears. Truly forgiving him made her lighter, easier in her own skin.

He leaned closer and touched her neck. "You don't know what that means to me. You really don't." Ash's voice was the merest whisper, but she heard him.

She reached up and touched his hand, and Brandt simply covered theirs with his as well.

The ride to Mirum took some time, so they all settled in and began to speak of the future. Something Brandt hadn't done in many years, because his life had become about the present and not thinking past the end of whatever mission they were on.

"Do you two live in Borran all the time when you're not on an assignment?" Sera asked.

Brandt twisted the end of one of her short curls around a finger. His body was turned toward her in the seat so he could see her and Ash both.

Ash had been shaken, he knew, by Sera's admission of what her life had been like and also by her forgiveness and understanding. He'd been quiet for a while, but he'd begun to perk up as they'd started talking about their plans.

"We have the compound in Borran, and we both have large residences in Ravena. I have a house adjacent to Family grounds in Majar as well."

Ash finally spoke. "As Brandt says, I've got a residence in Ravena and a small house here in Sanctu, just outside Mirum near the Family residences. I moved out of the house I shared with you. Kira and Perry sold it, I believe. I also have a few residences scattered through several 'Verses. Nowhere I'd call home, though. Funny how I never thought of it that way until you came into my life again."

Sera shrugged. "I don't have any residence. I had quarters in Borran, but they reassigned them when I was placed on your team. Having been in the corps as long as I've been, I don't have a lot of possessions. My parents came and packed me up. I imagine the few boxes are with them or in storage."

"Where would you like to live? When we're not out on assignment?" Brandt asked her. He wanted to buy her things, shower her with luxuries, but he knew they'd have to take it slow or she'd be offended. Whether she liked it or not, once they married, she'd be a rich woman.

"Not here. No offense, but I really think I'd like to avoid Sanctu and Majar just now and for the immediate future. I'm not going to be welcomed, you know. Borran is fine, if you two don't mind. Ravena is fine as well. I just want to be where you are."

Brandt supposed that was the exact point, but until they slept in the same bed every night openly, he'd be uneasy.

The outskirts of Mirum began to spring up around them as they drove. Residences, outlying neighborhoods. Because the atmosphere was breathable, there was far more sprawl than in the 'Verses like Nondal, where people needed to be in atmospherically controlled environments.

Ash leaned forward. "Let me take over, please. I'll take us to one of the bureaucratic divisions out here instead of dragging us into the chaos of the heart of Mirum."

Sera pulled to the side, but Ash didn't let her into the back, he simply scooted in, settling her in between them.

The small registry office was staffed by a very wide-eyed young woman who nearly fell from her chair when she caught sight of Ash as they entered.

Ash knew he was recognizable with the bald head and the markings. It pleased him in a sense, and it pleased him even more to know he'd be able to shed the indolent shell and let people know he was more than that.

"Mr. Walker! It's, oh my! Welcome. What can we do for you?" The girl looked at Brandt, her gaze moving from toe to head, and Ash wanted to laugh at the fierce look on Sera's face.

Brandt put the marital papers on the counter. "I need this witnessed and entered into Federation System records immediately."

"Of course." The girl took the sheaf of papers and looked through them, signing, stamping and entering different codes into the comm unit at her workspace. "Marital union. Congratulations." Her gaze flicked to Sera a moment. Sera stood tall and met her look until the clerk broke the stare and looked back to her papers. "Everything is in order. I need you both to enter your personal numbers and submit to blood and retina scan, and you'll be officially joined."

Sera entered a number on the keypad, and Brandt followed. The retina scan verified their identity, and the blood sample would go on record as well.

"Okay then." The girl gave Sera a tight smile and a warmer one to Brandt.

"It seems so cold for such a momentous moment." Brandt turned to Sera and kissed her. And then he kissed her some more. Sera wound her arms around Brandt's neck, and Ash heard her soft sigh as she opened her mouth to Brandt's demanding tongue.

An ache, sharp and deep, spread through him. He wanted her this way. He wanted to be her husband, was meant to be. If and when he got enough power to sway the Walker Family, he would abolish the rule that allowed the first and second sons to marry only with the head of the Family's permission.

Sera stood back, pressing her fingers against her lips. "I enjoy being married already."

Ash laughed and put his arm around her waist. Confusion slid over the clerk's face as she tried to figure out just what was going on.

He pulled his own sheaf of papers from his pocket and put them on the counter. "Now these, please."

She picked them up warily, her brows sliding higher and higher as she worked through each page.

"Mr. Walker, are you sure the names on this application are correct?" The clerk handed the papers to him.

He handed them back. "Yes. Ash Walker and Sera Ayers-Pela."

Color infused the clerk's cheeks then, and her cold gaze turned curious when she took Sera in again. Sera laughed and nodded. "I know. I can't believe it either." She raised one shoulder good-naturedly.

Brandt kissed her temple and squeezed her from the other side.

They went through the same process. Entering personal numbers, blood, and retinal scans.

"It's all official now. Anything else I can do?" The clerk's voice had gone a bit high.

"No, that'll be all for today. Enjoy your evening." Ash took Sera's hand, and Brandt took the other, and the three of them walked out together. *Together.*

Chapter 29

"All right then. I'll give that news about ten standard minutes to spread far and wide." Ash laughed. He did feel good. The ache had gone once the papers had been entered and Sera had looked to him, loving, trusting and happy.

"I imagine so. Let's go to your house, Ash, and get Sera changed. I want everyone carrying weapons. I know they're your family, but we don't know what some of them are capable of."

Ash knew only too well.

He drove the track around the edge of Mirum. The heart of the city was a snarl of commerce, residential space and all manner of vehicles. It could take longer to get from the outskirts of one side of the city to the next than to traverse the whole of the western regions of Sanctu.

He'd told Sera his home was adjacent to Walker lands but by adjacent, he'd meant within eight klicks. They wouldn't know he'd arrived as he'd changed the main security protocol to recognize his call alone and report any ingress to the property only to him.

As they made their way up the winding, tree-lined drive to the house, he realized just how much he'd been avoiding the place since he and Kira had broken up. He hadn't wanted to deal with his family if he didn't have to. Resentment, he'd figured, at losing what had been so important.

Sera touched him, caressing his neck. "Are you all right?"

"I'm fine, Freka. You're truly mine, and we will finally have a life together after so long. I think I'm just digesting it." He caught her hesitation in the way her hand had stiffened. "No, not that. It's a wonderful thing."

She relaxed. "I know this has to be difficult for you. I'm sorry."

He put his hand over hers. "Stop apologizing already. Now, we're here, and this is your home, too. Both of you."

He grabbed the bag holding her weapons and uniform while she got out, and Brandt followed.

"This is spectacular, Ash." Sera turned a full circle as they walked into the large common area. A wall of glass fronted the lake just beyond, the tree line and mountains in the distance framing it all.

"Thank you. Come on, let me show you the bedroom. You can get dressed."

Brandt laughed. "Undressed. And *then* dressed. We have time, don't we?"

"Again?" Sera threw her arms around Brandt, laughing. "You're a greedy little thing, aren't you?"

He picked her up, and she wrapped her legs around his waist. "Where you're concerned, yes."

"Don't get started yet. I need to catch up." Ash led the way through the long corridor back to the master suite, and he threw the double doors open. "Put our prize on the bed."

Brandt laid her down carefully.

"I expect after our interlude earlier you'll be a bit sore. But there's so much more than cock in cunt to do with you." Ash began to unbutton his uniform.

"*To* you," Brandt added.

She sat up and tossed away the sweater and lay back down to shimmy out of her skirt.

"No panties. You're naughty." Brandt moved over her body, kissing up her belly. Ash caught the wink of the necklace Brandt had given her back when they'd first left for Nondal. It'd seemed so long ago, he'd wondered if he'd ever touch her again, and now she was his.

"I hope to be." She smiled lazily up at Brandt as Ash joined them.

"Too late; you've been naughty a very long time." Ash tugged on her nipple ring, and she sighed her pleasure.

"Mmmmm." She rolled to the side facing him as he knelt, and she licked up his thigh and made her way over to his cock. "Even with all that work earlier, you're not flagging at all. I do love your stamina."

"I hope you can say that when I'm an old man." Ash looked down at her head bent over his lap.

Her hand surrounded him, sliding up and down his cock slowly as she licked the head. He shivered and locked his thigh muscles to keep from toppling over at how good it felt with her tongue sliding over the sensitive head.

His eyes flew open when she moved back and broke contact. But what he saw was his woman wrapped in an embrace with his friend, and instead of feeling bereft, it buoyed him.

What they had was miraculous. Amazing and complicated but utterly beautiful. The sweep of Brandt's dark lashes over his cheek, the line of Sera's neck as she arched into the kiss, the press of her breasts, small but perfect, against Brandt's chest, even the contrast between her pale skin and Brandt's darker tones thrilled Ash's eye.

He stroked his cock as he took them in, the woman he'd never ceased to burn for and the man who'd made their reunion possible. No, more than that, Brandt was part of him, too. He loved Brandt, felt a deep connection and bond with him. They came into the relationship with Sera with mutual attraction and respect, but their bond deepened over their love for Sera.

His blood stirred as he greedily took in the sweep of Brandt's hands down Sera's sides, over her back, down to cup her ass. All the while Brandt's mouth fused to Sera's.

Sera drowned in Brandt's mouth, fell into his spell as he touched her, bringing her skin to life. His taste rang through her like a bell, surging through her system, charging, racing, taking over as she held on and let him devour her.

The taste of Ash's cock lay on her tongue as she shared it with Brandt. Brandt's moan signaled he'd tasted it. Knew it himself. The idea made her restless, needy.

She pushed back, catching her breath. "I was sucking Ash's cock. Help me finish."

When she turned, she caught sight of Ash, fist wrapped around his cock moving up and off completely, over and over, starting at his balls, ending at the head.

"It's so sexy to see a man do that," she said moving toward him. A faint smile tilted the corner of his mouth.

"What, Freka?"

"You. So easy in your skin, assured of your sexual allure. It's very," she shivered, "engaging."

There was no mistaking the pleasure on his face at her words. "Can't be nearly as sexy as watching you on your hands and knees crawling toward me to suck me off."

She smiled. "That, too, I suppose." Reaching out, she grabbed him, sliding his hand away and taking over. "Now, where was I?"

"I think you were right here," Brandt said before showing her, taking Ash's cock into his mouth.

She nearly came right then at the sight. A sight she'd fantasized about ever since she'd learned they'd been together sexually. The fantasy had nothing on the reality. Gorgeous. That's what it was watching Brandt's mouth work Ash's cock in a slow descent and then back up, over and over, as she held her breath.

When he pulled off, he looked to her with a grin. "Well? Was it what you expected?"

She moved her lips, but no words came out. Ash laughed, and Brandt leaned in to kiss her, moving their mouths down toward Ash's cock. Ash's laugh turned into a strangled groan when they made contact in a tangle of lips and tongue against each other.

"Gods!" Ash gripped her hair as he seeped salty fluid.

"I love how your semen tastes," she murmured around the head, into Brandt's mouth.

It was Brandt's turn to groan as she reached out to grab his cock and give it a fondle, not too rough, not too gentle.

"Try this," Brandt said and she moved back to watch him take Ash into his mouth. "Now you."

Sera took Ash's cock deep once, and once again, and pulled off, alternating with Brandt over and over. Sensual yes, but also fun, carefree.

Ash interrupted their game after a while. "Enough. Sera, I want to come in your mouth."

Brandt moved back, and she positioned herself in front of Ash and began to suck him again. Licking, flicking, lapping at his cock and over the head.

Brandt stroked his fingers up and down the line of her spine, nearly in time with her movement over Ash's cock. Ash drew close. Her fingers joined with Brandt's, she cupped Ash's balls and tickled a bit over the pucker of his rear passage. He groaned. When the two of them pushed in a bit, he jerked, surprised.

Hmm. She figured a bit of cocksucking between them, sure, but neither one bottomed to that extent, she'd wager by the way he'd tightened up.

She hummed around his cock in her mouth just imagining it, the thrust and sweat between them, grinding and writhing. The play of muscles beneath the gleaming skin.

So engrossed in her fantasy, she didn't realize she'd moved one hand to her pussy to finger her clit until Brandt moved it away.

"Oh no, Sera. That's mine to touch. And I will in a moment."

Her snort of annoyance seemed to amuse them both. Soon Ash began to roll his hips, sliding his cock into her mouth at his own pace.

"That's the way. Yes, that's right, so good." Ash groaned, his muscles stiffening as he came, filling her with his taste, blinding her with the need to please him.

He collapsed, taking her with him to the bed, his arms around her.

"You're beautiful, Sera. Everything. So sexy I can't breathe sometimes." He kissed her temple and then down the line of her jaw.

"Thank you. I love you, too. I also loved sucking your cock with Brandt's help. We'll have to try that the other way."

Ash laughed. "Anything for you. He's got a very nice cock. You do a better job, but I'm always happy to render my assistance."

"First we need to see to our woman. She was fingering her clit quite feverishly some moments ago." Brandt pushed her thighs apart.

"You were? Hmm, did you get permission for that?" Ash raised a brow.

She sniffed her indignation. "I don't need permission to touch my own clit."

Brandt laughed. "Perhaps we need to make that part of our arrangement. No coming without permission."

It was her turn to laugh. "I think not. I love submitting to you both, but I won't cede something like that."

"Fair enough. What were you thinking about?" Ash spoke against her skin as he moved down to her nipple.

"You and Brandt. Oh, yes." She sighed when Brandt slid his tongue through her cunt. She'd just had sex—exhaustive, double penetrative sex—with them four hours ago, and she needed it again. What they did to her.

"Should I ask for more detail? You said it like you had a deliciously naughty secret." Ash tugged the nipple ring with the tip of his tongue, and she sucked in a breath.

Brandt pressed his face into the flesh of her cunt and brushed his lips over her clit from side to side. The slick slide of his mouth against her sensitive pussy sent bright threads of pleasure through her, painted against the backs of her eyelids.

"Just imagining the two of you, thrusting, writhing, covered in sweat." She gasped out. Brandt slid two fingers deep into her gate and hooked them, finding her sweet spot and brushing the tips of his fingers over it. "Have you ever taken each other like that? Fucked each other?" Just saying it made her flush.

Ash stiffened and then relaxed. "Hmm. Well, a little back door play with you is one thing. But no, we haven't. I don't know if it'll ever happen. Perhaps one day."

He kissed down her belly, and she raised herself on her elbows to watch him join Brandt.

They moved in concert, pushing her knees up and apart so she was on her back again, her knees against her chest, open wide to them.

A shiver worked through her at being so exposed, at the hungry look on Brandt's face as he lowered it to her cunt again.

And then Ash. Her every thought skittered away when suddenly two tongues licked at her. Fingers everywhere, pressing, playing, tickling. It was too much. So much it wasn't quite enough, either, and she hung there, suspended on a wave of intense sensation. Immobile, breath held, desperate to come.

"Give it to me, Freka. I want your orgasm. Brandt and I want it on our faces."

She wanted to arch, wanted to tighten her muscles, but she was held immobile in that position, open to their mouths and hands, and it was so good, so much. Her body didn't quite know what to do.

And then it began to happen. Wisps of sensation gathering in her toes, at the top of her head, in her fingertips. Building, building, building, until she began to push back the panic.

Before she could process it or worry, it sucked her under, and she heard nothing, felt nothing but the roar of pleasure as her body flooded with endorphins.

*B*randt looked down at her as he and Ash put her legs back against the bed. The light from the big windows lit her body, glowed against her pretty, pale skin, now flushed with orgasm.

Ash petted her, gentling those jumping muscles in her legs. Brandt watched, fascinated by the level of tenderness he'd never witnessed in Ash before Sera had stepped into their world.

Big hands, big man: Brandt had seen Ash wade into a group of brawling men and toss them aside as if they were nothing more than dolls. Ash was ferocious, feral, hard, arrogant, and fearsome, and yet he touched their woman like the precious gift she was.

Then again, it wasn't as if Sera was so very fragile physically. Brandt loved to look at the lines of her body: the muscled thighs and hard calves, the flat belly, the upper arms defined by holding weapons and humping around heavy loads of ammunition and packs of supplies. Despite that, she emanated an effortless femininity. Not of a helpless sort, but it moved him nonetheless.

All his life, Brandt had dealt with women who needed help. Women like his sister and his mother. Women who needed taking care of, or more accurately, were bred to believe it was their right and station to be taken care of.

That Sera submitted to their care in a sexual and romantic sense meant so much more because she didn't need to. She could make her own living. Had done for many years. Her independence spiced and enhanced their relationship, because topping her was a pleasure, a luxury in a sense.

He snorted inwardly as her blue eyes opened up and focused on him. No wonder he'd never found a woman he'd wanted to give himself to totally. None were this woman. None held her beauty and unique strengths and weaknesses. Because that was part of it, he knew, too. She had flaws, wounds, dark places within her, and he wanted to accept the flaws and wounds while filling her dark places with light.

"Your turn, Brandt." Her lips curved up into a smile.

"It's always my turn when I'm with you. You feed every part of me," he whispered as he lay beside her.

She blinked quickly, but he saw the bloom of emotion in her eyes. Loved that about her.

"On top. I'm tired."

She rolled her eyes but kissed him as she moved to straddle his hips. "You don't want me to suck your cock?"

"There's a lifetime for that. I want to be inside you."

Balanced above him, she went up on her thighs, and everything inside him went still for long moments as she came back down, taking his cock into her cunt.

"Are you all right?" He stayed her with a hand on her thigh. It hadn't been so very long ago he and Ash had fucked her at the same time. He'd forgotten. A lapse he felt ashamed of. Her wellness should always be his top priority.

"More than all right. You feel so good." She looked down at him, reassuring him.

She planted her palms on his belly and slowly rode him, rose and fell over his body all the while he hungrily watched her fuck him.

Ash settled in next to them, hands behind his head. "It's beautiful to see."

Brandt knew what he meant. Watching her with Ash made him feel the same mixture of awe, sexual desire and love. He only hoped they never swamped her with too much. Two needy men with an insatiable appetite for her body might be too much at times. They'd have to be aware of it.

His climax approached, he knew. It'd lodged itself at the base of his spine, metallic in his mouth. It would happen when it wanted to. He was content to just be with her there.

Ash reached between them to stroke her clit, but she squeaked, grabbing his hand. "I can't. You can make me come later. I promise," she added when she saw his look.

A soft exhalation left Brandt's lips, and he came, filling her. He caught a glimpse of her smile as her head fell back.

Chapter 30

Sera looked at herself in the large mirror as she adjusted her weapons belt. Professional. Strong. In charge. Still, a tiny glimmer inside her taunted her confidence. This was their world—Brandt's and Ash's—the world of the Ranking Families, and her place was subservient.

Not in the way she submitted to her men. Their world saw her as a lesser human being. They'd taken so much from her without a single qualm because of that perception. She'd dedicated her life to the Federation, and they still thought themselves above her.

She shook her head. That wasn't a place she wanted to go just then. Or ever, for that matter. Ash and Brandt weren't that way. She didn't want them to feel she compared them to that.

Her subcommander's pin shone on her shoulder. She'd earned it, and she would see this situation through to the very end, because it had to be done.

Bending, she placed a knife in the sheath at her ankle and smoothed her pants over it. Her rings glinted in the light, easing her tension a small amount.

As much as she longed to take out the people who'd betrayed the Federation and brought the deaths of those on the outposts, she did worry for Ash's feelings. It couldn't be avoided, so she'd do her job, eradicate the threat, and pick up the pieces when everything was over.

The two men were in the communication center when she found them shortly after she'd finished changing. She stood in the door-way, watching them both. She'd seen them in undercover mode and when they dealt with Yager, but this side of them was new.

Brandt communicated with a ground team of Federation troops who were moving into position to serve the arrest warrants on the Walker Family members. He spoke with command and precision. After their loving just minutes before, she'd replaited his hair, some-thing she'd loved to do as he'd leaned back into her touch. There remained no softness about him just then, only power. The soldier on the other end obeyed him quickly and without question.

Ash spoke with the comandante, who seemed to be setting up a press conference for after the arrests. She shoved her urge to sneer and wince way beneath the surface, instead holding herself like the officer she was as she entered the view of the comm units.

Ash signed off and turned to her, taking her in from the toes of the shined black combat boots to the top of her head. She'd ruth-lessly tamed her hair into obedience. It lay smooth and shining against her skull, but she knew from experience she only had a few hours before the curls would reassert themselves.

She touched her hand to her forehead, saluting him, and Ash snorted, returning it. "At ease, Subcommander. Are you completely armed? This may turn into a combat situation."

Nodding shortly, she turned to show him the belt. "I've got hidden weapons, too. When do we go in?"

"I've contacted my father and called a Family meeting. Everyone should be gathered within the hour. As a bonus, Perry and Kira are here, and they'll be in attendance."

Sera managed to keep her commentary to herself, but Ash saw the slight roll of her eyes and laughed. "Like I said back in Nondal, petty works for you."

"Stop it now." She shook her head and wrestled her smile.

"News travels fast," Ash murmured. "I've got an incoming comm from my mother. I'd wager it has to do with our afternoon activities. Well, the ones we did in public, anyway."

Sera blushed and stepped out from the line of the comm unit.

"Hello, Mother. I'll be seeing you shortly. What can I do for you?"

"Ash, is it true?"

"What?"

Sera looked to Brandt, who met her gaze and grinned.

"There's a rumor circulating that Brandt has *married* his concubine!"

"I'm receiving a message on the other line from Father. I'll be seeing you soon." Ash cut the transmission.

"She's currently lining up everything with a pussy and a Family name within this 'Verse. You know that, right?" Brandt clapped him on the shoulder on his way to Sera. "Are you ready?"

Sera nodded.

"Let's go then." Ash joined them. "There's a full house over there. I said I had to discuss financial issues, which assures every seat will be filled."

"The troops are in place. They'll wait for my signal and enter with the security codes you supplied us with." Brandt buttoned the last gold button on his uniform and straightened his spine.

They walked to the conveyance, and Sera got in the back. At that point, she was a member of the team, and hers was the lowest rank. She'd let them do most of the talking. She trusted them both to know just exactly how to handle the situation.

Once when she'd first moved in with Ash, she'd driven out to look at the Walker Family compound. Her younger self had been so impressed at the sight of the pale spires of the main house rising above the stone walls surrounding the large plot of land. She'd envisioned being at home there with her children, all with Ash's pale blue eyes.

Some lessons were learned best the hard way. The Sera she was now knew she'd never be welcomed behind those walls as anything other than a service worker. It had to be okay, because there was no other choice. She had what was important: Ash at her side, forever. She'd take that and be grateful.

The sentries saw Ash behind the wheel and opened the towering metal gates. An entire world exposed itself to her eyes once they came around a long curve in the track to the house. Although *house* was probably not a word she'd have ever used to describe the towering, gigantic structure they drove toward.

She leaned forward, mouth agape. "You grew up here? In that thing?"

Ash nodded. "In one wing, yes."

"Wow." She sat back without further comment. What else could she say? He'd grown up in a residence her own childhood home could fit in a thousand times over.

"Good for playing hide-and-seek with my siblings. It's awfully hard to get found in a place this size." Ash met her gaze in the mirror, and she smiled, thinking of Ash as a child.

"Paul would have just left me and run off to meet his friends."

Brandt snorted. "I knew I liked your brother."

Ash parked, and they all sat silent for a few moments.

"Showtime. Hold steady, Sera. Do you understand? I can see hesitation in your face. Don't. Not for a moment. Your place is at my side," Ash said just before getting out.

"You're my wife. You're his, too, even if the official license says mistress. You're also a highly ranked officer in the military corps, and you deserve respect. You may not get it in there, but you deserve it. Keep that in mind." Brandt spoke in low tones before they began to ascend the dozens of stone steps to the grand front doors.

Hard not to be impressed with such incredible grandeur.

"Mr. Ash, it's a pleasure to see you again," one of the guards at the door said, bowing low.

"You as well, Dortimer."

The guard swept the door open and announced them in a clear baritone. A voice Sera barely registered once they stood in the front entry.

The floor was decorated with a series of inlaid precious metals and rare hardwoods. Expensive and classic paintings lined the walls. The ceilings were open and rose up airily, making the place seem even larger. Every piece of furniture she could see was either ridiculously overdone or a collectible. Both, in many cases. The decorator clearly had no sense of restraint.

The three of them stood shoulder to shoulder according to rank as Angelo Walker approached with his wife at his left.

Ash stepped forward and let his father embrace his forearms. He dropped a kiss on his mother's cheek and moved back to them again.

"Why have you brought that disgraceful woman in my home?

Wearing the uniform of our Federation, no less. You insult me and our Family." Ash's mother's voice was babyish, breathless, and Sera had to fight a sneer.

"May I present Subcommander Sera Ayers-Pela?" Ash spoke without acknowledging his mother's theatrics.

"What?" She looked confused.

"Shall we go into the Family meeting? We can explain it all there." Ash indicated they should precede them, but his father stood unmoving.

"You're going to tell us why you've brought a concubine into our home, and you'll tell us now."

Sera saw the resemblance between father and son. The set of the jaw, the ferocity in the eyes. Angelo Walker wasn't simply a figure-head; that much was clear.

"Sera is not a concubine. She is a member of a military covert operations team. A team Brandt and I have led for six years now. She posed as a concubine, as I posed as a boy with more credits than responsibility. I have more to say, but I need to say it in the presence of the others. I also need your silence on what I've just told you until I reveal it myself. This is a matter of urgency and great import to the Federation. I need your trust on this."

Angelo sighed and nodded, his eyes flicking over Sera dismissively. "Let's go then."

Sera followed them all down the hallway, a space wider than most of the avenues in Mirum. She knew the effect was supposed to be impressive, but admittedly she thought it wasteful. Boastful even.

"*I'm sorry about that,*" Ash said through the link she'd nearly forgotten about.

"*Nothing to be sorry for. We knew it would be difficult.*" At that point, Sera felt worse for him than herself.

"Hold on. The hard part is to come."

"I've already lived through the hardest part, Ash. I'm fine now with you and Brandt at my side."

Through another set of enormous archways, and they finally reached an auditorium of sorts where dozens of people already sat, waiting for them.

Kira spied her and gasped. Several others did as well, and the chatter rose to deafening levels.

"Can I shoot her?"

Brandt's serious soldier look softened when his lips visibly trembled to hold back a smile. *"Try to hold off on that."*

"Bet she can't wait to hear I'm family now. Oh, can I be the one to tell her? Please?"

"Stop that. You're going to make me laugh," Brandt warned through the link.

They approached a front table on a raised dais. At least twenty people sat around it and watched their approach. Ash sat and looked at the gathered group.

Sera wasn't an idiot living under a rock. She knew who Ash's uncle was. Costas Walker sat glaring at her before he moved his gaze to Ash. Perry sat next to him, smirking.

"Ash, before we get started, I thought you should say hello to Pelli and Morga, they've come by just to see you." Agni Walker didn't waste time parading marriageable women in front of Ash, that was for sure.

"Mother, this is hardly the time or the place to do this. This is official Family business, and to add to that, I'm not looking for a wife."

"Of course you are! You can't remain unattached forever. You need to give the Family more children. It's your duty. You may think it fine to waste your time and frolic with unranked women," she actually jerked her chin at Sera, "but I'm here to remind you of your duty, and it's not to shame us."

"You would do well, Agni, to respect my wife when you speak." Brandt hadn't moved or raised his voice, but the threat was there, nonetheless.

Kira actually wailed and began to yell at him, "How dare you do this? How dare you marry a whore? Brandt, this will shame us all."

Brandt narrowed his eyes. "If you know what's best for yourself, Kira, you will sit down and cease this incoherent babble immediately. Sera is my wife. She holds my rank, which by the way, tops yours."

Really now? Excellent. Sera barely held back a snicker.

"There are many things to discuss. First of all, Sera is not only Brandt's wife, but I've made her my mistress as well. I would marry her if I could, but we know you'll never give me permission. Only one of us can marry her, anyway. There will be no other women for me. It has always been Sera, even when I was forced to give her up to marry Kira." Ash paused to let that one sink in, and after a moment of silence, the uproar began anew as they realized who she was.

"We need to deal with this insanity of you dallying with a woman who is not of your rank. After the fuss she made before, *now* she's willing to be your mistress. Have you asked yourself why, Ash? What is in it for her?" Angelo demanded.

Sera stiffened. She wanted to defend herself, but more than that, she wanted Ash to defend her.

"Ten years ago I did my duty to this Family. I lost a woman I adored. I hurt her deeply, and she left with her head held high. She comes back into my life by *my* interference. She did not ask to be my mistress. All my life I've been led to believe certain things. Chiefly that no one who isn't ranked is worthy of me. That everyone without rank seeks to gain something from us, else why would they bother with us? Such a mistaken way to believe. I realize that now in ways I did not before." Ash took her hand and kissed it.

"I hate the way you think of Sera. You don't know her or, frankly, anyone like her. She's a genuine person. Hardworking. Achieved her rank in the military corps through hard work and dedication. That she played a concubine was the height of ridiculous, because she's no more a concubine than I am a lazy child of privilege. No more than Brandt is a disappointment to his war hero father. As it happens, the three of us are part of a covert military team, and our presence in Nondal was necessary to follow up on the recent attacks on Federation outposts and relay stations at the hands of Imperialists. Imperialists who were given information by Federation citizens. Family members."

All eyes turned to Ash then as the room held a collective breath. Sera pulled out the file folders and began to spread out the evidence.

"Before we begin, I want to reiterate a few things. First, Sera and I are together. I will not marry another woman, so I suggest you save the effort and embarrassment of these lovely ladies and stop parading them before me. She may be married to Brandt, but she is mine as well, and I am hers. If we have children, they will be Family and ranked. Do not seek to harm her in any way." Ash looked around the table, and Sera was suffused with warmth. He'd defended her, he'd stood up for them and hadn't backed down. It was real, their future was real, and he wanted it as much as she did.

Brandt sat forward. "As Ash has indicated, our team has uncovered information that indicates involvement between some high-ranked members of the Walker Family and the Imperialists. Should any of you wish to confess your involvement at this point, it will be recorded and applied favorably when it comes time for sentencing."

"Such treachery is an executable offense, is it not?" Perry's voice cracked, and Sera wanted to slap his face.

"There's execution and execution." Brandt lifted his shoulders slightly.

"This is madness!" Ash's uncle shot out of his seat. "You come in here with your unranked lover and your boyfriend and accuse your own Family of treachery. It's unconscionable. You should be ashamed of yourself."

"I'm not accusing you of treachery, specifically. I'm charging you with treason and violation of the Federation Intra-Universe Credit Act." Ash wanted to throttle his uncle, but he wanted to see where his father and brother ended up.

Sera shuffled through her papers and began to speak in an even voice, totally unaffected by the fact that these people had just called her a worthless whore. "Perry Walker, on nineteen occasions, you've taken credits from Imperialists in exchange for information on the location and security coverage of Federal outposts." She looked up at him, waiting for a reply.

"Brandt, why do you allow this?" Kira yelled. "She's accusing my husband of treason. How can you sit there and let this happen? She's jealous and wants what she's not good enough to have. Can't you see?"

Brandt sighed. "I should add, Kira Pela-Walker, several incriminating communications were made through your network comm account to Imperialist-connected parties."

"You're out of your mind, Brandt! Why would I care enough to do something so stupid?"

Sera nodded. "Sit down and cease your wailing. As it happens, despite not being good enough, I agree. Not that you're not stupid. I think you are. And ridiculously shallow, selfish, petty and ignorant. Credit-hungry as well. But frankly, as I look over all the information and as I read your communications on a day-to-day basis, you're just not smart enough or bloodthirsty enough to engineer this sort of thing. You can get your credits in other ways; I think you're too lazy for this. I do think you're guilty on some level, but just not smart enough to attempt to bring down the Federation. Just greedy. Oh, and silly."

Ash stifled a laugh. Gods knew Sera deserved to say it after the way she'd been treated.

Dismissing Kira, Sera turned her gaze to Perry. "But you, Perry, you're guilty. Craven. Without many redeeming qualities, really." Sera tapped the stack of paper with her fingertip. "Page after page of truly incriminating communication with Owen Alder and Giles Stander. I would like to compliment your record-keeping skills. Thank you for that."

Perry stood and made to leave the room, but the soldiers Brandt had signaled stood in the doorway, barring his exit.

"I think you should sit back down, Cousin." Ash narrowed his eyes.

"Angelo, how dare you force us to sit here and be insulted and accused of such terrible crimes. You called us here to discuss financials." His uncle puffed his chest.

"Do you have proof, Ash?" his father asked.

"Yes. It's been entered and sent to the comandante. It's enough to have warrants for arrest and extradition to Ravena issued. Are you involved in this? I can't protect you if you are."

"We're supposed to trust you? You're nothing but a lazy drain on the Family, while Perry deepens our coffers. Even Kendal works harder than you," his uncle sneered.

Anger sparked deep. "Kendal. Ah yes, my little brother. We've also got evidence Kendal is involved in this scheme." Ash pushed the papers to his father, who looked at them, growing more and more pale as he read. The soldiers had moved closer to the table to keep order, but Perry had shut up when Ash told him it was either shut up or get shot in the head.

"What authority do you have? Father, don't you see, he's—"

Ash interrupted his youngest brother. "By the authority of the comandante of the Federation Military Corps as a commander of said military corps. And I'm what, Kendal? Jealous?" He stood and began to pace. "You see, I've been trying to understand why this was going on. We don't need the credits. Family businesses are doing extraordinarily well. We've always been solidly aligned behind the Federation. Ours was the second Family to proclaim allegiance to the Federation generations ago. So why are we suddenly aiding Imperialists?"

"Control. They want their line in control," his father spoke quietly. "Costas has been working to undermine me for years now. It's normal, you know, political infighting in Families. I expected it. But not this. Selling out our own people. Using my son to harm me. This will lay the Family low when it gets out."

"Angelo, do you believe I'd sell our universe out for credits and control of the Family? I can take over without that." Costas smirked.

Sera tossed a sheaf of papers down the table to Ash's uncle. "Would you like to tell us why you've had such a lively communication with several members of this conspiracy then? If you didn't do it for credits and control, why did you do it? Are you a true believer in 'Verse-wide fascism and enforced order? Do you think the Walkers will retain their holdings if the Imperialists edge into this part of the Universes?"

He wouldn't even look at the papers. "I've known Giles Stander and through him Owen Alder for some time. It's not a crime to have friends, is it?"

"Did I say the communication was to Alder or Stander?"

Costas swallowed hard. "No. But you named them earlier. I assumed you meant them."

"Father, why do you just sit there and believe Ash's lies? Have I not been right where you needed me always? Where has Ash been? Off traveling, collecting women, spending credits, all while I stayed here and did my part to help you." Kendal looked to Angelo, but his father just sighed.

"I don't want to believe any of it, but the facts here," he motioned to the papers, "are inescapable. My heart breaks to know my own son has not only betrayed me but his Family and government."

"Get ready to transport them to the docks to get them to Ravena." Brandt turned to speak to one of the soldiers near the door, and they dispersed, leaving the room to follow orders.

Costas leaned forward on his hands, still standing at the table. "Let us be reasonable here. Whatever you think you know, Ash, you're mistaken. This is all just a misunderstanding."

Perry nodded his head. Kira simply looked dumbfounded, and Ash nearly felt sorry for her.

"Why, Perry? Why did you do it?" Ash wanted to know.

"Were the credits worth dying for?" Sera added.

"I did it for my father! He wanted the connections, wanted the power. Your father has held on to control all this time, and what about our line?" Perry wilted right there in his chair, and Ash sat, dumbfounded by the confession.

Before Ash could comment, his uncle jumped at him, landing on him, sending his chair backward. He struck his head on the floor, losing focus momentarily, but it was Sera who flew across his body and shoved Ash's father down.

$\mathcal{B}$randt watched in horror, frozen with shock, as Costas jumped at Ash. He'd been reaching for his blade when he caught sight of Costas also reaching for a weapon, turning toward Angelo.

Sera had been a blur as she leapt at Angelo, knocking him down as Costas's weapon discharged, filling the space with the loud crack and the acrid stench of the powder.

Ash shoved up, knocking Costas down, while Brandt's blade landed true in Costas' chest. With his other hand, he pulled his blaster, holding it on Perry and Kendal. Soldiers had rushed toward the knot of activity, a shower of metal clearing leather and clicks as weapons were pulled and safeties thumbed off.

It wasn't until Angelo yelled out that Brandt truly saw Sera. She looked fine until he noticed the steady stream of scarlet dripping down her left wrist and hand.

"Arrest Perry and Kendal Walker. Confiscate their comm units and cordon off their personal residences. Take Kira Pela-Walker in for questioning and hold her for possible involvement in the conspiracy. Check Costas and see if he's still alive. If so, take him into custody, if not, toss him in an incinerator." Brandt said this all as he rushed to Sera.

"You saved my life; I'm in your debt," Angelo told her as he helped ease her to the ground.

Brandt swayed on his feet when he saw the smear of red on the wall where she'd slid down to sit.

"Were you shot? Sera, focus on me," Brandt ordered.

Ash made his way over, shoving others from his path.

"Yes, I think I was. If the burning throb and loss of blood means anything," she slurred a bit.

"Medic! We've got a soldier down here." Ash stood to look and direct the medic over to Sera.

The medic opened Sera's uniform jacket, and the snowy white shirt beneath bloomed a flower of blood over the left side of her chest and shoulder.

Brandt tried to keep it together, tried to keep in mind that he and Ash had been wounded before, and chances were one of them would be again in the future. But she was his wife, his woman, and the idea of her being killed suddenly became so real to him he saw little white lights in his vision.

Ash squeezed his shoulder, both of them wincing when the medic ripped the shirt off and began working on Sera.

"The bullet went straight through. Looks like some muscles were damaged. There's a helicopter landing on the grounds right now, and we'll get you to the military hospital right away." The medic spoke to her calmly, and she nodded.

"You two go on. Make sure they all get into custody and on their way," Sera managed to say.

Brandt looked at her like she'd gone insane, and Ash tsked. "I'm the one who hit his head, but you're the one talking crazy. We're not leaving you. When you're finished, we have a press conference to do."

"This is stupid. If I wasn't your wife, you'd both go." She made a soft noise of pain when the medic carefully laid her on a stretcher. Nausea swamped Brandt.

"I don't give a fuck what you think. Frankly, I don't care what we'd do if it weren't you sporting a hole in your chest. The fact is, *you* are." Brant followed the stretcher. "You can fight with me later. For now, I'm saying what goes, because you're too weak to stop me."

* * *

*A*sh stopped at the doorway for a moment and gave orders to the investigative team.

"I'll be sure nothing gets removed," his father assured him. "This will be difficult to weather. Tough times ahead for the Family. If you married, came back, and took a more active part in Family governance, things might be easier."

"I really can't believe you're bringing that up right now. She just saved your life! You still think she's unworthy of me?" Ash felt the last bit of love and respect he had for his father drain away.

"She's clearly a courageous young woman who did her job. Her job of serving and protecting. I think she's unfit for marriage to anyone of your rank. But that fool Pela solved the problem. You can have her *and* a wife. She's got a husband. Are you telling me you're accepting of sharing her with another man? You have a duty. Especially now." His father crossed his arms over his chest.

"My place is with Sera. It always will be. I'm *doing* my duty every day by serving in the corps. I did my duty when I married Kira. You have your first and third sons in political unions. The Pelas won't want to cause a stir with Kira under suspicion. You may as well know now, they're doing a press conference with the three of us when Sera is finished at the hospital. The new face of Family responsibility."

His father nodded. "That should help. You could do both." He exhaled sharply when Ash snorted. "I misjudged you, Ash. I apologize for that. I'm proud to know you did your duty. I know the cost was great. Even if you refuse to marry now, I've been guilty of thinking you an irresponsible wastrel. I was wrong."

"Thank you." It meant something to have his father say that, even with the qualifiers. "I have to run to catch up before the helo takes off. I'll be in touch. My men are here; stay out of their way, and make sure everyone answers questions, or they'll be taken into custody."

His mother just looked at him through sad eyes as he ran past on his way to the woman who loved him no matter what.

Chapter 31

"Are you sure you're ready for this?" Ash eyed her carefully.

"I told you at least five times, Ash, I'm fine. All I have to do is stand next to you two and look like the nice, token, unranked officer. It's not like I need much stamina for that."

"You were just shot two hours ago, Sera." Brandt paced, looking edgy and slightly feral. Both men hovered over her, asking how she felt every few moments. They'd badgered the doctor so severely they'd been banished from the room where she'd been stitched up.

Really, for two warriors who'd seen their share of blood and wounds, they acted as if it were extraordinary she was able to stand.

Not that she'd admit it, but she did feel dizzy and very tired. But all she had to do was stand there and look responsible. Even Kira could manage that. Maybe.

The nurse finished tightening the sling holding her shoulder and arm still and assisted her into a makeshift uniform shirt. The jacket would have to be draped over her left arm, and they'd call it done.

"Come on, you two, let's get this over with. I want to get something to eat, and then I want to pass out for many hours."

Brandt stepped before her, cupping her cheeks gently. "I could have lost you today. You don't know what it was like. The blood on your shirt, the look on your face. My heart stopped. I don't know what I would do if you didn't exist in my life every day."

She swallowed hard, choking on emotion. "Not right now, please. I need to hold it together, and there's been a lot today. I'm just barely—" She clamped her lips together to hold back the sob that threatened.

He kissed her softly. "I'm sorry. I don't want to upset you. Later. We will go home, and you can let it all go. For now, Subcommander, let's go."

Ash shoved Brandt aside with a snort. "*I'm* not done. I'm having you brought to the dais in a wheelchair. Don't argue, it's useless. As you and Brandt frequently forget, I'm the ranking officer on this team. You can stand once you get there but not until then. We'll be sitting at a table instead of standing throughout the press conference as well."

Sera wanted to be mad, but all she felt was relief. He'd taken care of her, and she needed it.

"Yes, sir. Pardon my lack of a salute, but the dressing is so tight both my arms have limited movement." She winked, and he kissed the tip of her nose.

Sera mentally thanked Ash myriad times for taking care to have all the attendees of the press conference sit. As she sat on the raised dais as the crowd pelted question after question at Ash and Comandante Ellis, she knew she'd have passed out if she'd had to stand for so long.

To say the Federation-Aligned Universes reacted with shock to the revelations that Families had cooperated with the Imperialists in the bombings and murders of Federation citizens was an understatement.

Several near riots had been quelled across the 'Verses in the hours since the news had broken, and it promised to continue to be a dangerous situation.

The populace, for the most part anyway, had trusted the Families to run the 'Verses and protect its citizens. That they'd taken that trust and betrayed it in such a heinous manner was not only shocking on a personal level but simply unbelievable.

There had been a lot of anger from the people, from the media, from the other Families, and all rightfully so. But through it all, Ash and Brandt had stood as what it meant to truly be a ranking Family member. They stood for what was right and what was just. Sera was so proud of them both as they handled the animosity and grief from the assembled press conference with humility and accountability.

The only notice that'd been taken of her had been when she'd been held up by the comandante as an example of what a citizen could achieve with dedication and hard work. The way the comandante spoke, Sera got the distinct feeling the Federation would make her their official "unranked citizen," at least until this all calmed down. *Goody.*

Thank the gods, their relationship hadn't come up at all. It would, she knew that, but it would at least happen when she wasn't nearly falling over after being shot.

Sera saw her parents in the crowd at the press conference and kept her gaze on them, willing them to understand she was happy at last.

Comandante Ellis closed the conference by conferring a commendation on the three of them and explaining that the members of the conspiracy would be put on trial in Ravena once they'd had a chance to procure a defense team. The Federation employees and military corps members who'd been implicated had been arrested. Several had confessed and were providing evidence to the Federation.

The supreme leader of the Imperialists disavowed any involvement with the plan, branding the charges as false and—what may be true—as instigated by rogue elements. Sera found the entire event totally ridiculous, but she'd not failed to notice the difference in the way Ash and Brandt both held themselves. She supposed years of playing a part would take a toll on them.

*B*randt watched her sleep as he sat in a chair near the bed, pretending to read. After the press conference he and Ash had wanted to get her straight back home, but instead they'd dealt with her parents.

After an intense and not so very pleasant session of angry accusations, crying and at last, acceptance, Sera had been sweating and barely awake.

Ash forced her to take the pain medication she'd been refusing, and once her mother had gotten on her case as well, Sera finally gave in. They'd taken a helicopter back to Ash's house and settled her in immediately.

And then Brandt had looked to Ash and shrugged, and they'd simply sat with her for the pleasure of being able to watch her without pressure. Without anything more than wanting to be assured she was well.

Ash had dozed off in the chair opposite Brandt's, not wanting to mistakenly roll over and jar her arm in his sleep. Brandt knew Sera would be grumpy about being alone in bed when she woke up, and it made him smile.

In the background, he heard the ping of his comm unit, and with a careful check of her breathing, he left the room quietly and headed down the hall.

He sat for a moment before accepting the communication. "Hello, Mother. Are you well?"

"Brandt Pela, are you insane? The buzz all over the 'Verse is that you've *married* a concubine!"

"No. Not a concubine. I'm sure you saw the press conference, so let's not play games. You know who and what she is. And you know I received permission to marry her. She's a Pela now, and I trust you'll receive her as such."

Not that he believed it, but he said it anyway.

"You had your sister arrested. How could you take this woman's side over your own blood?"

"There were no sides. There was incriminating evidence, and as a matter of fact, it's Sera who argued that she felt Kira should be charged as an accomplice instead of a member of the conspiracy. She's being questioned, and if she's innocent, they'll let her go. So I suppose you should hope she's getting another marriage dissolved, and you should start looking for another male for her to marry. Most likely a Walker, because I'm sure the taint of this whole thing will make other Families want to steer clear of us for a while."

Why that amused him, he couldn't say, but it did. He heard his father chuckle in the background, so it wasn't just him.

"Now, my wife is resting after having been shot in the line of duty, so I need to go back to her. I'll be in contact soon. My love to everyone."

He cut the communication and smiled. He was free. Free to live the life he wanted with his woman and his best friend. No longer did he have to pretend every day of his life. He'd save the ruses for those times when they went covert. The weight of judgment fell from his shoulders, and he walked back into the bedroom to face a life he'd never dreamed of but couldn't wait to live.

$\mathcal{S}$era looked through her laser sight and typed the measurements of the squat building in the distance on a keypad.

"*It's awfully large to simply be a supply depot. Infrared shows extensive underground tunneling and space. I doubt they need all that room for shoes and outdoor gear.*" She sat back, packing up the equipment and moving down the hill she'd been situated on while she staked out the buildings below.

Ash waited in the transport some distance away, waving as she and Brandt jogged to the doors.

She still hadn't gotten used to the wig he'd procured for the as-signment. Short, spiky, bright red hair. He wore green lenses in his eyes and had taken supplements to darken his skin. An odd combi-nation, but he looked like many other residents of Levin, one of the desert 'Verses on the frontier.

Brandt also had red hair and green lenses. A mustache and a fake scar on his chin marked his face, along with extensive tattoos on his arms and chest.

"Do you two need a lift back to the settlement?" Ash's accent was perfect. Rough. It made her shiver.

"Sure." Brandt opened the door, and she got inside, saying nothing as they drove into the tourist settlement on the edge of the vast nature preserve people traveled from far and wide to traverse and camp in.

It also seemed to hold some Imperialist agents moving their weapons around.

Back at their hotel, fairly luxurious for the area, she'd gone to her room and bade her "brother" good evening.

*A*sh snuck up the back hallway to his room and then knocked on her door, adjoining his.

When she opened it, she was naked. He looked his fill as he stalked inside. The whole mission had been like an elaborate sex role-play game. She stood there with short black hair, tipped with bright red. Her normally blue eyes were instead a brilliant green, and tattoos covered her whole body. Prosthetics had changed the shape of her nose, and while he knew it was Sera, the bit of *not* Sera thrilled him as much as he knew his changed looks turned her on. All the excitement of fucking a stranger but still being with your mate.

Brandt came in right as Ash had lowered his face to her cunt and breathed her in.

"Should have known you two would be at it already."

"Well, come on then, you're behind now." Sera laughed.

"I wouldn't want that." Brandt knelt, and she sat up, leaning forward to kiss him. Ash watched a few moments before adding his mouth to theirs.

"Perfect. What do you want to guess those other covert teams don't have nearly the fun undercover that we do?" Sera asked through the link.

About the Author

The story goes like this: A few years ago, Lauren Dane decided to quit her job and stay home with her brand-new second child. As a result, she had lots of conversations in a singsong voice but no real outlet for adult thoughts and words. While on bed rest during her pregnancy with the tiny monster, Lauren had plenty of downtime, so her husband brought home a secondhand laptop and she decided to "give that writing thing a serious go."

Lauren had no idea how fabulously wonderful it would feel to actually make a go of her writing and every day she's thankful people actually want to read what she writes! She's well aware of her good fortune and loves every moment of it, even when she has to edit and put Barbie's dresses back on over and over again. She still hasn't managed to figure out how to shut out the sound of the Backyardigans so she can write a love scene, though.

Visit Lauren on the web at www.laurendane.com.
E-mail her at laurendane@laurendane.com.
View her blog at www.laurendane.com/blog.